Love In The Dark

Copyright

Opening Quote

I'm never that good in a crowded room. But everything stopped when I just saw you. You seem like someone I could be myself with. No defenses. Maybe you like me the way I am. Even though you talk way too fast. I can't stop looking at your eyes. Heads turn every time you laugh. Baby, I'm in love.

Let's Go Home Together by Ella Henderson

Chapter One

⚔ Robby ⚔

I slip my phone in my back pocket as the door slams open. I just got off the phone with my boyfriend, Luke Massena, second in command to Ryan Crane of the Crane Mafia, the most powerful mafia in the world.

Quickly, I scan the surroundings behind the assholes coming through the door. Water. Definite smell of fish. Almost overpowering. I really am bobbing up and down like I told him I thought I could feel. I really do feel it. It's not just in my head.

"Get up," the guy I have identified as the leader of this entire shindig says to me. I haven't been able to see him well enough to know for sure, but I bet it's Matthew Lucinio.

"Fuck you," I growl. I get a swift kick to the stomach in return for my disobedience, but no fucking way am I going to obey this asshole.

"Get up right fucking now," he says again.

Two of his guards haul me to my feet. They were smart enough to disarm me. Had they not, they'd all be dead. I never miss.

What they don't know is not only do I still have my phone, I also have my fists. And I learned how to fight from Ryan fucking Crane himself.

"What do you think you're going to get from me? I'm not telling you anything," I growl.

"I think you will. I think you're going to tell me everything I want to know. Starting with Crane's security. How many guys does he have on Jessa and Lyric?"

"There's no fucking chance you're getting near either of them."

One of the guards holding me bends my arm back. I wince but don't let on that it hurts at all. I was trained well. I learned from the best.

"I'll ask you again before I allow him to break your arm. How many guys does that fucker have on the girls?"

"What's your obsession with Jessa and Lyric?" I give him my best 'fuck you' smile. The guard bends my arm further back. I wrench it loose and punch him in his face.

"Fuck!" the guard screams as he grabs his face.

I laugh as blood spurts from his nose. Spinning quickly, I punch the other one in the throat. He immediately falls to the ground gasping for air. Air he'll never get with a broken windpipe.

I slowly turn towards Matthew, clenching my fists. "You're gonna have to do better than that," I say dangerously. He gives me a low laugh, then puts his fingers in his mouth. He lets out a loud whistle. I grin. "Fuck, yes. I've been itching for a fight ever since I woke up from your sneak attack. Too scared to face me on your own?"

He smiles like Satan. I grin right back as his guards come in. "Why would I need to face you at all? I have them." He gestures to the men behind him.

I crack my knuckles and get into a fighting stance. "Your first mistake was not cuffing me."

"Cocky fucker, aren't you?" Matthew laughs.

"Sure. We'll go with cocky. Now, tell me. What's the fucking obsession with Jess and Lyric?"

"Don't you get it?" Matthew looks at me like I'm stupid. "Lyric is Josh's everything. Take her, Josh is nothing. Jessa is important to Ryan. The entire Crane family. But most of all? She reminds me a lot of Nick's mother. You figured out Nick is my son. You must have figured that out, too. She's the one woman in this world that I loved more than all of this power I wield. She was my world."

5

I chuckle. "Called that one. Does the big bad wolf have a soft spot after all?"

He holds up a hand to stop the guards advancing on me. "I want Lyric so I can destroy the bastard who tried to take me out. I want my son. And I want my girl. I don't care who the fuck I have to destroy to get them back. They're mine. I'll destroy that entire family to get them. Starting with you, little boy."

He puts his hand down. The guards approach me, surrounding me like vultures. I watch them, waiting for someone to make a move.

As soon as one of the guards throws a punch, the fight is on. I block him and duck as another fist comes flying at my face.

My fist slams into one of them. A satisfying crunch follows as his nose shatters under my hand. I land another punch to the midsection of another while I swipe the legs of one of the others.

Jumping back up and avoiding the fist of one of them, I step back and quickly count how many there are around me.

"Fuck," I say. Six with three more coming through the door. I take a deep breath looking for a way out. Matthew has the balls to laugh.

Fucker.

"Have fun, little boy. I don't see you making it out of this alive." He looks outside. The sun is just coming over the horizon. "Just in time. I gave your boyfriend until sunrise to find you. I have other ways to get that information I need. You, my boy, were just a fun intermission in this little play." Not saying another word, he turns on his heel and leaves. The nine guys in whatever the fuck hellhole I'm in all look at me.

"Come on. Let's get this over with so I can get home. I've been away long enough." My voice is dangerous and threatening.

One of the guards laughs. "You think you're getting out of here alive, little boy? You think you can take us all?"

"Oh, I know I can take you all. And I'm itching for the fight. The question is, how long it's going to take until all of you guys are bloody on the fucking floor?"

I raise my hands and signal them to come hither. As I thought, they all advance. But I'm prepared. My training was top notch.

The first fist comes flying at me. I step to the side. His fist slams into the wall behind me with a sickening crack. He howls in agony and goes completely silent as my fist connects with his jaw. I feel the bones shattering.

There must be something completely fucking wrong with me because the enjoyment I get from watching him drop to the ground is far more satisfying then it should be.

Two more guards come at me. I dodge out of the way only to be caught around the waist by another. I let myself drop to my knees as I disarm him.

"What the fuck?" he yells, grabbing for his gun.

"Now you all are in *real* trouble," I say menacingly.

I shoot him as I stand and spin out of the way of another attack. I meet the knee of another guard and gasp for breath. I refuse to allow myself to double over. Doubling over would mean sure death. That's not how I was trained. I was trained to fight through it; breathe through it.

This is a fight for my life. Losing means I die. I won't die today. Not when I finally found a reason to live.

Not that my family wasn't reason enough. But day to day life was boring and mundane unless I was on a mission or training. Hanging out with my family got me through. Lunch with Arianna. Coffee with Ryan. Touring project sites with Jessa and Jason just for the fuck of it.

Even helping out Taylor and his team track someone down with my unmatched hacking skills. Hanging out with Chase and Breetana, or swiping some of Nicole's unparalleled baked items got me through my day.

But it was being with Luke that really mattered. I would find ways to be around him. I would make sure all of my training happened on days I knew he'd be there. Just because I knew he'd be watching. Secretly, I hoped he'd be proud at how much of a badass I'd become since we'd met.

I fell in love with Luke Massena the second I saw him. I should've admitted to myself then that he was the one. But it took me a little while. It took him making the move. Touching my hand led to a kiss that awakened a part of my soul I thought had died.

I block a kick aimed at my ribcage, then turn and pistol whip my assailant before shooting him. Seeing other guards have started to grab for their guns, though, I know I need to get out. I may be able to take them all in a fist fight, but no way I can shoot all of them before they start shooting at me. I know I can't stop bullets.

7

With one hand, I deliver a brachial stun to the guard in front of me as I shoot the guard standing in front of the door. Both guards slump to the ground, one of them absolutely dead.

I leap for the door. By the grace of God, I don't get hit by any of the bullets that suddenly start speeding by me. Wood from the door as I sprint through it splinters around me as the bullets hit.

"Get him! Don't let him get away!" someone screams.

I hit the ground running, nearly falling through the soft wood. I was right. I'm at the docks. I'm at the end of a dock, to be precise. One that's sinking fast under the weight of the amount of people on it. It's rickety at best.

"Fuck!" I yell as my foot falls through a board.

Thankfully, I'm not far from shore. My foot goes through, but I only get water halfway up my shin before I hit sand. I quickly pull myself up as I turn and shoot at the guards following me.

My two shots take out the two lead ones. They fall to the ground, causing a comical chain reaction of other guards tripping over their bodies and falling over them or into the water in their haste to avoid the chaos unfolding in front of them.

I make a fast exit, crawling to the edge of the dock and finally hitting pavement. I don't stop running or look back. I can hear people chasing me.

"Get him, or I'll fucking kill all of you! Don't let him get back to Crane!" Matthew yells behind me.

I duck as low as I can and cover my head with my arms as I run. Bullets rain down around me. I need to find a place to hide swiftly. I know I can't keep outrunning them. I don't know how many bullets are left in the gun I took, so winning a shootout, despite the fact that I'm a crack shot, is unlikely at best.

I quickly glance over my shoulder. I'm definitely faster than Matthew's guards. They aren't gaining ground on me. Focusing my attention on my surroundings, I start looking for a place to dip into. I head for an ally and quickly look for open doors. There's nothing but abandoned buildings in this part of town. Hopefully one of them will be my savior.

One of the doors comes open. I breathe a sigh of relief. "Fuck. Thank God." I slip inside and close the door. Letting my eyes adjust to the dark, I start walking deeper into what I think is a factory. The voices of the now panicked guards fade behind me as I make my way through the building. I reach into my back pocket for my phone only to come up empty handed. "Dammit."

It had to have fallen out in the fight or during the run. I sigh as I continue making my way through the darkness. When I finally find another door, I see that it leads to the street I just ran down.

Knowing the area is swarming with guards, I kneel in a corner and stay away from the windows. Any light that comes in through them could give me away if anyone is looking in.

"Think, Robby. What do you do now?"

I wait. That's what I do. I can't leave this building right now. I think of the surroundings. This exit leads to the street, and the docks. The exit across the building leads to the ally. If I can find a door on the other side of the building, I'll end up on a fairly busy street. That's what I need to do. I have to get out of here.

I make my way to the other side of the building, being cautious to stay in the shadows. When I finally get to the other side, I'm relieved. I find a door and crack it open slightly. The early morning traffic is just starting to flow, and it doesn't look like too many people are on the streets. I watch before I exit the building looking for any sign of anyone who might be searching for me.

Seeing no signs there are guards on this side of the building, I silently open the door a little more. I jump when I hear a noise at the far side of the building. Closing the door so no light gets in to give away my position, I look to the other side of the building. Sure enough, I see guards come in.

"He's in here! I fucking know it."

"You said that about the last building."

"Well, he's in this one. I feel it."

I chuckle as I quietly slip out the door. "Time to go."

I close the door behind me, making no noise, and run across the street. I duck into another ally and make my way to the other side. I cut to the left and make my way into the busy city.

Soon, there are people and cars all around me. It's easy to get lost in the crowd. I flag down a cab and jump in as one pulls over. I give him the address to home as he pulls away from the curb. I slump in the seat as

9

my adrenaline comes down. I start to feel stabbing pain all over my body. I must have taken more hits than I thought.

"Hey, man. Your arm looks like it's bleeding. You okay?" the cabby asks me, watching me closely in the mirror.

I look down at my arm. I'm sure I look like hell. I'm wearing black tactical boots and pants with a black t-shirt. They took my vest gear.

I sigh. "Yeah, I'm good. Just get me home."

The cabby nods. I rip the sleeve of the t-shirt off. I feel the back of my arm and breathe a sigh of relief when I feel another hole. That means I have an exit wound. There isn't a bullet in me. At least I hope it didn't leave any fragments or anything.

Wincing in pain when I try to rip the sleeve. I place the fabric in my teeth to anchor it while I use my good arm to tear it. Continuing to use my teeth in place of my other arm, I wrap the t-shirt around the wound. The cabby continues to watch me as I work. I ignore him.

When I'm finished, I lean my head against the window and watch as the city flies by. We live on the other side of the lake on the outskirts of the city. Getting there from over here will take at least an hour, so I have no choice but to settle in for the long ride.

"Hey. Dude, you're home."

I jerk my head up. I don't know how the hell I fell asleep or when, but when I look around, I see I am indeed home. "Damn. I didn't mean to fall asleep."

"Looks like you needed it. That will be a hundred and six."

I nod and reach for my wallet. "Fuck." I shake my head, realizing I don't have it. I look over at the gate. "I lost my wallet during the fight, man. Give me a second to run in. I'll have someone pay."

"Sure. But I have to keep the meter running."

"No problem. Not worried." I step out of the cab and head for the gate. Drake sees me and opens it.

"They're going fucking crazy in there. They've checked a couple different places and couldn't find you. Luke is about damn near ready to tear the fucking world apart."

I smile at the thought of my boyfriend. I need him. I fucking need him right now to make me feel like I'm no longer in that nightmare I just came from. I need him to make me feel like I'm real. Like I didn't die in the gunfire back there and am now a ghost.

"Pay the cab, Drake. I lost my wallet and phone. I'll pay you back."

"I'll take care of it. Don't worry about it. Get in there. You're the only one who can calm them down right now. They raided the docks. No one was there. They think you're dead, dude."

"I almost was. If they had been a better shot or better at their job looking for me after I got away, I probably wouldn't be here."

"We're all glad you're okay. All of us." Drake heads for the cab as I head for the house.

I feel like I've been dropped out of a plane at thirty thousand feet and splattered all over the ground. I feel disassociated with my body, like I really don't exist anymore and am just watching everything unfold in front of me.

I don't feel real.

If I listen closely enough, I can hear my heart racing. I can feel myself sweating. Looking down at my arm again, I can see it's covered in blood.

Luke.

I know he'll make this better.

He'll make me feel alive again.

Being in his arms is all I need to make me feel whole.

Chapter Two

⚔ Luke ⚔

(Before Robby's Escape)

"This can't be happening. How is this happening?" I ask no one in particular.

Ryan Crane.

Most powerful mafia boss in the entire fucking world. Fierce protector of family. I've seen him in action. Ryan always gets his fucking man.

Until now, apparently.

"We'll find him, Luke," Shane Nelson, my mom's husband and my ex-boss, says as he lays a hand on my shoulder. I barely hear the words. I barely hear anyone's words. All I can focus on is the love of my life being taken from me.

"This can't be happening." I know there are tears falling down my face, but I can't find the will to give a shit.

I'm fighting for control of myself. All I want to do is rip the entire house apart. I want to punch Ryan in the face for letting this happen. For leaving an opening for that fucking asshole to even have the opportunity to take what's mine.

"Luke, we'll find him," Ryan says as he looks me square in the eyes.

I know this isn't Ryan's fault, but I need someone to blame for this. Robby isn't with me. If I had been with him, he'd still be here. If I'd been watching out for him, he wouldn't be gone.

"I need to get the fuck out of here," I growl. I need to calm down. I can't think like this. I can't fucking breathe.

I almost sprint out of the house. As soon as my feet hit the pavement outside, I'm running to my cottage. My place to retreat to when I need to be alone. It's a small house on Ryan's property that I moved into in order to be close to my little sister, Arianna, Ryan's wife. We have houses being built on the compound for me and Robby as well as Nick and Dani. It's a bright spot in all the darkness in my head.

My life over the past couple of years has been fucked up, to say the least. But I can't deny all of the good that's come from the chaos. I've never been as happy as I am with Robby.

I enter my cottage and sit on my couch. I force myself to breathe. Nowhere near enough oxygen is getting to my lungs. I'm hyperventilating when I should be focusing on how to find Robby.

Two years ago, my life changed forever. I didn't know it, but getting assigned to go undercover in the Ambrosio Mafia was the best thing that ever happened to me. It led me to finding out that I have a sister. Arianna was a seventeen-year-old girl when I met her. Her father was trying to gain enough of an alliance to take out the Crane Mafia.

I didn't know a lot about the Crane Mafia at the time. All I knew is that I was in the middle of a mafia war. My assignment as an ATF agent was to find the guns. That was my goal.

Until I found out about the Massena Mafia. I became obsessed because I knew little of my father. I'd never wanted to. I never really cared to know. I had my mom. That's all that mattered.

But forces I couldn't understand threw my curiosity into overdrive. I interjected myself into the Massena Mafia, not really knowing if the guy was or wasn't my father. But he had the same last name, and I wanted information. I knew they were involved in the weapons trade. That's what my case was all about, after all.

It didn't take long to find out about Arianna and her father. I got some DNA, ran a test through some contacts I had when I worked for the NYPD, and found out what I had suspected. I had a family I suspected existed but knew nothing about.

As soon as I met Arianna and saw how our father treated her, I went into overprotective mode. I found out she was dating Ryan Crane, but I didn't care. All I cared about was getting her out. I followed her everywhere, lied about her whereabouts to our father when he asked, and was lucky enough to gain her trust.

When she got married to Ryan, I was even more lucky to gain his trust. I learned a lot about him, and what he's all about. I became his second in command, but what's more important?

I became part of the family. I finally got everything I didn't know I wanted. I quit the ATF, but I gained far more.

And so did my mother. She married my ex-boss, Shane. She's liked him for a long time, but I never pushed it. She's never been happier. Fuck. We've all never been happier.

But that's not all. I knew as soon as I saw Robby Earnhart that he was it for me. Unfortunately for me, he was with someone. I saw through his girls' bullshit from the beginning. Thankfully, we all saw it.

Including Robby.

At first, Robby and I were just friends, but I saw the way he looked at me. So, I did all I could to be around him. We spent countless hours talking and being together. I knew his relationship with Renza was over because he had told me he was just keeping an eye on her for Ryan.

One day, I took the initiative. We were alone. I saw him looking at me. I grazed his hand. Not long after that, we kissed. And it was fucking amazing.

Robby and I have been inseparable ever since. The family supports us. That's all that matters to either of us. He's the love of my life. He's my entire world. I never thought I would ever find that, but I did with him. Our fifteen year age difference means nothing to either of us.

And now he's fucking gone. Taken from under my nose by that son of a bitch Matthew Lucinio. I rub my temple to try to ease the pressure in my head. My heart is racing. My chest feels like it collapsed a long time ago.

No matter how hard I try, all I can think about is Robby laying on the ground looking at me. His eyes pleading for help. And I couldn't do a fucking thing. I don't know where he is now.

And that fucker only gave me until sunrise.

I have three hours.

Three fucking hours to save him.

I look up at my door opening. Ryan walks in with Alex and Josh. Alex and Josh Lucinio. Matthew's twin sons. Alex and his brother are co-leaders of the Lucinio Mafia. At least for now. They took over after Josh killed Matthew, but Alex is going to step back as soon as Josh has a good handle on leading.

The problem, unfortunately, was that he didn't kill his father. He killed some asshole his father paid off and gave plastic surgery to so that he would look like him. Now, Matthew Lucinio is back. Bigger and better than ever. Or so he says.

I'm not in the mood for any of this. "If you don't have any information on where Robby is, leave. I need to think," I say, glaring at all of them.

"We have information. That's what I was coming to tell you," Ryan says.

I spring out of my seat. "Well, talk! Let's go! We don't have time to waste!" I run for the door only to be stopped cold by Alex and Josh. "What the fuck are you doing? Let's go!"

Ryan hauls me back as Alex and Josh push me into my house. I don't know what the hell they're doing. All I can think about is Robby. I need to get to him. I can't live without him. I won't. Not after I finally found the other half of my heart.

I fight with the three of them, throwing punches and kicks as I lunge myself for the door. "Just fucking talk to me on the way! We don't have time for this!"

"Luke! Stop! Fucking stop it and listen!" Alex yells as he shoves me back.

"I sent in a crew. They were already gone!" Josh says.

His words sink in, and I immediately stop fighting as I drop to my knees and dry-heave. My vision blurs and gets dark around the edges.

"No. Fuck…" I cough and grip my sides.

"Luke. Look at me." Ryan kneels in front of me. I look at him, pained. "We'll find him. I swear to you. We'll fucking find him."

Before I have a chance to respond, my cell phone rings. I push myself off the floor and quickly cross the room to grab it. "Robby? Shit, it's Robby!" I fumble to answer it. Not at all who I am. Confident and in control is who I fucking am. "Robby? Where are you?"

"I don't know, Luke. You gotta get me out of here." He's whispering. I put the phone on speaker. We all gather around to listen for any sound we can that may give his location away.

"Robby, tell me what you hear. What's around you?"

"I think I'm at the docks. I smell fish, but I don't know, Luke."

"Baby, concentrate. Anything you hear. Anything that you smell. It's all helpful. You smell fish. What do you see? What do you feel?" I force my voice to be calm because I know he needs me to be. It's not easy. Ryan puts an arm over my shoulders and nods.

"I… feel… uh… like I'm rocking."

"Good. Good, baby. What else?"

"Uh. It's wet. Damp. I can't see anything." We hear clattering. "Fuck. I gotta go."

"Robby! Don't you fucking hang up!" The line goes dead. The pain in my head hits me ten times harder than it had before. I squeeze the phone in my hand before throwing it onto my couch. "Fuck!"

"Luke? Honey, I just came to check on you. I'm so sorry all of this happened," my mom says as she walks in. She wraps her arms around me. Usually, her comfort would center me. Not today.

I slowly pull back from her and gently push her away. "Mom. Please go," I whisper. "I don't want you here for this." I know I'm about to lose complete control. I don't want to scare her. She's never seen me out of control before.

"Luke, I'm not going anywhere. I'm your mother, for Christ sake. I've seen you at your worst. You don't need to hide from me…" She runs her fingers through my hair.

"Please. Mom. I need you to go." I look at Ryan.

He takes my mom's arm. "Sonya, I need you to get Arianna for me. Can you do that?" He leads her out the door. She looks up at him then back at me before nodding and hurrying away. I turn away. I feel the last shred of control I have slip away from me. I let out a howl as Ryan turns back to me.

"Jesus," Alex says.

"Leave him alone. He needs to do this," Josh says.

My fingers dig into the chair in front of me. I squeeze it so hard, I feel the wood splintering beneath me. Suddenly, the rage is too much.

"Fuck!" I throw the chair into the bar near my kitchen with such force that it shatters in pieces and falls to the floor. I let out another howl as my coffee table follows the chair. I spin and look at Ryan. "Find him! You're so good at your job! You protect everyone else! Fucking find him!"

I grab another chair and start smashing it into the small kitchen table. The wood splinters and shatters until all I'm holding in my hand is the leg of the chair. I throw it, not really caring where. It hits a mirror, breaking it into so many pieces it would be impossible to count.

"Luke?" I hear Arianna's calm voice behind me. I flip the kitchen table as I let out another tortured scream. Arianna's small hand softly touches my arm.

"Go, Arianna. I don't want you near me. I don't want to hurt you."

"I'm not afraid of you. You wouldn't hurt me."

"You've never seen me like this." I feel all of my anger dissipate as she ignores me and wraps her arms around my waist. "I don't know what to do." I sink to the ground on my knees in her arms. I'm not able to function. I can't breathe without my Robby. I need him. "I've never been in love. Not until him, Arianna. I didn't know what it felt like to not be able to live without someone. If I lose him, I won't come back from that."

"You won't. You won't lose him. Ryan and Josh sent a team to the docks. They'll turn the entire place upside down looking for him. Just because he wasn't where we thought he was first doesn't mean we won't find him."

I look at her as I start to stand. But her grip tightens. She doesn't let me. "I should be out there with them looking!"

"No." She shakes her head and hugs me closer. "You need to be here in case he calls again. If you're with them, you could miss the call that saves his life." She tightens her grip around my waist even more.

I nearly collapse into her. "If anything happens to him…" I let the words die on my lips. I know I don't need to say them.

"I know, Luke. We all do. Save your anger for Lucinio. When Robby is found and comes home to you, he's going to need you. Not your anger. You."

I nod as she sits hugging me for only God knows how long. I bury my face in her hair as she sways with me. I hadn't noticed until we both stand, but Ryan, Josh, and Alex had left us alone.

I needed it. I needed her to center me again.

Arianna and I walk from my cottage to her house. The cool air soothes me more and more. Gives me a clearer head. I look at Ryan as his phone rings when we walk into the house. Arianna closes the door behind us as I watch him.

"What?" Ryan sits down in the chair closest to him and rubs his temples. "Check fucking everywhere," he growls. He starts to hang up, but puts his phone back to his ear. His expression becomes dangerous.

My heart stops beating. "What's happening?"

He holds up a hand. "Then, he's still alive somewhere because Lucinio wouldn't fucking pack up and not leave him for us to find. He would've left him there. Sent us a message. Have you checked the whole area?"

I collapse in a chair. Arianna sits on the arm of it and runs her fingers through my hair. Josh watches Ryan intently as Alex leans his head back on the couch. My body feels heavier and heavier the longer I listen.

Finally, Ryan hangs up. I just look at him. "So…?"

"They're combing the docks. They found the shed they think Robby was being held in. It collapsed into the water. But they found his phone. It was on the pavement. They think he got away. There are a lot of shell casings. Like there was a gun fight."

I nod. "He got away. He had to have."

Ryan stands. "Let's go. Lucinio is gone, but Robby is out there somewhere."

Josh stands and looks at me. "You need to stay here," he says.

I nod. "I know." I scrub my hands down my face. "Fuck. I know. I wouldn't be of use anyway. All I can think about is him. If he's hurt; fucking bleeding somewhere."

"You can't think like that," Alex says as he checks his gun. He looks down at me. "He'll call here. If he can get to a phone, he'll call you. You have to be here. Especially if he gets back here before we do."

18

Arianna rubs the back of my neck. "He'll come home. I know Robby. He's too stubborn. Tough."

I give her a soft, but forced smile. "I know."

As Josh, Alex, and Ryan head for the door, I close my eyes and force myself to believe it. Robby will come home. He'll fight to come home. Back to me.

He has to because if he doesn't, I won't survive it.

Chapter Three

☒ Robby ☒

I reach for the door handle to Ryan's house, but jump when it opens in a hurry. I take a step back as Josh, Alex, and Ryan start walking through it. Their expressions are all dark. Determined.

Ryan's eyes meet mine. "Fuck. Robby!" He throws his arms around me and drags me in the house. "Holy shit, we were going crazy!"

Alex closes the door behind us and Ryan pulls me over to Luke and Arianna. Arianna sobs as she hugs me. Josh pats my back and sits on the couch. Alex gives me a side hug before following.

But I only have eyes for one person. "Luke…" My voice cracks as I choke on my own sob. Ryan gently pulls Arianna away from me. Though, the vice-like grip she has around my waist makes it a little difficult to move.

Luke wraps his arms slowly and shakily around me. He buries his face in my neck. I can feel his tears. "I was terrified I'd never see you again," he whispers.

I mold myself to his body and hug him as tightly as I can. I shake my head. "For a little while, so was I. But getting home to you and this family… not letting him win. That's what got me through."

Luke nods and tightens his grip, swaying gently with me. I'm positive it's all he can do because I feel the same way. I can't form words right now. I can't think. All I want is to close my eyes and feel him. His solid frame against mine. His strong arms wrapped tightly around me.

Him.

Just him.

After several minutes of silence and Luke hugging me in the middle of the room, we finally pull apart. But only slightly. Luke sits in a chair and pulls me in his lap. I don't even care how ridiculous it looks for a man who is just over six feet to be sitting on the lap of another man who is only a couple of inches taller. All that matters to me is him.

All that matters is that I'm home.

Luke keeps me as close to him as he possibly can. I wrap my arms around his neck and rest my head on his shoulder. I feel us both start to relax a little more as each second passes. But there's no way either of us intend on letting the other go.

Lucky for us, our family isn't judgmental in the slightest. I look around the room for the first time since getting home and notice, though, that most of the family is missing.

I clear my throat and lift my head, looking at Ryan. "Where is everyone?"

"Jess and Nikki needed to tend to their boys. Tait and Jackson were fussy as fuck," Ryan says. "They were also about to drop, so Jas and Taylor took them both home. I think they needed a little time to decompress anyway."

"Dani and Nick are upstairs. They're just talking about everything," Arianna says softly as she cuddles into Ryan.

"Bree and Chase are in a guest room. Bree got really sick from all of the stress and worry," Alex says.

I look at Alex concerned. "Sick?"

He nods. "She's always been that way from what Chase was saying."

"I just sent everyone a text to come back because you're home," Ryan says.

I nod. "Okay."

"Our mother just got on a plane," Josh says. "Some of our team is escorting her. Cole and Lance will meet her at the airport and bring her here."

"Robby!" Lyric's eyes widen when they land on me, and she rushes over to us. She hugs me carefully with a watery smile. She steps back and sits next to Josh. He pulls her close, rubbing his hand up and down her arm.

"Oh my God, Robby!" Breetana Shaw squeaks from behind me. She slings her arms around my neck, nearly choking me as her silky blond locks cover my face.

I reach up and loosen her grip slightly as I hug her arms and turn to kiss her cheek. "I'm okay."

"We were so worried," she sniffles against my neck.

"I know, Bree. I know. I really am okay." I wince slightly at the pain in my arm. I completely forgot I'd caught a bullet and need to take care of it, but I don't have the option to say anything before Dani throws her arms around me from the front.

"Robby, we were so scared!"

I groan slightly when she squeezes my arm. "Fuck…" I hug her back. "I'm okay, Dani. But I need to take care of my arm. I forgot about it."

"Your… arm…?" Her eyes widen when she sees how much blood has soaked through my makeshift bandage. "Robby!" She looks at the blood on her hand. I expect her to pass out, but she doesn't. She turns and runs from the room. "I'll get a first aid kit!"

I just blink at her. "Jesus."

Nick Crane, Ryan's brother and Dani's fiance, chuckles. "We've all been worried as hell, bro. Ryan wanted to make sure we were all here when you got home or if you called. Ryan and Josh both sent teams out to look for you." Nick leans down and hugs me.

I reluctantly stand but don't go far. I sit on the footstool in front of Luke. "When everyone gets here, I'll tell you all what happened. Josh and Alex need to know all I found anyway."

"That wasn't the concern, Robby," Chase Shaw, billionaire CEO of Shaw Enterprises, a finance company and Breetana's husband, says, helping me onto the stool when I sway and groan a little. Chase is also one of Ryan's brothers, though not by blood. He starts untying the bandage. "The priority was getting you home."

I take a deep breath and swallow when I get dizzy and nauseated. "Fuck… I think I lost more blood than I thought."

Luke, not leaving my side, takes the wet cloth Dani hands him when she returns. He starts running it gently over my forehead. "Dizzy?"

"Yeah. Little weak," I lean against him when he positions himself behind me.

"Just relax, baby. I've got you." Luke kisses my shoulder just as Ryan's door flies open.

"Robby. Shit." Taylor Reddick, a Lieutenant with Chicago Police Department and another of Ryan's adopted brothers, runs a hand down his face as a very tired looking Nicole Reddick, Taylor's wife, comes through the door. Arianna stands and walks to Taylor, quietly reaching for a sleeping Tait, their young toddler son. Taylor hands him over and takes Nicole's hand as they head for me. Taylor kneels next to Chase.

Nicole hugs me and sniffles. "We were so, so scared, Robby." She cries against my chest as I wrap my good arm around her.

"I know. I know, Nicole. So was I." I kiss the top of her head as her tiny body quakes with her sobs. "It's okay… I'm here. I'm home."

She just nods as she cries. I hug her because it's all I can do. I'm tired. The adrenaline I had pumping through my veins long ago faded. I'm running off nothing right now. I don't even know how I'm still sitting upright.

"Bullet went through," Taylor says. Dani hands him some antiseptic. He looks up at me. "This is going to sting like a fucker."

I look at my arm. I can see the blood covering it. I can see the hole left after Dani cleaned it. "Doesn't matter. I can't feel shit right now."

Taylor nods. "Nikki, you might want to get up…" Nicole shakes her head and hugs me tighter. Taylor sighs. "Okay. Here goes." Chase holds my arm as Taylor begins disinfecting it.

I squeeze my eyes shut, expecting it to hurt. But, just as I thought, I feel nothing. Nothing but a little pressure. Even though I can see what's happening, I barely feel anything at all. Pretty sure that's not a good thing. But I push it aside when the door opens again. Jason Crane, Ryan's biological brother, and Jessa, Jason's wife, rush towards me with a screaming Jackson, their young son.

Ryan stands. "Here. I'll put him down for bed in the nursery." He plucks Jackson from Jessa's arms.

She drops next to me and wedges herself in next to Nicole to hug me. "Oh my God, what happened to you?"

"I'm okay, Jess. Really. I promise. I'm just glad I'm home." I shift and pull her into the hug with Nicole as Luke rubs my back.

Chase and Taylor finish wrapping the wound. Dani picks up all of the supplies. Nick picks up everything else and heads for the kitchen. Taylor and Chase follow to clean up. Luke stands and helps me up. I look up at him slightly confused as I stand.

He smiles as he leads me to a guest room. "You need to clean up a little. Trust me. You'll feel better in fresh clothes."

I chuckle. "I probably smell horrible right now."

He laughs. "Like dead fish and rotting worms."

I wrinkle my nose when the smell of myself hits me for the first time. "Fucking hell. Sweat and blood mixed in there, too."

A little while later, after all of us are freshened up and Doctor Chantau has checked me out, Luke settles me next to him on one of the large couches in Ryan's large den. I can't lie. Luke was right. I feel better. A lot better. More alive. When I lean into him, the night's events seem further and further away.

Ryan leans forward in the chair he's in as he looks at me. "Think you're feeling up to explaining to Josh and Alex all we've found out?"

I nod. "Yeah. I'm feeling better. Thought I was going to crash for a while there." I lean forward to open my laptop that someone put on the table for me.

Luke stops me and leans forward himself. "I got it." He grabs it and hands it to me, cuddling me back into him.

I smile at how caring and nurturing he is as I take the laptop he's put in my lap. I pull up all of my files and start explaining each and every one of them. One by one. I explain how I found Matthew. I tell them what I found about him paying someone off to get the plastic surgery to look like him. I tell them about Dani being the daughter of one of the men he'd employed.

I fill them in on everything regarding Jason and how Lucinio tried to have him arrested. I tell him about Taylor's Captain. The bribery and blackmail. Losing members of his team to Lucinio, but being able to save

Zekeih and his family. I pause and look up before getting to the part that they really want to hear. "With me so far?"

Alex looks at Josh before looking back at me. "Yeah. That's a lot to take in."

"Not even close to the end of it." I look back down at my screen.

"Looks like he had a hand in a lot of treachery for many years," Josh growls low. "I doubt we've even been able to uncover half of what he had us into. Even though it's been, what? Three years?"

"Something like that," Ryan says as he leans back on the couch and looks at me.

I take a deep breath. "I also found a few things I didn't expect. I happened on them by accident." I click to a screen and turn my laptop.

Josh and Alex both lean forward to look. Josh chuckles and shakes his head. "So, the son of a bitch was having an affair with Nick's mom."

Alex tilts his head. "Uh... No... Not exactly." He points to the screen. "Look. That's not mom's name." He looks at Josh. "He was fucking married to her."

"It was annulled," I say, showing him another screen.

"Jesus Christ," Josh says. "He..." He looks up at Nick just as Ethan, Ryan's father, walks in with Jenny.

Reading the room, Ethan sits down with Jenny. "What did we miss?"

Ryan stands and walks to lean over the couch next to Josh. "We just filled Alex and Josh in on everything Robby found out about Lucinio and... Well, all of this shit with the marriage and the annulment."

"Fucking hell...," Alex says as he looks up at Josh before he stands and starts pacing. "I don't get this. So he had an affair? Married her?"

Josh shakes his head. "I don't think so. I think he met her. Fell in love. Married her. She got pregnant with Nick. Then..." He gestures to the screen. "Then, I don't fucking know. Got an annulment? Why? If he had an heir in Nick, why get the annulment? Can that be figured out?"

I nod. "It'll take me a little time. But yeah. I'll start looking now."

I settle in and start my search, but I find nothing. I go through state by state as everyone around me talks. I tune them out and focus, barely noticing the food Luke puts in front of me.

I absently eat the food, but only because he damn near puts it in my face. I hardly notice the coffee I'm drinking.

I'm in my zone. The tunnel I always find myself in when I'm searching or hacking. It's like nothing else is around me. Just me and the electronic web of data. I see nothing but my code. Numbers. Letters. Lines. Strands. Like the DNA of the files I'm looking for is right at my fingertips.

But after what feels like hours to me go by, I finally have to admit it to myself. I'm at a loss on this one. I find no reasons for any of this.

I shake my head as I look up. For the first time, I see the toll the night has taken on everyone. Dani and Arianna are both curled up on the couch together fast asleep. Breetana and Nicole have fallen asleep together in a chair. Jessa is lying sprawled on the couch with her head on Arianna's lap. Lyric is curled up in the chair next to Arianna. She has her Kindle in her lap, but she's staring into space.

Alex and Josh are both pacing slowly around the room. Like they're stalking something. Ryan has his forearm up on the sliding glass door leading to the patio. His forehead is resting against it as he looks out. Though, I'm not totally sure he's awake. Nick is laying on the floor on his stomach. Jason is using Nick's back as a pillow. Taylor is watching CNN. Chase is doing something on his phone. Probably answering an email. One of the hundreds he probably gets a day.

Luke has his feet up on the table in front of us, eyes focused on my laptop. He's lightly rubbing my thigh. "Nothing?"

I shake my head and lean back. "Not a fucking thing. What time is it?"

"After noon. Josh just got word Rebekkah is on the way. Lance and Cole just picked her up. They flew to New York first and switched planes because they thought they were being tracked. She should be here anytime."

I yawn and nod, rubbing my eyes. "Were they?"

"Being tracked?" He shrugs. "Don't know. Better safe than sorry, though. The pilot felt a lot better after they landed and switched planes. Haven't heard word about if there's a track or not."

"Okay." I rub my eyes again and stand up, walking off the stiffness. I look over at Josh and Alex as they quit pacing. "Nothing. I've found nothing in any court documents anywhere. I'm still looking."

"I feel like my whole fucking life was a lie." Josh collapses on a chair.

I watch Lyric as she looks at him. She watches him for a moment before getting up and sitting on the arm of his chair. She wraps her arms around him in comfort. He pulls her into his lap and wraps around her, burying his face in her hair. I watch in amazement as he instantly calms.

Alex sits on another chair. Carefully. Like it physically pains him to do so. "You ain't the only one." Alex leans back and closes his eyes. "Find out we have a blood brother who is older than us. Who should have been the one the Lucinio Mafia was handed down to. But that can't prove any of it."

"I don't want it if that's what you're fucking worried about," Nick mumbles from the floor.

Jason groans as he sits up. He rubs his eyes. "He really doesn't. He's set to take over Crane Mafia if he needs to. You know, in case shit goes down before Christopher can."

Nick pushes himself up and sits, leaning against the couch. He looks up at Josh and Alex. "That didn't come out right."

Josh laughs the first genuine laugh any of us have laughed in some time. "I didn't think you did." He smiles. "You'd have to fight me for it anyway."

Nick laughs and shakes his head. "No fucking thank you. I haven't known you that long, but even I know you ain't one to trifle with."

"Considering he trained me in all I know with defense and weapons? I'd have to agree." Lyric murmurs, leaning her head on his shoulder.

Ryan jumps when someone knocks on the door. "Fucking hell," he growls, rubbing his face as he yawns. He looks around the room as he heads for the door. "Where are my parents?"

"They went upstairs to look after the kids. They're in the nursery," Luke says.

Ryan nods as he disappears around the corner heading for the door. The room falls silent for a few moments until Ethan walks into the room carrying Jackson and with Tait walking next to him holding one of his fingers. Christopher is burrowed into Jenny's neck with his hand gripping her hair.

"We thought we'd get the kids out for some fresh air," Jenny says quietly. "You can catch us up later. The least we can do is keep the kids busy while you all work." She gives a weak smile as she nuzzles Christopher.

"You both look pretty tired, too," I observe.

"It's okay, son," Ethan says. "The good thing about Ryan taking over is we do have time now to be parents and grandparents. Spoil our kids and grandkids. Be around when there's work to be done."

Ryan yawns as he comes back around the corner. "Feel like I've been awake for three days."

"You have been awake for three days," Arianna mumbles as she stretches. Jessa rubs her eyes. Dani yawns. "I can take the kids outside. We've napped. You both should get some sleep."

I chuckle. "Arianna Crane. Always the girl who takes care of everyone," I joke with a teasing smile.

She laughs. "Mafia King's Queen." She bows as she stands. "At your service."

Everyone in the room laughs as Cole and Lance walk in the room. Jessa beelines for Cole with a huge smile. He hugs her in greeting. Lance pulls a frightened looking woman gently in behind him. She looks rather frail. Tired. Like all of us. But she has an undeniable dark beauty about her. Dark hair. Dark eyes. Exotic.

"Rebekkah…?" Ethan asks, confusion laced in his voice.

All eyes snap to him. His mouth has fallen open. I thrust my laptop into Luke's hands and quickly stand, jumping over his legs. Ethan's grip on Jackson has loosened, and he's slowly slipping out of Ethan's arm.

I quickly grab him before he falls, looking at Ethan wide-eyed. "Mr. Crane?" I ask, alarmed.

"Ethan!" Rebekkah squeaks, putting a hand to her mouth as her eyes widen in shock.

He swallows hard. "Rebekkah…"

"Oh God…" Jenny sinks to the floor with Christopher in her lap.

I barely pull Tait out of the way before Ethan grips his chest and falls to the ground.

Chapter Four

✗ Luke ✗

"Oh God!" Arianna chokes out as she kneels next to Ethan. Ryan is staring at Alex and Josh's mother like he's seen a ghost. I quickly take out my phone and call our family doctor. "Ethan!" Arianna cries. She looks up at Ryan. "Ryan! Help!"

Ryan shakes his head like he's coming out of a fog. He slowly kneels down next to his father. "Dad?"

I look down at Ryan kneeling over his father. He looks defeated. The tears shining in his eyes as he tries to catch his breath throw me into a tailspin of confused emotions I can't grasp.

So, I force myself to focus on what needs to be done. First step. Get Ethan help. Second step. Figure out just what in the fuck is going on.

"Hello?" Doctor Chantau says into the receiver.

I step towards Ethan. "Ryan's house. Now. Ethan just went down clutching his chest."

"Be there in a flash, Mr. Massena."

I hang up as I kneel next to Arianna. Ryan is clutching his father's lifeless body with his head on his chest. Arianna is hyperventilating. Both

Jason and Nick are staring at the scene unfolding in front of them like they can't grasp it. Aren't comprehending.

"Dad! Get up!" Ryan yells, shaking him.

I put my hand on his back. "Ryan. Let me. Please."

He looks up at me, trembling. "I can't lose him. Not like this!"

"I know. Trust me. Please trust me." I remain as calm as I can be. That's what everyone in this room needs. So, keeping my steady hand on him, I turn to Arianna. "I need your help."

She nods and crawls to Ryan's side. She wraps her arms around him and sits on the floor next to him rocking him back and forth in her arms. She holds him as tightly as she can while he falls completely apart in her arms.

I lean down, listening for any breathing. I put my hand on his chest feeling for any movement. Begging for the steady rise and fall of his chest. I put two fingers on his carotid artery, praying to any God listening to me that Ethan still has a pulse.

Suddenly, I feel someone next to me. I look up. Taylor's eyes meet mine. He reflects the same level of confusion, but he pushes it back.

"Tell me what you need," he says.

"He's not breathing. We need to start CPR. I need someone to check on Jas and Nick," I command.

He looks up at Chase and points to Jason and Nick. Chase nods and does what he's told. Taylor meets Nicole's eyes and says nothing. Nicole nods and takes Breetana's hand. They split off to check on Jessa and Dani, who are both sitting on the floor hugging each other and staring wide-eyed at Rebekkah.

I've already started chest compressions on Ethan. Taylor leans down and gives him a breath on my command. Ethan doesn't move.

"What's going on, Luke?" Robby asks me as he grabs all three kids away from the scene.

I know he's scared. I can feel it. I can feel it from everyone. Confusion. Fear. Alex and Josh are both comforting Ryan's mother while we work on Ethan.

I shake my head. "I don't know, Robby."

After the fifth round of compressions, I'm starting to feel it. My arms are starting to tire out. Pins and needles run through my hands. I hiss and wince.

"I'll take over," Taylor says. All I can do is nod as I try to figure it all out.

I look up at Jason. "What is this? What's happening?"

He just shakes his head. "We... thought... she was dead."

"Breath!" Taylor commands.

I do as I'm told, then look back up at Jason as Taylor continues with another set of chest compressions. "Who? Rebekkah?"

Jason nods. "We were told..." He shakes his head. "We were told she was dead."

"Wait. Wait a second. How do any of you know my mom?" Alex asks.

Rebekkah stares at everyone both sadly and quite shocked, but no one answers Alex. Lyric has moved to Rebekkah's side. She is hugging her close, watching the chaos with wide eyes. Jenny has transformed into a trembling mess and burrowed herself into Josh's chest. He's hugging her tightly, not knowing what else to do. Lance and Cole look helpless and as confused as the rest of us as they stand next to Rebekkah.

I look down when Ethan starts coughing. Taylor quickly turns him to his left side towards me as Jason, Nick, Ryan, and Jenny all scramble towards him.

"Ethan!" Jenny screams. She breaks free of Josh and buries her face in Ethan's neck, cradling his head on her lap while she cries.

Josh walks to his mother and hugs both her and Lyric. Doctor Chantau hurries through the door. I back up and stand when Doctor Chantau takes my place next to Ethan.

Robby wraps his arms around me from behind and rests his head against my back. I close my eyes and lean back into him, reveling in how he always knows exactly what I need when I need it. Right now, I need him. I need to feel him to center me, so I know the next step to take.

I turn and take him in my arms. He hugs me close, kissing my cheek and neck. I bury my face in his shoulder. "I don't fucking know what to do right now," I whisper.

"Yes, you do," he whispers back. "Ryan put you in the position he did because he knows if he's distraught or can't lead, you can." He kisses me again softly before pulling back to look in my eyes. "So lead."

I nod, strength filling me once more, as my mother and Shane appear. They quietly take the kids outside. I look at my watch. It's time for family dinner. I silently thank Ryan for making family dinner's mandatory and both my mother and Shane for always being so punctual. I'm grateful to Shane for never failing to know exactly what to do when things get chaotic. They're here for dinner, but he stepped right up and took the kids without asking questions, even though this isn't the type of scene he usually walks in on.

They've moved Ethan to a couch in the den. Doctor Chantau has hooked up monitors to him so quickly that my constant amazement at the guy's efficiency is surpassed yet again. Jenny is holding Ethan's hand. Ryan is on his knees pushing back Ethan's hair. Nick and Jason are both leaning over the back of the couch.

I take a deep breath. "Doctor Chantau. How is Ethan?"

He looks up at me and nods. "He's going to make it. Yours and Taylor's quick actions saved his life today. I need to run a few more tests. But it looks like he's had a heart attack. Though, I don't recall a weakened heart or any heart conditions in the family's history."

"Run your tests," I say. "Do we need to get him to a hospital?"

"Yes. I don't have the necessary equipment I need here." He turns back to Ethan as he starts to sit up. "Oh no, you don't." He gently pushes him back down. "Tests are good from what I could run. But we need to find out what happened."

I nod. "Ryan. Jason. Nick. Help the doctor get your father to an SUV. Jenny. Go to the hospital with them. I'll follow with Jessa, Arianna, and Dani. Robby will come with me. Taylor. I need you here. I'll be on my cell. Call if anything comes up."

Robby kisses my shoulder as everyone starts acting on my commands. Before long, we're speeding to the hospital in near silence with more questions than answers running through our heads.

XXX

Dragging myself out of bed the next afternoon might be the hardest thing I've ever done. I groan as I start to sit up. Robby's head is on my stomach and his arms are wrapped tightly around me, effectively immobilizing me.

I chuckle and run my fingers through his hair. "Honey. Time to get up."

"Five more minutes," he grumbles into my stomach.

"No. Now." I reach down and slap his ass as I shift him off me. I start to sit up.

He grabs my dick with a wicked grin. "How 'bout now?"

I drop my head back knowing I'm not going anywhere. But I try to plead my case anyway. "Baby, we have work to do. We need to check on Ethan and make sure Ryan and our family are okay."

"Pretty sure we'd have gotten a phone call if we were needed at the house." He strokes slowly, taking his sweet time.

I'm instantly hard for him. There's no fighting it. "Fuck…"

I can feel him smiling as he takes my dick in his mouth. "Mmm…" He moans deeply and low against me as he slowly takes me further and further into his mouth.

I grip his hair as I close my eyes, allowing myself to feel him. Nothing but him. His warm mouth. His strong hand slowly working my throbbing cock as he sucks.

Harder.

And harder.

He flicks his tongue and nips just under my tip. I jerk into him, pulling his hair as I gasp. He knows what I like. He knows when he hits that spot, he'll have me coming in seconds.

But that's not what Robby wants today.

He pulls back and starts licking from my balls to my tip and back down again. He takes each of my balls in his mouth and sucks gently before he licks and sucks up the vein running up my length until he gets to my tip once more.

"Jesus, Robby." I look down at him just as he takes me into his mouth once more.

When I hit the back of his throat, he looks up at me. He swallows around me with a moan as he starts stroking the part of my large cock that he can't fit into his mouth. My dick twitches as my stomach tightens.

Robby grins and begins bobbing his head up and down matching his fast strokes. He nips my tip and instantly knows he has me where he wants me when I moan and push into him, silently begging for release.

I push him back down on my dick until I hit the back of his throat again. Reading me, he moans and swallows around me as he strokes my length.

"Holy... God..." My back jolts, and I come hard, shooting my load down his throat as he greedily swallows all I give him. My dick jerks and throbs as I thrust my hips. He sucks hard and flicks his tongue over my tip and around it as he swallows, sucking me dry.

When he's done, he slowly releases me and sits up, licking his lips. I sit up and kiss him so deeply, it takes both of our breath away.

But I don't have the option to take it further. I groan when my phone starts ringing. I look at Robby apologetically when I see it's Ryan.

"I'm sorry, baby."

"For what?" he laughs. "I got what I wanted. You got what you needed. It's a win for both of us." He kisses me as he gets up and heads for the shower.

"Hey, Ryan," I say, shaking my head with a smile at Robby as he disappears in the bathroom.

"First off, thank you. I don't know where this family would be had you not taken the lead yesterday."

"You don't need to thank me, Ry. That's what family does."

"I know. But you did it with no explanation. No idea why things were happening. I can never thank you enough for that. Your loyalty means everything to me. All of us."

I smile at the praise. "That's the job. I told you when I took it that I'd follow with no question and lead when you needed me. That's what I did. You don't need to thank me. I'm just glad that Ethan is okay."

"Yeah," he sighs. "Fucking hell. He scared us this time. He's never just... gone down like that. Well, I guess I can't say that. But the only other time it happened was when he had a bullet in him."

"I understand. So, what did Doc say? Did he call with the results yet?"

"Uh... Not a heart attack. He was shocked. That shock led to his heart beating at an erratic rate that he just couldn't keep up with. My father is resting comfortably. But that has a lot to do with my mom. She's told him if he gets up, she'll kill him herself." He chuckles. "Anyway. Josh is on his way over with Alex and Rebekkah. I'd like the whole family here for this."

"You mean when you tell us who she is and what the fuck is going on?"

He chuckles again, but it's a lot darker. "Who she is, yes. What's going on? Man, I don't fucking know. Just get over here. I'll call everyone else. Breakfast is being cooked."

I smile despite the graveness I'm feeling in this situation. "Can't say no to that."

"Gives me something to do with my hands. I'm fucking on edge right now. But I can't say I'm not thankful that Lyric is helping. She was here first thing. I'm pretty sure she hasn't slept." He sighs. I can tell he doesn't like the idea of her not sleeping. We might have only known her for a few years, but she's family. And after what happened the last time she went so long without sleep, I can understand the worry. "Maybe Josh can get her to have a nap today. We don't need her collapsing again."

"Can't blame you for that. She scared us all last time. We'll be there shortly." I hang up and quickly clean up.

Robby and I walk into the house a little while later immediately feeling the difference in mood.

Somber.

Heavy.

Quiet.

It's the quiet that throws me. And judging from how uncomfortable Robby is next to me, I can tell he's feeling it, too.

Chapter Five

⚔ Robby ⚔

I sit down and wait for Luke to sit next to me and settle.

Ryan waits for everyone to sit before he stands to address us. "There are a few people in this room who are probably confused. I'm sorry for that. Last night's events were scary as hell and dragged out this conversation. I'm sorry for that, too."

"We just want to know what happened," Taylor says. "We don't need you to apologize for events out of your control."

Ryan smiles, but it's weak. Everyone can see the toll this has all taken on him. "But these events were in my control, Taylor. Everyone here is family. But a few of you don't know some things that others do. I've always vowed that would never be the case. No matter how small or insignificant the information seems."

"I'm so sorry," Rebekkah says. Josh whispers in her ear and hugs her. Lyric rubs her thigh soothingly from the other side of Alex.

I tilt my head curiously when Ethan reaches over and takes her hand in his from the reclining chair he's sitting in. Jenny is settled next to him, making sure he's comfortable. I take Luke's hand, sensing whatever is about to be said is going to change the dynamic of this family. Whether it will be good or bad is something I don't know and fear immensely.

Luke rubs gentle circles on the top of my hand with his thumb comforting me almost instantly. He sweetly kisses the top of my head. I'm reminded once more that despite his position of power, Luke is by far one of the most gentle and caring men I've ever met. The others I know are all in this room.

Ryan takes a deep breath. "When we were kids, we were playing in the attic of our family home. Nick had just been adopted by our parents. Looking back, it was probably us bonding. But then, we thought of it as us being kids and trying to scare our little brother. We told him the attic was haunted. We made noises. Freaked him out. We were being boys."

Nick smiles softly. "I hated you fuckers for days after that."

Jason chuckles. "Not all bad came from that day."

Ryan nods slowly and takes another deep breath. "Nick called us a few choice names and turned to leave the attic. But he tripped over a box. It had a lot of dust on it. Looked like it had been up there for a long time. Naturally, we decided to open it, even though it said not to touch. What we found was a lot of pictures and a few belongings for a woman we'd never seen and didn't recognize."

Ethan kisses Rebekkah's hand. "They came down from the attic with the box, and a lot of questions."

I crease my eyebrows and look up at Luke, then back at Ryan. "Rebekkah... is family?" I ask as my brain works.

Ryan sits down next to Arianna and leans forward as she gently rubs his back. He nods at me, watching Rebekkah. "Family. She's our aunt."

There is a collective gasp throughout the room. But no one is more surprised than Josh or Alex. Alex leans forward, resting his elbows on his knees as he chuckles and shakes his head.

Josh, his arm still around a frail and terrified looking Rebekkah, looks down at her. "This is why you refused to say anything to us last night?" he asks quietly.

She nods. "I thought... being here... with everyone." She sniffles. "That would be the best for you. All of you."

"Ryan," Ethan says as he slowly sits up. "I'd like to be the one to explain." He meets Ryan's eyes as Jenny helps him get comfortable in his new position. Ryan nods and sits back, cuddling Arianna into him. Ethan takes a deep breath once he's settled. "When I was a young man, just turned twenty-one, I got news that my sister, Rebekkah, was killed in a car accident on her way home from college in the summer after her Freshman year. She was just barely nineteen. She'd just told me she'd gotten engaged to the man she'd been dating all through high school."

"I was happy," Rebekkah whispers. She squeezes Ethan's hand.

Without hearing the words, I already know what both of them are going to say. Suddenly, everything from yesterday makes perfect sense.

"I was devastated," Ethan continues. "Rebekkah and I were very close." He looks at Alex and Josh. "As close as twins. We had that kind of a bond. And it was because of that bond, that I didn't accept that she was dead. At least not right away. I didn't feel it. You'd think I'd feel if my sister was dead, you know? But I didn't. Not until the funeral a couple of weeks later. And only because they had an open casket funeral. She was made up. She looked alive. But if you looked closely, you could see that her chest was crushed in. Her cheekbone was disfigured. I couldn't argue with an official autopsy report. Certainly not with a body that matched what it said right in front of me. And one that looked just like her. So, I forced myself to believe she was gone."

"It wasn't long after that when he saved me," Jenny says softly. "But he was still reeling from the loss of his sister. We thought... the best thing for him to do... was..." She takes a deep breath. "Was remember her. In his heart. But things like pictures. The other things he kept. We decided, together, that in order for him to move on, he had to put those things away."

"But it was also pressure from my father and mother both," Ethan says. "In order for me to be the leader that I was meant to be, I had to push all of those emotions down and use that anger I had about her death to do what I needed to do. Many people thought I was the ruthless one. But that wasn't me. At least not at first. That was always my father. As time went on, I suppose I became numb. I didn't feel. But when I came home, I had my family. I had always vowed to treat my family like gold because that's not how my father treated us growing up. He was always cold and aloof. I didn't want that. I lost Rebekkah. I wanted to give that love that she should have felt to my family. In her honor. That's how I'd always remembered her. How I honored her."

38

"When we found those images," Ryan begins. "Dad and mom sat us down and told us everything. Dad told us about her and how ambitious she was. How she looked forward to college and starting a family. How excited she was that day to come home and see him. Spend the summer with him. They intended to go hiking in the Rockies. They had a lot of plans. He told us how close they were. He described everything about his sister in such detail that we could almost envision her standing right in front of us."

Nick pinches the bridge of his nose. "But we believed that our aunt was dead. A tragic car accident over a cliff on her way home from Maine."

"When I saw Rebekkah walk through that door," Ethan starts. "I honestly thought I was seeing a ghost." He looks at Rebekkah. "I'm still not convinced I'm not."

Rebekkah's eyes shine with tears. She kisses Ethan's hand. "You're not. I'm real."

I nearly deflate against Luke. He tightens his grip and rubs my arm. I rub my eyes. "You were sold off into an arranged marriage," I say, knowing I'm right.

Everyone in the room looks at me, but Rebekkah's nod confirms what I'm sure everyone feared. Jessa sniffles. Arianna wipes her eyes and hides in Ryan's chest. Nicole whispers something I can't hear as Breetana lets out a strangled sob.

"Why? Why would anyone think that's right? It's horrible," Dani says.

"It's how most mafia's work," Jason answers. "It may be how it used to be done, but it's not how we grew up. It's not how Ryan runs it. It's not how dad ran it. It's one thing that we've never agreed with. Arranged marriages are an archaic way of doing things."

Rebekkah sniffles. "But our father didn't agree." She sits a little straighter. "I didn't know that my father had faked my death. I arrived home. Ethan was out. Our father and mother met me at the door. My things were packed. There was a man there I'd never seen. He was about our father's age. I thought he was someone he worked with. I was used to seeing people come and go. But seeing all of the luggage, my luggage, I was instantly on edge. I was scared. My father said that I was to be married to a person in another mafia. That it had been in the works for a while."

"Our father," Josh growls.

Rebekkah looks down and plays with her fingers. "Yes. But I didn't know that. Not then. I thought he was joking. But mom, she said that it was no joke. That the deal had been made. That I needed to do this. It was my destiny. My role within the Crane Mafia. I instantly tried to run. I was screaming for Ethan. I was hoping he was there. That they were lying when they said he was out. I knew Ethan wouldn't allow this to happen. He wouldn't allow me to be sold off like a piece of property. We'd seen it happen in other mafias. We'd talked about how terrible we thought it was. How he'd never allow that to happen in his family."

"I really was out," Ethan says. "I didn't know at the time, not until just now, but it was a set up. I was sent on a surveillance mission. But the whole time I was out, they were selling off my baby sister. And she's right. I never would have allowed it."

Rebekkah smiles a pained smile. "I was dragged from the house kicking and screaming. Literally. I was shoved into a vehicle and slapped. Hard. But I still fought. Then I was punched. When I came to, I was in a room in a house I'd never seen. Everything was different. The smells. The air. The feel of the sheets. The bed. It took me quite a while to realize what happened. As soon as I did, I immediately ran. But I was locked in the room. I had no phone. No means to communicate at all. I tried picking the lock. I tried breaking a chair against the handle to get out. But nothing worked. I was stuck."

"When did you know who you were being married off to and why?" Luke asks.

"That night. Or at least I think it was that night. It wasn't long after I woke up. I was in the process of throwing myself at the door when it opened. I threw myself right into the arms of a young man that I hadn't seen up to that point."

"Father," Alex says as he leans back.

"Yes." Rebekkah nods. "And believe it or not, he was actually kind. He sat down with me and we just talked. He told me he didn't want this sham of a marriage anymore than I did. He had gotten married the night before." She looks up at Nick.

His eyes widen. "You knew he married my mother?"

"I didn't know that she was your mother. Not for a very long time afterwards." She looks back down at her lap. "At first, he told me he'd planned to break the pact that his father and my father had stupidly entered into. And I believed him. He promised to help me. He told me that we needed to fake it for a couple of days until he could figure out what to do. So, we did. And his plan, though I never really knew what it was, worked. He came to me with his marriage license and said that that day was the day. That I could go home. I was so happy. I just hugged him for a long time as I cried."

"But… that's not what happened…" My heart breaks the more and more I hear.

She looks up at me sadly as she shakes her head. "No. It's not what happened at all." She bites her lip. "He took me down to his father's office. We were going to break the news to him. But his father had already found out about Matthew's secret marriage. He found out where Matthew had hidden her. He had pictures of her tied up. Bound and gagged. Bruised. Scratches all over her. Matthew was shaken to the core. He begged for her life. He begged his father to let her go. He promised he'd do whatever his father wanted as long as he left her alone."

"And you were caught in the middle," Chase says near a whisper.

"I was. I didn't want to see another person get hurt. So, I stayed quiet. I stayed in the back of the office like a good girl. That's the way I was raised. I listened to his father saying the reason this arranged marriage was happening is because it forged peace between our two families. It was our responsibility to our families. The merger of our two families would make us the most powerful families in the world. It was good for all of us."

"Why didn't you call?" Ethan asks.

"I tried. Several times. But I'd always gotten mom or dad. Eventually, the phone had been disconnected. I had no way of contacting you. I'd even tried to write. When I didn't get a response, I assumed that I just had no one left. Eventually, I guess I thought that no one in my family wanted me anymore. And it didn't help that I was being told exactly that by Matthew's family. I guess what I would say now is that all of my letters had been intercepted. Just as my calls had. After two years of trying, I gave up. I didn't know that they had faked my death so you thought I was dead."

"What about the papers?" Taylor asks. "The Lucinio family is all over them. So is the Crane family. You would have had to have seen them. Seen what's going on," Taylor chokes out.

Ethan shakes his head. "Rebekkah was never on them. I knew he was married. We all knew he was married. But he kept her very well hidden. She was never seen. She was only referred to as Matthew's wife. Most of the shit in the papers involving him was a company he'd taken over or a woman he had on his arm for some event. Rebekkah was never seen publicly."

"And I never knew what happened because I wasn't allowed to read the papers or watch the news. I'd get severely punished if I tried."

I shake my head and look at Ryan. "I'm not trying to disrespect you, but you and Alex have been friends a long time. Like brothers. How have you never seen his mom?"

"It never came up," Alex responds.

Ryan looks at me. "I never needed to know. Alex hadn't seen my mom until I married Arianna."

"The only times Ryan had been to my house was when we were on missions. The first time was when Josh called me in the middle of the night saying dad had fucked him up and had taken our mother somewhere. Ryan never saw her face. He guarded the door while I covered her up and the doc saw to her wounds. The second time was when we went in and took out the person we thought was my father. But Josh and I had already gotten our mother out."

I nod and rub my forehead. "So, she's your aunt. Which makes Alex and Josh cousins."

"Essentially," Luke says with a chuckle. He looks up at Rebekkah. "So you're with him for two years at this time."

Rebekkah nods. "He had found out about Nick just about a year or so into our marriage. I guess I'm not too sure. But I know that Nick was an infant at that time. He wanted custody, but his father wouldn't allow it. He made him relinquish all duties of fatherhood. All responsibilities. Then he paid her off and moved her someplace else so Matthew wouldn't go after her. Matthew was distraught about it. He'd just come to accept what was happening to us. But that, well, that upset him. He decided then and there that he would never give up looking for her. I couldn't blame him. I felt the same way. But I knew that I couldn't reach out to the person I loved because when I did try contacting him, things were intercepted. They had to have been. I'm sure of that now. At the time, though, I thought he abandoned me, too."

"I'm so fucking sorry, mom," Josh says. He hugs her tighter. "I wish I'd known all of this sooner."

She reaches up and touches his cheek. She leans forward and kisses his forehead. "It wouldn't have mattered. There would have been nothing you could do, my boy." She lets her hand fall to his lap. "For years, Matthew searched. But every time he got close, his father did something to make her disappear, and he'd have to start all over. Finally, he found her. By chance. I really don't even know how, but he did it. He told me that this was about to be over. That I'd finally get to go home. I'd hung onto that for the whole ten years I'd been with him. I held onto the hope that as soon as he had her, I would be free. Matthew was kind to me that whole time. He never forced me into a sexual relationship, but that did happen in time when we both started to lose hope." She pauses. "We really did love each other. In our own way. To everyone looking, we had the perfect marriage. Two adorable kids. And behind closed doors, we were almost happy. We were in our own way. We were a team. So, when he said it was about to be over, I believed him."

"But that was a lie," Nick says.

Rebekkah looks at him sadly. "He didn't mean for it to be. He really thought that he had her back and that he had you. But his father somehow found out. He'd ordered a hit. He had believed up until then that keeping your mother alive was somehow keeping Matthew in line. He thought that Matthew would eventually give up and forget. He underestimated his son. So, he ordered Matthew's contact to kill you all. Only he did it pretending to be Matthew. I had overheard the entire thing, but we didn't have cellphones and email then. I ran upstairs as quickly and quietly as I could. I called Matthew at the number I had for him. It was his hotel. He'd gone to New York so his contact could bring you both to him. But he had already gone by the time I'd called to wherever he was supposed to meet his contact for you."

"My father...," Dani whispers. Nick kisses her forehead as he hugs her.

Rebekkah's eyes widen. "Your father?"

She nods sadly. "He was Matthew's contact. We just found that out a few days ago. Well, Robby. Robby did. We thought my father screwed up. That it got out of hand, and he killed them. That's how it looked from what Robby found. And it fits with what I remember happening. He came home that night and..." She turns and buries her face in Nick's chest as she starts crying.

"He went home and was confronted by Dani's mother," I finish for her. "She had evidence that he was into some shady shit. We found records of the money he was paid by Matthew. We thought it was for the hit. We thought he was trying to kill Nick's parents and take Nick back to Matthew. But it makes so much more sense now with the other things we found. Like the marriage certificate between him and Nick's mom."

"He got back home after believing the love of his life and son had been killed. And he got my message, but it was too late. He was irate with his father, but even more irate with me for not getting to him sooner." She takes a deep breath and closes her eyes a moment before opening them. "Things changed that night. He couldn't have her anymore, but he had me. I became a possession. A game. He became cruel. Suddenly, I was owned by him."

"That's so awful," Jessa sniffles.

Rebekkah gives her a kind smile. "Matthew really lost it at that point. He thought he lost Nick. He'd planned on Nick being his heir. But without him, he had to finally bend to his father's will. So…" She looks up at Alex and Josh. Almost apologetically.

I meet Luke's eyes. He's suddenly just as uncomfortable as me. He shifts slightly and cocks his head curiously. Much like everyone else in the room who caught the expression.

Alex shifts. "So…?"

Rebekkah stands and paces for a moment before turning back to her sons. "I want you to know that I wanted to tell you all of this a long time ago, but he threatened me. He threatened to kill me. He threatened to break the pact and go after Ethan. My whole family." She turns towards Jason and Ryan. "Both of you."

"It's okay, mom. We know better than anyone the way he was. What did he do?" Josh asks as he watches her.

She's silent for a few moments as she gathers her thoughts. Finally, she looks at both Alex and Josh. "It started with him switching information on your birth certificates," she says quietly.

"Switching… information on our birth certificates…?" Alex looks at Josh then back at Rebekkah.

"Shit…," I whisper, glancing at Luke. His eyes widen in disbelief. I know he's caught on. Lyric's sharp intake tells me she has, too. She moves to Josh's side and hugs him tight.

"Yes...," Rebekkah says slowly. "Josh... you..." She closes her eyes again a few moments before opening them. "You were born first. You were born with the umbilical cord wrapped around your neck. You weren't crying. They had to perform life-saving measures on you. Alex came out a few minutes later. He was reaching for you. Screaming for you. Matthew used that. He didn't have Nick. He didn't know then if he ever would. He decided that Alex was the stronger twin. He was the leader. A backup plan to the real leader, but the leader nonetheless. He went through a bunch of legal measures that I don't understand. He paid a lot of people. In the end, he had legal documentation that made Alex the older twin. But..."

Josh looks up at her, even as he leans into Lyric. "But... I'm the older twin."

She nods. "Yes."

Josh looks at Alex with slightly widened eyes. "Why the fuck would he do that? Our whole life he pitted us against each other. Why?"

"Because he's fucking psychotic," Alex answers simply.

"You said there was a pact. Your marriage was to merge the Crane and Lucinio families," Taylor says. "But he went after the Cranes."

Rebekkah nods sadly again as she looks at him. "He found out that Ethan had adopted Nick. He had thought Nick was dead, but when he found out he wasn't..., well, he tried to get him. No matter how many people he tried to pay off, though, Ethan's money went a much further distance. Matthew couldn't get to Nick."

"I didn't know that he was trying," Ethan says sadly. "If I had, maybe we could have stopped it all before it started."

Rebekkah shakes her head. "Don't you see? That's where it started. Nothing you could have done would have prevented what happened next. He became infuriated, Ethan. He knew then that you were and always would be more powerful. He went back to his father and tried to get him to break the pact. His father was a cruel man, but one thing he could always be counted on for was loyalty. Even though, by that time, our father had died, he still honored the deal he had made with our father. And that was that you would work together and continue to grow."

Ethan shakes his head. "I didn't know we had any dealings with him at all. Even after I'd taken over."

"I know," Rebekkah says. "Because they were never directly with him. They were with his affiliates. And it was mutually beneficial. But

45

Matthew didn't agree. He felt like the pact was holding the Lucinio Mafia back. He tried to convince his father, but it didn't work. He started taking his aggressions out on me and our kids at that time. At first, I fought back. But after years, he beat me down. I was so afraid of him that even his voice made me cower. I kept throwing myself in front of both of you when he went after you." She looks at both Josh and Alex. I become furious over all they went through. "He started going after you when I wasn't around. When I was in the library. Or garden. When he knew I couldn't get to you in time."

Josh stands and starts pacing the room angrily. We all watch as his expression darkens. Rebekkah sits next to Alex. He hugs her tightly. Lyric stands and steps in front of Josh. She puts her hand on his chest moving him backwards until his back hits the wall. She cups his cheeks, pulling his forehead against hers as she speaks to him softly. Too low for us to hear. I don't know how she does it, but she has this incredible calming effect on him. Hell. On all of us. I know she's helped calm the girls more than once when the kids have overwhelmed them.

"I got news that the Lucinio Mafia leader had died, and his son was taking over," Ethan says. "It wasn't long after that we found ourselves in a war with them. To me, they were a new mafia. I hadn't dealt with them. I didn't even know how long they'd been around. My father never talked to me about them. I'd never dealt with them."

Rebekkah nods and looks over at him, taking his hand once again. "As soon as he died, Matthew decided the pact died with him. He knew that you knew nothing about it. He knew you thought I was dead. But I didn't know that. I thought you had agreed to marrying me off. I was angry. I felt betrayed. But I still loved you and this family. And he knew that. He used it against me more times than I can tell you. He always threatened harm to you and my kids. I begged him to leave you alone. I said if he went after you, then I'd leave and take the boys with me. I didn't wake up for two days after that." She looks down.

Josh growls from the wall he's standing against. He's hugging Lyric to his chest. "He beat the hell out of her. We didn't know why. We heard the fight."

"Couldn't get to her, though," Alex says, swaying gently with her. "He'd locked the door. Had guards guarding it. We fought to get to her. By the time we did, it was too late. We thought he'd killed her."

"But he hadn't," Josh says. "He told us that we would do what he said and go into this battle with this huge mafia, or he would kill her, and it would be our fault. We didn't expect the attack that night, though. We were blindsided. He told us the girl we had, the one he'd had some guys kidnap from New York, was Ethan Crane's daughter. That it was his way of luring him to us. But we thought we had a day to prepare. He told us about an hour before you showed up that you were coming. I don't know how he knew."

"That explains why things seemed so fucked up that night," Nick says. "When we walked in, we expected to blindside you. We didn't expect the fight we got. And that girl wasn't a daughter. It was Ryan's on again off again girlfriend. The Police Commissioner's daughter."

"He was beyond angry that he couldn't have you, Nick," Rebekkah says with a nod of understanding. "For a very long time, he hated both me and Ethan for corrupting you. Even though I had nothing to do with it. Then, when Ryan took over and grew exponentially, he grew more and more infuriated. More abusive. More out of control. I tried leaving several times, but I never made it and always ended up paying for it. After a while, I just…"

"You couldn't fight anymore," Lyric finishes in a whisper. But she didn't have to. The room is so quiet, a pin could drop and it would sound deafening.

"I didn't have the strength," she says quietly.

"I think we need a break," Josh says. "I just…" He pushes off the wall. "I need to go for a walk." He takes Lyric's hand and pulls her with him, heading for the patio doors. I don't need to ask where they're heading. They'll end up at Jaxon's Garden. It's their place. Theirs and their sons. I know they both have been down there a few times since they flew in.

"I think we all need a break," Luke says as he stands. He pulls me up with him as everyone else follows. He leads me outside, keeping my hand in his.

No words are said. We don't need them. Both of us are lost in our own thoughts. Both of us have questions. I can tell by the way he's chewing his cheek and clenching his jaw that he's trying, like I am, to put it all together.

But the pieces are so fractured and broken that fitting them together is complicated.

So we walk.

Hand in hand.

We think.

We go through section by section as we silently work through it as the Chicago sun sets over the lake in front of us, bathing us in a peaceful sense of serenity that I'm sure won't last long.

Chapter Six

✗ Luke ✗

I wait for everyone to settle after we had taken our breaks. I can tell from the expression on everyone's faces that, while we've learned a lot, we've managed to work through it all. All that truly matters is that a broken family is reunited. Rebekkah is where she belongs.

Josh clears his throat. "Alex and I talked about it. We've decided L.A. holds nothing for us. Our family is here." He looks at each of us in turn before turning to Ryan. "With Matthew on the loose..." He trails off.

Ryan nods. "She stays here. As do the both of you and Lyric. The construction of all the homes for our families is nearly complete. You can work with Jason and Jessa for your design. I assume you'll want to be close to everyone, as we all did. Until it's done, you can take a guest room in the house."

"Speaking of Jessa," I begin. "I'm curious. I feel like I know the answer. What was Matthew's obsession with her?"

"She looked like Nick's mother," Rebekkah says. "I knew as soon as I saw her. The resemblance was uncanny." She tries to smile, but it falters. "It still is."

Robby settles into me. "When he had me down at the docks I asked him what the obsession with her is. He simply said she's important to Ryan but that she looks like her. Said she was the one woman in the world he loved more than all the power he wields. I think he thinks Nick is a lost cause. He's a Crane through and through. But if he can get her…"

I nod. "He can get that heir he's always wanted and lost when he lost Nick."

"His goal is to destroy the Cranes. That's always been his goal," Rebekkah says.

"But his ultimate goal is to secure his legacy," I say. "We need security on Jessa. More than usual."

"I want Jessa here," Jason says. "I learned from last time. Safest place is here."

"And guards with me all the time. Even if you or Ryan or Nick are with me," Jessa says quietly.

"She's not the only target this time," Ryan says, meeting my eyes.

I sigh, not wanting to admit what's been playing in my mind since getting Robby back. "I know." I look at Robby and pull him closer. "Robby and Lyric, as well."

Robby blinks, trying to hide the fear. But I know my man. I can see it behind the brave facade. "I think we're all targets…," he says quietly.

"You're right. We are," I say. "But you're the one who figured him out. You're the one who forced his hand. He wasn't ready to come after us yet. You made him come out of hiding when you figured out he wasn't dead. When you tracked the money. When you cracked the web he thought he'd done so well at weaving."

He slumps into me, folding his arms over his chest. He sighs. "What about Dani and Arianna? They both have the same look as Jessa, and they're important to Ryan, too. He's going after what he knows will hurt Ryan just as much as he is going after a replacement heir. And he mentioned Lyric. He said Lyric is important to Josh. Losing her would destroy him."

"Maybe everyone should stay here," I say, picking up on Robby's silent plea and looking at Ryan.

Ryan nods and looks at Arianna. "We have ten rooms."

50

"I don't think we have a choice," Arianna says quietly. "We need to be together now."

Ryan leans forward. "Okay. Everyone in this room has a bedroom with things in them. Get whatever else you need. There's three extra rooms. One for Josh, Alex, and Rebekkah. Arianna is right. We don't have much choice. We need to stick together. Plan how to take him down once and for all."

"Lyric will stay with me," Josh says firmly. He looks down at her. "I know that will make you feel better. And maybe you'll be able to sleep at night knowing you're safe with me." She smiles shyly and nods. I can sense the tension release from her.

"I thought…"

Josh shakes his head. "We're friends. Family. It may not have been the best time to break up, but we've been discussing things for a long time. I'll move my stuff into the room she's been staying in."

"That… would explain why she stayed here last night," Robby says. "I'm sorry, man. I didn't know."

"Don't be," Lyric smiles shyly. "Josh and I are a lot better friends. Best friends. Family…" She blushes and hides her face in the fleece she's wrapped in.

Josh hugs her even tighter. I'm completely shocked but find myself happy for both of them. They may not have found their happily ever afters with each other, but they will. I'm certain of it.

"I, for one, would like to get to know my family," Rebekkah says with a shy blush.

"I'd like to know how things are going to change," Alex says a little nervously. "It's one thing to be close as brothers, but we share blood that we didn't know we shared. What does that mean? Nick is our half-brother. You and Jas. You're our cousins."

"I don't think anything needs to change," Jason says. "Everyone in this room is extended family. We're just as close as we were before all of this. Still have a strong bond. Blood or not. That doesn't change."

I watch Alex visibly relax. I smile and start to get up. "Let's get everyone settled. I'm sure everyone needs to get some things despite what they have here. Sooner we get that done, sooner we move on to everything else."

"Couldn't agree more," Chase says as he stands and helps Breetana up.

Robby stands with me. "Luke," he says quietly. He grips my hand.

I turn to him. Seeing his worried expression makes my heart skip a beat. "Yeah?"

"I don't think anyone should be going anywhere without guards," he whispers. "He's not fucking around anymore."

I lean down and kiss him softly. "Okay. I'll take care of it." I gently caress his cheek before calling the guard's quarters to have escorts meet us and escort two couples at a time, unwilling to let more than that go at once.

Less targets.

When everyone is back and has everything they need, I take Robby's hand. I lead him down the path to my cottage where we both have been spending most of our time. To ease his fears, though he still hasn't admitted to having any, I make sure we also have protection trailing us.

"Thank you," Robby says as we start the walk back to Ryan's house.

"You don't need to thank me, baby." I squeeze his hand. "I know you well enough to know when you're scared. But I also know you well enough to know you'll always portray a strength that you don't feel because you think your fear is weakness."

"You know me too well," he says so quietly I almost don't hear him.

I bring his hand to my lips and kiss his palm as we walk. "You don't need to pretend you're okay around me if you aren't feeling it. I don't view you as weak if you're scared. Fuck. I'm scared. When Matthew took you, I'd never been so scared in my life."

He chuckles. "By the looks of your living room, I would've thought you were more pissed off. Not scared."

I can't help but laugh. "I was. I was pissed I'd let him get near you. I was angry he'd gotten to you. I was beyond livid that he'd done it right under our noses. Mostly, though, I was scared to death I wasn't going to see you again. That he would win in whatever the fuck game he was playing. Part of me knew you'd fight. Deep down, I knew you'd get away, or that we'd find you. But that wasn't the part of me that had control. I was fucking terrified."

"So was I. I thought I was a goner a few times." He looks down at the ground as we reach the house.

I lead him inside and to our bedroom. I smile at the scent of whatever delectable dish Ryan is preparing for dinner and close the door to the bedroom. Robby sighs and stands in the middle of it rubbing his forehead.

I take his hand and lead him to the bed, pulling him down next to me. "Talk to me. Tell me what's going on."

He looks down at the hands he has folded in his lap. "I'm scared. I'm terrified. And I don't like feeling like that. I keep running through every moment down at the docks. When it came down to it, I relied on my training and the confidence I have in myself. But I almost died down there. They were shooting at me. What if they'd been better shots? What if the one who got me in the arm had moved his gun just a couple of inches?" He looks up at me. Tears are shining in his eyes. "What if -"

I lean over and kiss him, cutting off his next words. I pull back slowly. "No more what if's. You got out. That's all that matters. Next step is to take that fucker down."

"I don't know how…"

I reach up and wipe away the tear that's snaking its way down his cheek. "What is it that Ryan is always saying?"

Robby gives me a small smile as he sniffles. "Trust your team."

"Trust your team." I lean in and kiss him softly once more. "Trust your skills. Trust what you bring to the team. You can fight. You can shoot. You can protect. And you have unmatched fucking hacking skills. No one comes close to you."

Robby chuckles softly and blushes as he looks down at my lap. "I don't know about that. There's a lot of good hackers out there."

I tilt his chin up so he's looking at me as I grin. "I'm sure there are. But I don't know any that have CIA backing."

He smiles and laughs. "That's because of Ryan and his contacts."

I shake my head. "That's because you have skills that have helped them. You've proven yourself."

"If I wasn't on Ryan's team, I'd be on the world's most wanted list."

It's my turn to laugh. "There's a reason for that. Because you're good. I'm sure everyone is thankful that you're using those skills to help instead of draining the Government's bank account."

"Our Government?" He cracks up. "We're over a trillion dollars in debt. There's no money for me to steal even if I wanted to."

I smile. "My point is that you could. You could use your skills to do a lot of harm. But you don't."

"I understand." He puts his arms around my neck as I slip mine around his waist. "Thank you. I think I just needed a little pep talk."

I reach up and run my thumb along his lower lip. "Is that all you need?" I ask huskily.

He inhales sharply and gently kisses my thumb. "I always need you."

I smile and let my hand wander to the back of his neck as I lean in. I kiss him deeply, letting my tongue dart in and play with his. I shiver when he nips mine gently and sucks on it softly. He lets his hands trail down my chest to the waistband of my jeans. He untucks my shirt and pulls back from our kiss only long enough to tug it over my head.

When our lips meet again, the kiss is far less gentle. Far more needy. Hot. I nip his lip. His tongue darts back into my mouth and starts a war with mine. He tugs my hair with a groan when my tongue wins our battle for dominance. I always win. Robby may hold a lot of control in life, but not with me. With me, he lets all of it go. I fucking love it.

I pull his shirt over his head and toss it onto the bed. I let my hands start a journey over his perfect ridges as I kiss his neck, blazing a fiery trail to his throat. I suck his Adam's apple tenderly as he lets his head fall back with a moan. He grips my arms as I trace his abs and continue my mission to the other side of his neck with my kisses.

His quiet moans and soft sighs drive me to the brink of madness with the desire I have for him. The insatiable need to show him who he belongs to makes the blood coursing through my veins buzz with the electricity only he's ever been able to bring me.

Robby reaches for the buckle on my belt and tries to hastily undo it. But tonight isn't about a fast lay. Tonight is about showing him what he means to me. Easing fears. Showing love and adoration for the man who is my entire life.

So, I grip his wrist and pull his hand back while I nip his shoulder, running my tongue along the mark to soothe the burn. I'm rewarded with a delicious low moan that leaves me wanting; needing more. Needing all of him.

I shift and kneel on the floor in front of him. With a slow smile, I begin undoing the button on his jeans. I love him in jeans. Something about a man in worn out jeans is sexy as hell, but when he wears them, my mouth waters, and I start thinking very inappropriate thoughts about everything he holds underneath.

He looks down at me, gripping the blanket beneath him. "Luke…"

I smile as I lean forward and kiss his well-toned abs while, at the same time, jerking his pants off his hips. He gasps as I pull them down and tug them off with a nip to his stomach.

Taking his already erect and beautiful cock in my hand, I begin my torturously slow strokes. I kiss up to his chest, nipping the hardened peaks waiting for me there. He jerks into me, his body trembling under my touch.

With my other hand, I slide it slowly up his leg to his thigh. I let it fall to his inner thigh, then make my way to his balls. I kiss back down his body while I roll his balls gently in my hand. He groans deeply and spears my hair with his fingers as he leans back, giving me more access to his God-like body.

I tug each of his balls lightly and start licking from the base of his magnificent dick standing at attention just for me. I know he's watching without needing to even look. Robby loves to watch me take him. Just like the sounds he makes for me make me harder and harder.

I moan as I lick at the salty and slightly tangy bit of come that sneaks out of him. "I love the way you taste," I say against his dick, my deep voice rumbling and sending waves of pleasure through him.

"Fuck, Luke…" He arches his hips into me as I gently scrape my teeth along the vein running up his length. "Oh fuck."

I smile against him moaning before taking all of him in my mouth. Deliberately. I stroke to the pace of my sucks. He pants and arches. His stomach tightens. His dick throbs as he moans. His thrusts into my mouth become slightly frenzied.

It's my cue. My cue that he's close to losing control. Giving me what I crave.

Him. All of him.

I grin. "Come, baby. Give me what I want…," I rumble low.

"Fuck, Luke!" He falls back on the bed as he comes, gripping my hair and pulling me closer to him.

I swallow around him moaning as his hips jerk and his dick releases the part of him I've been dying for. I lap it all up like a starving man. My strokes slow further and further as he comes down. I lick him clean and kiss the tip of his dick.

After a few moments, I release him and stand. He looks up at me when I lean down and kiss him. He melts into the kiss, relaxing for me; showing me that I've succeeded in my mission to calm him. I slowly stand, pulling him up with me.

I run my fingers through his hair as I smile lovingly down at him. "Shower for you. Take your time." I help him stand. "Enjoy it. I'll get our stuff put away. Dinner should be ready soon by the smell of it."

He leans in and kisses me. He pulls back with a teasing smile. "Sir, yes, sir." He winks as I laugh. I unashamedly watch his firm, tight ass while he walks to the bathroom.

After I put everything away and he's done with his shower and dressed, we both walk hand in hand to the dining area of the house.

The rest of the night is filled with story after story of the Crane brothers growing up. Everyone regals Rebekkah with memories of how they met Ryan and became involved with him. There's laughter. Excitement. Happiness. The mood is light. The room is filled with the greatest type of warmth anyone could ever hope for within a family.

And it's something we need. All of us.

Because the battle that looms ahead of us is going to be cold and unpredictable. Family is all we're going to have to rely on to get through it.

My hope is that we all do indeed get through it.

Chapter Seven

☒ Robby ☒

(Two Days Later)

A couple of days later, I drum my fingers on the desk in Ryan's office. It's early in the morning. Blessedly, no one is awake except Ryan. But that's only because he thinks working out at four in the morning is normal.

I lean back in his smooth, leather chair in his office and link my fingers behind my head. My laptop sits open in front of me. I've hooked it up to Ryan's desktop computer so I have two screens to work with. Why I haven't thought of this before is something I'll have to tackle later.

Right now, sifting through this information is my priority. Putting it all together. Making sure nothing has been missed. We need to be prepared for the Lucinio Mafia. And then we need to prepare beyond that. We need to be so ready for them that we can predict their moves before they make them.

That's where I feel I come in. Preparing my team. That's my role. Maybe not tactically. That's Ryan's job. Luke's. But arming them with knowledge. That I can do.

So, I start organizing. I take each piece of information and put it all together until the entire puzzle makes one big fucked up picture.

I lean forward. "Start from the beginning, Robby," I mumble. "There's still something missing in this puzzle."

The beginning. Well, that starts with Rebekkah and Ethan now. The pact their parents made. Not to merge. More of a partnership. Two separate mafias that vowed to work with each other to rule the world. Bonded by a marriage between a daughter and son. Neither of whom wanted it.

A secret marriage between Matthew and Nick's mother. Aubrey. The one woman he couldn't get out of his mind. Never forgot. A secret child. Nick. Matthew's heir to the Lucinio Mafia.

But not according to his father. Matthew's destiny and fate laid in the hands of his father as well as in the hands of a man he'd never met. And it crossed with Rebekkah's. A young, sweet girl who was engaged to marry the man of her dreams.

I write down questions in the notebook next to my laptop that I come across as I form them. The newest one is who exactly is the man Rebekkah was engaged to. Did he look for her? Was she told she was dead like Ethan was? It would make sense. If he thought she was dead, perhaps he wouldn't look for her. But I still want to know who he is. How he's connected. If he's connected at all.

I yawn as I finish the beginning of the timeline. I've been at this for a couple of hours now. I feel like it's important. We've learned so many things over the past few days that keeping it all in order feels like a priority.

I glance up when I see Ryan walk past the open door to his office. He stops and peeks in on me. He's got a towel around his neck. It's all he's wearing besides his gym shorts. I can tell he's had a good workout by the amount of sweat he has dripping off him.

He smiles as he wipes his face. "Why are you awake so early? I'm used to being the only one."

"Couldn't sleep. My mind started running away with me. OCD, you know. The shit that we've found out about Lucinio isn't organized." I pause and lean back again, slumping a little. "And I feel like there's pieces we don't know. Unfinished story."

He nods. "I get it. You hate unfinished things."

"I also hate unorganized things. I have all of this information in different folders. It's chaotic. Driving me fucking crazy."

He grins. "Well, I'll leave you to that. I know better than to get in your way. Breakfast in an hour."

I chuckle. "Yes, sir."

"I mean it. I know how you get when you get in the zone."

"I promise."

He nods and disappears down the hall. He's not wrong. I have a very nasty habit of losing myself in my work and not eating. I've been better about it. Especially with Luke around to make sure of it.

I chuckle a little at the thought. Luke has quite literally taken my laptop and moved it out of my grasp. Then put food and water in front of me, forcing me to eat. Interestingly enough, it works. I've always been built. Tall and muscular. But definitely nothing like now.

The past year has changed me in all ways, including physically. I'm a lot more muscular now. Toned. Healthier. I give credit to Ryan and the intense training I've been through as a guard, but I give most of it to Luke.

I go back to my screen, murmuring. "Matthew finds out about Nick, but his father threatens him and hides them consistently." I make sure it's all in order in my file. "Matthew doesn't give up. They have kids about five years into their marriage. He finds and goes after Aubrey again. His father has her and her husband killed. Nick hides. Is never found." I pause. "Fucking lucky. Thank God someone was looking out for you."

"Talking to yourself?" Luke asks from the doorway.

I smile and gesture to my screens. "Organizing."

"I know how much you like organization. Files for everything." He sits in front of me and props his feet on the desk. "I love watching you work."

I can feel the blush creeping into my cheeks as I look away. "Ryan sent you in here to make sure I come to breakfast, didn't he?"

Luke holds up his hands playfully. "Guilty as charged. But you got some time."

I chuckle. "Good. You can make sure I don't miss anything with my mumbling."

"Okay. His parents. Killed by Krins."

I nod and look back at my screens, grabbing files and putting them in order in the proper folder. "Krins is Dani's father. Kills Dani's mother for figuring out a secret. Still don't know what the secret is. The assumption is what he's done."

"We don't assume."

"We don't assume," I repeat. I write down a reminder telling myself to dig into what his secret could be. "He flees. Leaves Dani. Little while later, Ethan adopts Nick. Still having no idea Rebekkah is alive or anything about a pact of peace between Lucinio and Crane Mafias." I let out a long sigh. "I feel like there's a lot of unanswered bullshit."

"We know Matthew tried to get to Nick. But Ethan's pockets are deeper."

I look up at him. "Wouldn't that mean he had to know? He had to have been paying people off."

Luke shakes his head. "That isn't how mafias work, baby. At least not completely. I mean, yes, Ethan had to have paid some people off. Like the adoption agency. Maybe a judge. But unless they come back to him for more money or tell him that Matthew had been inquiring, he's not going to know a thing." Luke leans forward. "Write down to question Ethan about that. Who he paid off. Might need to know later."

I nod and do as told. "Okay. So then, Matthew's father dies. Matthew views the pact as over."

"He goes after the Cranes."

"From what Ryan has said, there were a few smaller gangs that they dealt with. Then his friend was kidnapped. They figured out who it was and went after them. Ethan didn't know about a pact even existing."

"He didn't know about business dealings either. They must have ended before he took control."

I write down a note to ask. "They go after the Lucinio Mafia, who Ethan didn't know much, if anything, about. Ryan and Alex forge a friendship. Ethan nearly gets killed. Jason and Nick leave the mafia. Technically. Go off on their own. Ryan takes over, but another peace pact is born because of his friendship with Alex."

"It's because Alex always thwarted plans, but also because Matthew realized he wasn't big enough to take on the Crane Mafia. He needed to grow. Which is what he spent years doing."

"Then, Alex meets Jessa. Matthew sees the resemblance between her and Aubrey. Formulates this sick fucking plan to get from her what he's always wanted. The heir and the girl, but fails with epic proportions when he comes up against Ryan again."

Luke nods. "I think that's when he devised the plan to split Ryan's attention."

This is the part I'm struggling with. I tap my pen against the keyboard. "It's odd to me how he knew about Taylor."

"He'd been researching. Just like you. I think it was more a stroke of luck than planning, but if he was trying to figure out ways to weaken Ryan, he'd know about Taylor. They're close."

"So, he finds out about Taylor. Opportunity arose with Chase and Breetana. He uses his cartel contacts in an attempt to get to her."

Luke shakes his head. "I think that was more of an opportunity to get Ryan out there. The cartel is fucking huge, but I think he underestimated just how big Ryan is. How many contacts he has. I don't think he expected Ryan to beat the cartel. I think he expected the cartel to take out Ryan for him. End it right then and there. But even the cartel isn't stupid enough to fuck with Ryan."

I chew absently on the cap of my pen and nod slowly. "So, Breetana, Chase, Taylor, and Nikki were just pawns in that."

"That's how I view it."

I nod as I add it to my timeline. "Then we have Taylor and Nikki a second time. The gang that went after her. Krins was involved in that. Paying them. I went over that with Ry. We know he did Matthew's bidding. Probably as some kind of way to pay back for killing Aubrey."

"No assuming."

I nod as I write down a note about figuring out Krins' and Matthew's relationship. How it came to be. "Alright. Massena and Ambrosio. They were involved with Lucinio. We know they were a ploy to split Ryan's attention. Keep his focus on them and all the other smaller battles he was in so Lucinio can grow. We know that Krins was Dani's father and deeply involved with Lucinio. We need to figure out just how deeply." I shake my head as I finish. "I hate feeling like I'm playing catch up."

Luke looks at the clock. "Finished just in time."

I log out and shut down as I stand. I grab my laptop and notebook, then follow Luke out to breakfast. "I've been meaning to ask…"

Luke takes my hand. "What?"

"I still don't understand how he got to me. How he got me out of that house without anyone seeing. We had a fuck of a lot of people there. And with everyone Josh had with him? How did he get to me?"

It's something that's been on my mind since I woke up with Matthew's gun pointed at my head. Whatever scenario I play out in my mind leads to the same conclusion. There's no way he could have gotten to me. There were too many people.

"We interviewed the guards. Cal. He was the leak. He shot Krins. Right before he was shot, Cal said he had to take a leak. Returned just after. Just as another guard was questioning him about where the hell he went, he started screaming about having company coming from the basement. Thing is, we didn't have surveillance on the basement. None of the cameras could see that far down. It was a fucking bunker. We didn't know anything about there being a basement." He sits down at the table, pulling my chair out for me.

I sit next to him. "Fuck."

"He took off running right after. He was seen in the house by a couple of guards right before Josh's team got upstairs and guns started blazing. You were next to me then. Every guard that we questioned said you were there then. No one saw him disappear or you. Matthew came on the screen right after that. We all were distracted by him. But two of the guards outside took off after Cal. They found him a block away. He'd been shot. But we don't know who did it."

I look up as Josh sits across from us. "We think one of Matthew's guards. But we can't prove it."

"No one else saw anything?" I ask.

Josh shakes his head. "Nope. But we're sure that he was the only one paid off."

"What about the two that took off after Cal?" My heart starts racing a little at the thought of more guards within our own mafia being paid off by that asshole.

Luke squeezes my thigh under the table. "It was all caught by other surveillance team members. The story from all of them is exactly the same."

"Matthew said that he'd paid off a couple guards, but we believe that was a ruse to distract us from going after you," Alex says as he sits next to Josh and others start trickling into the room.

Luke leans into me and kisses my ear as he whispers, "Baby, you're safe. No one is getting to you. I won't let them. Not again."

I don't know if it's the confidence he portrays, or the promise behind the words, but I believe him. I lean in and kiss him softly as the sense of calm only Luke brings to me begins to snuff out the feeling of fear I'd allowed to creep in.

As the rest of our family surrounds us, the perception of safety once again becomes the dominant sense. The laughter around me is the final key to warming my soul and bringing that peace I needed.

As Luke's thumb lightly rubs the back of my hand, his fingers entwined with mine, I feel lighter.

Content.

Chapter Eight

☒ Luke ☒

"Yeah?" I answer into the intercom box next to me.

"We have a Gavin and Marissa Vandenberg, Damon Knight, Cole Westwood, and Lance Engle here," a deep, rich voice responds. "They're on the guest list, but not meant to arrive until later."

"Let them through. They're part of Josh's team. Make sure they end up on the approved list so they can come and go. Get pictures and ID's."

"Yes, sir."

"That really necessary?" Josh chuckles from the doorway of the den.

I chuckle. "We have a lot of new guards since I became Ryan's second. FBI. CIA. DHS. We have an entirely new system that Nick sat down and devised. Even if you were approved before, you aren't now. Well, unless you're family."

He nods as he sits across from me. "That explains why we had to go through the fingerprinting and other bullshit again. Lyric was shaken by it."

"My fault. Sorry. You won't have to again. I put you on the family list. You still have all the same access you had before to Ryan's buildings and planes. Everything."

"I wasn't worried." He leans back in his chair watching me. "And she calmed down pretty quickly. She knows how important our safety is. Especially after the threats that were made against her."

I pause the surveillance video I'm watching from the night Matthew made his ugly as fuck appearance. I know I've missed something. Anything that will lead me to where he is. Because, once again, that son of a bitch has disappeared like a fart in the wind.

"What do you need?" I ask.

"Nothing. Just curious why you're watching the same surveillance video you've already watched twenty times."

I sigh and lean back in the chair. "Because I feel like I'm not seeing something. Something that could lead to where ever the fuck Matthew is hiding."

"I don't think you're going to find that from the surveillance video. Only thing that will lead us to him is tracking his fuck ups. And we know he's not that smart."

I give a weak chuckle, feeling slightly defeated. "He seems to get to us pretty easily. He paid one of our guards and took Robby. He grabbed Jessa right from under the guards. He used the cartel to get to Bree and Nicole. He used a gang to get to Nikki again. He used Arianna's own father to get to her. Then used Dani's father to get to her. He paid off three of Taylor's team and his Captain to get to us. Seems pretty fucking smart to me."

It's Josh's turn to chuckle. "Robby got away. Without us. I'd say that's Matthew being stupid. Jessa was taken when she trusted that she was safe without guards. She wandered too far away. And the guards never should have left her fucking side to begin with. That's not him being smart. That's us fucking up. The gang, cartel, and his stupid as fuck plan with Massena and Krins is him thinking he's better. But he was outsmarted on every single level. He's not smart, Luke. The only reason he was able to get anything off as he was is because we didn't know he was alive. Now we do. We weren't on our game. Now we are."

"I guess you're right. I know you're right. Doesn't make me feel any less fucking helpless."

"That's all part of it. The trick is to focus on what you can do. Get yourself ahead of the game. You were ATF. Same thing. This is no different than a case you were working. You found your guys. How?"

I lock my hands behind my head as I think for a moment. "Tactfully. We used technology a lot. We used informants. Eyes on the ground. That's what we called them."

"That's what you do here. We have one of the best hackers in Robby. Kid is a fucking wizard behind the screen. We have another hacker. Lance. Those two together are unstoppable. And most of all, we have a huge fucking team. We have my contacts. We have Ryan's. Our eyes on the ground. There's no way he can stay hidden for long."

"We just need to work together."

"Exactly. Do what we already are. I don't care how fucking big he says he is. Take the Italian Mafia and Irish Mafia. Both huge." He gives me a cocky smile. "Then combine us. No competition. We'd completely crush them."

I smile. "I get it. I see where you're going with it."

"We stick together, combine our forces. We can't lose."

We both look towards the hall when we hear voices. Ryan leads Alex, Gavin, Lance, Cole, and Damon into the room. Robby trails behind. I smile when I see his nose is behind the screen of his laptop. Sometimes, I wonder how the fuck he sees his surroundings and doesn't run into walls. It's just another one of my Robby's many talents.

I raise an eyebrow as Alex closes the door. "Where's Marissa?"

"She was on the phone with one of her friends," Gavin says. "I sent her to the sunroom. She's a little fucking bitchy today."

Damon looks at him incredulously. "Today? She's been that way as long as I've known her."

"She's my least favorite person," Cole says. "Matthew Lucinio not included."

"We'll need to keep her away from Lyric. She's this close to attacking her." Josh chuckles dangerously, making a tiny gesture with his fingers. "Did you know Marissa told her it was her fault she had the miscarriage? That she deserved it?"

"The fuck?" Damon asks, incredulous. That's one of the most vile things I've ever heard. And I worked under my father before Arianna fled to Ryan's side.

66

"Yep. I wanted to kill her. Lyric who let it go. She'll be civil whenever she sees her out of respect for Gavin, but fuck if I didn't want to tell her to go ahead." Josh shakes his head.

Lance chuckles as he looks at me. "None of us like her. We don't see what Gavin sees in her."

Gavin plops in a chair. "Honestly, neither can I. We've been on the outs for a while. I know Jessa has forgiven her for what she did, but it's been a pretty big riff between us. I couldn't just leave her home at a time like this, though. Never know what Matthew is planning."

"What did she do to Jessa?" Robby asks as he sits next to me. I put an arm around him.

Alex chuckles and shakes his head. "Before we broke up when Josh was fucking with us, she'd confided in Marissa and Damon's friend Tia. Tia told her she should talk to Damon because with her new job, she barely saw any of us even though she still lived with us at the time. Jessa told her she would, but never did. So, at least Tia *thought* she had spoken to Damon. Marissa, on the other hand, didn't do anything. She didn't go to Gavin. Didn't come to me. She sat there and told Jessa she was crazy."

"Had she gone to one of them, any of them, they would have figured out something was wrong." Josh rubs his temple. "Jessa is a very forgiving person by nature. She's like Lyric in that aspect, though that girl can hold a grudge. I think it's the Brit in her. Marissa had a huge hand in messing up Jessa's life, though."

Gavin sighs. "I've tried to forgive and forget. Follow in Jessa's footsteps. But I'm not as forgiving as she is."

"One of the best things about you," Alex teases.

We all laugh as everyone settles. Robby leans against my shoulder. I can feel whatever tension he was carrying slowly melt away. I look down at him curiously, but say nothing when he closes his eyes. One of my favorite things in the world is being able to make him feel comfortable enough to let the stress he carries on his shoulders go.

"Alright. Let's get this started. Gavin, Lance, and Damon. You all know why you're here," Josh says. "We need to get our guys together. I want our factions meeting up with Ryan's all around the world."

Lance whistles. "That's a lot of factions, Josh. That's going to take time to pull together."

Ryan nods. "It is. And it will. That's why I want you and Robby on the emails to the heads starting right now. This is a direct order from the leaders. We team up. End of story. Questions, comments, or concerns, come to me or Josh. Anyone has a problem, they answer to us."

Robby sits up slowly. "Okay. What do you want it to say? It's going to have to come directly from you. Your email. And Josh's."

I keep my arm over his shoulder as Ryan dictates the email. Josh adds in what he wants to be in there. I watch him type everything they say proficiently and professionally. My pride grows with each stroke of his fingers flying across the keys.

Mine.

My Robby.

And I'm beyond proud to call him mine. It's never been easy to show who I truly am. I suppose deep down I always thought that being a gay man in law enforcement, or being a gay man who is a leader in one of the most powerful mafias in the world, would come with consequences.

If I'm being honest, I was probably right. If I'd been in any other mafia, or come out while I was working with NYPD or the ATF, I doubt I would have gotten the reception I have. There's not a single person I lead who has an issue with who I am. In this family, this mafia, it's all about the skills. And I have those in spades.

We're all close to each other. If anyone has any kind of issues with me, they've been good about coming to me to work it out. But not a single issue has stemmed from my sexual orientation. It's both a relief to me and a surprise. It's unexpected given the stigma that surrounds gay men in positions of power like I have.

I never really felt like I had a fear of coming out until recently. I'd always been comfortable with who I am. I never felt like it was anyone's business who I chose to sleep with. But I realized that I was wrong. I suppose I knew the family would be accepting. But when Robby shared his fears of coming out to me, I started to question my own.

Good thing my fears were unfounded. I'm not sure where I'd be or what I would have done had I faced any backlash. The awareness of how lucky I am compared to so many other men, and even women, in my position, is very real. Infuriating. Just because I'm a man who loves another man shouldn't matter. It doesn't make me weak. Doesn't make me any less capable of doing my job.

I hate that there are people in the world who think it does, though. That no matter how often I, and people like me, prove otherwise, there will always be someone who disagrees. Someone who wants nothing more than to bring us down.

I absently rub Robby's shoulder as Ryan and Josh continue to dictate their messages. I glance towards the door when Nicole quietly appears. She bites her lip as she looks at Josh and Ryan. Nicole silently motions for me.

I shift and kiss Robby's temple as I squeeze his shoulder and get up. I make my way to the door and quietly close it behind me as I meet them. But before I can say a word, Nicole puts her finger to her lips as she takes my hand, silently leading me to the sunroom where Lyric is waiting. She's hidden out of sight of the door and leaning against the wall.

I look at them both questioningly but say nothing, trusting their instincts.

"I have to get back to the kids," Nicole whispers. I nod and lean against the wall next to Lyric as she twists her fingers. I fold my arms over my chest and wait. It doesn't take long.

"Look. You aren't understanding me. I can't take the goody two shoes act that Jessa is constantly portraying."

I raise an eyebrow and look down at Lyric. "Is that Marissa?" I ask, keeping my voice no more than a low whisper only she can hear.

Lyric nods. "She's been talking for a while," she whispers back. "I was coming back from the garden. I heard her mention my name. Nicole came up behind me as I paused to listen. I sent her to get one of you." She smiles in the direction Nicole left. "Just after she left, she said something about feeling like she's a female version of James Bond with all the sneaking around and shit."

"It's driving me crazy," Marissa pouts. "This whole family drives me crazy. Jessa and Jason are both insanely and sickeningly sweet. They flaunt it so bad. Breetana and Chase are just so stuck up."

I stop myself from laughing by biting my lip and looking down at Lyric. She shakes her head with a smile as she pinches the bridge of her nose.

"I know there's no use in complaining, but I'm really pissed off. You aren't here. You don't know what I'm dealing with trying to get your stupid information. I mean Taylor and Nicole act like they're God's gift to the world. Arianna and Ryan literally think they're like royalty or something. Oh. And that Robby and Luke? Seriously fucking annoying. Luke acts like he's the leader or something. And his boyfriend thinks he's like the best at everything. Josh and Alex have been strutting around following Ryan's orders. It's like they're just weak or something and incapable of making decisions on their own. That bitch Lyric is here, too. I don't know why. It's not like she's anything important now that she's not carrying Josh's brat. She's so weak, she couldn't even do that simple task. And psycho Dani and her precious Nick?"

I squeeze Lyric's hand when she looks down at Marissa's comment about Jaxon. I'll have to remember to mention that to Josh. I have a feeling that might have her needing a little more comfort. Marissa pauses, but it sounds more like she's been cut off. I look towards the door, curiosity peaked. She's silent for so long, I wonder if she's hung up. But just as I'm about to check, I hear her sit down.

"Fine. Fine. But just so you know, if my father were in charge, I wouldn't have to be doing your job for you."

Nicole looks up at me, bewildered. "Father?" she whispers.

"Okay. Okay," Marissa sighs. "Damon and Lance are scarily close. I mean, like, if I didn't know they were into women, I'd say they were fucking each other on the side. Cole is stuck like glue to Josh, but he's still a cop. I don't know how he gets away with it. So is Taylor. He's a cop, but he's just all about Ryan. And Gavin is being super stingy with money and everything. And he's always near me. I can't seem to get a second alone. But he's standoffish ever since he found out that I kept what Jessa said about Alex to myself. He barely even wants sex. He hardly touches me and it's been so long."

"Who the fuck is she talking to?" I whisper, getting more and more pissed off.

"Rebekkah is here, too. I heard Alex tell Gavin that she'll be staying with Ryan and bonding with her family. But that's not something either of them have told me, and I don't know what that means."

Lyric looks up at me. I simply shake my head and continue listening, absorbing all of the information she's spewing into the phone. I'm hoping she fucks up and says the name of whoever she's talking to, but I'm not that lucky.

70

"Oh. Okay. That makes sense. I'll try to get more information. I've gotten pretty good at eavesdropping. And everyone thinks I'm stupid, so they don't ever suspect anything." She pauses. "I understand. I promise."

I pull Lyric with me into the bathroom off the sunroom and silently close the door when I hear Marissa getting up. I wait until I hear her walk past the bathroom. I noiselessly open the door and peek down the hall.

Seeing no one, I turn to Lyric. "Have Nicole grab Taylor and the guys. Have them come to the den. Then gather the girls. Act like you know nothing around Marissa. Tell them they need to keep her distracted. Do whatever they need to do. We're going to have a pow-wow."

"You don't want me to help the girls?" she asks quietly as she looks up at me.

"No," I say firmly. "I want you in the den with us. After what she said, I know you need Josh right now. And we need him in the pow-wow. Besides, I'd like you to tell everyone what you heard. Make sure I have it right."

"She's obviously betraying us, but who do you think she was talking to?"

"I don't know, honey. But we're going to find out. Tell the girls that the guys will fill them in when we're done."

She nods and takes a deep breath. "Okay."

I give her a reassuring hug. "You did the right thing. Keep your eyes and ears open. Grab the guys for me. Then tell the girls to stay inside. If she's out of their sight for even a second, they text me or come here." I kiss the top of her head before leading her out of the bathroom. I duck back into the den as she heads for the stairs.

Ryan meets my eyes. "Everything good?"

"Nope." I sit next to Robby. "We have a huge fucking problem. I just sent Lyric to grab the guys then get the girls together. She's giving them my direct orders to text me or come to this room if Marrisa is out of their sight for even a second, then Lyric will be joining us." I look at Josh. He raises an eyebrow curiously. "She needs you right now, but we need you here, so I told her she would be staying. I'll explain when she gets in here."

Ryan raises an eyebrow. "Marissa."

I only give him a nod as the room falls quiet. Gavin gives me a quizzical look, but doesn't push it. I silently send him a thank you because I don't know what the hell I just heard.

What I do know is I want my brothers here as we figure it out. Things have been very fucked up since I've been involved with the Crane Mafia, but one thing that never falters is that this family is stronger together.

Chapter Nine

✗ Robby ✗

"So, hang on. You're saying you think Marissa is working with someone?" Gavin asks Luke.

"That's exactly what I'm saying," Luke responds.

Gavin sits back in his chair. I lean into Luke and rub my temples. I just want a fucking break. Just one little fucking break to catch up. To make sure that everything we've learned up until now makes sense and fits in this five thousand piece puzzle we're trying to put together.

Luke just explained everything he and Lyric heard during the phone conversation Marissa had with Mr. Mysterious. Visions dance in my head of Hawaii. Renza. The house up in flames. Not knowing if everyone was out. Being terrified that Arianna was dead. That I had lost Luke. All at the hands of my vindictive and selfish as fuck ex.

"I have so many questions," I say after a few moments of silence.

"Man. You ain't the only one." Chase rubs his head. "Who the fuck is her father?"

I nod. "And why would he be in charge? In charge of what?"

"Why would she be talking shit about us?" Jason asks.

"Who is this random dicktard she's giving information to?" Lance asks.

"Alright. Enough." Ryan holds up a hand to still the room. "Lance and Robby. I want you both working together. Someone needs to get us a tap on her phone."

"I'll call in my team," Taylor says. "Dane is the quickest at it."

"Okay. Good. I can track a phone like no other. Tapping takes me time," Lance says.

"Give me a firewall over a phone tap any day of the week." I smile, but even I can tell it's weak.

I just want to be done with this shit. I'm sick of people fucking with my family. I'd have nothing without the people in this room. I wouldn't have Luke, the love of my life. I wouldn't have the family I've always wanted.

"Dane can get a tap going. I want that done. Priority." Josh hugs Lyric closer, and tighter. "We can't really do much else right now."

Lyric has been in his lap ever since Luke told us what they heard Marissa say about her. It made his comment about her needing Josh make so much sense. She still struggles when it comes to her miscarriage. And I know that even though everyone has told her that it wasn't her fault, she still partially blames herself. I know it's something she's working on. He presses a kiss to her head.

"We're lucky Lyric heard her on the phone," Nick says with a proud smile.

"Definitely." Josh grins down at her. "Good girl for keeping your ears open, little one." She blushes and ducks her head with a shy smile. I'm glad to see it. Her tears were like a knife to my chest.

"Good job, Lyric." Ryan smiles at her. He turns back to us. "Josh is right that there's little we can do. Most we could manage right now is digging into her background," Ryan says. "Robby and Lance. That's on the both of you. I want to know everything about this girl. Everything."

"Starting with who the hell her father is," I grumble.

"We need to get Lance caught up with everything else we found. There's a lot of information," Taylor says. "If we're going to be working together, you all need to be up to speed."

"I agree." Ryan looks at me. "Robby. Take Lance. Go to my office. Get him caught up."

"Watch for Marissa," Luke warns.

I kiss him as I stand. I grab my laptop and wait for Lance to gather his. A few moments later we're settling into Ryan's office. After I get set up, I settle into Ryan's chair.

"Ready for some really fucked up shit?" I ask.

He chuckles as he settles back looking up at the wall I have my screen projected onto. "Bring it."

I launch into the data of every single thing I've found up until this point. Everything from where Matthew Lucinio started his obsession with the Crane family all the way to finding out Adam Krins is Dani's father. I show him where all of the money over the years has come from and been funneled to. I show him the marriage certificate and the annulment.

When I'm done, Lance leans back and whistles. "Fuck. That's a lot."

"Lots of unanswered shit. Like who Ethan paid off in Nick's adoption. He had to have given someone a lot of money. Otherwise, he would have known that someone was inquiring about Nick. And all those business dealings between the Lucinio and Crane families. What happened to them?"

"I think only one man can answer that. We need to talk to Ethan," Lance says.

"I'll text him." I quickly text him to see if he can come to Ryan's office. "We need to figure out this Marissa thing in the meantime."

"I'll start digging into her background. See what I can find. Maybe dig into her finances. As soon as we figure out who her dad is, I can dig into his."

"While you're doing that, I'll talk to Ethan. He's on his way."

I chuckle when Lance doesn't answer. I like this guy already. A man of few words. Just gets right to work. Doesn't dawdle and ask questions. A man after my own heart. Too bad it's already taken.

I look up when Ethan comes through the door. I don't say anything as he closes it. I just wave him closer. Ethan takes a chair across from me in front of the desk. I lean forward, a little unsure how to ask this incredible man the questions I need to without sounding like an asshole.

Luckily for me, Ethan is just as intuitive as I've come to learn his kids are. "You don't need to be worried about asking or telling me hard things, young man. I can take it." He gives me the signature Crane smile.

75

I'm instantly relaxed. "I have some questions about Nick's adoption, sir."

Ethan nods and leans back. "Okay. Shoot. It was a while ago. But maybe something will jump out at you and help out. What do you want to know?"

"Well, you said you had no idea that Matthew was inquiring about Nick. Only he can say for sure, of course, but I believe that he thought he was dead. How did he find out you were adopting him?"

"Keep in mind, now. Matthew had eyes on me before I even knew who he was. I've always had deeper pockets. But he knew who I was before I had a clue about him. My father never told me about a deal. He knew I wouldn't allow him to sell off Rebekkah to the highest bidder for a business deal."

"But you would have been told someone was inquiring. Right?"

"I had a team of lawyers who dealt with all of that for me. My job at that time was to give that boy a good home. If anyone got paid off, it went through my team. I have an account for that. It's not anything I wanted to be bothered with. We decided the kid was ours. That was final."

I look at him slightly incredulously. "Sir, with all due respect, what if someone came for him who was extremely loving and caring? You could have potentially kept Nick from knowing who his family is. I mean, aside from the fact that we now know who it is, but what if it wasn't?"

He gives me a reassuring smile. "Robby. I admittedly made mistakes when I was younger. I'll be the first to admit that. I inherited my father's and grandfather's mafia. It wasn't mine. I was following their rules. Yes, I was the leader. Yes, my grandfather had long passed away. My father, though, was still very much involved, right up to his death. A lot of his procedures were still in place long after I took the reins, including the team of lawyers who had their orders from him. I hadn't thought to give them new ones. Things were working just fine. No need to change it."

"When did your father die?" I ask.

"A little less than a year before we adopted Nick. But, like me, his power came to a pretty abrupt end. I took over when I was rather young. I was barely eighteen. That's why when it came to things not related to missions, my father was still very much in control. So, while Rebekkah was off to college, I was learning how to command a fucking army. Which worked for me. It's what I wanted. I didn't want her to be sucked into this

76

life. I wanted better for my baby sister. I wanted her to never have to worry about what I did. I wanted her to be happy."

I play with my pen as I think. "So, the deal. The one with Matthew's father."

"I wasn't in control of part of the mafia. The missions. Territory. That was all me. Not the business. My dad was still teaching me how to control the guys I commanded. He was still sending me places he needed me as he was teaching me. I had to grasp things very quickly."

"When he died, though, what happened with the deals he had with Lucinio?"

"I couldn't tell you even if I wanted to. We didn't have dealings with them by that time unless they were fronts for him. I'll gladly give you access to all of that, Robby. But it's a lot to sift through. We went through major changes over the years. Things back then were a mess. No computers. It was all paperwork."

"You have all of that?" Lance asks, looking up from his laptop for the first time since Ethan came into the room. "I mean it has to be boxes upon boxes of records."

Ethan smiles as he looks at him. "The wonderful thing about being in a position of power is that you have the ability to pay people to do things for you. I have each year of everything in a nice document stored in my safe at home."

"Well, that's... convenient," I say. "Still. There has to be a lot of shit."

"There is. But if you want to figure out what happened, it will be there. I didn't pay too much attention to what my father had done before. Maybe I should have. I was too focused on growing and turning my mafia into something I wanted. Mine. When he finally gave me control of the business dealings, Lucinio wasn't a part of it unless we were dealing with front businesses that I wasn't aware were part of Lucinio's dealings."

I scrub my hands down my face. "Okay."

"I don't know if we'll need to do that much digging, Robby," Lance says. "It might not matter. We might not need it."

I furrow my brows. "It might lead to more information that we need."

"I think it just answers curiosity at this point," Lance responds. "We have a lot of shit to sift through. If we need to do it, we will. For now, let's focus on Marissa. We know that Ethan had a team of lawyers involved. No one wants to fuck with their paperwork. And we know that his father likely ended business dealings with the Lucinio Mafia long ago."

"I do know that we have no dealings with them at all now. When Ryan took over, he and Jason went through everything with a fine tooth comb." Ethan rubs his eyes and yawns. "At this point, there's no way we have dealings with them. I suppose if they were a front company, it's possible Ryan would have missed it, but I doubt it. He and Jas caught a lot of front companies for other mafias that Ryan wanted nothing to do with."

I shake my head. "No. I know all of his business dealings. I know all the companies and who they belong to. He ran me through all of that after things settled down last year."

"Then, we pick our battles. We have our hands full with Marissa," Lance says as he goes back to his search.

I nod, feeling a lot better. Ethan yawns again. I stand with a smile. "Tired, old man?"

He grins. "I didn't sleep well last night with that storm that rolled through. Jenny was tossing and turning, too."

"You should go take a nap. Don't people your age do that these days?" I tease.

Ethan roars with laughter as he stands. "Watch your mouth, boy! I can still whoop your ass!"

"I don't doubt you could!" Lance says, cracking up.

"Get out of here, old man. We can take it from here." I smile widely, enjoying the tease. It's something I love about the family. No one is too high and mighty. No one sits on a throne of gold and can't take a little bit of razzing.

"A nap does sound like a good idea." Ethan pats us both on the back as he heads out the door.

I sit down again. "Okay. What do you have so far?"

"I know that her mother's name is Patricia. Her father's name is Jack. Last name is Benz. Mother's maiden name is Anderson. Both were investment bankers. I say were because they're both deceased. Murder suicide. He got caught embezzling. She shot him then herself."

I blink in shock. "Well, fuck. That's a little… backwards. Usually the other way around."

"Gets better. You weren't around when Alex and Jessa were together, but Marissa came to Jessa one day and said she had been disowned. Her parents didn't like the program she majored in at UCLA. She said they disinherited her. She had a trust fund, but they took all of that from her. She was living with Alex and Jessa. Gavin was there, too, because Alex knew that his dad knew about Jessa. He didn't know about the obsession, but he moved Gavin and Damon into the penthouse with him to help protect her."

"And Marissa moved in with Gavin."

"She said her parents refused to pay her tuition. She had nothing. They took everything from her."

I raise an eyebrow. "I don't like where this is going."

Lance turns his laptop towards me. "Take a look."

I study the screen. "Looks like she has a lot of money in a private account."

He nods. "Yes. Marissa Vandenberg has a nicely padded private account worth a cool million. Ironic that that's what her trust fund was for."

"Huh." I cross my arms over my chest as I think. "Why would she do that? Lie?"

"I have a few guesses, but I need to dig. Want to check out her bank account while I research?"

"Yeah. Sure." I grab the account numbers and start my search as Lance researches his hunches.

Before long, I'm neck deep in some very shady shit. My notepad is filled with things I hadn't expected to find when I started this. Deposits to her account from her father's account. Deposits to her father's accounts that come from accounts I have yet to trace.

"Shit…," Lance says, letting out a breath and locking his fingers behind his head.

I look up, shaking my head. "What?"

He glances up at me, then back at his screen. "Patricia was clean as a fucking whistle. Not even so much as a parking ticket."

I raise an eyebrow. "Why do I feel like there's a 'but' coming…?"

"Oh… because there is. Patricia really was clean. But Jack? Not as clean as he appears. In fact, Jack Benz isn't even his real name." He turns his laptop towards me.

79

My eyes widen. "Holy... shit..." Staring back at me is Adam Krins. I lean back in my chair. "Adam Krins... is..."

"Yep. Marissa's father."

"Marissa is Dani's half-sister."

He nods. "Half-sister. Same father."

"Which means... Fuck..."

"Either Krins is still alive, or she doesn't know he's dead."

"And the person she was likely talking to..."

"Was Matthew Lucinio himself."

I run my fingers shakily through my hair. "Is that possible? I mean that he's still alive?"

"We didn't think Matthew was still alive. I fucking watched Josh shoot him in the head."

"But Matthew. He said something about Krins being dead. Didn't he? I swear Nick said something about it."

"I know. But until we know for sure, I'd question it."

"We need to ask Ryan. There's no way he wouldn't do something to know for sure it was Krins. Especially after the fiasco with Lucinio."

"What did you find?" he asks, nodding towards my laptop.

"I got into Benz's account. Or Krins, I guess we know now. There's a lot of fucking deposits from a few random accounts. I haven't tracked them yet." I pause and look at him curiously. "What about his death? I mean, you said Jack Benz was dead. Murder suicide."

"Haven't gotten that far yet. I need to break into the Medical Examiner in Los Angeles. I swear I've done it so much, I should just have my own access at this point."

I laugh. "One thing about erasing people and faking deaths. Gotta change that documentation."

"A lot easier now that everything is automated." He throws me a wink as his phone dings. He looks down and reads a message. "Josh says Taylor's team is here. He wants us back in the den. He said Ryan put guards on the girls and has a guard by the door in case Marissa tries to spy."

"Fuck, I swear that man is so detail-oriented. I didn't think of that."

He shrugs as he stands with his laptop. "He has to be. It's his job. Josh is the same way. He doesn't miss anything."

"He learned from the best, though. Between Ryan and Alex, Josh is on track to be even more powerful than even Ryan."

I grab my laptop and follow Lance to the den as he agrees. As crazy as it sounds, one of the most fun things about being part of the Crane Mafia is watching Josh grow as a leader. I love watching him work with Ryan and ask for advice.

But one of the greatest things about the guy is something that no one else, other than those in his circle, really get to see. The persona he projects is much like the one Ryan does. Ruthless. Hard. Uncaring. But really, the guy is one of the most protective people I've ever met.

I sit down on the couch next to Luke with a soft smile. I say one of the most protective people because I know a couple. But the one who is the most of all?

The sexy man I get to call mine.

All mine.

Chapter Ten

☒ Luke ☒

Robby leans over and kisses my cheek as he sits down. "We need to talk."

I drop my arm over his shoulder. "Oh? What did you find out?"

"Nothing good. Do we know if Krins is for sure dead?"

I narrow my eyes. "Why…?"

"Lance just figured out who Marissa's dad is."

I look at him in complete consternation. "Krins?"

Robby nods, not flinching or blinking as he looks at me. "Jack Benz is Adam Krins."

I shake my head trying to follow. "How the fuck do you know that?"

"Because after Jack Benz died at the hands of his wife, he didn't bother to change his looks in the slightest when he miraculously came back to life."

"The fuck?" I pinch the bridge of my nose and close my eyes. "Start from the beginning."

"Jack and Patricia Benz. They were investment bankers. Jack was caught embezzling. Patricia killed him, then herself. That's what the official police report says." He pauses.

I open my eyes and rub my temples. I've had one fuck of a headache coming on during the day, and it just hit. "Okay."

"Lance has an image of him. Same guy. Unless the fucker has a twin. I haven't been able to dig that deep, but it looks like Adam Krins is Marissa's father."

"I heard her say if her father was in charge. If Krins is her father…" I trail off. I don't need to finish.

"Then we have a problem. Either he's still alive, or she doesn't know he's dead."

"It had to have been Lucinio or someone working with him." I shake my head and glance towards the door as one of my guards nods at me letting me know he's there. I nod back as he closes the door. "We need to bring this up to Ry before we get started with Taylor's team and that tap."

"Couldn't agree more," he says as he settles into me. I kiss his temple and start to pull him closer, but he shifts. "Let me take care of you for once." His voice drops low. His beautiful eyes darken. Before I have a chance to respond, he starts rubbing my neck. His thumb hits a nerve or something, and the tension in my head immediately starts to release.

"Fucking hell," I groan as my eyes close on their own.

Robby nudges me forward. My body obeys on its own. I lean forward as he slides in behind me and starts rubbing my neck and back. I force my eyes open, but silently beg Robby not to stop rubbing as Ryan stands. Thank fuck he hears my quiet plea.

"Listen up," Ryan says. It never ceases to amaze me that the man doesn't have to raise his voice in the slightest to command the full attention of the room. It's deep, commanding, and dominant as fuck. "Taylor already explained to you all why you're here, so I'm not going to reiterate. I just want everyone getting to work immediately. Dane. I want that tap done. Right away."

"On it," Dane says.

"Next. Robby and Luke. Tell me what you found. Where are you at on Marissa's history?"

Lance glances at Robby before clearing his throat and turning his laptop for the room to see. "Meet Marissa's father, Jack Benz."

"That... looks... suspiciously like someone else we know," Nick growls.

"Holy Christ," Jason says, exasperated.

"Lance and I haven't had a chance to prove that he is, in fact, Krins, but there's a chance," Robby says as he continues rubbing my head and neck. The pain lessens more and more the more he massages.

"We were wondering if you had assurance that the man shot was Krins," Lance says.

"We tested his DNA," Josh answers. "We aren't taking chances after our fucking father came back from the dead."

"Then our conclusion right now is that Krins has a twin or, the more likely option, he is Marissa's father, and she doesn't know he's dead," Robby says. "Which would mean that the person she was talking to is either someone working with Matthew or Matthew himself."

"And whoever it was is holding back the information of her father's death. Because it really doesn't sound to us like she knows," Lance finishes.

"I can't be sure if she knows or not," I say. "She might. Maybe she was saying that because she believes if her father was still alive and in charge, then he'd be a better leader. We can't assume anything right now."

"Speaking as a cop, he's right," Taylor says. "We need hard evidence. All we know right now is that Marissa was talking to someone. Everything else needs to be backed up."

Lyric clears her throat softly. She's moved from Josh's lap to his side. I watch as she sits up. We all look to her. She squeaks a little at the attention. "I don't believe she knows. Not long after she and Gavin arrived, I heard her on the phone. It sounded like she was leaving a message. I didn't linger long as I hate being near her, but she definitely told her dad to call her back." She looks up at Josh. "I didn't think anything of it, so I didn't mention it."

"That's okay, honey. You wouldn't have known what we do about her parents. You didn't know her then," Alex says.

She smiles up at him as she sits up straighter. She squeezes Josh's hand as she stands. "I'm going to grab a drink, and then join the girls so you all can keep planning."

I watch as she leaves the room, closing the door softly behind her. I look back at Ryan to see him share a look with Josh and Alex. Josh nods to the silent question. What that is, I have no clue.

Ryan nods, turning back to us. "Let's get the both of you back into researching it. I want answers. Next up. Taylor. Josh and I have been talking since they decided to move to Chicago. Cole was his law enforcement contact while they were in L.A."

"Say no more," Taylor says. "We'll get him on my team. He'll still be a contact."

"While I appreciate that, I wasn't going there." Ryan gives him a half-cocked smile as I raise an eyebrow, curious as to where he *is* going. "As a Lieutenant, you have credentials to get me information no one else is able to. Working with organized crime is a huge plus that will come in handy for both of us. What we were thinking, though, is a whole new team." He gestures to Dane.

"You… want Dane leading a team…?" I ask. Robby kisses the back of my neck as he stops rubbing and settles next to me.

Taylor leans back on the couch across from me, folding his arms over his chest. He cocks his head. "You want my Sergeant?"

"I'd like him promoted. Same rank as you," Josh begins. "I'd like him leading a major crimes unit. He'd still be working closely with you."

"We already have a major crimes unit," Nick says.

"We already have an organized crime unit, too," Taylor counters. "My team is used to help ease the caseload." He looks at Dane. "It's a good idea. Their caseload is worse than organized crime. I bet we could get team approval without having Ryan or Josh influence anyone."

"Still need them for the promotion. And I'll want Cole on my team. He'd have to get transferred and promoted to my Sergeant. You'll need a replacement for me, too."

"I don't want it," Jesse says.

I chuckle at how quick the words came out and nod to Reed. "What about you, Reed?"

"Fuck no. Are you kidding? I see the shit Dane puts up with."

"Zeke?" Taylor asks.

"Nope. I want to be home with my wife and kid. She hasn't recovered from the idea that I'm back to work. She hates everything about me going back to the team. When I told her I was being called in today, I thought she was going to divorce me."

"Then, Nick. It's all on you, bro," Ryan teases.

"If that's what I need to do, I'll do it," Nick says. "But I don't want to hear any shit about my rank in relation to how long any of you have been with the department."

"Won't hear any from us," Jesse says. "You're doing us a favor."

"I'm working on taking on a couple other people to my team to replace Adam and Mark. If I'm losing Dane, too, I'm going to have to take on three people," Taylor says, looking up at Ryan.

"You're concerned about them being okay about working with the mafia," I say.

Taylor looks at me. "Up until a couple years ago, I hadn't told my team about Ryan. But we've been working closer and closer with him."

"We need people who we trust to bring into the fold," Nick says.

"We'll work on it," Ryan responds. "Josh will need to work closely with Dane and Cole, too. We don't need to be worrying about if we can or can't trust the people we'll be working with."

"Ryan and I will deal with the promotion and team influencing," Josh says.

I look up as the door to the den quietly opens. Everyone falls silent and looks towards the door. Rebekkah walks in near silently with a tray full of beverages. She smiles at us all as she walks to the table and sets everything down without spilling a drop.

She pushes her hair back out of her face as she stands with a brilliant smile. "I thought you all could use something to drink. I have dinner in the oven. I made a roast."

Dane gasps and sputters. "M-mom...?"

Everyone looks at Dane and back to Rebekkah with the same bewildered expression on their face. Rebekkah's mouth drops open, and she stares like she's seen a ghost. The reaction only succeeds in confusing us more. I glance at Robby before looking back at them.

"I..." Rebekkah starts backing up towards me. "K-Kent...?"

"Mom?" Josh asks. He starts to get up.

"Who's Kent?" Alex asks, shaking his head as he furrows his brows. He shifts and starts to get up, too.

86

"Mom…" Dane looks between Alex and Josh, his mouth slightly open, like he's trying to make sense of what he's seeing.

Rebekkah continues to walk back directly towards me. Josh stands and starts walking towards her. Alex, sitting next to Robby, looks at Dane. Dane meets his eyes, sharing the same bewildered expression.

"Whoa," I say as Rebekkah runs into my leg and falls into my lap. She's trembling, so I do the only thing I can think of and hug her. "What's going on?"

"K-Kent…" Rebekkah's eyes are wide as saucers.

Josh rushes to her side, kneeling in front of her. But she doesn't meet his eyes. Her gaze is fixated on Dane. Alex moves to my other side and pushes Rebekkah's hair out of her face. He looks down at Josh, sharing a perplexed look. Not a single person in the room looks like they're understanding any of this. Everyone is just as confused as I am.

Robby looks between Rebekkah and Dane for several moments before he seems to finally get it. "Holy… shit…" He motions between the two. "The similarities between you. I can even see it between Dane, Josh, and Alex."

"Care to enlighten me?" Taylor asks. "Because I'm fucking lost."

Just like that, the lightbulb goes off. "Jesus Christ. He's your son." I look at Dane. "It's so obvious. I don't know how I didn't see it before."

Josh looks up at me. "Son?"

I nod. "Dane is her son."

"Hang on. Hang on." Ryan waves his hands. Almost like if he waves them enough, everything will make sense.

I chuckle. "Rebekkah," I say gently. "How about you explain a little more about that guy you were engaged to."

She takes a deep breath and gulps a few times as she nods. Josh stands and helps her up when she tries to shakily stand on her own. Josh and Alex help her to a chair. They both sit on the arms of it, protectively surrounding her as they each hold a hand.

"His name. It was Kent," she sniffles.

"That's my dad," Dane says. "My dad's name is Kent."

Rebekkah looks up at him. "Matthew told me you were dead. He said his father killed you right after he… took me…"

I raise an eyebrow. "Matthew told you that?"

87

She nods and looks over at me. "He said that's what his father said. He said he saw pictures. He told me his father had a team go after Kent and my son. It was... after... a few years. I had tried contacting you..."

"You never said you had a son," Ryan says, still trying to follow as he sits down.

"Maybe you should start from the beginning, Aunt Rebekkah," Jason says as he rubs his brow. "You hadn't mentioned much about the person you were engaged to before you were traded off for that stupid business deal."

She nods sadly, her eyes pinned on Dane. "I... got pregnant near the beginning of my first year of college. I was able to hide it pretty well for most of the time. It was just the last couple of months I struggled with. I'd never gotten truly huge, but the last couple of months you could tell." She swallows. "I had you about three weeks early. But I stayed in school. Even when it was hard. Kent brought my work to me. I worked with my advisors. But I knew that my parents would be upset. I never told Ethan because I didn't want him to be put into a position with our father that was uncomfortable. Keeping a secret that big for me."

"So dad. He never knew?" Nick asks, looking at Rebekkah.

"No. He never knew. When I got home that day and was met by our father and Matthew's father, I tried to plead with them. I told them I had a little boy who needed me. I even told them that I was already engaged. They didn't care."

Listening to her talking breaks my heart in so many pieces that the thought of being put back together is difficult to envision. This girl has been through so much at the hands of a stupid fucking business deal, it's unbelievable to me. The family was torn apart because two guys thought it was best for business. So stupid.

"I was told you were dead," Dane says, still trying to wrap his head around everything.

"Everyone was told she was dead," Ryan tells him. "Even my father. The story was that she was in a wreck on her way home to visit. My father was out on some surveillance mission that his father sent him on. He knew my father would never allow what happened to happen."

"Wait. Just wait. Back up," Dane pleads. "Let's just pretend for one second that I don't know what the fuck is happening." He looks at

Rebekkah. "Just tell me who you are, why you're here, and how the hell you came back from the dead."

She smiles softly and wipes her eyes. "I just can't believe you're really sitting in front of me…"

Dane gives the room a pained look. "I have a picture in my wallet." He reaches for his wallet and takes out a picture. He puts it on the table. We all lean forward and look.

"That's definitely Rebekkah," I say. "Younger, but there's no question."

"Rebekkah is my aunt," Ryan says, leaning back. "When she was younger, just started college, my grandfather, her father, basically sold her off to a rival mafia in order to form a business alliance."

Dane rubs his eyes. "So, she's Ethan's sister."

"Yes," Nick continues. "The rival mafia was the Lucinio Mafia. She was basically handed to Matthew on a silver platter."

"Matthew Lucinio," Dane says as he follows along. I watch as everything begins to come together for him. His eyes widen as he slowly looks back at Rebekkah. "I was told you were killed in a wreck just about a month or so after I was born. My father said he'd gone to your funeral and was told by your father that he'd do whatever he could to make sure my father and your son stayed safe. My father said he'd been given a lot of money. Enough to live comfortably forever. I inherited a trust fund. I've never had to worry about anything, but I was raised to make my own way in life. I followed in my dad's footsteps and became a cop. My dad never forgot you. He never let me." He nods to the picture.

The mistiness I see in his eyes makes me tear up. "It's why you carry the picture," I say quietly.

Dane looks at me. "Yes." He looks at Rebekkah again. "Your father made sure we were okay."

"That's one good thing he did." I can hear the anger lacing her voice.

"So, if he's your son…," Alex looks down at her then back at Dane.

"He's our brother," Josh finishes.

"And our cousin." Jason chuckles and gestures around the room. "Welcome to our very own fucked up rollercoaster ride."

89

I lean back and look down at Robby. "Just gets more and more fucked up, huh?"

"I'm beyond sad for her," Robby says. He leans his head against my shoulder. "Fuck. What she's been through..."

"What about your father, Dane?" I ask. "I mean, my heart is fucking broken over here. At least tell me he's still alive."

Dane chuckles. "And pining for the girl he lost?"

I smile. "Call me a romantic."

Taylor laughs. "Out of everyone in this room, you're definitely the most romantic."

He's not wrong. I've planned many romantic dinners with Robby that includes all of his favorite things and spent many hours sweeping him off his feet. One more thing that my family gets to see, but others absolutely do not. The dark, brooding second to a powerful man. That's who everyone else gets to see.

"My dad got married when I was really young. I always knew she wasn't my real mother, but there was a lot of love." He smiles softly at Rebekkah. My heart hurts. I fight back a groan of frustration. I really didn't want to hear that. "He never forgot you, though. His wife died a couple of years ago. Breast cancer. I... uh... I know he'd like to see you."

Rebekkah blushes. "I'd like that."

"I hate to say this, Dane, but we need to bring your father here," Josh says. "Not just for her, but because if Matthew knew about him, he could be a target."

Chase sighs. "If he's using Marissa as his eyes like my instincts tell me he is, then as soon as we bring him in, Matthew will know."

"I don't see a choice here, Sarge," Reed says.

Dane nods. "Yeah. You're right. I'll call him. You and Jesse go pick him up. I want to get this tap going."

Reed and Jesse nod and head for the door. I look down as Robby discretely adjusts himself and leans forward. I rest my leg against his. He looks up at me as the others talk around us. But to me, it's just us. Whenever I look at him, everything else disappears.

"Problem?" I say low with a sexy grin.

"You being romantic. Kryptonite. I hate you."

My smile widens. "We got some time before dinner."

"Don't tempt me, you asshole. I have work to do."

90

"It can wait. You need a break anyway. You haven't slept well the past few nights."

His eyes darken with the desire I know is reflected in mine. "You don't play fair."

"No one in this family plays fair. I learned well."

He chuckles and adjusts himself again. "The timing is inappropriate. There's a lot of work to do."

I raise an eyebrow. "I don't really recall giving you a choice here. Go to our room. I'll be there in a couple of minutes."

He bites his lip as he looks me up and down whimpering just loud enough for only me to hear. I shift slightly so no one can see what his submissiveness does to me. When he quietly closes his laptop and slips out of the room obeying my command, it's almost my undoing.

I give myself a few minutes before I excuse myself and head for the bedroom. Robby is right. It's an inappropriate time to disappear for a fuck, but I also know him. His energy is fading, and he has a lot of work ahead of him with this Marissa bullshit. He needs a break.

And my job is to take care of him and his needs. No matter what they are, or when he needs them. He's number one for me. My priority.

So, as I close the door to our bedroom behind me as I enter it, I have one thing on my mind.

Him. And making him forget everything for just a little while.

Everything, that is, except me.

Chapter Eleven

☒ Robby ☒

I nervously crawl into our bed in the bedroom. Why I'm nervous, I can't say, but I'm always on edge before sex with Luke. I've never understood why. I doubt I ever will. It's not like I don't think he likes it. It certainly isn't because I don't.

I think it's because I'm used to being the one in control of things. When I was with Renza, I never allowed her to have any type of control in the bedroom. Not that she'd know what to do with it anyway. Most of the time she'd tell me she wanted it, then just lay there. She barely participated. After a few times, I admitted to myself that I didn't want anything to do with her or any other woman.

That seemed to be just fine with her. I turned a blind eye to all of her illicit affairs, playing the good and very naive boyfriend. It suited both of us well. As long as I didn't have to be the one to stick my dick in her, it was all good with me.

I look up when Luke closes and locks the door. He turns and leans against it. I shiver under his heated gaze as it travels up and down my body. I learned pretty quickly that when he tells me to go to the bedroom and wait for him, that he also expects me to be naked and ready for him when he walks through the door.

Not to say that's the way it is all of the time. There are plenty of times when Luke is very in tune to what I need. And instead of the quick fuck I'm about to get, he takes his time. He'll make sure that both of our needs are met, but he always puts mine first. There isn't a single time I can think of where Luke took what he needed while not giving me what I did.

I watch him as he slowly stalks across the room. His sharp and strong eyes burn into my soul and leave scorch marks all over my body as he takes me in. I'm as cold as ice and hot as lava. I shiver under his stare, but feel like I'm going to burst into flames at any given moment.

Luke smiles as he stops at the edge of the bed. He leans down and pins me under him as he kisses me long and deeply. His tongue finds mine and starts a war that he knows he'll win. He always wins because he likes the dominance. He likes me being submissive to him. He loves the control I give up to him.

And I love it just as much. I love letting myself go with him and giving him all the control.

I reach up and run my fingers through his hair, moaning into his kiss. There are far too many clothes between us, but I don't try to remove any of his. That's not what he wants. I know that if I follow all of his rules and obey every command, the reward will be worth all of the sexual tension I'm about to experience. I wouldn't want it any other way.

Luke pulls back slowly and straddles me. He runs his fingertips down my chest until he reaches my throbbing and hard as steel cock. But he doesn't touch. He gets a sexy smile on his face that only succeeds in making me harder. I bite back the groan and give him a small moan instead. My eyes zero in on his jeans where his large length is making one hell of a nice bulge.

Luke knows what he has to offer. He knows he's the full package, complete with rock solid abs and a dick that's droolworthy. He doesn't need anyone to tell him. I'm not ashamed to show him, though. One of my favorite things to do is stare at the beautiful man in front of me.

Luke slowly pulls off his shirt. "I've been waiting all fucking day for you."

I can't help the slow smile that spreads across my lips. "Then take me."

I'm rewarded with a sexy as hell smirk. "Oh, honey. I intend to." He unbuckles his belt and pulls it taut, making a snapping sound that makes me jump and my dick twitch.

I look up at him then back at the belt both curiously and in some weird as hell anticipation of what he's going to do with it. I've only ever heard of belts being used as punishment. I've never been smacked with one.

"What are you planning to do with that?" I finally ask after the curiosity gets the best of me.

"You'll see."

He keeps it in his hand as he shifts further down the bed. He bends and licks my dick, wrapping his hand around it. I arch into him, begging for him to relieve the pressure he's built up just by being around me.

"Fuck…" I jerk into his mouth when he takes my dick deep into his mouth as he strokes long and slow. I tremble as I moan.

Luke nips my tip and sucks hard, keeping pace with his torturously slow strokes. I grip the bedsheets with one hand and his hair with the other. I thrust my dick into his mouth silently begging him to let me come. I know he can tell by the uncontrollable twitching and spasming of my hips and cock that I'm close.

"You know what I want." Luke's voice rumbles against my tip sending vibrations down my length to my very core.

"Fuck… Luke, please let me come," I whimper as I plead with him.

He nips my dick again making me jerk. "Come for me, baby. Give me what I want."

I pull his hair as I push him down on my dick. I come so hard, it feels like it's being ripped from somewhere deep within. My stomach clenches. My hips thrust up. My body arches. My mouth opens to scream out his name, but all that comes out is a low moan and satisfied sigh because I can't form words.

I close my eyes as he sucks me dry. He slowly pulls back. I feel him get up, but opening my eyes as I'm coming down isn't an option. They're too heavy. He always appeases every single part of me no matter what he does, but when he goes all dominant like that is when I really feel the most satisfaction and contentment.

94

He doesn't give me much time to recover, though. My eyes fly open when that belt comes down on my thighs dangerously close to where my dick is hanging.

"Holy fuck!" I look up at him in both shock and wonder. "Why the hell did that feel so good?"

He smiles. "Because I know what I'm doing." He motions me up with his finger. I obey as he unbuttons his jeans. He helps me to stand. "I only use it for pleasure. I'd never hurt you."

I chuckle. "I know. I wouldn't be with you if I doubted that."

He kisses me as he turns me around so my back is to him. He trails the kiss across my jaw and down to my neck while he slowly runs his hands down my chest to my hips. I lean my neck to the side, giving him more access. I feel his jeans slip down over his hips and groan when his length settles against my ass.

I push back against him silently pleading with him to remove the boxer briefs.

But he loves playing this game too much.

"If I didn't know the reward would be sweet, I'd be on my knees begging for you right now."

He nips my neck. "Good thing you know I'll make it worth it then, huh?" He licks my neck and keeps himself pressed against my back as he tugs the jeans and underwear down, scraping his teeth along my ass and my back on his way back up.

"Jesus…" I close my eyes and try not to pant when he drags his fingertips up my legs to my thighs.

I'd almost forgotten about the belt, but feeling it follow his fingers creates goosebumps all over my body. Once again, I find myself thinking how fucked up I have to be to anticipate the feeling of that belt against my skin again.

Luke steps back and runs the belt along my ass. Just when I'm about to look over my shoulder at him, he brings the belt down against my ass. Such a delicious slap. I moan and bend over, placing my hands on the bed.

"Holy fuck." I drop my head on my arms.

I don't have to see Luke's smirk to know it's there. "You like that?"

"You know the answer to that."

"I do. But I asked and expect an answer." The belt hits my skin again. My dick is so hard that touching it at all against the sheets underneath me physically hurts.

I arch, sticking my ass up further. "Fuck. Yes, Luke. I like it."

He chuckles. "That's better." He drops the belt and slides his glorious dick deep inside me with a low groan that sounds far more possessive then it should.

"Oh God, yes." I push myself back against him as he grips my hips. He slides deeper and deeper until he's buried so far inside me that it feels like he's a part of me.

He starts thrusting slow and hard, just the way I like it. He pulls me back into each pound of his dick as I push back against his hips. The duel action makes him sink deeper with every single plunge. I grip the sheets, tangling them in my fists.

Each drive sends me closer and closer to the edge. His smooth, steel cock hits every place of pleasure I have. When he starts twisting his hips as he pushes his dick into me, though, is when I lose all control. I bite down on the sheets so I don't scream out for him, alerting the entire house to what's going on in this room.

"Fuck, Luke!" The sheets thankfully muffle my scream.

Luke reaches around and grips my dick. He strokes just as hard as he's thrusting. He pumps my dick faster and faster, keeping pace with the new speed of his thrusts as he pounds into my ass. My dick thickens and throbs for him. When I feel his do the same, it's almost too much to take.

Luke leans over my back and kisses my shoulder blade continuing his heavenly infiltration of my ass. He kisses up my neck stopping just behind my ear. He buries himself in me, holding himself as still as possible, but I can feel him jerking inside me.

"Come for me," he whispers in my ear.

The command is all I need. I come hard, making an instant mess of the sheets, my thigh, and Luke's hand as he strokes me. My ass clenches and pulses uncontrollably around him. The feel of him coming just as hard deep inside me, our dicks jerking in unison, drags moan after moan from me.

He thrusts with each spasm of his dick until both of us are emptied and spent, able to do nothing more than pant and tremble as we come down.

After several moments, Luke slowly pulls out of me. I can feel him dragging his come with him. Why I like the feeling of it dripping from me is something I don't think I'll ever understand. But I do. It's one of my favorite feelings in the world.

Luke drops on the bed on his back next to me. "I don't know how you manage to make each and every time better and better."

I laugh and turn my head towards him, releasing my grip on the sheets. "Me? You're the one who controls the intensity."

He smiles and turns his head towards me. "But you're the one who responds to me. And your response just keeps getting better and better."

I can feel the blush creeping into my cheeks before I have any time to stop it. He turns and kisses my cheek with a chuckle as he gets up. I crawl my way completely onto the bed so I'm laying sprawled over it on my stomach.

A few minutes later, I feel a warm cloth against my skin. I moan, content and relaxed, as Luke cleans me up. When he nudges me to the side, I slowly turn so he can finish taking care of me like he loves to do. When he's finished, he kisses my hip and gets up once more. He returns a few seconds later with a glass of water filled with crushed ice from the small fridge we have in the room.

I smile as I take the glass. "If they could only see you now. Badass mafia commander by day. Tenderly takes care of boyfriend at night."

He leans in and kisses me. "Don't be telling everyone my secrets." He gives me a teasing smile so filled with love that my heart melts. He takes my water glass when I'm done and sets it on the nightstand, then he lays down next to me and starts rubbing my back and neck and shoulders.

"Mmm... How did I live so long without you?"

"An age old question." He hits every point that hurts with practiced ease, slowly but confidently rubbing the remaining tension out of me.

"I needed this." I close my eyes, relaxing completely.

He kisses my shoulder. "I know what you need. It's part of my job to know."

I shift slightly as he continues the massage and turn my head to look at him. "I don't know if it's immaturity on my part, but how? How do you know?"

He runs his fingers through my hair before continuing to rub my back and neck. "I've always been good about reading people. I guess it's part of my job. With you, though, I just know you Robby. I know what you need because I know you."

The sweetness of the statement melts me even more. "If I wasn't in love with you already, I would be now."

"I can remember the very second I fell in love with you."

"This I have to hear." I give him a teasing smile.

He kisses the smile and increases the pressure of the massage, digging into my muscles with the perfect amount of pressure. I groan in pleasure as I feel myself loosening even more. Muscles I didn't know were tense are relaxing.

"It was the night we kissed for the first time. On Ryan's yacht in the middle of the Mediterranean Sea. Nothing but the water and stars overhead. Just the two of us on the back of the yacht when everyone else was asleep."

I smile. "That was one of the times I felt the most peaceful. Despite the bullshit going on with Renza and Arianna. And then, of course, your father."

"I don't know what it was about right then. But I knew. I wasn't even really with you. The talks we had, and the intense flirting. I think maybe even the fact that you were technically off limits. I think all of it combined for me, but that was the moment I knew."

"I think it took a little bit longer for me to realize it. Truthfully, it was probably love at first sight. I had feelings right away for you. But I didn't realize it until later."

"When?"

"When Ryan's and Arianna's house was set on fire in Hawaii. When we didn't see you or Arianna on the lawn with everyone else, my heart stopped beating. It was after that when I knew for sure. I guess I knew before, but then? Then I knew I couldn't live without you."

My eyes get heavier and heavier the more relaxed he makes me. When his lips hit my neck, I know he knows I'm a goner. He knows what to do to make me fall asleep. I don't think he cares about the fact that it's the middle of the day.

He really does know me well. He knows I haven't been sleeping because I feel like I need to find all of the information I can knowing that

Matthew Lucinio is out there. He can feel the stress he's slowly rubbing out of me.

This. This is Luke Massena. Not the tough, cold, unemotional asshole that almost everyone else knows him as. The real Luke is the caring, loving, protective man next to me.

"I love you," I whisper just before I crash. Luke pulls me close to him. I melt against his chest and sink deeper into his arms.

"I love you, too." He kisses just behind my ear as he holds me possessively.

Perfect, I think to myself as I lose the battle and finally give into the sleep I need.

Chapter Twelve

⚔ Luke ⚔

(One Week Later)

"Please tell me that everything that just came out of your mouth was a joke," I say, looking up at David, one of our guards, and a previous ATF agent who wanted a better life for his family.

"Sorry, Mr. Massena. But no. She was seen."

I let out a long breath. He's just informed me that Renza is, in fact, alive. We suspected, but without proof, it's been hard to really determine one way or another. I had been holding out hope that she died in the damn fire.

As unlikely as it was.

I growl. "Get the surveillance footage to Lance. Robby is busy with other shit."

"Yes, sir."

I get up from the weight bench I'm using and grab my shirt from the other bench I threw it on. This information has just thrown our entire plan into a complete fucking tailspin. I had hoped that we'd be able to deal with one thing at a time. I should have known better, but it still pisses me off beyond reason.

I wipe myself down with a towel and grab deodorant from my gym bag. I throw a shirt on and spray myself with my cologne. I don't have the time to change. I need to talk to Ryan about this shift in our game.

"Fucking hell." I jog up the stairs and across the yard from the guards quarters to Ryan's house. I walk in through the kitchen nearly jumping out of my skin when Ryan pops up from behind the counter. "Fuck…" I rub my chest.

"You look like a man on a mission," he says as he bends to check something in the oven.

"What's that delicious smell?"

"Croissants. They're going with tonight's dinner." He takes them out and puts them on a cooling rack. He then puts his hand on the counter. "It sounds insane, but I miss this."

I sit on a barstool at the counter and raise an eyebrow. "Miss what?"

"Zoning out. Focusing on nothing but cooking. The steps. Measurements. Making it all perfect. But the best thing? Watching my family's expressions. Enjoyment for them is like music to my soul."

"If anyone heard you talking like that…"

He laughs. "I know. Reputation would be ruined."

"Not just ruined. Torpedoed. Blown up. Destroyed to the point of no return. You'd never come back from it." I give him a teasing smile as he turns to continue his culinary work of art.

He laughs again. "Don't I know it! So, tell me what has you running into the house wearing gym clothes. I don't think I've ever seen you dressed down like that unless you were actually in the gym."

"Well, I was in the gym. David came in, though, and ruined my workout with news I didn't need."

"What news?" He takes the lid off a pot and stirs.

I choke back the groan at whatever the delicious smell coming from it is. Spicy. Beefy. "Uh…" My stomach growls. I look down at it incredulously, but ignore it. "Uh… Renza. She was spotted by one of our affiliates in Cancun."

Ryan puts the lid back on his pot. "Tell me they got surveillance."

I nod. "They did. I had him bring it to Lance. I'm hoping he can see more than just her."

He turns and folds his arms over his chest. "You're hoping they get Lucinio."

"Fuck yes. Then we can really focus down there instead of just suspecting that's where he might be."

"Call down there. Keep eyes on her."

"I'll make the call, but I'd hope that goes without saying."

"One thing I've learned in the years I've been doing this is nothing goes without saying. You'd be surprised at how many people I've lost because someone fucked up. It's like if they don't have the command, they think they've done their job."

I nod. "I'll do it now."

"Grab everyone for dinner, please. Stew is done. Arianna is upstairs. Not feeling well. I need to bring her some soup. It's warming. Almost done."

I pause by the door, my phone to my ear. "What's wrong with Arianna?"

He chuckles. "She's stressed. She's trying to be the good and strong Mafia Queen and take care of everyone that's staying here, but it's hard on her. It all brings back what happened with her father and Chad. Things she would rather forget. Add in all the new information that has been unloaded on us all, and she's exhausted. She wants to be there and support everyone, but she's neglecting to take care of herself in the process. Putting everyone else above herself."

"Well, that sounds familiar," I chuckle as I look at him.

He chuckles. "She learned from the master."

"I'll make the call. You finish the soup. I'll bring it up and check on her."

"Deal."

I lean against the wall and pull out my phone, finding the number of our Cancun contact. I wait for him to answer as Ryan finishes the soup as the stew simmers.

"Morales," a highly accented voice answers.

"It's Massena," I say. "You got me surveillance on Renza. I want you to stay on her."

"Yes, sir. She's at Le Blanc Spa and Resort."

"She alone?"

"No. She's got someone with her. A woman. I don't recognize her. Lucinio hasn't been seen. You want us to grab her?"

"Fuck." I rub my temple. "No. I want you to stay on her. Don't approach her. We're hoping she'll lead us to Lucinio. Find out what you can about the other girl. I'll get our guys on the surveillance you sent and what she checked in under."

"Yes, sir. She's in a penthouse. Top floor. Suite two."

"Got it." I hang up and look up at Ryan. "She's got a woman with her. Don't know who she is. They haven't seen Lucinio. They know the room. I'll have Lance look while he's checking the surveillance footage."

"Okay." He puts the soup, some crackers, and some Ginger Ale on a tray. He hands it to me. "Get that to my girl. Tell her I'll be up in a little bit. I just need to get the family settled."

I smile. "On it." I take the tray and head upstairs, making sure to tell everyone on my way that it's dinner time.

I quietly enter Ryan and Arianna's room. Arianna is curled up in the middle of the bed wrapped in more blankets than I would ever know what to do with. I chuckle as I set the tray on the nightstand. I sit on the edge of the bed and lean over pulling blankets aside until I finally find her at the bottom of the pile.

She looks up at me and sniffles with wide eyes. "Luke?"

"Not feeling so hot, huh?"

She shakes her head sadly and pulls the blankets closer to her. "I'm freezing."

"Well, I have some chicken noodle soup for you. Courtesy of your husband."

She smiles shyly. "He's one of a kind. But I don't think I can eat."

"I think you can. How about we get you sat up? Maybe if we get something hot in you, it will warm you from the inside out and you won't be shivering so much."

"I don't even know what's wrong with me."

"You have this nurturing quality about you. And you tend to let it overtake everything else. You want to take care of your family, but it's managed to overwhelm you a little bit. There's a lot of people here that you're trying to take care of. Add the kids on top of it, and you're just a younger version of Ryan. Always putting everyone else first."

She ducks her head. "I don't mean to. I just... I really want to help in any way I can. Ryan can't do everything."

"Well, honey, neither can you. Now, come on. Sit up."

She obeys the command and starts to slowly sit up. She puts her back against the headboard and pulls the blankets up as she shivers. She looks miserable, but I have my orders. So, instead of making her come out of her cocoon, I start spoon feeding her the soup.

I grew up an only child, but when I found out Arianna is my sister, I took on the big brother role quickly, and it fit. Arianna is an amazing woman. Getting to know her has been incredible for both of us. But having the connection we have has been even greater.

Sometimes, Arianna is the only person, beyond Robby, who is able to get me to calm down, be rational, and think. My mother had always been that person, but never fully. Arianna just has a way about her. A calming aura that makes everyone around her center themselves. It's no wonder that her and Robby are so close. They have the same way about them. It's a rare quality not many possess.

"How do you feel?" I ask her as she finishes off the bowl of soup.

"Better. Surprisingly."

I give her a teasing smile. "Hmm... Could it be there's actually someone in this world who just might know a few things, too?"

She gives me a mock surprised look. "You mean... I'm not the smartest person in the universe?" She gives me wide eyes and blinks adorably.

I crack up. "Maybe in this family! But Einstein comes to mind when I think of the smartest person in the universe."

She laughs. "There are far smarter people than Einstein. But... I mean, he's dead... so..." She shrugs her shoulders.

I laugh. "Oh my God."

"Seriously, though. You think this is all caused by me and my need to want to take care of everyone? Make sure they're okay?"

"Yeah. I think it has a lot to do with it. You wear yourself out because you're trying to lessen the load on everyone. Which is commendable, but you can't take care of them if you aren't taking care of yourself."

She chuckles softly. "That sounds like the same advice Nick gives to Ryan all the time."

"Well, Nick is kind of smart."

We both look up as Ryan walks in the room. I give Arianna a wink as Ryan settles next to her with his dinner. I stand, heading out of the room. I close the door behind me glancing back at Arianna cuddling into Ryan. He engulfs her. I'll never get used to his size compared to her, but it's one of those extremely adorable things that warms my heart to see.

Especially since I have to deal with this new tip. I'd much prefer Ryan and Arianna spend some time with each other, though. If I can lessen the responsibilities Ryan has on his shoulders so he can take care of himself and my sister, I'm game.

After dinner, I make my way to the den. It seems to be the place we've all congregated to share information. It's also where Lance has set himself up, and I want to know what he found. I want this all behind us so we can get back to normal. Whatever that is for a mafia family.

When I walk in, Damon moves away from Lance and sits some distance away from him. I raise an eyebrow but say nothing. I lay down on the couch and watch him do whatever it is that he does. He's a lot like Robby. He gets lost in his work and barely notices anything going on around him.

"So… Damon," I start, trying to make conversation. "You aren't seeing anyone? I figured you'd have brought her here if you were."

"Oh, uh…" He rubs the back of his neck uncomfortably. "I… was dating someone. But she didn't want to leave her old life behind."

"Old life?" I ask.

Damon leans back with a sigh. "Yeah. She's a great girl. But mafia life just wasn't for her."

"I get it," I say. "Kind of seems like Gavin and Marissa. Doesn't seem like mafia life is for her either."

Lance chuckles. "Marissa is a fucking gold digger. Tia was never like that. All of us liked her. We still do."

"You still keep in contact?"

"Kinda. She's doing well. We talk sometimes."

I nod and shift, resting my arm on my head. "So, what did you find, Lance?"

"A lot of shit. I'll need Robby to help me make sense of it. Help me track the account. I have my skills. His are better."

"I have him doing a few things right now, but he'll help. What do you got?"

"To start, the surveillance. They caught Renza. Followed her. There's a guy in the background. I can't make him out, but from what I can see? It looks like Matthew. Dude is on the phone in a private cabana. He's wearing sunglasses. I think I can clean it up, but I need a different program then the one I have on my laptop. I have one I hacked and downloaded from the LAPD."

"Talk to Taylor. He'll get what you need. I doubt CPD's programs are different," I tell him.

"Okay. I also went through the surveillance and got images of the other woman there. I'm running her through every system I can think of. I have AFIS, FBI, CIA. Everything. So far, there's nothing on her. I have no identification. Nothing. My next step is going to be running her image against known criminals in every single system I can think of. See if maybe she could be related."

I raise an eyebrow. "You can do that?"

"He can," Damon says. "He can at least get a list of people she could be related to. We can run that against people we know are affiliated with Lucinio. And those we don't recognize, we can find out about."

"It's a process. She looks a little like Damon, but if this pulls him, I can easily rule him out. I think between me and Robby, we can get it done. First step, though, is figuring out who this person is. Morales said that they didn't see Matthew down there. So, I don't know if this person is or isn't Matthew."

"Get on that. I want to know for sure. I have Morales keeping an eye on things down there, but if you get information that it was him, I want to move in fast and hard with everything we have." I sit up. "I need to grab Ryan. We need to come up with a plan on who is staying here with the girls if we have to move."

"I asked Josh that very question," Lance says. "He said he wants to leave the guards we have here on property in the guard's quarters. That's twenty-four. He wants Jason, Chase, Taylor, me, and Damon here with them."

I nod slowly. "I can see Ryan agreeing, but we still need to run that by him. He might want Taylor for the SWAT experience, but I can also see him wanting him here for the leadership just in case shit goes down. I also doubt he'll just want twenty-four guards. I can see him pulling in all of the forces we have in this entire fucking city. What else do you got?"

"Last thing. There is no Renza Gregorson checked into Le Blanc. There is no Matthew Lucinio. But… There is an Ari Lussane."

I pause mid-stretch and look at him. I slowly put my arms down. "What?"

"You heard me right. I don't know what the fuck it means, but I don't think it's a coincidence. Ari is way too close to Arianna. Lussane is really fucking close to Lucinio and Crane. I think he's sending a message. And if he isn't sending a message, then she most certainly is." Lance looks up at me. "Last thing. For real this time." He turns his laptop.

I lean forward and look at the image he's pulled up. "Fucking hell." With shaky hands, I take out my phone and dial the only person I can think of to make sense of what I'm seeing. Because my mind just went into fucking overdrive.

"Yeah?" Ryan answers.

"Den. Get down here. Now. And bring Arianna. I don't care if you need to carry her. She's not to be alone. Period."

"What? What the fuck is going on?" I can hear him shuffling, but I know Ryan. He's doing what I say because he trusts me.

"She just became as much of a target as Jessa, Dani, and Lyric."

"We're coming down."

A few moments later, Ryan strolls into the den with a wide-eyed Arianna wrapped in a blanket. Robby and Josh both follow him in. A guard stands outside the door. Ryan settles on the couch next to me with Arianna in his lap.

"Tell me what's going on," Ryan says.

Josh sits down on the other side of Ryan. Besides me, Taylor, and Ryan himself, Josh is one of the people she feels safest with. Him being here goes a long way in making me feel better, so I know it's helping keep her calm. Despite the fact that she's buried herself in a blanket and burrowed into Ryan.

I point to Lance's laptop, but say nothing. Robby and Josh both look at the screen. Ryan follows, though very hesitantly, locking his gaze on the laptop. Arianna stays cuddled into his chest. I can't blame her for not wanting to look.

"Son of… a… bitch," Ryan growls.

Arianna whimpers. "What...?"

Josh reaches over and rubs her back. "It's Renza, honey. Fake name."

Arianna sniffles and turns to look at the screen. She instantly starts shivering again. "Th-that's R- Renza..." She starts crying and curls into Ryan, making herself as small as possible. I didn't think it was possible to make herself any smaller than she already is, but fuck if she didn't just prove me wrong.

Ryan hugs her tighter. "Ari Lussane. There's no fucking way that ain't a message to us."

"The question is who's sending it? Her or Matthew?" Josh asks.

"Matthew. We know damn well she's working with him. Evidence or not." Ryan runs his fingers through Arianna's hair. "Is Lucinio with her?"

"Don't know for sure yet," Lance says. He fills him in on everything he told me as I call Taylor.

"What's up, bro?" Taylor answers.

"I know you're busy tonight wrangling the gang you've been working on, but we have a problem," I tell him as I stand. I walk to the other side of the room so I don't interrupt Lance's explanation.

"What happened?"

"Lance found some disturbing shit. We found Renza at a resort in Cancun. She's checked in under a different name." I pause and take a breath. "Ari Lussane."

"Sounds a bit like Arianna Lucinio Crane."

"That's... exactly what I thought. Actually it's what we all thought."

"We're doing the bust now. I'll have the guys process everyone when we're done. I'll get home."

"I need access to some of the department's software. I'll explain when you get here."

"Whatever you need, you got it. I'll be home in a bit." He hangs up.

I take a second to compose myself. I know Arianna needs everyone to be calm for her. If I walk over there now, she'll sense my rising panic. We don't need that.

Robby meets my eyes and slides closer to Arianna without me saying a word. I take a second to close my eyes. We know Jessa is a target just because she looks like Nick's mother. Matthew's fucking obsession. We know Dani is a target because of her relationship with Nick. We know Lyric is a target because even though they've broken up, she still means the world to Josh. We know Robby is a target because Matthew knows his value to us because of his ability to find out information.

But Arianna? Why? Just because of Ryan? Is it like Lyric with Josh? Or is there a deeper reason? I shake my head with a low, imperceptible growl. It doesn't matter. He isn't getting near her, Robby, or anyone in this family.

Not as long as I'm breathing.

Chapter Thirteen

⚔ Robby ⚔

"I am positive. One-hundred percent." Arianna sits in front of Ryan in one of the chairs in front of his desk. Her hands are folded into her lap. She's looking back at him, unflinching. Ryan's mouth is slightly open in surprise.

My jaw is nearly on the ground. "What?"

She turns her head towards me. "I know. I'm sorry I didn't remember it. I totally blocked it out, I think. I just chalked it up to her thinking of a letter or seeing a name or something and accidentally almost saying it."

Ryan clears his throat. "Baby, when did that happen?"

"The day we got married." Arianna looks back at him.

"She said she was excited to start her life with Robby, but started to say a name that started with 'M'." Ryan leans back in his chair.

"It was more like 'Ma'. Like she was starting to say Matthew, but stopped."

I lean forward. "It makes sense."

"I just never thought of it after," she says.

"Until this morning when you woke up from that dream," Ryan says.

Arianna nods. "I'm sorry. I think with the events of last night... I mean, seeing Renza and the fake name. Talking about Matthew..." She shakes her head. "It just came back to me. I'm sorry."

Ryan shakes his head. "No, baby. There's nothing to apologize for. That entire time was traumatic as fuck. Besides, at the time, it didn't seem that significant. I'm just glad you remembered now. It's more and more likely that she's with him."

I look up as Luke walks through the door on his phone. Ryan and Arianna both look at him. A very pained and pissed off expression plasters his face. All of his muscles are coiled. Tense. Like he's ready to strike. It puts me instantly on edge, but when Lance hurries in behind him wearing the same expression, I know something is wrong.

"You were given a direct order. How did this happen?" Luke asks as Lance sits down next to me.

I look at him. "What the fuck just happened?"

"I verified that the guy in the surveillance footage I thought was Matthew was, indeed, Matthew. Luke just called his contact. He hasn't been happy since."

I look back up at my boyfriend as he glares at the wall and grips the phone so tightly in his hand, I can't believe he hasn't shattered it. Arianna looks up at him slightly alarmed. Ryan watches him. After a few moments, Luke glances at Arianna. Seeing this isn't the time or place to lose his temper, he shakes his head.

"I'm not the one you need to answer to for this colossal fuck up." Luke hands the phone to Ryan. "Morales. They lost them."

Ryan narrows his eyes as he snatches the phone. "What the fuck did I just hear?"

Luke collapses in the leather chair next to the one Arianna is cuddled into. "Fuck. One fucking break. That's all I want."

"Are you fucking kidding me?" Ryan stands and paces behind his desk as he rubs his temple, but the venom in his voice makes us all jump and snap our eyes to him. "You were told to keep surveillance on them! How the hell did they escape?"

"How the hell did this happen?" I ask Luke quietly.

He looks at me. "Fuck if I know. They had him. He was in the resort. Next thing I know, I'm being told they left."

"Left. Just left?" I slump against the couch. "Fuck."

"Listen, Morales," Ryan growls. "Find… him. Because if you don't, I will take all of my anger and frustration out on you. Do… not… call… me… unless… you… have… him… Got me?" Ryan hangs up the phone with a frustrated howl. "Fucking Christ!"

Lance looks at him a little frightened. Luke has absolutely no reaction. Arianna hasn't moved an inch. Ryan drops Luke's phone on the desk as I stand. I grab it and motion Lance and Luke out of the office with me. I know Arianna is the only thing bringing Ryan back from that.

"I don't think I've even seen Josh or Alex get that pissed," Lance says as I close the door to the office. "Was he levitating? I think he was levitating."

"He got pretty pissed off a little while ago when we were dealing with Krins," I say as we walk down the hall. "Best to just walk away. Sounds like a dick move to say leave him to Arianna, but since they met, she's been the only one who is able to calm him down."

"Arianna has a way about her. It's not something I can explain, but she's got a very calming effect," Luke says with a chuckle as we turn and walk into the den.

Josh is laying on the couch with a pillow over his head. "Go away." He says. "I can't take anymore bad news today."

"I take it that means you know Matthew slipped through our fingers?" Lance asks as he sits in a chair and watches Josh.

Josh groans and throws the pillow at Lance. "What the fuck did I just say?"

Lance catches the pillow, looking at Josh incredulously. "You mean you didn't know?"

"Does it look like I knew that?" He looks up at Luke. "How?"

"Not a fucking clue. They had him," Luke says. He sits on another chair in the room and pulls me into his lap.

I glance at him, but don't question why. If it's what he needs, I'll gladly give it to him. Lance settles with his laptop in his lap once more. I settle between Luke's legs and pull out my own laptop. I did find a few things I'd intended to tell Ryan before Arianna rushed into his office.

"What kind of bad news have you had today?" Luke asks.

"None. But considering all of the shit yesterday? I need just one day to formulate a damn plan. I can't believe the amount of crap that's happened in just the past fucking week."

I glance at him. "Well, I don't know how you're going to like this."

He sits up and motions at me. "Just bring it." He glances up at Lyric when she comes in with a steaming cup of something. She sets it on the table and smiles softly before turning to leave again. "Stay." His voice sounds a little like a growl.

Lyric bites her lip and furrows her brows as she lets him pull her down next to him. "You okay?"

"Nope. And I doubt that's getting better." Josh looks back at me. "Just lay it all out."

I nod. "I tracked the card Renza used at the hotel," I start as Gavin walks in the room. He sits on the other side of Lyric and looks at me as I talk. "The account is under her fake name, but I tracked the account. It tracks to an account under the name Matthew Lussane, but that account tracks to Lucinio. It wasn't really that hard. He didn't funnel money through near as many accounts before landing in hers."

"Hang on. Lussane?" Gavin asks.

I nod. "Yes. Ari Lussane. It's Renza Gregorson's made up name. She's the one -"

Gavin holds up a hand. "I know who Renza is. She's the one who started that fire in Ryan's house in Hawaii. And the one Arianna was in before she was with Ryan. The one at Renza's house. But Ari Lussane. This is her alias?"

I glance back at Luke, unsure where Gavin is going with this. Luke has his brows furrowed. I nod again as I look back at him. "Yeah. Her alias."

"You got a picture?" Gavin asks.

"Yeah." Lance says, looking at him a little confused. He pulls up her image and turns his laptop.

Gavin blinks and leans back. He links his fingers behind his head and laughs. "Son of a bitch."

We all look at each other, then him. I lean back against Luke. "Care to explain?" I ask Gavin. Luke wraps his arms around my waist.

"Ari Lussane. She's Marissa's fucking best friend." He nods to the screen. "That's her. Same girl. They met in Marissa's favorite coffee cafe last year. Hit it off. They do everything together. Talk to each other all the damn time. Text. Everything."

"Wait," I say. "We thought Matthew was somewhere in the Caribbean. We know him and Renza are working together. And given the surveillance footage we got, I think they're more than just working together. Now you're saying she and Marissa are friends?"

"Yep. That's exactly what I'm saying." Gavin drops his hands to his sides.

Lyric's eyes are wide. She turns to Josh, trembling, and whispers something in his ear. Josh growls low. He hugs her a little tighter as he takes a drink of whatever Lyric brought him. He leans over and whispers something to her that seems to calm her.

He takes a breath and looks at Gavin. "We need to know what she knows about Renza. Or Ari. Whatever the fuck she's going by. Where's Ryan?"

"Calming down," Luke says. "I'll touch base with him. He needs to take a breath."

"He know about Matthew disappearing?"

I chuckle. "He may or may not have threatened Morales' life."

Josh laughs quietly. "Sounds about right. Morales better hope he redeems himself, though. Coming up against Ryan isn't the wisest of decisions."

I look up as Nick walks in the room. He sits on the couch near Luke and I and lets out a long breath as he rubs his head. We all quietly watch him sensing there's something on his mind but knowing enough to wait him out.

"Dani is starting to freak out a little bit," Nick starts. "I don't want to go to Ryan about this right now. He's… a little tied up." He rubs his eyes. "I haven't slept since I told her about Marissa being her half-sister. Sharing the same father. Actually, she hasn't slept. Which means I don't sleep. I don't even know what the hell day it is."

Luke kisses my back. My heart actually feels lighter. The effect he has on me is still something I can't quite grasp. But I love it. I love all the sweetness he only shows me. I love all sexiness only I get to see. I love all of him.

114

I link my fingers with his and look at Nick. "How is she freaking out?"

"Well, we all know. All of us. Marissa doesn't. Knowing they share blood is hard on her. I think the reason is because she feels like she can save her. If that makes sense."

I nod. "It does. She thinks if Marissa knew she has real family within this one, it might affect her opinion and role."

Nick leans forward. "The problem is that I think she's right. But I also don't want to set us back with Matthew. I want Marissa to get us information, but I'm in agreement with Dani. I think if we open up to her, we might be able to get more out of her."

Gavin chuckles and shakes his head. "I appreciate your girl has a heart, Nick, but you don't know my wife. The past couple of years have been pretty fucking unbearable. I would have divorced her a long time ago, but with Josh taking over Lucinio Mafia, he's needed us. I'm hardly ever home anyway, so I only have to deal with her shit for a day or two before I'm gone again."

"Don't you think that might have a little to do with you being gone?" I ask.

He shakes his head at me. "Marissa has always been a little crazy. I honestly thought she'd calm down the older she got, but I was wrong. When we found out that she kept everything from me that happened between Jessa and Alex and Josh, I fucking lost it, but I tried to make it work. I took a page out of Jessa's book. She wanted to forgive and forget. I figured I could."

"But Marissa has gotten worse," Josh puts in. "I think it's because she's working with Matthew. We'll find out. As for letting Dani talk to her?" He shakes his head. "I don't think it's a good idea, bro. I think we need to let this play out."

"Fuck. I know you're right. But she's miserable," Nick says. "I hate seeing her like this. She's down. She doesn't want to do anything with the girls right now because it involves being around Marissa."

"Then you should find a way to distract her," Luke's velvety voice says against my shoulder. "You don't need to go out to show her a romantic night. What she needs is time away from all of this. To forget it. In fact, I think we all need a break. Downtime. We've had a lot of shit thrown at us. It's taking a toll. And if we're all tired and stressed, none of

115

us are going to be at our best. That's when mistakes happen. We can't afford mistakes."

"Couldn't agree more," Josh says with a smile. He looks at me and Lance. "Laptops down. Go have fun."

I laugh. "Spoken like a true leader."

He shrugs cockily. "Well, you know. Now, get out of here. I'm going to take a long nap. And since Lyric hasn't been sleeping so well, she's taking one with me. We can't do anything until we track that fucker down again anyway."

"Shouldn't we be doing that?" Lance asks.

Josh shakes his head. "That's what we have other forces around the world for. You both have alerts on their accounts set up. And now we have Renza and that Ari Lussane account. We'll get them." He looks over at Damon. "Go. Take your boy. I ain't telling you again."

I raise an eyebrow as Damon and Gavin both crack up. Lance turns a shade of red I've never seen. I look back at Luke. He shakes his head and shrugs and he nudges me up. I follow him out of the den hand in hand.

"Was that weird?" I ask.

"Yes. That was definitely weird." He leads me to our bedroom. "I'm getting fucking cabin fever. I want to go for a drive or something."

"Then let's go for a drive." I sit next to him on the bed and lean into him.

He chuckles. "We can't, baby. Not right now. I'm not only second in command, but I'm head guard. With the whole family here, I'm needed here. Best I'll get is the pool."

"Okay. Then let's go to the pool. I wouldn't mind seeing you shirtless and wet." I smile, teasingly.

I can tell he's just as on edge as Ryan. He needs the break just as much, but he'll never admit it. Just like Ryan. The two are a lot alike considering they aren't actually related. It's kind of unnerving to someone who isn't used to them. I think it's the reason they work so well together.

"Pool it is. I'll get a few laps in. I could use them." Luke stands and wastes no time stripping his clothes off.

The guy is unfairly gorgeous. I have a theory. I'm convinced he's secretly a God, and that all of the other Gods were jealous of him. His abs. His body. His strength. His dominance. His looks. So, they kicked him out of his place with the Gods and sent him here, thinking that would solve

116

their vanity problem. But it didn't. Not even a little. Instead, Luke thrived and rules the entire world.

Now, here we are. Luke the God picked me to be his mate. And I'm the lucky one who gets to watch every single muscle in his body flex and move with God-like grace and ease. He's perfection. A complete and utter masterpiece.

I stand and walk slowly to our dresser. I quickly change and turn to him. I kiss him as deeply and slowly as I can, wrapping my arms around his neck. His arms encircle my waist. He pulls me closer and tighter against his body. I submit instantly to his dominance of the kiss and mold myself against his body. He drops his hands to my ass and squeezes as his tongue meets mine, deepening the already demanding and hot kiss.

He pulls back slowly with a smile that disarms me. "Is that what you were looking for?"

"I can't help that you're walking sex."

He laughs and takes my hand. "In case you haven't looked in the mirror lately, so are you, baby."

I can't help the smile that plays across my face as we walk to the pool. I also can't help the pride I feel at walking next to him just like I'm supposed to be with my hand in his just like it's supposed to be.

All his.

When we get outside, we immediately dive into the pool. The cool water is just what I needed. When I resurface and see Luke casually swimming laps, I know it's just what he needed as well. The calm and serenity of the water around us is so soothing, it's almost like we've entered a magical alternate universe.

I smile. An enchanted land just for us. The thought makes me nearly laugh. The man has turned me into a sensitive sap or something. I mean what the fuck kind of man thinks of a fantasy land like it's his very own fairytale? It's right. It's so right. Perfect.

Unfortunately, my own personal Heaven doesn't last long. Somewhere in the distance, I hear a shot ring out. What surprises the fuck out of me, though, is that the water in front of me ripples. What looks like a mini torpedo sails through the pool.

"What the ever living hell?" I ask myself, confused. I jump when I hear another shot and once again see something shoot through water.

"Get down!" Luke yells.

But my body doesn't obey.

I watch in both horror and fear as I realize what's happening.

Someone is shooting at us.

On Ryan's property.

Someone is shooting at us on Ryan's property. I look around quickly, trying to decipher where the shots are coming from, but I don't have a chance. Like a missile, Luke shoots towards me and tugs me under the water. He pulls me with him until we're on the other side of the pool.

When we resurface, he forces my head to stay low. Just the top of our heads to our nose is out of the water.

But there's still shooting. The bullets are hitting the water dangerously close to where we are. We have to get out of the pool. I look at Luke trying to get him to understand, but he shakes his head. His eyes are dark. Dangerous. Above all else, I trust him.

Moments later, I hear people running to our defense. My racing heart begins to once more regulate, but the shooting doesn't stop. I hold onto Luke like he's my life raft, and if I let go, I'll drown.

"Out of the water!" Taylor yells. "Move!"

Trusting my team and Luke, I quickly pull myself out of the pool. I don't need to look or feel Luke to know he's right behind me.

"In the house!" Nick commands.

I run for the house, staying low to the ground. Luke's hand drops to my back, both giving me comfort and propelling me into the house. As soon as I hit the tile by the door, though, I slip and fall flat on my ass. Luke trips over me, but stays on his feet. He grabs me and pulls me towards the kitchen where there are no windows.

Luke pulls me behind the counter. We both nearly fall over Marissa and Dani who are cowering behind the counter in the kitchen. They're hugging each other and crying hysterically as they grip each other frantically.

"What the fuck are you doing?" Ryan yells. "I said upstairs!"

They both jump and start scurrying towards the stairs, but I pull them both back. "Stop! Too late now! Stay down!"

Marissa cries as Dani lays nearly on top of her, keeping them both on the ground. Marissa covers her ears as Dani hugs her, keeping her head against her back. They both tremble.

Luke holds me close against his back as the shooting stops. He kisses my shoulder. "Fuck…," he breathes. "Fucking hell."

I look back and see Ryan crouched at Luke's back with his Glock aimed at the door. He glances at us all. "Don't move until I say."

Like a flash, he's gone. We all obey, staying huddled in the same position that he left us in. Partially out of fear. Mostly us obeying our leader.

Luke soothingly kisses my neck and shoulder and cheek as he holds me as close as possible to him. As tight as he can manage.

Despite everything, I feel safe. I feel like nothing will get through the man holding me. He's impenetrable. Invincible. My very own indestructible superhero.

As he whispers soothingly in my ear, I calm further and further. While I don't know what the hell just happened, Luke at my side reiterates that I'm okay.

Safe.

Chapter Fourteen

☒ Luke ☒

I pace angrily around the room filled with guards in the guard's quarters. I haven't said a word, but every so often, I glare at them. My plan is to wait until Ryan walks in the room. I think having him here will keep me from murdering everyone in this room for allowing an attempt on Robby's life.

Fucking again.

"Sir," one of them begins.

"Stop," I growl, not making eye contact. "If you want to live, don't fucking talk."

"Probably a wise idea," a buttery smooth, deep voice says behind me.

I turn to see Josh behind me with his arms folded over his chest. "Where's Ryan?"

He casually leans against the door frame. "Calming down the girls. Arianna is hyperventilating. Jessa is in a panic attack unlike any I've ever seen. Dani has managed to make herself as small as humanly possible. She's crawled underneath the couch and refuses to come out. Which surprised the fuck out of me. I didn't think anyone could fit under that thing. Well, other than a kid. Or dog. But she did it. Bree and Nikki are making squeaking sounds I can't decipher. Marissa has gone eerily quiet. And Lyric has literally burrowed into Alex. She jumps every time anyone else moves so much as a centimeter."

My heart breaks for all of them. "It's not every day there's an attack on our own fucking property." I turn back to the room. Everyone's eyes are on their hands. No one makes eye contact with me. They don't dare.

"Want me to deal with this?" Josh asks.

I bite back the vicious growl forming from somewhere deep within and threatening to escape. "Probably." I take a step back and lean against the wall. "I can't deal with this."

"You're too close to it." He puts a hand on my shoulder. "Let me help." He steps forward and snaps his fingers. "Eyes up."

Not a single guard disobeys. My eyes widen. "Well, shit," I whisper. Josh is far more commanding than I thought. He's settled into his role as leader just fine.

"What do we know about what happened?" His voice sounds far more powerful than any I've ever heard. And that includes Ryan. Everyone starts talking at the same time. Josh holds up a hand. "Enough!" Everyone stops and stares at him. He drops his hand. "One at a time. What happened?"

The guards look at each other before one of them clears his throat and stands. "They weren't on the property. We think they were on the lake."

"I was out there. I didn't see anyone on the lake," Josh says.

The guard looks at the other guards before back at Josh. "We think he was in the water."

Josh and I both stare at him like he's grown another head. After a few moments, Josh clears his throat. "How did he get a high-powered rifle in the water without it getting wet? It wouldn't have shot."

"I don't know that yet, Mr. Lucinio, but I'm confident that it came from the water."

I push off the wall. "It's possible if they waterproofed the gun. We've done it on missions when I was with the ATF."

Josh looks at me. "How?"

I shrug. "Wrap it in plastic or something. A diver could have jumped off the boat further up the lake. Swam with it strapped to his back. Chose his spot. It's hard to look for nothing but a head in the middle of the lake. When he's done, he just dives back under and swims away. No one is the wiser."

Josh scrubs his hands down his face. "Fucking hell."

"The angle those shots were coming from, and the distance... It just makes sense," the guard continues. "We combed the grounds. We found no shell casings. Just the ones from our guns. Nothing that matched the bullets we found in the pool."

"So, we have them coming out of the goddamn water now," I growl.

"We think the best thing to do at this time is allow no one outside in the back of the house." The guard sits back down.

Josh looks at me. I meet his eyes and sigh. "I don't see another option. Shades closed on that side of the house. We'll have to use the front for any coming and going. And no one sits outside."

"That's going to piss Jenny and my mom the fuck off."

"It's going to piss everyone off, but we don't have a choice. We still have Chase and Bree going to work. We have Nikki going into the bakery. Taylor and Nick are going into the precinct. Jessa and Jas are still going into the office. They all have guards and protection with them. I think we need to be just as cautious at home."

"They're going to feel like prisoners. Trust me. I know how that goes. It feels like shit. Takes a psychological toll."

I nod. "I know. But we don't have a choice. I'm not tempting fate. This is the second time I've almost lost Robby." I look up at the guards. "If I do lose him, Ryan isn't the one you'll have to worry about." I turn and head for the door.

I take out my gun. I hate everything about what I'm about to walk into. I don't like the idea of being forced to walk across to the house carrying my Glock in my hand. This is our property. Home. We shouldn't have to go through this shit on our own fucking turf.

Josh falls into step with me. "I know you're pissed, but this isn't the time to show it. Robby is probably scared, but I've come to know he's definitely not going to show it. Everyone in there is scared. Even Ryan.

Hell. Even I am. This is a new type of attack. And it's vicious just like Matthew. You don't know how vicious he can actually be."

"I'm trying, Josh. But I don't know how to deal with this shit. This is so far out of my league. All I've been thinking is shit like why did Ryan make me second to him? I can't even keep Robby safe. And he trusts me to keep his whole family safe? Command his fucking army?"

"Luke. Stop it. You know better. You know how good you are. You want to sit there and blame yourself for this shit, but really? It's just as much mine as yours. Taylor's as yours. Alex's. Ryan's. Nick's. We all have just as much responsibility for everyone else as you do. You think Ryan is the only one responsible for Arianna?"

I look at him and shake my head as we walk in the house. "No. Fuck no."

"No. He's not. I am. You are. We protect each other. Just as much as we protect ourselves. So quit with the blame game. Put that energy into finding out who did this and why."

"I know who did it."

Josh shakes his head. "Think like a cop. What evidence do we have to definitively say it was Matthew? We know he hires other mafias or gangs to deal with his bullshit for him."

I turn to him. "You think it was a hire?"

"Don't you?" He puts his gun in his holster.

I sigh as I follow suit and put mine in my holster. "Fuck. You're right. I know you are. Which makes me like it far fucking less."

"There's nothing to like about this shit, Luke. Nothing at all. It's one more thing to figure out. But right now? We have a scared as hell family that we need to step up for."

I nod. "Okay. Okay. I get it."

Josh leads me to the living room. The sight before me makes my heart stop. Not because everyone is very obviously upset, but because there isn't a single dry eye in the room. Including Robby. Tears always get me. But tears from the eyes of the man I love is something I just realized I can't deal with.

The girls are wrapped in the arms of their significant others. Nick and Dani are sitting on the floor. Nick is rocking her back and forth and has somehow wrapped himself around her, engulfing her. Jason has a trembling Jessa underneath him. Her face is buried in his chest. Her nails are gripping the waistband of his pants. Breetana is sitting on Chase's lap wrapped in his arms. Her face is buried in his neck as she shakes with sobs. Nicole has made herself as small as possible and is burrowed into Taylor. Ryan is hugging Arianna so tightly, I'm not convinced she can even breathe. Lyric is leaving marks in Alex's arm with her fingernails.

In the middle of the floor is Jackson, Tait, and Christopher. Surprisingly they're happily playing by themselves. Even though Marissa and Gavin are next to them wrapped in each other's arms. Jenny is sniffling as she leans on Ethan's shoulder. Shane is swaying gently with my mother and Eve. Even Lance and Damon are leaning together like they're exhausted.

It's hard not to read the room. The fear. The anger. The confusion. The insecurity. It all slams into me at once with a force that's staggering. But I still put one foot in front of the other because Robby needs me. I hated the thought of leaving him for a second, but I had to figure out how the hell people got to us on our own turf.

Looking at Robby, though, as I cross the room to him, I know what a mistake that was. I should have let Josh or Alex take the lead. I put my responsibility over Robby. That never should have happened. The realization is like a kick to the nuts. I inhale sharply as I slowly kneel in front of him. I take both of his hands in mine and kiss them before laying my head in his lap.

"I'm sorry, Robby," I whisper as I wrap my arms around him.

He runs his fingers through my hair. "Why? You didn't do anything."

"I left you here. I shouldn't have left you here after that."

He cups my face and lifts my head up so I'm looking at him. "You needed to find out what happened. How it happened on our property." He kisses me so softly it makes me want to cry. "I can't fault you for that."

"I don't deserve you. I don't know what I did to end up with you in my life."

He leans down and kisses me again, tugging my hair. "I know what I got into when I decided to be with you, Luke. I know what your job entails. But most of all, I know that your entire reason for going to the guard's house was for me. I'm a big boy." He smiles. "I can take it."

I smile and stand slowly. I pull him up with me and sit down in the oversized chair he was just in. I pull him down next to me and hold him close. He shifts and wraps his arm around my waist, tucking his head under my chin.

After checking on Lyric, Josh remains standing. He clears his throat. I can tell he doesn't know if he should say what he's about to, but I'm grateful that he's the one doing it. I need to be able to focus on Robby. He's what matters. He's what will always matter.

Regardless of him telling me that he's okay, I still hate that I left him during this time. I know he won't admit it, but he needed me to be here for him. I wasn't, and it breaks me in more pieces than I know how to deal with.

"I know you all are wondering what happened," Josh begins. He takes a breath. "We believe the shots came from the lake." He looks over at me before looking back to the room.

Jessa lets out a strangled sob, clutching Jason harder as he whispers soothingly in her ear. "Why can't he just leave us alone!" she cries out as she sobs.

Josh, thrown off slightly at the pain I know he feels from everyone, takes another breath. But it's shaky. I watch as Lyric makes her way to his side, taking his hand and squeezing. He gives her a grateful smile and wraps an arm around her. "I don't... know, Jess. I don't. I wish I did."

"How did they do it from the water? There wasn't a boat," Taylor says. "Across the lake, maybe? Long-range, high-powered rifle?"

"No. Shots were coming in too fast for that," Ryan says.

"The trajectory that we saw, shots coming from the lake would make sense." Josh sits on the arm on the couch near him. He pulls Lyric between his legs, hugging her close. "We saw no shell casings from any weapon that would match the bullets we found in the pool. All of the shell casings were from our guns. The only location that makes sense is from the lake."

"How did the weapon not get wet?" Taylor asks, visibly confused.

"When Luke was in the ATF, he explained they'd wrap guns. Keep them from getting wet. Then they'd initiate their attacks. They'd leave the way they came."

"Through the water," Taylor says. "Holy fuck."

I clear my throat before Josh continues and looks at Marissa. I can see she's perked up at the conversation even though she's hiding her face in Gavin's chest. Josh looks towards them. I can see his wheels turning.

But he doesn't have a chance to say anything. Marissa sniffles and stands up slowly. "I can't handle anymore," she says quietly. "I'm not used to this. I'm scared." She looks down at Gavin, and I'm surprised to see she actually does look terrified. "Can I please just go to the bedroom? Maybe I could take the kids to the nursery? Something to just…" She wipes her eyes as she trails off. "Something to just help me come down from this. Help me calm down."

Gavin looks at her as he stands. He reaches down for Tait when Tait reaches up for him. He picks him up. "Yeah. I'll go with you. I need a second to breathe after that. Maybe playing with them would help."

Marissa gives him a soft and terrified smile as she nods. "Okay. I'd like that."

The two gather the kids. Gavin shoots Josh a wink over his shoulder. I have to wonder if the fucker is a mind reader or if he's just that good at picking up signals and reading them accurately. Gavin and Marissa disappear upstairs.

Josh waits a moment before he starts talking again. "The other thing." Josh looks a little hesitantly at me.

I take a breath. "We don't think it was Matthew. In a sense. He hires out for shit like this."

"You think it was another mafia?" Ryan asks.

I nod. "Another mafia. Another gang. We have a lot on Lance's and Robby's plates right now. I think we need to find other hackers. Or maybe bring in some of your contacts from high places. We need to track Lucinio's accounts. We need to figure out where he's starting and trace backwards. Figure out who the fuck he's paying. Where his money is going."

"That's the only way we're going to be able to get ahead on this," Josh finishes. "We can't ask Lance or Robby to do this. We have them doing too much other shit."

Ryan sweetly kisses Arianna's forehead as I tangle my fingers in Robby's hair. Everyone is quiet as they digest the information we've just shared with them. I kiss Robby's head when he tightens his grip around my waist and grips my shirt.

"What about if we call in that guy who works with the CIA?" Arianna asks quietly. "I think his name was Pierce. I remember you used him a few years ago when you were helping Taylor in Minnesota."

I chuckle a little when Ryan looks down at her in shock. "You remember that?" he asks.

"I remember a lot of things. But I remember that because I was the one who answered the phone when he called you with your information, and he kept calling me bird."

I laugh. "Bird?"

She shakes her head. "I didn't get it either."

Ryan grins. "I'll get a hold of him. We'll have to fly him in from D.C."

"You should get a hold of him now," Josh says. "We need to get a jump on this. If we can get to whoever he hired to do this before he does, maybe we can get them to lead us to him."

"I agree." Ryan takes out his phone.

Robby yawns into my chest. I kiss the top of his head again. The infamous adrenaline dump. I wondered when it would hit him. I also know he'll fight through it. But not tonight. Tonight he gives in whether he likes it or not.

Chapter Fifteen

✗ Robby ✗

Waking up the next morning is like coming out of a haze or something. Like I just got the deepest, most peaceful sleep I've ever gotten in my whole life. I smile when I feel a pair of strong arms wrap tighter around me and pull me back to him so I'm as close as possible.

"How do you feel?" Luke asks.

"How do you do that? Just know when I wake up. Even if I don't move a single inch."

I feel his lips curl into a smile against my back. "Your breathing is different. Not as deep. And even though you think you don't move, you do. Ever so slightly, but you do. You push back into me."

"I do not. I'd feel that."

He chuckles. "You do. But you're just coming out of sleep, so you probably don't feel it. Now, tell me. How do you feel after what happened?"

"I'm not sure anyone can really feel great after being shot at. I'm not really sure I even really comprehended what happened until I saw everyone huddled together. But really I think it was Marissa that made it feel real. I didn't expect her to fall apart like that. Seeing her threw me off. Then I started to really feel it."

"I know you were okay with me taking off to the guard's quarters after that, but I'm not doing that again. You needed me. I wasn't there."

I smile and shift so I'm turned towards him. I take his face in my hands and lean in kissing him deeply. My tongue tangles with his. I can feel the sparks exploding around us when the kiss gets more and more heated. When he lightly catches my tongue in his teeth, I let out a deep moan and shiver.

He responds by pushing me back slightly and covering me with his body. My fingers tangle in his hair. He pushes against my dick making me instantly rock hard. I push up against him, rubbing myself against his naked cock and throwing my head back with a groan.

Luke kisses down my jaw to my neck continuing to rub and thrust against me until we both can't take anymore. He reaches down and takes both of our lengths in his hand. He strokes and squeezes with the perfect pressure as we both thrust against each other.

It doesn't take a lot for Luke to turn me on. It takes even less for him to have me begging for him. But I've never lost the ability to talk with anyone other than him. He always makes everything feel so good that all I can focus on is the build up to the release I know he's about to bring. Talking is not only unnecessary, but it's impossible.

He starts twisting his wrist and giving us both a little more of the pressure we need before he backs it off. He keeps repeating the motion making us both arch and moan as we thrust against each other. I kiss his neck before crashing my lips to his. I suck on his tongue lightly as he continues to build the pressure until we're both thick and panting.

"Come. Now, baby" he says against my lips.

I nip his lip before I hungrily and greedily kiss him again. I come at the same time he does, drenching his hand, thighs, and dick. I feel his hot climax spill over my balls and base of my dick. He continues stroking, but slows his pace, helping us both come down.

My stomach quivers as I shiver. He pulls back gently and slowly from the kiss. He straddles me as he sits up on his knees. He gives me a sexy smile that makes me groan as he licks our come off his hand.

"Fucking hell. You're killing me."

His smile widens as his eyes darken. "Best breakfast I've ever had."

I laugh as I sit up and lick his hand before kissing him again. "I love you."

He kisses me softly. Sweetly. "I love you, too."

He finishes licking us both off his hand as he gets up. He pulls me with him and leads us to the bathroom to shower. Several orgasms for the both of us later, we finish getting dressed. I feel lighter than I have in days, and I can tell Luke has had a lot of stress taken off his shoulders, too.

I look up to a knock on the door. "Yes?" I call as I button my jeans.

"Unc Luck! Unc Ruby! Bakefast!" an excited voice calls through the door.

I raise an eyebrow and look at Luke. "Unc, Luck, Ruby, and bakefast?" I laugh.

Luke smiles. "We're coming, Tait!"

"Hoowy!" Tait says. I can hear Nicole laughing and pulling him from the door.

I laugh harder at his attempt at words. "At least he's not calling me Booby anymore."

Luke laughs. "The first time he called you that, I damn near pissed my pants laughing so hard."

I laugh. "I was so fucking shocked I just stood there staring."

Luke pulls a black t-shirt on and takes my hand after I pull on my own t-shirt. He leads me down the stairs and to the dining area. I sniff the air, trying to decide what kind of dish Ryan is creating. I smell bacon and something baking that smells fucking divine. My stomach growls right on cue. Luke takes a seat, but instead of sitting next to him, I gravitate to the kitchen. My curiosity has gotten the best of me, and now I need to know what he made.

It's always been like this with me. I have a habit of working far too long without eating, but when Luke and I started seeing each other, he began making sure I ate when I was supposed to. Since then, Ryan's cooking has been my favorite food of all time. It doesn't matter what he cooks. It's my favorite.

I pop into the kitchen, my nose leading me, and stop dead in my tracks at the scene. Ryan is in the middle of the kitchen with flour on his face having some kind of a flour war with all three kids. Jackson and Christopher are squealing as they throw flour at him. Tait squawks every time Ryan hits him with the flour, then throws a giant fistful back at him.

Ryan looks over at me. "Well, don't just stand there! Help me! They're ganging up!"

I laugh and walk the rest of the way into the kitchen. I eye the rest of the flour in the bowl as I watch the kids. They all stare at me wide-eyed, but when I pick up the bowl and dump the rest on Ryan's head, they all start laughing. Ryan's mouth drops.

I laugh. "I'm a kid at heart."

"Betrayal! You're going to pay for that," he says with a smile before he starts laughing.

I turn to the kids as they all reach for me. "See? I'm always on your side."

I watch Jackson's eyes widen. He points behind me, but I have no time to react before Ryan has me in a bear hug. He shakes out his head over mine and covers me in the excess flour on his shoulders and clothes. All of the kids laugh hysterically as Ryan lets go.

"You all are traitors," I say as I grin and laugh with them.

Ryan laughs. "So, what brings you into the middle of my battle?" He bends and pulls a few things out of the oven that look as good as they smell.

"My nose led me here. I smell a lot of delicious things. I was wondering what they were."

"We have some baked eggs with peppers, onions, ham, and cheese. We have hashbrowns with cheese, ham, peppers and onions. And we have some croissants. Freshly baked." He bends down one last time taking a smaller pan out of the oven. "And especially for you, I made a couple of extra slices of bacon."

I smile so widely, it causes the kids to smile. "Thank you."

"You're welcome. Help me take this out. I need to clean up the kids."

I laugh. "We all need to clean up."

I take the dishes he hands me out to the dining area and return for the rest. After they're all set up on the table, I head back for the kitchen to clean up. I help Ryan take the kids out to the table and settle them all into their seats before taking my own.

"What was that all about?" Luke asks, knocking flour out of my hair that I must have missed when I shook it out.

"Flour war in the kitchen. I walked into the kids attacking Ryan with it. He was losing. He asked for some assistance. So naturally, I dumped the rest of the flour over him. He proceeded to bear hug me and get all of the flour that was on him on me."

Luke laughs. "As long as it was fun."

"A nice reprieve from the seriousness of the past week or so." I lean my head on his shoulder as Ryan settles.

"Oh! Josh, I have the designs done for your house," Jessa says excitedly after everyone is settled and beginning to eat. "I'm almost done with yours, Alex, but I'm struggling with one of the rooms. It's not quite the way you described."

Josh chuckles and nods his head. "As long as I have a room for Lyric when she visits, I'm happy with everything you come up with. I trust your talent." He nudges Lyric, who smiles.

"I'm sure that however you designed it is perfect," Alex says.

"That reminds me. I need to talk to you and Lyric about Jaxon's garden. I was thinking of putting it behind Rebekkah's home as more of a..." She tilts her head adorably as she thinks. "More of a centered location?"

"I'd love that," Lyric says quietly.

Jessa smiles brightly and turns to Alex. "The slight issue I'm having with yours is the angle of the room with the door leading to your pool. It doesn't work with the retractable roof around the pool."

"You need to make it less rounded?" Alex raises an eyebrow as he thinks. Then he shakes his head and waves his fork. "Nope. I told you that I wanted you to have free rein. If you think it needs to change, then change it."

"Really?" She bites her lip as she thinks. "I really want it to be what you want."

"Jessa. I've seen your designs. I trust you."

I smile when Jessa's brightness fills the room. She loves design more than anyone I've ever met. The way she lights up when she talks about it, or the way she concentrates so hard when she's putting a model together is incredible to watch. The girl is truly gifted at what she does.

"What about ours, Jess?" Gavin asks. He grins. I know he's trying to make sure the conversation doesn't turn to anything sinister.

"Oh gosh. It looks so good! I'll have Jason help me bring it down later. I think we can break ground this week on all of them if I can get Alex's pool area to cooperate."

"I don't want to move here," Marissa whines.

"Well, you don't really have a choice in the matter," Josh says with a slightly wicked grin. "He goes where I do. You don't like it, you can leave. No one here would have a problem with it."

"Gavin would have a problem with it," she says through gritted teeth.

"You sure about that?" Damon asks.

She glares at him. "I just don't want to live near you."

Damon folds his arms on the table and leans forward slightly with a grin. "Is that because I refused all of your advances over the years?"

"No. It's because you're an asshole. And you're -"

"Stop it," Ryan cuts her off. "Kids are around. I don't want you upsetting them."

Marissa pouts. "He started it."

I hide my snicker. "Well, Ryan just finished it. And really? What are you? Three? Honestly. Tait is better behaved then you are."

Josh chokes back a chuckle and shakes his head. "Enough. Like I said. You don't like it? There's the door." He points in the vicinity of the front door.

Marissa looks up at Gavin like she can't believe he's not defending her. He shrugs. "Don't look at me. I agree with them. This is my job. Josh is my boss. If he says move, I move."

"Why couldn't you just go into the family business?" she asks. "You'd still have plenty of money."

"Because I didn't want the boringness of a bullshit nine to five where I'm working my ass off for less than I'm worth. Just because I would have inherited the business doesn't mean I'd be making the amount of money I am to give you this lavish life you feel so entitled to. I may have inherited millions. Doesn't mean that's what I'd be making if I took over the business."

"But why do we have to move?" she whines. The fake tears that start falling from her eyes fool no one.

"Because that was the order," Gavin says simply. "Because Josh wants to be around family. This is his family. But most of all? Because it's mine. Josh, Alex, Lyric, Damon, Cole, Dane, and Lance. They're my family. The people in this room have become my family. So to reiterate what Josh said, if you don't like it, there's the door. Have fun. I'll gladly give you a fair settlement so you can live out your days lavishly, but fuck if I'm going to stay in L.A. when everything I love is here."

"This is completely ridiculous. To just uproot like this?" she wipes her eyes. I have to fight myself to keep from telling her that her tears are really not getting her anywhere.

"Oh, for fuck sake," Lyric mutters, finally as fed up as the rest of. The difference? She has no fucking filter, and we all love that. "No one is falling for your crocodile tears. Knock it the fuck off." She reluctantly starts eating the food that Ryan points to. I love seeing how they all interact with her. With her living so far away, none of us get to spend much time with her, but we love when she's here.

"Bitch." Marissa glares at her. We all growl at her, making her cower.

"I'd think you'd be happy about it," Gavin says. "After all. You have Damon right here to throw yourself at, right?"

Her eyes snap to his. "What are you talking about?"

"Honey. Come on. You think I don't know all of the times you've pranced around the house in next to nothing when I was out on a mission and asked him to guard you if we didn't need him with us?"

Lyric snorts. "Don't act so innocent. I've seen the way you throw yourself at him when Gavin isn't looking. I know you've been trying to spread your legs for the guards he leaves behind whenever you can. Luckily for them, they have fucking taste, so it never works."

That shuts her up immediately. She says nothing more. She focuses completely on her plate and pushes around her breakfast. Gavin winks at Lyric. She smiles softly, and starts eating again. I lean back after finishing mine and lean into Luke. He looks at me, hiding a smile.

"Well that was fun," I whisper. "Nothing like a little family drama over breakfast."

He chuckles. "Sometimes, this is where you learn the most about people."

Marissa sniffles and gets up from the table. She leaves the room as all of our eyes follow her, despite the cheerfulness of the conversation that has resumed around us. Dani watches her with the most concern of all of us. But when she starts to get up, Nick gently grabs her wrist, shaking his head.

"She's upset," she says quietly. "I should comfort her."

"She's going to call Matthew," Nick says just as quietly. "Let her. Dane will catch it on tap. We have more proof to confront her with."

Dani sits down with a very sad expression that makes my heart hurt for her a little bit. Who am I kidding? She looks for the best in everyone and has a habit of seeing good qualities in people that none of us do. My heart doesn't just hurt a little bit. It hurts a lot for her. I hate seeing how torn she is.

Luke kisses my head as he stands and starts cleaning the breakfast dishes. Despite the little detour, everything about right now is perfect. It's the type of calm family time I know I've needed and feel like everyone else has as well.

Just being around everyone seems to replenish our strength. Strength I know we'll definitely need in the coming days.

Chapter Sixteen

⚔ Luke ⚔

I stand stretching after an intense Lego session with Tait. I can't believe how smart he is for a kid his age. He's barely three. Yet, the kid was able to build a building that actually looks like a building instead of a stack of blocks. It's incredible.

I look around the room. Everyone just being together is peaceful to me. Relaxing. Jessa and Lyric are reading a book in the corner. Ryan is getting his ass kicked in Scrabble by Arianna. Taylor and Nicole are playing Monopoly with Jason and Breetana. Chase and Robby are playing with the two younger kids. Even Josh and Alex are taking a time out and playing Battleship. Gavin, Lance, Nick, Dani, Marissa, and Damon play some intense card game I've never seen. Even all of the parents seem calm and at ease as they watch everyone.

Tranquil.

Just as I'm about to sit down again, there's a knock on the door. I glance towards it. I don't think we were expecting anyone. At least not until later when Pierce, Ryan's CIA contact, arrives. I also don't recall hearing the call from the guards saying anyone was here.

Ryan smiles. "It's okay. It's Dane. He texted a little while ago."

Rebekkah smiles brightly as I head for the door to let Dane in. Since finding out about him, she's talked to him every single day, even though she hasn't seen him every day. It looks like she's becoming a lot more comfortable with the knowledge that her entire life was a lie. She's by no means okay with anything that happened, but she *is* coming to terms with everything that happened.

I open the door after making sure it's Dane by looking through the peephole. I raise an eyebrow at the man next to him, though. If they didn't look exactly like each other, I may not have opened the door.

I smile. "Hey."

He grins back. "I was going to block the peephole, but given what you all just went through, I decided that might not be the best idea."

I laugh. "No. It wouldn't have been. We're all a little on edge." I close the door behind him. "What brings you by?"

"Uh..." He looks over my shoulder. "I got the tap going. Marissa made a call today."

I nod. "I know. Did she give you any information?"

"A lot. But first." He turns to the man next to him. "This is my dad. Kent. He just got back from Spain."

"Spain, huh? How was it?"

He gives me the same cocky smile Dane does. It's obvious where he gets it from. "It was warm, but not all it's cracked up to be. Great culture. Great people. Very iffy hotel. Noisy. I'm glad to be home, crazy as that might sound."

"Chicago definitely has a hold on its people," I say. "I didn't think I would, but I love it here. We're in a quiet area, though."

"So are we," Dane says. "I love our neighborhood, but it's getting a little crowded. Jessa has been calling non-stop because she wants to design our new house."

I laugh. "I have news for you. She already has. I snuck a peek earlier. I didn't know you lived together, though."

"Yeah, a house to myself just got to be too much after my wife passed," Kent says, looking anxiously over my shoulder.

I smile and turn, waving them along. "Say no more!" I lead them into the living room and enjoy my front row seat to what I think is going to be a very happy reunion. "Everyone." I wait for attention to be on me before I step aside and gesture to Kent. "This is Kent. Dane's father."

"Shit...," Marissa whispers with wide eyes.

I'm sure she has no idea how many people actually heard her because she clears her throat and immediately disappears from the room, pushing past me and hurrying down the hall to the sunroom. I stare after her in disbelief as she closes herself in the room.

"Well, that was fucking brazen as hell," Dane says quietly.

"No shit," I say.

"Don't worry about it. Jesse is on tap detail. He'll hear everything."

I nod and turn back to the room as both Kent and Rebekkah wipe their eyes vigorously and move slowly towards each other. Almost like they can't believe they're standing in front of each other. Like they can't fathom the other exists.

"I thought you were dead..." Kent chokes out. "I didn't believe Dane when he said you weren't. I got back from my trip as soon as I could."

I lean against the wall and cross my arms over my chest as everyone watches the two of them with soft smiles on their faces. Robby stands up as the kids crawl over to Jenny, Ethan, and Eve. He walks over to me and turns with his back to me. He doesn't need to tell me what he wants. I pull him against me and wrap him in my arms as we watch the beautiful moment unfold in front of us.

Rebekkah lets out a strangled sob. "I didn't dare believe I'd ever see you again."

They hesitate when they're in front of each other. I silently will them to hug and admit their undying feelings for each other. Then, I quietly chuckle at myself for being a romantic sap who just wants to see the happy ending. But holy shit. If anyone deserves it, it's these two.

Just as Dane, who has a bigger smile on his face than any of us do, is about to take matters into his own hands and push the two of them together, they both take the final steps and embrace each other tightly. Kent squeezes her hard, burying his face in her hair. Rebekkah clenches his shirt tightly in her fists and burrows her head into his chest. Both of them tremble with sobs as they sink to their knees on the floor holding each other.

I hug Robby tighter and lean forward. I kiss his neck. "It's beautiful, huh?" I whisper against his neck.

"It's miraculous when you think of it. The shit they went through to get to this point," he whispers back.

"What happened? Where have you been?" Kent asks. "What happened to you?" He runs his fingers through her hair as they both tremble. I'm sure Dane has told him the story, but I know how it feels to need to hear it directly from her mouth.

"My f-father used me as a b-bargaining chip for a business deal with another mafia!" she sobs into his chest. Her nails dig into his back. "E-Ethan had no clue!"

Kent rocks with her, but I can see his body racked with sobs just like her. "He said you were dead. I was at your funeral."

"It was faked," Ethan says. "I thought she was dead, too. Until she showed up here with part of Josh's crew. I found out she had a whole other life. None of us knew."

"They told me you were dead," she whispers.

"Ethan's father told me that they didn't want anything to do with us. He gave me a very large sum of money and said it was to take care of our son. I… thought Ethan knew. He stayed away from me during the funeral."

"I was in shock," Ethan says. "I couldn't believe any of what was happening. I don't think I really had any conscious thought for days afterwards."

Kent just nods. Once again I find myself hurting for how much this family has been through at the hands of Matthew Lucinio. The pain he's caused is nothing less than astounding to me. Even though, in this case, it was his father and her father that started this trainwreck, the fact that he continued on with the charade and gave her hope that she'd one day be reunited with her family is so beyond heartbreaking. No one could watch this and not feel like a thousand knives are being stabbed through their heart.

"I moved to Chicago almost right away. I finished school and just left. I was angry that they didn't want anything to do with our son. I was angry at all of them. By the time Ethan took over, my anger for the entire family consumed me. I hated the idea that Dane was even working with anyone connected to them."

"E-Ethan didn't know," Rebekkah cries quietly. "Everyone th-thought I died in a wreck. I thought you were dead. That's wh-what I was told by Matthew. He said his father killed you and our s-son right after they took me."

"Oh, honey. No. No. That isn't what happened. I was threatened. I was given a large sum of money and was threatened. I was told by Ethan's father that I had to stay away. My life would be in danger if I didn't. He told me to take the money and run. He said that your family wanted nothing to do with us, but they'd protect us. He told me to not contact them or not only would we be in danger, but my whole family would be in danger. I did try contacting Ethan after that, but I never got through to him. All of my attempts were intercepted by your father or mother. The last time I tried, I was told to stop calling, or I'd be killed, and our son would lose both of his parents."

Rebekkah cries harder. "Why? Why would he do that?"

I'm positive if she digs her nails any harder into Kent's back she'll draw blood. To his credit though, he doesn't flinch or tense. He just holds her and lets her grip him as hard as she needs to as he rocks back and forth with her, crying himself.

"The only conclusion I've been able to come up with is that he himself was being threatened and was trying to, in some way, protect you and Dane," Ethan says. "There were things that happened over that period of time that I didn't understand. He'd never explained them to me. One of the most important things, though, is that he changed our phone number. I didn't get that. And he told me that you didn't want anything to do with us. He'd said you'd moved."

"I don't mean to sound like a dick right now, but I think worrying about any of that at this point is going to do nothing but piss us off and give us all headaches," Ryan says. "The only things that matter are that Rebekkah is home where she belongs, and that you and Dane are here. You've been reunited. Other than that, nothing else really matters. It's time to move forward."

"I have to agree, dad," Dane puts in. "We have her back. We have what we always wanted. We have more than we've always wanted. I have two brothers I didn't know I had. Cousins. We've gained so much."

"Now is the time to celebrate. Talking about everything that happened can come later," I say.

Kent and Rebekkah nod, still gripping each other tightly as if they'll never let go. If I'm being honest, it's an adorable sight. It's really

140

beautiful to see two people who had so much love for each other at one point in their lives come together again. It's obvious that the love they once shared has never died. It's burning in the way they hold each other; the way they touch each other. Even the way they look at each other. It's the type of love everyone strives for.

I glance at Dane when his cellphone beeps. He glances at the screen then glances down the hall. After a couple of moments he clears his throat and catches Ryan's eye. He tilts his head down the hall before turning and walking down it. Robby looks up at me slightly confused as I reluctantly let him go, but I take his hand and quietly lead him out of the room, following Dane with Ryan close behind us.

He steps into the den. Ryan closes the door behind us and looks at him expectantly. My heart skips a beat. Not out of fear, but out of excitement at possibly being able to move forward with whatever information he just got.

"I got the tap info," Dane says. "She's on the phone right now, too."

Ryan nods. "Just a second."

He disappears from the den as Robby, Dane, and I settle. A few moments later, Ryan comes back with all the guys. They all find seats as Dane furiously texts. We all wait patiently for him to finish. Robby leans against me. I drop an arm across his shoulder.

Finally, Dane looks up. "Okay. Here's what we have," he says, keeping his voice low. He glances towards the door. "Is there a guard out there?"

Taylor nods. "Yes. Marissa is still in the sunroom."

"Good. She's talking to Matthew right now. She called him earlier today, too. Earlier, the conversation threw me. I don't know how close they are, but maybe not as close as we thought." Dane pauses. "Earlier, she was telling him that she wanted out. She couldn't do this anymore. He told her that if she didn't continue, he'd let Renza kill her."

Robby's mouth falls. "So, we know Renza's with Matthew," he growls.

Dane looks at him and nods. "It looks like it. Can't be totally sure, but it's starting to sound like it. Marissa said she didn't care. Anything was a better fate than being stuck in a loveless marriage around people she hates. She begged him to pull her out. He told her no. Then threatened her again. Except this time, he told her that if she didn't do as he told her, he'd kill her father just like he did her mother."

Gavin shakes his head and rubs his temples. "I'm so fucking confused. I thought she thought her father was dead. I went to their funeral with her. I mean, I get it. Her dad faked his death. But if Matthew is threatening her with killing her father, then she had to know her father was still alive after he allegedly died. Which means she's been working with that fucker for years."

Robby leans forward. "No. She's been being blackmailed by him for years."

"There's more," Dane says. "In this call, she said again that her father is the best mafia leader. She said that she doesn't know what he has over her father, but when she finds out, she's going to take Matthew out."

"It sounds to me like she's starting to get scared," I say. "People who have little power and are scared often make threats like that to make themselves seem more powerful than they are. It's what makes them so unpredictable."

Dane nods. "And she just became one of the most unpredictable parts of this whole situation. Not only did she make that threat, but he turned around and told her that she needs to get him the information he wants, or he'll just call up one of his contacts to blow up our entire complex. She told him to do it and hung up. We can't get a location, but it was Matthew she called. She made another call. Jesse traced it. It was to her father. He, of course, didn't answer."

"We can't stay here," Nick says. He looks at Ryan. "We need to get to the safehouse. Now. We need to confront her and get the fuck out of here."

"We can't leave her," Chase says. "I know she's done some fucked up things, but we can't leave her to him. He'll kill her without a second thought."

Gavin takes a deep breath and lets it out. "He's right. I planned on drawing up divorce papers. I still will, but we can't leave her out there to fend for herself. She won't make it to daybreak."

"We can't take her to the safehouse either, Gav," Lance says. "She'll give us up."

142

"Then what do we do? Huh?" Gavin glares. "I can't fucking leave her out there alone! She's not the best of people, but fuck. She doesn't deserve what he'd do to her!"

The entire room erupts into an argument. Raised voices become angrier and angrier as everyone tries to get their point and opinion across to everyone else. Repeated attempts from Ryan to quiet the room fail with epic spectacularity. Though I try a high-pitched whistle to gain everyone's attention, it doesn't work.

Finally, Josh stands. "Enough!" he commands above the din in the most dominant voice I've ever heard. Even more so than Ryan. Everyone looks up at him, instantly quieting. "Fucking hell. What are we? Kids? No! We're fucking adults! Act like it."

Ryan scrubs his hands down his face. "I don't want to hear another fucking word about leaving her to fend for her fucking self. We have ways of making sure she doesn't give us up. One is taking her damn phone. The next is checking her for any type of GPS tracking device. That means any that have been injected. We have the best technology in the world at our fingertips. We need to start taking advantage of it. When this is over, she can leave. For now? Her leaving is a danger to her and to us."

"Now. Dane. Anything else?" Josh asks as he sits back down rubbing his temples.

Dane nods. "Only other thing is something about the Department of Defense. It didn't make any sense. She asked if the Department of Defense was a go. He said yes. I have no idea what the fuck that means. Jesse said she hung up, but she seemed pretty upset. Sounded like she was crying."

"I'd be crying, too, if I knew my life was about to be over," Damon mumbles.

"Stop it," Josh warns. "We need to take this information and run with it. We need to take her phone. We need to get someone here to check for GPS devices. I don't have contacts who can do that."

"I'll call in my contact," Ryan says. "Don't worry about that." He takes out his phone to make his call.

Josh nods. "Then we get the fuck out of here. Nick is right. We can't stay here. Especially if he thinks she's going to betray him. I don't know what he'll do."

"I wouldn't put dropping a bomb on us past him," Alex grumbles as he rubs his eyes. "I'm so fucking sick of this."

"You aren't the only one," I say. "We have Pierce coming in within the next hour or so. I'll secure the safehouse."

I lean forward as I make my own call while the room suddenly becomes alive with a nervous energy. I grip Robby's thigh, feeling like he needs the contact. I don't know what Matthew's plans are for us, but I do know Nick is right. We need to leave.

Now.

Chapter Seventeen

☒ Robby ☒

Marissa flies by me like a flash of light. I don't even have a chance to stop her before she's reached Ryan and is grabbing his arm.

"Don't! They're fake!" Marissa screams.

Ryan looks at her alarmed as he starts to open the door. He pushes her back slightly. "What the fuck are you talking about?"

"It's the Department of Defense! They're fake!" Marissa cries, trying to slam the door.

"It's the fucking Chicago P.D. Now, would you back up?" Ryan pulls her away from the door, but before he has her fully back, the door slams open, knocking both him and Marissa to the ground.

"Holy shit!" I dive behind a couch as bullets start flying.

I don't know whose gun they're coming from. All I can think of is the girls and kids. I take the gun from my holster and peek out from behind the chair. Arianna has the kids in the middle of the room, trying to pull all of them to safety. I scramble up and run to her, shooting towards the door on my way.

The uniformed cops who busted through the door have taken cover by the staircase. I grab Nicole's hand and Breetana on my way. Dani has managed to grab Jessa and Lyric. Jason is covering Dani as she pulls both of them away.

Suddenly, I feel a hand on my back. "With me!" Taylor shouts. "Let's move!"

Amid the flying bullets, I manage to usher Arianna and the kids down the hall. Glancing behind me, I see that Ethan is pushing Breetana, Nicole, Jessa, and Jenny in front of him. Dani is pushing Rebekkah, Kent, Eve, Lyric and Sonya. Taylor is behind them, pushing them down the hall while he walks backwards.

I push and guide everyone into the den. "Go! Go! Stay low!"

Ethan hurries to close the blackout shades as everyone else huddles. Arianna tries to soothe the screaming kids. Nicole and Lyric try to help her.

"In here! Now!" Taylor commands a couple of guards at the end of the hall. They both run towards us. Taylor shoves them both into the den with our family. They don't need any other commands. They know what they need to do.

I close the door to the den and follow Taylor back out to the living room. Ryan has taken cover behind a chair. He has Marissa on the ground next to him. Her ears are covered as she cries and squeezes her eyes shut.

Taylor and I duck down behind a shelf near the stairs. One of the cops makes eye contact with me and aims for us. I push Taylor down as the wood of the shelf splinters and rains down around us. My heart quickens when I realize that not only has our perimeter been breached a second time in such little fucking time, but it's the second time the shooters are after me.

"Not today, you fuckers." This time, I'm armed. They don't know it yet, but they don't stand a chance.

Reading me and my body language, Taylor moves aside and behind me. "You got a shot?" he asks so only I can hear.

I shake my head. "Not yet, but I will."

"Don't let that Robby fucker get away!" one of them yells. "He's worth millions to us!"

I chuckle. Nice to know Matthew thinks I'm that valuable. But it doesn't matter. They won't be seeing that money. I lay on the ground and catch Ryan's eye. Nodding, he pops around the chair and starts shooting.

146

I take the distraction to slither my way to the stairs. I hear a gasp, but I don't turn. I can't. Even a second could ruin my plan. They could see me and shoot. I wouldn't have a chance. Not in my position. I have to take them first.

I quickly jump into a crouching position and shoot them both, using the railing for my cover in case I miss.

I don't.

Both collapse in a heap on the floor on the other side of the stairs. We all stay in our positions for a moment as we catch our breath. It's not until we see the blood oozing across the white linoleum towards the open door that anyone dares to move.

In that instant, Luke's arms wrap tightly around me, almost cutting off all air. But I'm completely okay with it because being in his arms as the adrenaline seeps out of me might be all that's keeping me standing.

"Fuck," I say as I turn around. I wrap my arms around him.

He holds me tight and close as he sways with me. "I saw you going after them. If they had seen you…"

I shake my head into his neck. "Don't. Don't think about that. I saw an opening. I took it. Ryan provided the cover I needed. He was the only one in position to."

"What were you thinking? Baby, you could have been killed," he whispers in my neck. I feel him start to tremble. Only slightly. Anyone watching him would never be able to see it, but I feel it.

"I'm okay, Luke. I promise."

"I-Is everyone o-okay?" Marissa asks meekly.

Luke spins on her so fast I have to hold onto him or I'll fall. "No fucking thanks to you!"

I grab his arm before he can chase after her. "Luke, it's okay. She tried."

Marissa shrinks behind Ryan. "I'm sorry…"

"Sorry?" Luke asks. "Fucking sorry? You think that's going to just fix everything miraculously? You almost got Robby killed! Fucking again! Did you have your hand in the pool incident, too? Huh?"

He breaks free of my grasp and starts for her, but Josh steps in front of him before he even takes a step. He puts his hands on Luke's chest. "Stop. That's not going to help anyone. Turn around. Robby needs you."

Luke glares at him. "If she hadn't been playing this fucking game in the first damn place, he wouldn't have just been shot at!"

"And if she hadn't warned us when she did, he might be dead. So would Ryan. Fuck. Maybe more of us, if not all." Josh lets the words sink in as we all watch Luke.

Finally, I reach out and take his arm, rubbing soothingly. "Luke, she did the right thing. The end is all that matters. I'm okay. They're dead." I glance at the guards coming silently through the door. They immediately start to clean up.

Luke takes a deep breath. "This is the third time he's come after Robby. We need to get out of here. I'm not going through this shit again. I've almost lost him three times now. I can't do this anymore."

"I couldn't agree more," Ryan says. "But we have measures that we have to take, Luke. You know that. We aren't going to leave in broad daylight. We have people coming to help deal with all of this shit. We have to wait for my experts who can deal with the GPS bullshit."

I step closer to Luke and kiss his arm. He wraps his arms around me and kisses my forehead as we hug each other. He nods against my neck as he kisses it. Ryan barks out commands. For us, everything stands still while Luke sways with me, taking the comfort that he needs in the fact that I'm okay.

But there is a thought running through my mind. "How did they get through security?"

"There's a flaw in my system," Nick says. When he ended up next to me I don't know, but I look at him anyway. "They had to have been able to give themselves fake CPD jackets. Got some CPD uniforms. Or they are real CPD officers who were paid off. I don't know. But from here on out, no one gets through our security without being on an approved list. I don't care if it's the goddamn President." Nick walks away, heading for the den.

Luke chuckles. "He's pissed."

"I think we all are. Matthew managed to attack us on our own property twice now."

Luke kisses my neck and pulls back slowly. "We need to identify them. Track who paid them."

"I know, baby. I'll take care of it."

"Everyone to the den," Ryan says. "Cleanup crew will deal with this shit."

Luke takes my hand as everyone obeys Ryan. He starts tugging me to the den, but I pull him towards the bodies. "I need their ID's, and I need to touch base with the guards at the gate. I need to see what it pulled up when they ran them."

"We'll call up there, but you aren't going out there. Matthew has a hard on for you, Robby. You need to stay indoors until we leave. And this fucking house is going to be covered with guards."

I kiss his hand as I let go and bend to retrieve their wallets and anything else I can use to identify them. When I have everything, I follow Luke back to the den. It's crowded with everyone in it, but this is the second safest place in the house. The first is Ryan's bedroom.

I sit on the floor against the wall away from everyone. I don't expect Luke to sit next to me, but he does. So close that if he could be on top of me, he just might do it. I lean into him as he wraps his arm around me.

"I'm not letting you more than a foot away from me," Luke says.

I turn and kiss his jaw. "I love you."

"I love you, too."

I look up when Lance sits next to me. Damon sits on his other side. "Thought you might like some help. And if you don't, then give me something to do, man. Because I want to kill Marissa right now. And I'd have no fucking regrets doing it."

I chuckle. "Trust me when I say you aren't the only one. I think half this room wants to kill her. Why do you think she's stuck to Ryan's side like glue right now? He's the only one she feels she might have a chance with when it comes to protecting her."

"I think Ryan would step aside if I leveled my Glock at her," Luke growls.

"I'm not so sure about that," I say. "I think he thinks she might be useful."

Luke growls. "He's right. Doesn't make me less pissed off. Though, he wouldn't keep her so close if it had been Arianna targeted."

I elbow him. "Luke. Stop."

He looks down at me. "Come on. You really think he'd allow her to be that close if those fuckers came in and started shooting at Arianna?"

I scrub my hands down my face. "I know you're pissed off, but me being a target isn't his fault. If he thinks she's better off alive, then you have to trust him."

He lets his head fall against the wall. "I know. I do. I trust him, but this is three times, Robby."

"How many times did Renza assist in targeting Arianna after Ryan suspected she was working with someone?"

"And she almost got killed in a fire," Luke hisses.

"We can't fall apart right now. You know as well as I do that he's learned from that. We all have."

"I'm pissed, too," Damon says. "But we need to trust them. We can't fall apart now."

Luke grumbles, but I know he knows we're right. I also know he's upset and saying things he doesn't mean. He knows Ryan wouldn't be treating this any differently if it were anyone else, including Arianna, because Marissa can get us information that we would never be able to get otherwise.

"Listen up," Ryan says. "I know everyone is scared. Pissed off even. I am, too. But before we even start, I don't want to hear a single word about Marissa being left to fend for herself, or shot, or any other bullshit."

"I wouldn't mind taking the bitch down a couple pegs," Lyric mutters under her breath. Josh smirks at her and kisses her head.

"Hanged, drawn, and quartered would be nice," Luke whispers.

"Ssh...," I whisper back with a half-smile and a quiet chuckle as I shake my head.

We all look up at the knock on the door. A guard in the room answers it. He opens it a little wider, letting in a younger looking man with a laptop and other equipment that I'm jealous of. The man is wearing a suit. He's blond. I'd guess late 20's.

"I don't want to know what happened out there," he says.

"It's better not to ask," Ryan says. "Everyone. This is Pierce. He's with the CIA and is going to help Robby and Lance with all of the tracking and tech stuff. He's gone through more checks and scrutiny than I care to explain. He can be trusted. Pierce, I don't want you to set up yet. We're moving to a safehouse. I'm waiting on one more person to get here before we go. We can't leave if I feel we're being tracked."

"You call in Oscar from Homeland?" Pierce asks.

"Yes. Only person I know who can do what I want quick and discreetly," Ryan answers. "Take a seat." He waits for Pierce to find a seat before he continues. "Next up, Marissa." He turns to her. She cowers and hides her face in her arms as she draws her knees up to her chest.

"I'm so sorry," she whispers.

"Just start with how the fuck this happened," Gavin growls. "We already know you're talking to Matthew."

She looks up at him wide-eyed and startled. Like a deer in the headlights. "W-what?"

"Did you think we're stupid, sweetheart?" Luke drawls. "Because we ain't. We know how to run a fucking tap. Track. We know you're connected to Matthew. And we know you're connected to Renza. Though, you know her as Ari Lussane."

Her lip quivers as she sniffles. She fights back tears. "He k-killed my mother," she whispers. I don't know if anyone else can hear her, or if just those of us close to her can. Before I have a chance to say anything, she clears her throat. "He killed my mother. He helped my father fake his death after a huge scandal involving embezzlement. It was then I found out that my father was a mafia leader, and that the life we had was a cover. The embezzlement scandal that hit the papers was actually a money laundering scheme that was covered up with the embezzlement story."

"Huh," I say. How the fuck did I miss that? I make a mental note to dig into that.

"I went to that funeral," Gavin says. "You were bawling your eyes out. World class act if you knew he was still alive."

She shakes her head. "I didn't, Gavin. At least not then. It wasn't until a few days later. I was approached by a man dressed all in black who pulled me into an alley by my favorite cafe. It was my father. He told me everything. He came totally clean. He told me he needed me to keep his secret. Of course I was going to. He's my father. He told me that he's working with another mafia, and that when it's all over, we'll be in a place of power and control that our family deserves. He told me our real family name is Krins. And that his first name is Adam."

"How did you end up on Matthew Lucinio's payroll?" Ryan asks her.

She pauses a moment before taking a breath. "I found out that I have a sister…" Her eyes fall on Dani. "I… asked my father about her. Well… you… He told me about you. He told me that he left you when you were just a young girl. Only a year older than I was at the time. He said that your mother found out he was living a double life. That he was a cold-blooded killer. That he was a mafia leader. And that he was working with Matthew. He…" She closes her eyes and wipes them. "He told me that he was still working as a contract killer for the same man he was then. That he was trying to get out from under his thumb. He had a plan. He was going to have the Crane Mafia take out this man and his mafia."

"Matthew," I say, keeping track of everything she says in my head so I can sit down later and dig through everything to verify her.

She looks down at me from the couch and nods. "I… thought… I could save the war. I couldn't talk him out of it, but I hated the idea."

"So, you knew Matthew was alive. How long, Marissa?" Josh growls.

She flinches at him and curls into herself. "Almost immediately after you thought you'd killed him," she says softly. "A few days…"

"Fuck," Alex says dropping his head in his hands. He looks back up at her after a moment. "Do you have any idea how many lives you could have saved by telling us that?"

She hesitantly nods. "I… actually went to Matthew a couple of weeks ago. I begged him to leave my father alone. I even told him in good faith that he was trying to stay out of everything and let him fight the Crane Mafia on his own." She sniffles again. "He seemed to be receptive to my plea, but he said that he can't let him go until he finishes his mission. I knew he wouldn't ever let him go. I called my father right after. I told him that I wanted to help. I wanted to meet my sister. I told him that I thought he should team with the Crane Mafia. I knew Dani was with Nick at that time."

She flicks her eyes to Lyric then Josh and back to Alex. "I also knew that he had had someone watching Lyric. He knew about the baby. About the miscarriage. My father told me that Matthew had expressed interest in her. So, I knew Josh would have been brought into this at some point."

"You knew she was a target and never said a fucking word?" Josh snarls at her. Lyric shakes her head and wraps her arms around herself, snuggling close to his side.

Marissa flinches. "I thought if we could team with you, then we would also have Josh since I knew you would bring him in on this. I thought we could defeat him that way. And maybe my father could take over the mafia Matthew built up. I'm still hoping that. I'm just trying to get a hold of him. I haven't been able to."

"You thought you could get him to team with us... And then we would let him take over Matthew's army? Are you fucking delusional?" Nick asks.

"No! I thought it through. Really."

"You're missing half the fucking story here. What about Renza?" Ryan asks, getting slightly frustrated.

She looks up at him, confused. "You keep saying Renza, but that I knew her as Ari Lussane. I only know of one person named Renza. But I don't have contact with her. Ari is my friend."

"Bullshit," Dane says. "I tapped your phone. I know he told you he'd have Renza kill you if you didn't cooperate."

She blinks at him. "Dane, Renza is Matthew's new wife. I've never met her. But he's always saying things like she's a cold-blooded assassin. He's threatened me with her numerous times. Ever since he found out that I knew he was alive."

"Hang on," I say, holding up a hand. "When did you start talking to Matthew?"

"He contacted me about a year ago. I knew he was alive, but I hadn't talked to him. He threatened me right off. He told me that he would rip me up into little pieces if I didn't do what he wanted. He told me he'd kill my father. He said he'd already killed my mother. He told me that from that moment on, I was working for him. I was to get him any shred of information on both Josh and Ryan as I could. But I hadn't done it. Not until a couple of weeks ago when I contacted him."

"So, you've known he was alive for how long?" I ask. "Three years?"

She nods. "Since just after Josh thought he killed him."

I pull up an image on my laptop and turn it towards her. "Who is this?"

"That's Ari. What does she have to do with this? Why do you have a picture of her?"

"Because that's not Ari, Marissa," Gavin says. "That's fucking Renza. And it's the same person who approached Lyric twice and freaked her out enough to come here."

"When did Matthew get married?" Luke asks.

"U-Um…" She shakes her head. "A little over a year ago."

"That's…" Arianna lets out a sob and turns to Josh, who's sitting next to her as Ryan paces. Josh puts an arm around her and Lyric and hugs them both. "That's just after…"

"I know, baby," Ryan says, soothingly to her before shooting a withering glare in Marissa's direction.

She cowers even more. "I know I'm the most hated person in the room, but… I did try to get him to stop. I've even told him he could kill me. But he started threatening you, Dani. He said if I didn't cooperate, he'd kill you. I tried to get him to believe that I hate everyone in this room. I spewed so much shit about all of you. Then he started threatening my father. He said he'd kill him if I didn't fall in line."

"Your father is fucking dead," Josh snarls. "Matthew had him killed the day we left L.A. That very night. He'd paid off one of Ryan's guards to kill him."

Marissa bursts into tears and hides her face in her arms again. "I knew it! I knew it." She cries hard. It's difficult not to feel something for her. Something other than hatred. "I'm sorry! I'm so sorry! I was trying to protect the only family I knew I had!" Her body turns into a trembling, shaking mess.

"Oh my God," Dani says, beginning to cry as well. She breaks out of Nick's grasp, shoving him back a little bit as she rushes to Marissa's side. She wraps her in her arms.

Marissa turns, burying her face in her hair. The two embrace in what would be a very touching moment if I felt any sympathy at all for her. Even though I feel a little bad for what she went through, I can't feel the sympathy for her that Dani obviously does. Not after everything we've been through with her. The two attempts on my life after surviving one already were attempts she could have stopped long ago from happening.

154

"Why didn't you say anything to me?" Gavin asks, slightly pained. "You know I could have helped you. You didn't have to do this. You've caused so much irreparable damage I don't even know where to begin."

"I know. I'm really sorry." Marissa grips Dani as tightly as Dani is gripping her.

I have to hand it to Dani. She might be the only person in this room with a heart big enough to see past all of the reasons we're all so pissed off. Maybe it's because of the relationship between the two.

Unfortunately, Marissa has dug her grave on this one. And I don't think it's one she'll be able to come back from.

Chapter Eighteen

✗ Luke ✗

I stand against the wall with my arms folded across my chest watching the room. I'm not happy with anything happening right now. I want to be gone. I want to be on the way to the safehouse like we should have been three fucking hours ago.

But I know better than to question Ryan. I know he knows what he's doing. It's not that I don't trust him. My problem is that I want Robby away from all of this. I don't like that he's had a direct attempt on his life three fucking times since Matthew waltzed back into our world and turned everything upside down.

I'm impatient. I want our family safe. I want Robby safe. I want to regroup in a place where no one knows where the hell we are. I want to figure out how our security is being breached. We have the highest levels of security of anywhere that I've ever worked. I worked for a fucking federal agency. Ryan's security is far more advanced than the ATF could dream of.

So, why the hell were two cops able to get through and try to kill Robby? How is someone able to take shots from the fucking lake without us seeing? Where's the flaw? Where are we failing? There should be no way anyone can get to us here. Not on our own property.

"You look deep in thought," Josh says quietly as he stands next to me. He leans against the wall and surveys the room with me.

"I just don't understand how it was so easy to get to Robby. Three fucking times."

"The first time he paid off a guard, Luke. There isn't a damn thing you could have done about that. None of us could have. Matthew was a really good fucking distraction. No one expected that. It was easy to grab him when no one was paying attention. You can't sit here and blame yourself or anyone else other than Matthew for that."

"I know. But part of me believes something in our security design is fucked up. It shouldn't be so easy to breach us."

"All he needed was one guard. I don't care how good of a boss Ryan is. There is no way he can make every single one of his people happy. No way. We're always going to have to worry about a guard getting paid off here or there. And when it happens, we deal with it. In this case, Matthew did that for us. As for Robby getting shot at from the water... No one expected that either. Maybe we should have. All we can do now is what we already are. Patrol the water."

I sigh. "I'm fucking tired of all of this. I just want my family safe. They shouldn't have to worry about being attacked in their home. I shouldn't have to worry about Robby being attacked like he just was."

"You're right. You shouldn't have to. I agree with you. But it happened. Sitting here and reliving it is going to do nothing more than piss you off. So, instead of picking apart everything that happened and how fucking wrong it was, put that energy into fixing it. We need to put up a wall. We shouldn't have to, but we know that the lake is a weak point in our security. Jessa will hate every fucking second of it. So will Arianna. Everyone will. But in the end, everyone will understand."

I nod, knowing he's right. "Every time someone makes an attempt on my family, I just want to explode. But taking a shot on Robby?" I shake my head.

"You want to go gamma ray level and destroy the universe."

"You have no idea."

"Oh, I do. When I figured out everything Matthew had done to my family, I felt the same way. Seeing all the shit he put my mom through?"

He pauses. I look over at him. His jaw muscles are working, and his muscles are tense. After a couple minutes, he looks over at me. "It took a lot to remain calm. Lyric played a large part in that. And I know she's struggling herself. So, I do understand, Luke. I'm pissed, too. But we have got to channel that energy into dealing with the problem."

"You're right." I yawn into my hands before running them through my hair. "We need to get the fuck out of here. I can't think."

"As soon as Oscar is finished checking for GPS tracking on the vehicles and getting us all a scrambler so we can't be tracked. Just in case that's what that fucker is doing."

"It's what we'd do."

Josh nods. "If he's smart, that's what he'd do. When I was after Jessa, first thing I did was went for her phone. Hacking phone companies isn't as difficult as you'd think."

I chuckle. "I've seen Robby hack into fucking Government agencies. I'd believe anything is hackable if the hacker is good enough."

Josh laughs. "I can't believe some of the shit he's hacked into. Lance is good, but fuck. Robby could be the world's biggest enemy. Thank God he's on the right side."

I smile. "You know, when he was in eighth grade he hacked into his math teacher's computer and changed his entire test. The reason? Because the teacher said something stupid about his system being like Fort Knox. Took Robby less than five minutes, and he did it in class."

Josh raises an eyebrow. "How?"

I shrug. "Not a clue. He said the kids had tablets or laptops in the class because that's how the guy taught. He'd give them references they could look up if they didn't understand something. And he'd do a lot of interactive stuff. Robby said it didn't take much. Some hacking software and boredom. It was done before he knew it."

"How did the teacher find out?"

"He didn't until he went to print off the test. Robby erased everything and typed out something about how Fort Knox should get better security." I smile as Josh laughs.

"Mr. Massena?"

I glance over at a guard who has just come into the room. "Yeah?"

"Vehicles are all ready to go. We have scramblers installed in them. We also have a couple for the safehouse and the perimeter. When we get there, we'll install them. Until then, though, we should communicate by radio. All phones off."

"Okay. What about the kid's and the rest of the family's personal items?"

"We've got everything packed. I've sent out guards ahead of us in vehicles that have been cleared."

"And the guards at the safehouse know we're coming?"

"Yes, sir."

"Okay. Thank you."

"One more thing. We have an issue at the gate."

I glance at Josh before looking back at him. "What issue?"

"There's a few people there that we've had no contact with at all. They aren't an ally. That we know of anyway. We did run them. They belong to a motorcycle crew. Viper's Venom."

I raise an eyebrow. "I've heard of them. They're pretty vicious. Cutthroat. What do they want?"

"Didn't say. Just that they want to talk to Mr. Crane or Mr. Lucinio. Preferably both."

"Like hell," I growl as I push off the wall.

Josh grabs my arm. "Whatever is going on out there, Ryan needs to be aware of it."

"After what just happened? We were attacked in our own home. No way am I letting him go out there."

"The need to protect your family is almost overpowering sometimes, but you know as well as I do that he's going out there with us." He pushes off the wall and catches Ryan's eye. He waves him over.

I sigh. "I hate that you're right."

"Right about what?" Ryan asks when he gets to us.

"Everything. Literally everything," I say. "We have a problem at the gate. Motorcycle crew named Viper's Venom."

Ryan looks down at the guard standing next to me. "Why?"

"Didn't say, Mr. Crane. Just said he wanted to speak with you or Mr. Lucinio. He said it was important."

Ryan crosses his arms over his chest. "Did he say why it was so important?"

"Nope. He wouldn't say anything more. Just that he has information for you that you want to have."

Ryan looks at me and Josh. "Okay. Let's go."

"This is a terrible idea," I say as I follow them out of the room. "Truly terrible."

"Well, we aren't letting them in here. And I'm not sending anyone else out there," Ryan says. "If I'm walking into a trap, I have you both for back up."

The guard chuckles. "I don't think any of us would dare go against you, Mr. Crane. We all value our lives too much. Besides, you treat us well. Not many jobs out there where you get room and board paid for. And sometimes get treated to a lavish meal by your boss. Everyone here loves this family. All of you."

Ryan gestures to him. "See? It's all good."

I grumble under my breath as Ryan chuckles. I can't really argue with the guy. Ryan really treats all of his guys very well. I've never worried about the people who are on duty to protect the family. But after Cal, I worry about all of the rest of them. They *are* all paid well, but it's not hard to see that a lot of them are bitter about not being on family security detail. The job is prestigious. Everyone wants it.

I've become very suspicious and cynical of everyone over the past few weeks. Guards who have been with Ryan for years are all suspect to me. Truthfully, I should listen to Josh. Deal with the guards who turn on us as they come. But I've never been good with waiting for things to happen. I prefer being in control of the outcome. Even when it's impossible.

I'm not that different from Ryan or Josh in that aspect of things. But they're both far better at dealing with all of that than I am. I need to learn how to take things as they come a little better than I do. Like right now. I don't like that Ryan or Josh are coming out here. I want to be the one to screen whatever the fuck these guys want. I want Ryan and Josh both safely away from the unknown.

I also know better. Ryan and Josh aren't the type of people who would allow that to happen. Not only are they both the kind of leaders that are in the thick of things, but they also choose to be there. They won't let others fight their battles for them.

I sigh as we reach the gate. Guards are armed with assault rifles at our side. It looks a little like a military base. All of the guards are dressed in tactical gear. Most are wearing helmets and night vision goggles. I know we have snipers on the roof of Ryan's house right now because I commanded them up there. There aren't a lot of people in the world who would dare fuck with us.

Which is why I don't like that this crew is currently standing outside our gate like they have nothing in the fucking world to fear. They should all be terrified; shaking in their leather fucking chaps. Instead, they're leaning casually against their bikes with their arms folded over their chest.

"Mr. Crane," the dude I assume must be the leader says as cockily as he possibly can as he stands up and walks to the still closed gate. "I'm Alec. My friends call me Ace." He sticks his hand out but stops before reaching through the bars. He looks at them suspiciously. "I'm not going to get electrocuted, am I?"

"Maybe," Ryan says, keeping his arms to his side and regarding Alec with a cool detachment I admire. "What do you want, Alec?"

Alec watches us all a moment before dropping his hand when none of us make a move to shake it. "Okay." He glances over his shoulder then back at us. "Look. I won't waste your time. Over the past couple of months, we've had some serious problems. Girls have gone missing. Last week, we had one of my guys' girls go missing. The week before, we had a daughter of one of my guys disappear. The month before, Tyler here." He pauses and gestures to a guy behind him. "Tyler had his sister go missing. And just today, my sister vanished. I got a call from her about two hours ago. It was all static. Nothing since."

"What does that have to do with us?" Josh asks.

Alec hesitates slightly before running his hands through his hair. "All evidence leads to you. The Lucinio and Crane Mafias. The problem is I know your rep. Any reputable mafia, gang, or crew knows who you all are. When we discovered it was all connected with you, we knew there's no fucking chance. It had to be a set up."

"We don't go around kidnapping women for the fuck of it," Josh growls low.

"That's not how we operate," I say.

"We know," Alec agrees. "Which is why we're asking for help. And as a sort of a good gesture, if you will, word on the street is the Berlusconi Mafia is after you and your family. They're the ones who took shots at you guys. I hear they had someone do it from the lake. And they paid off a couple cops to come here."

We all look at each other. I clear my throat and furrow my brows. "We took them out. They shouldn't exist."

"They've been reborn," Alec says. "And they've been in my business."

Ryan looks at me. "Am I crazy? Did I not take them out?"

I chuckle and shake my head. "Matthew fucking Lucinio came back from the dead, Ry. Mafias we obliterated are coming out of the swamps we buried them in. We took them out, but it doesn't surprise me at this point."

"We're happy to team with you if you need us to," Alec says. "But please help us. One of those girls is my sister. A few others are practically family to me. To all of us. We have no information on them. It's like they've just vanished. I want my sister back. She's my entire fucking world. We want our girls back."

The three of us look at each other again, but I already know we're doing this. Ryan would never walk away from this. Neither would Josh. The two of them have an overwhelming sense of protection. Especially when family is involved.

"I don't just allow anyone to team with me," Ryan starts. "Neither does Josh. You need to prove yourself. We have to check you out. Everyone is after us."

Alec raises his hands a little in front of him. "I get it. Do what you need to do. I'm on the up and up. Your guards have all of my information."

"We'll be in contact," Ryan says. He steps forward and slips his hand through the gate to shake. Alec regards him warily, but steps forward and takes it. Ryan shakes his hand but doesn't let go right away. He tightens his grip instead. "We aren't the kind of people to fuck with. If you're here as some kind of a distraction, I will hunt you all down and kill you without a second thought. Understand that."

"I understand, Mr. Crane. I'm not here to fuck with you. I need your help. And I'm offering my services in any way you need. Information. Added forces. Name it. We aren't stupid. We know better than to get on your bad side. All I care about right now is my family. That's what you stand for, and it's what I'm counting on."

Ryan lets go of his hand. Alec nods and turns to leave. His crew jumps on their bikes. At almost the same time, they all roar to life.

Moments later, they're gone. We all watch them in silence until we can't see them any longer.

"I'll have Robby start looking into the Berlusconi Mafia as soon as we get to the safehouse," I finally say as we all turn to walk back to the house.

"We'll have to go in and capture them. Question before we destroy them this time," Josh says.

"I don't want to put all of our cards in one hand," Ryan adds. "We look into Berlusconi. Have Lance and Pierce do it. I want Robby looking into Viper's Venom. Find out about the missing women. See if we can figure out who took them. He said it's connected to us. That means we're being set up."

"Which means Matthew likely has a hand in this," I finish.

"Correct." Ryan opens the door to the house. "Get everyone together. Everyone takes different routes. Nick, Taylor, me, Luke, Josh, and Alex are the best drivers. That means we take the family. Two guards to each vehicle with us. Two vehicles with us. One in front. One behind."

"Got it," I say.

In a flurry of activity, everyone gets ready to go. We all pile into the vehicles. Robby climbs in next to me. Breetana and Chase climb in the back with Eve. When everyone is settled, we all take off on our planned routes, separate from one another.

I hate the idea, but it's necessary. More targets to chase spread out over a far distance means it's less likely for anyone chasing us to catch us. It's far easier to avoid a tail with a couple of vehicles than it is for many.

The farther we get from the city, the less anxious I feel. The hope now is that everyone gets there safely.

Chapter Nineteen

☒ Robby ☒

"Are we the first ones here?" I ask with a yawn as I look around.

"Looks like it," Luke says. He parks the vehicle. We both get out. "Stay with them, baby. I need to check in with the guards inside."

I nod, but stay outside the vehicle. My AR-15 is across my chest and in a low ready position just in case I need it. I can feel how tense Luke is. It's radiating off him in waves. I don't think he'll feel relaxed until everyone is here and safe.

Of course, it may take hours for that to happen. We all took different routes to get here. Traffic in Chicago is unpredictable on its best day. On the worst? It's like an apocalypse. I would go as far as saying it's worse than New York.

I look up when Luke comes back out. "We're clear." He opens the door for Chase as I open the other on Eve's side. "They're installing the scramblers, so keep the phones off."

We all grab our things and head inside the huge house set back in the deepest part of the woods possible. After we get our things put away in our room, I grab my laptop and settle in a quiet corner of the office. I want to get all of the information I can on Viper's Venom. Especially if they're bank rolled by a particular mafia boss and just fucking around with us.

"Hey," Luke says from the door of the office.

I look up at him. "Hey." I raise an eyebrow at the expression. Worry? Anger? There's a storm going on that I can't place. "You doing okay?"

"No." He shakes his head. "I'm not. I don't like that we're all separated." He goes quiet for a moment before sighing. "At the risk of sounding like an asshole, I need you out there, Robby. I… I don't want you away from me."

I give him a soft smile as I stand. Without question I gather my things and walk towards him. When I reach him, my laptop tucked under my arm, I kiss him. I push him back against the doorframe when I deepen it, nipping his tongue. When he moans into my mouth and tangles his fingers in my hair, I smile. I pull slowly away and kiss him once more, softly this time.

"I'm okay," I say against his lips.

He runs his fingers through my hair and tugs. "I know. But I don't want you away from me."

"Then I won't be." I kiss him again and take his hand. I let him lead me out to the living room.

Chase and Breetana are both sitting on the couch. Breetana is in Chase's lap. Eve is leaning against them. Chase has a blanket around them all as he holds them. I smile when I sit on a smaller couch. I expect Luke to sit down next to me, but he doesn't. Instead he paces, and I realize that he will until everyone is safe and under this roof.

So, I go back to my search. So far, Viper's Venom is a real merciless crew. They've been involved in everything from illegal drug trade to weapons. Shake downs. Hire for murder. Not the type of people I want any of us involved with. It's obvious the side they chose to ally with is the side that pays the most.

That is until a few years ago when they all but dropped off the radar. Very interesting. I smile because I know what's about to come. The type of research I love to do. Digging deeply into people who really want to keep their secrets. Unfortunately for them, they've come across me. Secrets have a habit of not staying hidden for long when I'm on the case.

I crack my knuckles as I get ready to really discover all I can about them. Enough piddly shit. I want the real story. I want to know what they're doing now. Why they don't look like they're into all of the illegal shit they used to be anymore. I want to know where their money comes from. I want to know what the leader's favorite color is. Just because I can.

But before I can, the radio that has been quiet all night suddenly crackles to life. I look up as Luke answers it. He looks about as on edge as I feel.

"Go ahead," Luke says.

"It's Josh. I'm leading a tail straight to you. Grab a few guards. Meet me outside."

Luke nearly chokes as my mouth drops. "Are you insane? Why the fuck would you lead them here? They could have a fucking locator!" Luke yells.

"We have a scrambler, Massena."

"Fucking Christ! Where the hell are you?"

"Coming up the long ass drive now. You better get me vehicles to block, and I'm sure these fuckers are armed."

Luke turns to me. "Stay with them." He runs for the door.

"I don't know whether to be pissed off or trust that asshole knows what he's doing," Chase grumbles, hugging his mother and wife tighter and casually putting his feet up on the table. "If he gets us killed, I swear to God I'll come back just to fucking haunt him."

I can't help but chuckle. "I'd be right behind you."

"How are you so casual and calm about this?" Eve sniffles and burrows closer to them both. Breetana hugs her tightly.

Chase drops a kiss to the top of Eve's head. "Bulletproof glass, mom. Reinforced steel on the doors. Even the siding of the house is protected."

He's right, but the words don't seem to ease her fears. Breetana looks like she's become numb. I can't really blame her. The girl has been through so much. This has to be bringing up memories for her. And I'm sure none of them are pleasant.

"Nick to Robby."

I take out my radio. "Go ahead."

"I assume Luke is outside with Josh. We're coming up on the entrance. I'll need an all clear."

166

"I don't hear gunfire yet, but stay back until I know."

"We're pulling off," Nick says. "But we're hidden in the trees at the top of the drive. I don't want to risk being on a road, no matter how secluded we are back here."

"Yeah. 10-4." I put down the radio just as I hear squealing tires outside. It doesn't take long to hear shooting followed by almost immediate silence.

"Well, that didn't take long," Chase says.

"Can't be sure. At least not until they're in here."

"What's going on up there, Robby?" Nick asks over the radio. "It's far too quiet for what it should be."

I sigh as I get up. Unfortunately, he's right. It's far too quiet. With my gun at my side, I make my way to the window next to the door. I move the shade ever so slightly and peek out. Josh, Lance, and Luke are both hauling three people off the ground. They're all cuffed with their hands behind their backs. They've been disarmed and are being led towards the shed off the side of the house. Shane and Cole are standing near the vehicle on guard.

"It looks like they have everything under control, but I'm not giving you the all clear until they say. They have three guards in cuffs being led to the interrogation shed."

"I want them checking that vehicle for any tracking equipment. Why the fuck Josh would lead them there is beyond me."

"He said the scrambler emits a signal that would have jammed up anything they have."

"Where are the guards he had with them? Why couldn't they take them out while Josh got away to safety? That's why they were there."

"Not a question I can answer, Nick. I'm not in Josh's head." I love all of my brother's, but sometimes they have a habit of pissing me off. Particularly when they ask me stupid questions they know I can't answer. Like why something happened the way it did when I had absolutely nothing to do with it.

I watch as they come out of the shed. They all head for Josh's SUV. They begin grabbing bags as Shane helps a trembling Sonya out of the SUV. He hugs her tightly and helps her into the house. The rest of the guys follow.

"Nick is at the end of the drive hiding in trees," I say to Luke. "Should I give him the all clear?"

"Yeah. He's good. They're locked in the shed. Too fucking bad it's kind of cool and there's no fucking sun. It would be kind of fun to watch those fuckers bake to death."

"Luke!" Sonya barks as she glares.

Luke adorably jumps at her tone and drops his head. "Sorry, ma'am," he mumbles.

I chuckle and go back to looking out the window. "You're good, Nick. You can come up."

"Be there shortly," he responds.

True to his word, Nick and the two vehicles filled with guards fly up the drive a few minutes later. They all park and take out bags. Nick glares at the shed as he drops his hand to Dani's back. Damon carries Christopher with him.

I stare out the window a few moments after they all enter the house to make sure no one followed them in. I really should trust the millions of guards roaming the property, but I'm suddenly just as on edge as Luke. At least he knows why, though. I have no idea. Not having everyone here is a little off-putting, but there's something else. I just don't know what.

When I spot one of our guards roaming the property, I decide staring out into the night is useless. I really need to find out all I can about this motorcycle crew. I don't like the idea of them showing up out of nowhere with information directly related to the battle we're facing at this moment. And to be being shot at. They know way too much fucking information.

So, I do what I do best. I sit down at my laptop and I knuckle down. I lose myself. I tune out everything going on around me. I vaguely feel Luke kiss my head and hug me from behind. I hardly register the drink he sets down in front of me when I start coughing and clearing my dry throat.

All I'm focused on is the numbers in front of me. The code I'm inputting. The data coming up when I make the command for it. Account information. Backgrounds. Criminal history. Names. Dates of birth. Everything and anything I need for all of the names I've found who are members of Viper's Venom.

When Taylor arrives with Nicole and Dane, I take a second to stretch and help them put Tait to bed with Christopher in the nursery. It's the first time I've seen the time. I yawn and look for Luke. As I thought he would be, he's looking out the window with his arms folded over his chest.

"It's two in the morning," I say against his back when I wrap my arms around his waist from behind. "What the hell is taking Alex and Ryan so long?"

He wraps his arms around mine, taking my hands in his. He turns and kisses me. "Alex is on the way. He said he ran into some trouble. Took a while to lose the tail he had. But they boxed the tail inside Lucinio territory. Some of his guys were able to help them. Alex got away with our guys. He got word that the guys tailing him were killed. No other choice."

"Well, we have three guys here. We'll be able to get what we need from them. I don't really understand how we all had tails, though."

"He's watching us, baby. He had people waiting for us. Lucky for us, the idiots tailing us got tired."

I chuckle. "I don't think they got tired. I think you lost them so quickly, their heads were spinning, though."

"I wonder if they're still scratching their heads somewhere downtown." Luke smiles as we see headlights coming up the drive.

I keep my arms locked around his waist and rest my chin on his shoulder as we watch Alex and Gavin get out of the vehicle. After they both look around a few moments, they open the back doors. Rebekkah gets out looking more tired than any of us. Kent gets out of the other side carrying Jackson. Alex and Gavin grab their bags and everyone hurries inside.

I let go of Luke. We both turn to the door when they come in. Everyone finds their rooms and puts their things away. Kent and Rebekkah put Jackson down. Alex comes back to the living room with Gavin.

Alex looks around at everyone. "Where's Ry?"

"Hasn't gotten here yet. We haven't heard from him," Luke says.

"He probably ran into some trouble," Gavin says. "We had a pretty relentless fucking tail."

"We knew we'd have them," Josh says from the chair he's almost fallen asleep in. Lyric is curled into his side asleep. His hand is rubbing her back lazily.

"We had a tail, too," Nick says with a yawn. "Dani, here, is one fuck of a co-pilot, though."

She giggles from where her head is in his lap. "I had a hand in it."

Nick grins. "She's back there screaming out directions at me. Telling me which direction he's coming. I damn near died of laughter thinking how fucking confused the guy must have been with the directions we were going."

"It was pretty entertaining when he ran into the fire hydrant trying to avoid the fire truck that turned in front of him," Dani says as she laughs.

"And Josh here, decided to bring us all presents," Taylor jokes.

Josh chuckles. "Asshole."

Alex raises an eyebrow. "Presents?"

Luke sits on the arm of the chair I sit in. I take my laptop once more and continue what I'm doing as they talk around me. I can't help but chuckle when Alex scoffs at Josh leaving the three guys in the shed to sweat a little bit before they talk to them.

"What about you?" Alex asks. "You find anything on Viper's Venom?"

"Yeah. A lot actually. Starting with how much illegal shit they've been in for damn near their entire existence. I can tell you every single leader they've had since they were created in 1957. I can tell you every single crime every member has been convicted of. I even have some of their allies. I have accounts. It doesn't appear they have dealings with Matthew or the Lucinio Mafia before Josh took over. But the most interesting thing is what happened three years ago."

Josh sits up and looks at me. "What happened three years ago?"

I grin. "Three years ago the leader was overthrown." I pause for dramatic effect for no other reason than because I can. "By his own son."

"Well, fucking hell." Josh laughs as everyone else joins him.

After a few moments, I continue. "Turns out Alec, or as he's known, Ace, didn't like the way his father was running things. What set him off? His father attempting to marry his sister off to an older biker. The guy was in his sixties. His sister was only eleven at the time."

"The fuck?" Taylor shakes his head. "Who would do that?"

"That hits a little close to home," Alex says.

"Far too close to home," Rebekkah says, burrowing into Kent.

I nod. "So, he overthrows him. Turns his entire operation legit. And because he did the law enforcement community a favor…" I trail off, looking around the room.

Nick chuckles. "They let him go. Looked the other way."

I nod again with a smile. "And now he works with them. Gives them information on big kingpins in the area. They get credit for the bust…"

Josh leans back with a smile. "They leave him alone when he does a bunch of illegal shit to help them bring the bad guys down. How did you find this out?"

"Off the record law enforcement files mostly. Some newspapers. Court records." I yawn.

"So, Viper's Venom. They're on our side?" Taylor asks. "I've never heard of them."

"From what I can find, yes. They are on our side. For the most part. I still can't figure out exactly how they make their money, but I can say for certain that they aren't getting paid off by anyone. Other than a few businesses, though?" I shrug. "I haven't been able to dig that far."

Josh looks at his watch. "Three in the morning already? Anyone try to get Ryan on the phone or radio?"

"His phone is off," Nick says. "I just tried. Thought I'd give it a whirl since Oscar said everything was installed with the scramblers. As for the radio, I think he's out of range. I can't get him on that either."

I can feel the mood in the room change instantaneously. The nervous energy is very suddenly buzzing. Everyone falls silent. I can almost feel the tension thickening the air around me. Words don't come as Nick tries again to get Ryan on both the radio and the phone. The only thought I imagine running through all of their heads is the same that's playing in mine.

Where in the hell is Ryan?

Chapter Twenty

⚔ Luke ⚔

"It's been hours. Where the fuck is he?" I ask myself for the thousandth time as I look out the window. The sun is just starting to peek out and brighten the pitch black sky. "Fuck." I turn to Josh. "Have we heard anything from the guards I sent out to look for them?"

He shakes his head. "They followed his route all the way here and back. But if he had a tail, he could be anywhere. They're looking. They're combing the whole city. We all have our phones on now. He can call. And he will if he can."

I look at Taylor. "Call the P.D. See if there were any accidents. Anything."

"I already did, Luke. I'm waiting on a call back. Jesse is looking into last night's call log. There were seven accidents. He's going through to see if any of them involved Ryan's vehicles. He and Reed are the only people who have Ryan's vehicle information. To everyone else, it looks like they're registered to a company."

"There's no way he wouldn't have contacted us if he could have," Nick says as he stands impatiently for the millionth time. Much like me.

"Something had to have happened. I've left him voicemail after voicemail and sent a hundred texts. He would have answered."

"I've called Arianna and Jessa," Dani whispers as she sniffles and curls up into the vacant place on the couch Nick just left.

"I called Ethan," Rebekkah says just as quietly. "No one is answering. Everyone's phone is off."

She's not wrong. I've called the guards assigned to their detail. I've called Jason and everyone else myself. I've even had Gavin call Marissa. No one is answering the repeated messages or texts any of us have left. I'm starting to hate every second of it more and more as each moment passes.

I go back to staring out the window. Lance, Robby, and Pierce, who arrived with one of the guards, are all working on Matthew's accounts to see who it is he's working with so we can systematically destroy every single one of them.

I scrub my hands down my face. "This is fucking ridiculous. I'm going out there to find them." I start heading for the door.

"Luke. Stop!" Taylor commands. "Jesse just texted. There was an accident on the east side of the city. Ryan's vehicle was involved. When they got there, they found nothing but the vehicles. He's looking into it."

I watch as everyone goes silent and slumps. The entire family curls into whoever is next to them as collective sniffles, gasps, and sobs hit my ears. I lean against the door. I can't hear my heart beating anymore. I think my blood has stopped flowing through my veins.

I catch Robby's eye. I can tell he's hyperventilating by the horrified expression on his face, but I can't force my legs to move to go to him. I can think of nothing more than Ryan being detained somewhere while that sick son of a bitch took our family God only knows where.

"You..." Nick chokes back a sob. "You only said Ryan's vehicle."

Taylor focuses on his phone as he wipes his eyes. "It just says Ryan's. Two vehicles involved. The other one wasn't his. I don't know where the two vehicles that were escorting him are. There were no bodies. But there was blood and bullet casings."

"Shit...," I whisper as I slowly sink to the floor. Right before I hit it, though, I hear the rumbling of several very loud engines nearing us. I jump back up. "The fuck?" I get to the window just as Josh does. I peer out with him.

"We have company!" one of the guards yells into our radio.

I look at Robby and Shane. "Get everyone out of here."

They both act quickly, ushering everyone out of the room and upstairs. Taylor, Alex, and Nick crowd in next to us. Moments later, the rumbling grows louder as a group of bikers lead two SUV's up the driveway. We all look at each other as we grab our guns and walk cautiously for the door.

By the time we get outside, though, the guards around the property already have them surrounded at gunpoint. We all join them as the bikers have their hands raised. I don't recognize any of them, and I can't see inside the SUV's with their blacked out windows.

"Who the fuck are you?" I ask.

"And how the hell did you find us?" Josh asks.

"Calm down, man," one of the bikers says, fear lacing his voice. "We're Viper's Venom. You talked to Ace earlier. He's in the lead SUV. Right behind me. Ryan is with him."

"The fuck do you have Ryan with you for?" Taylor growls.

"There was a wreck outside our shop," he says. "I swear to fuck we didn't come here to start a fight with you. We're trying to help."

My eyes flick to the SUV, and I nod at two of our guys. "Open it."

They nod and do as they're told. They open the driver side door and tell the driver to get out. Alec gets out slowly with his hands raised. I breathe a sigh of relief, but don't put down my gun. We all keep our weapons trained on the crew.

"Ryan is in the passenger seat," Alec says. "He's banged up, but he's okay. I have his wife and brother in the back."

"Why?" I ask. "What happened?"

"There was a wreck outside my tattoo shop. Viper's Den. I heard it and went to check it out. Next thing I know there's gunfire. A lot of it. I got a couple of my guys. I didn't recognize anyone at the time, but they were dragging a girl to their vehicle from the vehicle they rammed. We rushed out there and started laying down cover fire. I ran for the girl, but they got away."

I glance at Josh. I'm suddenly very shaky. I don't want to know the answer to the question I'm about to ask, but I do anyway. "Who was the girl?"

"I think you need to talk to your boss, Mr. Massena," Alec says. "Your guards can see him. He's right there."

Nick takes a couple of steps over so he can see inside the door of the vehicle. "Holy fuck. Ryan." He runs to the passenger side of the vehicle and opens the door. He helps Ryan out and hugs him harder than I've ever seen anyone hug another person.

"Weapons down," Ryan says as he hugs Nick back. "They aren't here to fuck with us."

We all obey and hurry to help Jason and Arianna out of the backseat. Arianna collapses against me as soon as I get her out. She wraps her arms around my waist and cries so hard my t-shirt instantly feels wet.

"They got them! They took her!" she sobs as she grips my shirt. Her knees buckle. I have no choice but to pick her up in my arms.

"Who, honey? Got who?"

She doesn't answer me. Instead, she cries harder. Nick releases Ryan and hugs Jason just as hard. I hadn't noticed it, but both Jason and Ryan are crying. Not as hard as Arianna, but it's obvious they've been crying for a while. Their eyes are red and bloodshot. They seem weakened. Defeated.

"I think we should get everyone inside," Ryan says. "I… have something to tell you all." He gives me a pained smile and starts ushering everyone inside.

"What happened?" I ask.

Ryan says nothing. I follow him inside carrying a still sobbing Arianna. I notice the way he walks isn't as confident. His swagger is gone. His shoulders are slumped. Ryan is a big guy. He's six feet five and built of titanium. But for the first time in the entire time I've known him, he seems weak. Unsure. I look around uncomfortably.

"Wait a second," Nick asks from behind me. "Where's mom and dad? They were with you. Where's Jess? And wasn't Marissa with one of your escort vehicles?"

Jason pushes him gently when he stops walking. "We need to get inside."

"What? Jas, where the hell is our family?" Nick asks.

"Nick. Please don't make me say it again." Ryan's voice cracks. It's enough to make us all obey and not ask questions. Ryan looks over his shoulder. "Bikers come in with us. Trust me when I say they just might be our greatest allies. We fucking need all the help we can get."

None of us question. The heated look that flares in his eyes when he looks at us all sends chills down my spine. I know whatever is going on is bad. But if I'm going by Ryan's looks and demeanor, I know it's far worse than I ever dreamed.

After a few minutes, we've gotten everyone settled once more downstairs. Per Ryan's command, though, we're all outside in the back of the house. Alec has lit a fire in the fire pit. Though the sun is coming up, it's chilly.

We all take seats on one of the many wooden benches around the pit. Robby takes my hand in his. It's cold. I can feel him shaking, but I can't tell if it's because of the chill in the air, or the fear we're all feeling at what's to come.

"I really don't like this," Robby whispers as he squeezes my hand.

"I don't either." I hold his hand tightly and watch as a guard comes up to Ryan. He leans down and whispers something in his ear. I watch as Ryan solemnly nods. The guard leaves.

Ryan rubs his eyes as he slowly stands. We all watch him, except Jason and Arianna who are both huddled together on the bench Ryan just stood from. All of the bikers are standing back from us, but within ear shot. They're all watching. I've already come to six thousand conclusions as to what's going on. I don't like any of them.

"As you've all seen, we're missing four people," Ryan finally begins after a long pause. "On the way here, we were rammed from the side. I didn't see it coming, and I don't know what the fuck happened. All I remember is rolling a few times. When I woke up…" He glances back at Alec. It takes him a moment to compose himself when he looks back at us. "When I came to, I was on a couch in Alec's tattoo shop. Jason and Arianna had woken up just before me. The three of us had been knocked out in the wreck. As for everything else, I'll let Alec fill you in."

I can tell Ryan can barely finish. When he sits down, he puts his face in his hands. Jason pulls him into Arianna and him as he breaks down. I don't need to hear anything else. I already know. I squeeze Robby's hand before wrapping my arms around him and hugging him as close as I can. Matthew finally got what he wanted. At least a huge part of it. I can feel it.

Alec steps forward. "I heard the wreck. I was on my way to the front of the shop when I heard the gunshots. I grabbed a few guys right away. We ran out there laying down our own fire. The guys were in masks dragging someone away from the wreck. She looked like she was out cold, but she started fighting about the time they got her to their vehicle. There were a couple of guys around the wrecked SUV, but I didn't know if they were friend or foe until they'd killed all four people from the other two vehicles. I found out later they were Ryan's guards."

Robby slumps against me with a sob. "Fuck no," he whispers. I run my fingers through his hair and kiss his head, knowing he's figured it out, too.

"There was also a woman laying on the ground near the first SUV. Looked like she had been thrown from the SUV," Alec continues. "Ryan told us it was a woman named Marissa."

"Jesus," Gavin mutters, looking up at him wide-eyed.

Alec looks down at him. "She didn't make it. We have her in the back of the other SUV." He puts his hand on Ryan's shoulder. A show of comfort and support as he, Jason, and Arianna all cry. "Along with Ethan and Jenny who died in the wreck."

"No!" Rebekkah cries. Kent immediately pulls her into him. Alex, Lyric, and Josh all wrap around her as she crumbles. "No! Ethan! I just got him back!"

I pull Robby into me when I feel him break. Holding him as close and tightly as I can, I look up at Alec. "What about Jessa?"

He takes a moment to compose himself. I wouldn't have guessed it, but it looks like the deaths are affecting him more than he cares to admit. "Jessa… was… the girl they took."

As if hearing that was the last straw, everyone starts crying. No one even attempts to remain strong for anyone else anymore. Not even me. I turn and bury my face in Robby's neck. I let loose, sobbing tears that I've been fighting.

I knew something was wrong. I sent people out to find them long ago. When they kept reporting nothing, the thought formed that Ryan had been targeted. It never left. I started thinking he couldn't get away. That they'd killed everyone.

Except Jessa. Somewhere deep within, I knew they'd take Jessa. Matthew wouldn't allow anything else. He doesn't get his perfect son, so he'll take his idea of the perfect girl to create his perfect son once more. A second chance at the life he wanted but couldn't have. The epic ending to his saga with the Crane family. Get rid of the leader. Get rid of the man who had been a thorn in his side for so long. Take the girl.

I'm sure he wasn't counting on Ryan walking away from this. I don't think he thought anyone would. I breathe in Robby's strong scent as I tighten my grip. I'm not stupid. I know damn well if this had happened anywhere else, Ryan, Jason, and Arianna would not have made it out of that alive. Whoever he has working for him was definitely under orders to kill everyone and take Jessa. Thank fucking God it was in front of Viper's Den. Thank God for Alec.

Alec clears his throat. "I know that was a lot. I'm sorry. But Ryan said he didn't want anyone left behind. We assumed he'd want all of the…" He pauses. "Uh… Everyone cleared out before the cops showed up. It's what I would want done. So, we took the two SUVs that were still drivable and cleared everything out. Including the guards." He squeezes Ryan's shoulder again. "He wants to cremate them, and make sure their families get their remains."

It's there that Alec's voice cracks. No one needs to look at him to see the emotion has hit him, too. There isn't a single person here who has a dry eye. Everyone is heartbroken. It's written all over their faces when we all start to finally look up from whoever we'd buried ourselves into.

I don't know how long we all stay outside comforting each other, but when Ryan finally takes back a little of the control that he's allowed others to have while he composed himself, the sun is high in the sky. I pull Josh and Ryan aside, suddenly remembering our guests. And I'm not talking about Viper's Venom.

"I know we have a lot going on," I begin. "But we have three assholes in the shed who need to be questioned. Given the sun is up and has been beating down on us, I don't know that they're even still alive."

"Guests?" Ryan asks, folding his arms over his chest.

"I had a tail. I talked to Oscar about the scramblers and how it would work if they had any tracking devices. He said we were safe. It would scramble theirs as long as they were within a certain distance. So, I led them here. I kept them within the distance to assure we weren't tracked," Josh says. "But it wasn't necessary. Oscar checked everything.

There was no GPS. No tracking. Nothing. There were three of them. They're in the shed."

Ryan nods. "The measures were necessary. You couldn't have known until you checked. Get them food and water. Check on them. Let them out for air."

Josh raises an eyebrow. "Seriously?"

I chuckle. "Have to keep them alive long enough to talk to them."

Josh sighs. "I guess you're right."

"We have more important things to do right now anyway," Ryan says. He takes a deep breath. "My parents and guards need to be dealt with. We need to know what Gavin would like done with Marissa."

"I'll deal with the guests," Josh says. "You deal with our family." He leans in and hugs Ryan hard. "I'm really fucking sorry, Ryan."

Ryan hugs him back. He says nothing. Just nods and takes the comfort. It's difficult for me to watch this incredibly strong man deal with all of the shit he's dealt with. To add this on top of it seems so unfair to me. Wrong. So very undeserved.

I hate that all I can do for anyone here is be the support they need. When I look over at Robby, I see him doing and feeling exactly the same as I am.

We'll be the one providing the hugs. We'll give the pats on the back and be the shoulders to cry on because that's what our family needs right now.

Love.

Chapter Twenty One

☒ Robby ☒

Ever since we finished the ceremony for Ryan's parents, guards, and Marissa, I've stayed out of everyone's way. Not because I don't want to be supportive. It all has to do with my newfound insatiable need to gain justice for the lives taken so soon and fucking viciously.

So while Luke, Josh, and Ryan are all outside dealing with the assholes in our shed, I'm holed up on my own in the office. My efforts are no longer on Viper's Venom. Ryan trusts them. So, does everyone else. With the information I've gathered, we all came to the conclusion that the crew is legit and on our side. There's no connection to Matthew. Of that I'm confident.

Lance and Pierce are focused solely on Matthew's accounts. They've made some incredible progress. We've already sent out crews to take down some of the targets we've discovered he's working with. Between the Crane and Lucinio Mafias, there's no chance for any of them to defend themselves. There's too many of us in relation to them.

With them locking that down, I'm free to dig into the Berlusconi Mafia. Given Ryan, Josh, and Luke have been outside for a few hours now,

I'm positive that they need something to use as incentive to get the assholes to talk.

Luckily, I think I figured out how to give them the edge they need. I have to smirk a little bit because the more this day goes on, the more pissed off I get. I'm fucking tired. I haven't slept in fucking almost two days. Topping it off with this attack on my family is my last straw. I have no more boundaries. They want to play dirty with us, then they'll get dirty right back.

I leave my laptop on the desk and head out to the shed. I'm surprised to see the sun has gone down, and the sky is darkening. I didn't realize it was already that late. All the more reason to end this. Right fucking now.

I reach the shed just as Ryan's black boot crashes into the face of one of the asshole's with a crunch that might make me sick if I wasn't so pissed off. The asshole collapses on the ground in a heap as blood spurts from his mouth.

"Who is Gertrude Brambleberry?" I ask as I cross my arms over my chest and lean against the doorframe behind Luke. Every person in the room, except the one who just collapsed, looks at me. "5461 University Avenue. Age seventy-nine. Nice old lady. Lives all alone."

Luke looks at me a little confused. Josh chuckles. Ryan stands up to his full height. His head nearly touches the ceiling. The two assholes not passed out stare. But no one says a word. The attempt at keeping the information quiet is truly touching. Unfortunately, I already know the answer.

Ryan gives them both a cocky grin as the bloodied asshole on the ground groans. He kicks him hard, but doesn't look at him. "One of you guys holding out on us? That's not very nice."

I grin far more smugly than I should as I look down at them. "Is she a grandmother?" I ask. "Frail old granny getting taken care of by her sweet little grandson. I bet she wouldn't be able to defend herself against the big bad biker crew I'm about to send after her."

"Stay the fuck away from her!" The asshole in the middle somehow manages to get to his feet and lunge for me, but Josh sticks out his arm and clotheslines him so hard that he slams against the back wall and falls into a whimpering heap.

"I think maybe it's time you start talking then," I say, not moving and unflinching.

"I'm not saying a fucking word to you," he spits back at me.

"Hmm… Well, that's too fucking bad. I hate when we have to take things out on old ladies." I turn away from him and call over to Alec, who's working on something on his bike. "Hey, Ace! Get over here!"

This idiot doesn't need to know that we aren't like that. We'd never in all of the Hells go after an innocent party to get to anyone. Especially someone's defenseless grandmother. But the incredible thing about having the reputation that we do as a ruthless mafia is that all we need to do is say it and people believe we'll do it.

"What's up, kid?" Alec pats me on the back, playing along without me asking him to.

"Turns out asshole number two here, the one in the middle, has a grandmother in the city," I say.

"Oh," Alec says with a grin. "Want me to take the boys and play with her? One of my guys has a grandmother fetish."

Ryan grins. "I think he'd like that. Maybe grab her and bring her here. We can have some fun right in front of him."

"Sure. I'll grab a couple, and take an SUV." Alec turns to leave.

"Wait! Okay! I'll talk. Just don't touch her. Please."

I grin. "Looks like he got himself a soft spot for granny."

Alec turns around. "Well, damn. I was hoping I'd get to have myself a little fun tonight. Getting a little boring just dicking around with my bike."

"I'll talk. Okay? I'll talk. Leave her out of this."

"That's a good boy," Josh says. "Now. I believe the question was how long have you been in Matthew Lucinio's pocket?"

"It's been a couple of years. We were having some trouble with the cartel. They were coming down on us for missing drugs. We were skimming off the top. Taking profit for ourselves."

Ryan laughs. "Come on. Matthew just swoops in and says he'll help?"

"No. It wasn't like that. We'd heard he was looking to align with other mafias. We didn't know why. We approached him. He said he'd get the cartel off our back if we helped him distract you and his kids."

"So, you started a battle," Luke says with a chuckle. "And lost."

"We weren't supposed to win. We knew we wouldn't. We knew we'd lose guys, but that wasn't the goal. The goal was to distract you so Matthew could continue to grow and align with others. We sacrificed, but that was our job."

"What was the end goal?" Ryan asks. "What did he promise you?"

"A key role in the most powerful mafia in the world. An opportunity to grow exponentially. And most of all, protection. Protection from you and his kids."

Josh bellows. "Well, that's one more promise he didn't keep."

"Among the many," Ryan says. "Tell me about the attacks on my family. Robby getting shot at was only the beginning. You obviously intended for me to be killed last night."

"That was the job. He told us to watch the house. Robby was a target because he's been able to track everything he's been doing. All of his money. Everything. Robby is a huge threat, and Matthew recognizes that. He was our target. When we saw you were leaving, he told us to follow. We gathered everyone we had to do it."

"Bullshit. That was organized," I say with a shake of my head. "How the fuck did you know we were leaving?"

He looks fearful. "I don't know the answer to that. I don't. I swear."

I chuckle and look at Alec. "Go. I'll send the address to your GPS."

Alec turns again. "On it, boss."

"Wait! Fuck! I swear I don't know. We got a call saying that you were going to a safehouse. We were told to organize a team and follow you. That you'd split up. We were to send a team specifically after Ryan and everyone else! The team after Ryan was meant to. That's what we did. That was our orders!"

Alec leans against the other side of the doorframe. "Where is he? Your boss."

"I'll lead you right to him as long as you leave my grandmother alone." He looks at us all with pleading eyes. "He knows where Matthew is. He can give you Matthew."

"Well, if you're going to be a good boy and play ball with us, we don't need either of these fuckers." Ryan shoots both of the other two guys in the shed then kneels down in front of asshole number two. "As an act of good faith, I'll have someone come out here and deal with these two. I'll even be nice and get you some food and water. Tomorrow morning, you'll be taking me directly to your boss. But you jerk me around, I'll let Ace and his buddies here go have some fun with your grandmother. And I'll sleep just fine tomorrow night after it happens. We understanding each other?"

"Y-Yes, sir."

"Good." Ryan stands and follows Luke and Josh out of the shed. I lock it behind them. Ryan hands the key to a guard. "Grab two guys and clean up in there. When you're done, go to the kitchen, and get him some food and water." He pauses. "Make it good food. I really want to make him like me." He smirks and keeps walking.

"Yes, sir."

The four of us follow Ryan into the house silently. It's quiet. Everyone has retired to their rooms and fallen into an exhausted sleep. Except for Lance and Pierce, who are still working side by side. Damon is on the couch next to Lance fast asleep. Gavin is on his stomach using his arms for a pillow, also asleep. We all walk to the back of the house where we won't disturb anyone.

"I thought Jason would be down here," I say, a little surprised to see that he's nowhere to be found.

"Arianna forced him to try and sleep," Ryan answers. "He kept telling her no. So, she appealed to his protective Alpha side."

Josh chuckles. "How the hell did she do that?"

Ryan sits and rubs his eyes with a smile that looks something like pride. "Told him that she didn't want to be alone while I was outside at work. He almost instantly gave in and followed her to our bedroom telling her he'd stay with her while she slept. I checked in before I walked out there. They are both asleep on the bed. Jason has Jackson and Christopher on his chest and is hugging Arianna and Lyric both. They're all out like lights."

Luke sits next to me with a smile. "She's clever."

"Fucking smartest person I know," Josh says.

"You should have seen her in high school," I say with a smile. I try to fight the yawn, but it hits me hard anyway. "Fuck."

We all jump a little when Josh's phone goes off. "Jesus. I forgot I even turned it on." He looks at the caller ID. "Oh fuck." He quickly answers with wide eyes and puts it on speaker. "Jessa?"

184

"Dead. Finally," a deep voice that sounds far away says. We all look at each other confused before focusing back on the phone.

I run to grab my laptop. Opening it on my way back to the den and scrambling to get my tracking equipment, I slide in next to Josh on the couch as quietly as I can. I plug the cord into his phone, hoping I didn't miss much of the conversation as I rush to trace the call.

"I don't care about that. I want to know. How the hell do you know? There weren't bodies, you idiot," another male voice says.

"Because I checked the motherfucker. He was dead. Same with his parents and pain in the ass brother."

"You can't go to Matthew and say that. You have no evidence. Besides, there's still the other brother and Matthew's kids to deal with."

"Matthew is a fucking fool. He'll believe any damn thing I say."

The other guys scoff. "We have a job to do. Get the girls so we can get them to Matthew and fulfill this part of our deal. I want to be done with that guy."

"Don't let him hear you say that. We want to be on his good side. Remember?"

"Come on. Come on," I whisper. "Just a few more seconds." My laptop is triangulating a location, but I need time to do it.

"Josh," Jessa whispers. I can hear the tears in her voice.

"We're here, honey," Josh whispers back. "Robby is tracking you. Give him a few more seconds."

"I don't know if I can. Please tell me my family is safe." Her breathing is labored. Josh looks at Ryan.

"We're okay, Jess," Ryan whispers.

"Thank God. Thank God." She sniffles. "They're coming back."

"Almost, Jessa. I've almost got you. Don't hang up," I whisper as calmly as I can. But I feel her panic.

"I have to hang up."

"Five seconds, Jess." Fuck. Please. Please don't hang up. But she does. "Fuck!"

Ryan looks at me with both hope and panic. Josh throws his phone in frustration. Luke simply deflates. Alec takes several deep breaths as he leans back in the chair. I stare at my screen in disbelief at the signal lost message flashing at me. I have the overwhelming urge to throw my laptop against the wall. It takes everything in me not to.

"Did you get an area?" Alec asks.

I nod, frustrated. "Yeah. Chicago."

"Just Chicago?"

I look at him. "Yes. Chicago. All of Chicago. If I'd had a couple more seconds I could have triangulated her signal off the nearest three towers and gotten you a better location, but she hung up before I could get that far. Five seconds. It's all I needed. Another five seconds after that, and I would have had her!"

I close the laptop and toss it with such force onto the couch as I stand that it bounces. If Josh hadn't reached out and grabbed it, it would have fallen on the floor. Fucking serves it right. I run my fingers through my hair and tug as I pace. When I turn, I run directly into a solid wall.

Luke grabs my wrists and hauls me against him, wrapping his arms around me. "You did what you could. None of us thought to trace it. I didn't even know you could fucking do that."

"Her phone is off. She shut it off," I grumble. "Why not just hang up? I can't even track her by GPS."

"She had to have her reasons, Robby. She's smart. She's been a part of this family for a while." Luke hugs me close and sways with me gently. "Trust me. We'll find her."

I let him hug me as I close my eyes and rest my head against his shoulder. It's getting harder and harder not to break totally down. The only thing getting me through right now is Luke's arms. Knowing Jessa is alive gives me the fuel I need to know what I need to do next.

"I'll let Lance and Pierce know. They can set up an alert. If her phone comes on, we'll know. It will automatically start tracking her. If all three of us are doing it, chances are we'll get her."

"That's my man," Luke whispers in my ear as he kisses it.

"That call gave me an idea," Josh says. Luke leads me back to the couch. I grab my laptop as I listen and set up the alert. "It sounds like they think you all died in the wreck."

Ryan raises an eyebrow. "Yeah?"

Josh leans forward and puts his elbows on his knees. "Let them. Let them think you're dead. Let it get back to Matthew. He knows Nick doesn't want your position, but he also knows he has a strong sense of family. He'll think Nick will try to take over with the help of Alex and me.

186

And he doesn't think we have what it takes. Obviously, Nick won't have what it takes if he's being trained by us."

"Easy takeover," Ryan says.

"We can fake the reports. I'll have Dane make some calls. Let Taylor sleep. Dane can go back to sleep when he's done. We'll pay off the media to keep the story quiet. All they have right now is an accident. They aren't going to report on that. No bodies. No drama."

"So, you want to fake his death?" I ask.

Josh nods. "Leak it throughout our allies. Tell them the truth, but have them spread the word. Then whatever story these assholes are feeding him turns out to be true. It buys us time to find him."

"Then when Ryan shows up, Matthew is thrown completely off his game," Luke says with a small laugh. "I like it."

"I think he'll even try to contact Nick," Josh says. "Without Ryan and Jason to help him and having no one but us, I think he might feel like he can get Nick on his side. That would be the ultimate revenge, right?"

I can't help but chuckle a little. "Killing the guy who was your biggest enemy. Killing the guy who took over. Taking the girl who looks strikingly similar to the love of your life. Then getting the son you lost but wanted as your heir to side with you and combine to form the largest mafia in the world while simultaneously destroying the one you hate. Sounds to me like the perfect ending to the psychotic dream of a sociopath."

"Too bad that dream is going to come to a violent fucking ending," Ryan growls dangerously.

Josh chuckles. "We need to get some sleep. No way we're going to get anywhere if we don't."

"I'll agree we need it," Alec says. "I want to take that son of bitch in the shed right now into the city and end this, but I don't think any of us have the strength or energy to do it."

"I don't think Jessa is where he's going to be leading us anyway," I say. "It doesn't make sense. I think we need to go in fast and hard before the sun comes up. It gives us a couple of hours to recharge."

"Where do you think they'd keep her?" Luke asks. His voice is becoming gravely. I look over at him and smile. His head is against the back of the couch. His eyes are closed. I can tell he's fighting to open them.

"In a shed. Storage area. Something. I really don't think they'd be stupid enough to keep her where they're actually staying. They know how good our team is. It wouldn't surprise me if they kept moving. Less chance of being tracked." I squeeze Luke's thigh and look around the room.

Everyone is fighting to stay awake. If I'm being honest with myself, so am I. The events of the past few days have taken us all for a ride we never expected to be on. An out of control expedition that we need to take back the authority of.

The only option at this point is to take a time out. We need to recharge our minds and bodies. Refuel. Then, and only then, can we dole out the kind of retribution that only we're capable of.

When we start tearing apart their world, though, may God have mercy on their souls.

Chapter Twenty Two

⚔ Luke ⚔

"Luke. Get up," a deep voice says to me chasing away the deep sleep I'd fallen into with my body wrapped around Robby.

I open one eye and see the sun isn't up. "Walk away," I growl.

"I can't do that. It's time to go."

I turn and see the voice belongs to Ryan. I groan. "Tell me again why I agreed to working with you?"

Robby chuckles. "Something about family. Your sister. Saving the world. Blah, blah, blah."

I swat his naked ass with a laugh. "Fucking sassy in the morning." I feel him smile against my chest as his dick hardens. Good thing we're under blankets.

Ryan laughs. "I made breakfast. I got a little concerned you were too tired to set an alarm when I didn't see you down there."

"That may or may not be true." I yawn. "Okay. Okay. We're getting up. Be down there in five. I want to get this shit over with."

"You and me both," Ryan says as he leaves the room.

"Too bad we don't have time for a quickie," Robby says as he gets up. He groans a little at the pain his hard dick is causing.

"I'll make it up to you, baby." I start to get up myself, but I can feel my body is depleted of energy. I go a lot slower than usual and stand with a groan.

Robby looks over at me. "You okay?"

"Feel like I was in a fight." I stretch my arms over my head and grin when I catch Robby looking. "Like what you see?"

"I hate you," he says with a teasing smile as he shakes his head and pulls his jeans up. He tucks himself away with a couple of sexy groans that make me smile.

I walk over to him and kiss him with everything I am as I push him against the wall. As my tongue plunges in his mouth, he lets out a sigh and digs his nails in my ass as he pulls me closer. Feeling his rock hard cock straining against his jeans makes me feel awful that I don't have time to do anything about it. Or the energy.

I pull away slowly with a cocky smile. "No you don't. You love me."

He grins. "So much." He gives me a soft kiss before we both pull away and finish dressing.

A little while later after eating a very quick breakfast and forcing Ryan to stay at the safehouse, Robby and I are driving with a cuffed prisoner towards the city. What we haven't told him is that Lance got us a location on his boss before he went to sleep last night. So, if he so much as breathes the wrong way or utters a single lie, I'm shooting him.

"Where's your boss keeping the girls?" I ask after several minutes and a few miles of driving in silence.

Maybe he'll tell me. Maybe he won't. Maybe he doesn't know. But I know I have to try because we couldn't get anything on Jessa after she called Josh. Her phone is still off. She hasn't been able to call back. I don't know if that means she can't, or if she's in an area where it's not possible, or worse. It's the worse that I refuse to think about.

"I don't know. I really don't," he answers. I can tell in his voice he's telling the truth.

"Why is he taking them?" Robby asks. "We know it's more than Jessa. And we know we're being set up for it."

The guy sighs. "Orders. We were told who to take and when. We hold them. They're shipped somewhere else. I've never been a part of the holding. I'm not that far up in the chain of command. I've only ever been a part of taking them and bringing them to the leader's home. That's where I'm taking you."

I look over at Robby. "You think there's a chance they're still there?"

"Possible," he says. "I hope so, but it depends how fast they move them."

"Before you ask, I don't know. I do my job. I go home."

I watch as he leans his head against the seat. He's struggling. Weak. He took a beating and believes if he doesn't cooperate we'll go after the only person he cares about. It's a fuck of a way to control someone. Tried and true.

"Chances are he moved them already, though," Robby says quietly.

I nod. "I know."

"Turn here," the guy says. "His house is at the back of the road."

I look at Robby. He looks down at his GPS of the coordinates Lance gave him and nods. I make the turn and cut my lights.

This might be the only mission I've ever been on where we haven't done surveillance first. But we don't have time. So instead, we've come in with a huge force. The numerous number of men I have compared to the satellite footage we have of the few we know he has gives me a sense of confidence.

"Alright, we're coming up on the house," I say into our earpieces. "The plan is to run this like a SWAT mission. Team One and Two on me and Josh. Team Three on Alex. Team Four on Drake. Questions?"

There are a chorus of no's over the earpieces just as I see the house. I take a deep breath and step on the gas. I whip onto the grass. Robby and I jump out as our other vehicles skid to stops near us. We surround the front of the house in what looks a lot like an FBI takedown.

We all duck down when we're met with an almost immediate hail of gunfire. Robby crouches next to me as I'm pulling our guy out from the back of the vehicle.

Like an idiot, he immediately starts screaming. "It's the Cranes! Scatter! Scatter!"

My mouth drops at the utter stupidity I'm witnessing. In my state of shock, I let go of his arm. He instantaneously takes off running and is met with gunfire from his own side. I watch as bullet after bullet makes contact with his body. As if he's being tased, he drops to his knees convulsing with each hit. Robby and I both watch in complete fascination until he finally falls back into the dirt.

"Well, that was fucked up," Robby says.

"There aren't words," I say. "Ready to do this?"

"More than."

"Team Four. Cover fire!" I command. They do exactly as they're told. "Teams break! On your leaders!"

We all run to the house amidst the flying bullets. Team Three runs to the back. The rest of us take the front. Team Four stays outside continuing to provide us cover and take out anyone who may try to escape. We have a very well-oiled strategy that's been tried numerous times and works like a charm.

"All teams enter now!" I command.

My team enters the door in the front first and at the same time as our team in the back. Josh's team follows. We split off, clearing each and every single room in the house taking out the few guards here.

"Left!" Robby yells to me when he sees someone come out of a room that I don't.

I don't question. I simply turn and aim while still moving. I take my shot and hit the guy in the neck. He falls back gurgling as he holds his wound. He pushes against it like he can get the blood spurting from it to go back into his body. I put him out of his misery and shoot him in the head.

We continue moving methodically through each room in the house until we've gotten through them all. Our team outside has taken out everyone. There's no more gunfire, but I feel uneasy. We're missing someone very important.

"Where's the leader?" I ask.

"Where were they holding the girls?" Robby asks. "I didn't see anywhere they could've hidden them.

"Something isn't right." I shake my head. "Where's Josh?"

"Basement," he whispers over our earpieces. "Get your asses down here."

I look at Robby slightly panicked as we all start running as quietly as possible down to the basement.

"Team Three, stay upstairs. I don't want to get ambushed," I whisper.

"Yes, sir," Alex whispers back.

We meet with Josh's team outside a closed door with light coming through the crack. I look up at him questioningly, a little baffled why he hasn't gone through the door already. He puts his finger up to his lips and gestures for me to listen.

I put my ear to the door. I hear quiet cries and sniffles. Listening closer, I hear teeth chattering. I look up at Josh, mouth slightly agape. He continues listening, so I follow his lead. Moments later I hear someone shushing the room. I'm hoping I'm not hearing what I think I am. My stomach twists into a sickened knot.

Josh taps my shoulder to get my attention. He gestures me backwards and counts down from three on his fingers. When he makes a fist, we both kick open the door with such force that it shatters in a brilliant show of splintered wood.

We go in low, leading our team. There are two men armed with automatic, military style rifles, but they have no chance to raise them before Josh and I both take our shots. They fall backwards, guns flying across the floor.

There's a line of ten women chained together on the floor by their ankles. They're leaning against the wall. All have dark brown hair. They're covered in dirt and hugging each other. Not a single one isn't trembling, but I don't know if it's because they're all completely naked and cold, or if they're afraid. Probably both.

"Don't move!" I hear one of our guys yell.

Josh and I both turn quickly before we have a chance to deal with the women. Sitting in the corner of the room with ten AR-15's aimed at his head is a man who looks to be somewhere around my age. He's looking at us all wide-eyed. Fear is all I see covering his delicate features.

The guy doesn't strike me as a person in a position of power. His blond man-bun makes me think he's an alfalfa, wheat-grass drinking, electric car driving, tree hugger who does hot yoga three days a week. He doesn't look like he has an ounce of muscle on him, though he tries to make it look like he does with his tight t-shirt and white skinny jeans.

I grimace. "There's no way those jeans can be comfortable unless your dick is the size of a button. Who are you?"

Josh chokes back a laugh. "My guess is daddy's little protege."

193

The guy whimpers and shakes visibility. "He's not here." His words are hardly more than a whisper.

"Who are you?" Josh asks, repeating my question. "Don't make us ask again. We're all a little trigger happy."

"I'm Theodore Berlusconi." He sniffles, trembling. "Sean Berlusconi's nephew. Unwanted nephew. He always made sure I was aware of that after my father died. He took me in."

I look over at Josh. "Rich kid who had the world handed to him, but it still wasn't enough?"

Josh purses his lips as he studies the terrified guy. "No. I'm thinking more young kid who wasn't quite enough. Maybe grew a conscience and got caught. How old are you?"

"Twenty-two, sir," he says shakily, but a little louder this time.

"Well, I was way fucking off," I say a little disgusted with myself. "Usually, I'm a far better age guesser than that. What are you doing down here?"

Theodore looks at us all before focusing on Robby. He takes a deep breath. "I asked him why he had all of these girls coming and going. He told me that it wasn't my business. I asked if it was an illegal sex trafficking ring. I've been studying them in school. I told him that I would call the police." He looks down at the floor. "He didn't like that answer. I snuck down here. I was trying to help them escape, but I got caught. My uncle told me I could stay down here until he got back. He locked me in here." He swallows, still not looking up. He starts crying.

Josh looks at me before looking back at Theodore. "Why not just kill you?"

Theodore shrugs his shoulders as he cries. "It's not how he works. He prefers to let me sit and wonder what he's going to do. It's his own form of torture. The punishment is never the same."

"Where is he?" I ask.

"He took two girls with him. I don't know where. He only wanted to take one of them. An older one." He looks up at us a little sheepishly. "She was really pretty. Long dark hair and blue eyes."

"Jessa," Robby says with no hesitation. It's what we're all thinking.

"I don't know her name, but the other girl. She was young. Really young. Younger than any of the girls in this room. She had dark hair, too, but she couldn't be more than a teenager."

"That has to be Ace's sister," Robby says. "She'd only be fourteen right now."

"We can't be sure of that," Josh says. "But I feel like you're right."

"The older one you call Jessa," Theodore continues. "She forced my uncle to take her, too."

"Forced?" I raise an eyebrow.

He smiles for the first time. "She said if he didn't take her with, she'd make sure that Matthew cut off his balls and fed them to him right after she had him shove his dick up his nose. I don't know who Matthew is, but it worked. My uncle must be afraid of him because he took her and the girl."

Josh laughs. "Sounds like Jessa. Playing whatever fucking hand she's dealt."

"We can't leave him here, Luke," Robby says.

"I know." I lower my gun. "Check him for weapons and everything else." Robby obeys and starts checking Theodore. I turn back to the shivering women, trusting him to take charge of the entire situation with Theodore.

Josh kneels in front of them, lowering himself to their level. "I'm Josh Lucinio. I'm here to help you, okay? I don't know what the fuck the plans for you were, but you're safe now. You have nothing to fear from me or any of my guys." He looks up at me. I follow his lead and kneel down in front of the girls. Josh looks back at them. His voice portrays nothing but kindness and protection. It almost instantly soothes them. "This is Luke Massena. He's also here to help you. You're safe now."

"Are you the police?" one of the girls on the end whispers.

Josh looks down the line. "No. We're not the police."

I watch as the girl breathes a sigh of relief. And she's not the only one. My instincts are instantly on high alert. "Why the relief, honey?"

Her eyes snap to mine, but she doesn't say a word. It's one of the girls directly in front of us that speaks up. "Because they were the ones who brought us here," she chokes.

I look at Josh. "The fuck?" I whisper.

He only nods before focusing back on the girls. "I know me asking you to trust us is a little like throwing you in shark infested waters covered in steak, but I can assure you that we are absolutely not going to hurt you. We're here to help you. We have several safehouses all over the city and the world. I don't know if you all are from here or not, but my goal is to get you home or wherever it is that you want to be."

"We have a team of people all over the world who can help us with whatever you girls need. But you need to trust us to make it happen."

"Please. No police. I just want to go home," another girl whispers.

I look up as a couple of our guards come in with blankets. One hands me keys. "We raided the house. We found blankets and some clothes we thought might fit. And we found those keys. They look like they might fit the shackles on their feet."

Josh and I both nod. I start getting to work unlocking the shackles. Josh continues soothingly speaking to the girls and reassuring them. He answers every question they have with honesty and openness.

By the time we have them free and dressed, he has a list of where they're from and which safehouse they'll be sent to. Those who have families to reunite with are given phones to contact them. One of them is Tyler's sister. Those who don't have family to contact are given the opportunity to start a new life anywhere in the world they choose.

For the first time in days, I feel like we've done something good. Even though we aren't any closer to Jessa, I feel good about being able to help these women.

At least they won't have to suffer anymore at the hands of a madman.

Chapter Twenty Three

☒ Robby ☒

I flick the strap on my vest absently as Luke drives. The trees go by in a blur as I stare straight ahead. We've been gone for a long enough period of time that the sun has gone down. Every single girl has gotten the resources she needed. Theodore has been shipped with his girlfriend to a safehouse. We're hoping maybe his uncle will contact him.

But ever since I sat down in this vehicle, I've been troubled. Disturbed. So many things don't sit right with me, and it's making me physically ill. My stomach is turning. I think I've given myself acid reflux. I reach up and rub my chest.

"You okay?" Luke asks quietly.

I look over at him briefly before looking back at the road. "Yeah. No. I don't know."

He reaches over and takes my hand. Almost right away, the storm churning inside me calms. Luke is the only one who can do that for me. Just with a touch. A look. It's like everything is okay again. I'm steady.

"Tell me about it." He rubs his thumb gently against the top of my hand.

"Just questions. Why the hell were all of the girls left? Why did they all have brown hair? Why did they all have striking similarities to Jessa? Why take them from all over the world? One of those girls was from Paris. Another from Pakistan. I just don't fucking get it. And then Jessa? Where did they take her? Who is this other girl? Why did she have a particular bond with her?" I squeeze his hand and take a breath.

"Robby, I know your beautiful mind is turning, but there are things we need to deal with. Things that I think will answer those questions the more we dig."

"But I don't know where to start." I look at him. "I'm at a total fucking loss. And then adding in Chicago PD on top of it? Other cops? What the fuck is going on?"

"We have a sex trafficking ring, baby. And you have two other people willing to help you with the tracking stuff. You aren't alone. We have an entire army willing to help with this. And I bet you if Ryan asked, we could probably get the literal Army to help." He grins.

It eases my mind. Ryan does have a lot of contacts. I don't think Luke is wrong. And I also think Matthew probably doesn't realize just how many allies Ryan has formed over the years. It's suicide for anyone to go after him. Purely stupid.

My problem is how many lives Matthew has to fuck up before he simply dies. I can't understand how any human can be as callous and calculating as him. Even with everything we've discovered the guy has been put through. I can't understand how he turned out the way he did.

"So, he's decided to start a sex trafficking ring with a bunch of Jessa look-alikes. I can't understand it."

"I think understanding his mind is only going to drive you as mad as he is. Those are all things that we may never have answers to. At least we got Tyler's sister back. I think one of the others was from his crew. She said something about being held in sex slavery there for a long time. Right now, our priority is to find Jessa and the girl she's become so protective over. My guess is that it's Alec's sister, and Jessa is feeling the way she is because the girl is so young. Those other girls were all adults. If I know Jessa, and I do, the idea of this entire ring is killing her. But a fucking kid? Jessa wouldn't be able to stomach that."

I smile because, once again, he's right. "No. She wouldn't. She'd do whatever she could to make sure the girl was safe."

"Look. Wherever they took her, they aren't going to hurt her. Hopefully, we can find her before they get her to Matthew, but if we don't, he's not going to hurt her either. In his mind, she's his. He'll use her for leverage. There's no doubt. But to him, Jessa is his girl. I don't doubt that she'll fight him. I don't doubt she'll end up with some bruises. And I don't doubt he'll try to force himself on her. Jessa will fight. Jason, Josh and Alex taught her how to defend herself. She'll use everything she has to her advantage. We need to trust that so we can focus on finding her and dealing with him once and for all."

Luke turns into the drive for our safehouse and squeezes my hand again. I smile a little because what we did accomplish today was a lot. We saved a lot of lives. We reunited families. We did what we do best.

As Luke parks, I notice something is slightly off. "Uh... Why the hell is the house decorated in white streamers and whatever the fuck all that other shit is?"

Luke squints. "I... Um... I don't know."

We both get out of the vehicle slowly. Josh and Alex join us in looking up at the house. We all share a confused moment before heading to the back of the house where some kind of joyous music is playing.

"Okay, what did we miss?" Alex asks.

"Not quite sure," Josh answers as we all round the corner to the back of the house.

We stop and take in the sight before us. White tea lights and small twinkly lights that give off a warm glow are strung throughout the yard. Everyone is in the back gathered around the firepit. I've managed to surpass confusion and hit bewilderment.

"What's going on...?" I ask Ryan when we reach him.

He smiles. "Go get cleaned up. Nick and Dani have decided life is too short. They've decided they're getting married." He smiles wider. "Now."

My mouth drops. "Like now as in right now?"

He nods. "Right now."

"Damn. They haven't really been together that long," Alex says.

"Well, when you know you know," Josh says with a chuckle. "Let's get cleaned up. I'm sure they don't want to wait."

We all head off to our rooms. Luke and I quickly strip down and head for the bathroom. We share the shower, somehow managing to keep our hands off each other as we quickly wash off the day's grit and grime.

When we're finished and dressed, we walk back outside hand in hand. There's a table filled with covered food on one end of the yard. There are camping chairs to sit in on the other. In the middle, there's a makeshift aisle leading to the firepit. It's lit with more tea candles and covered in white flower petals.

Ryan is standing by the firepit next to Nick. Both are wearing jeans and a black button down shirt. I glance at Luke as we take seats. I'm glad we decided to dress semi formal because everyone is dressed up. At least a little. The girls are all in summer dresses while all of the guys are wearing jeans or dress pants and a button down shirt of some kind.

After a few moments, the music switches to something slow with a little bit of a country feel. We all turn towards the house and stand as Dani appears dressed in a plain white dress that just grazes her knees and hugs every curve of her body. Her hair is piled onto her head and held up with something that has shiny, clear rhinestones all over it. The girl is definitely a vision in white. She's truly beautiful, but the smile on her face radiates a beauty that's rare.

I steal a glance at Nick as Jason starts escorting Dani down the aisle. The guy couldn't be smiling any wider if he tried, but it's the tears shining in his eyes that fills my heart. The love between these two is something to be envied. A person doesn't have to look at either of them to feel it crackling in the air.

Did you know that, baby
You're the bluebird in my sky?
I only wanna make you happy
'Cause I love to see you fly.

The words to the song as Dani reaches Nick seem perfect. Like a symbol of the deep-rooted love the two share. The support they both show each other, and the sweetness between them both is adorable and beautiful.

I lean into Luke and rest my hand on his thigh as Nick take's Dani's hands in his. Luke puts his arm over the back of my chair and pulls me close to him as we watch. Ryan grins and starts the ceremony, but Nick and Dani are totally and completely focused on each other. I'm not even certain they realize he's talking.

"I'll be honest in saying I never thought I'd see this day," Ryan begins. "Nick has been adamant for longer than I can even remember that he would never get married. The idea of dating made him run. Since we were young, he's been perfectly content to live his life as both of his brother's had before we'd met our soulmates."

I chuckle along with everyone else. "A commonality with Crane boys," I whisper to Luke. He grins in agreement.

"After his ex, none of us thought this day was possible. But we're all beyond proud. Even mom and dad are looking down smiling." Ryan chokes up a little as we all look towards the sky for a brief moment.

"I know they're proud," Jason says. He wipes a tear away as do we all.

Ryan takes a breath. "I couldn't be happier with your choice. Dani is perfect for you." He smiles at them both. Dani blushes. "I'm honored and beyond proud to be standing up here in front of all of our family performing this ceremony tonight. I love you both."

"We love you, too, man," Nick says, smiling up at his brother.

Ryan looks down at the cards in his hands.. "Let's get this show on the road, huh? Want to start with your vows?"

Nick smiles and looks down at Dani. "Ry wasn't kidding when he said I stayed far away from relationships for a long time. I wanted nothing to do with them. Beyond a date here or there and a casual night, that was it. I had rules." He reaches up and runs the pad of his thumb along Dani's lower lip. "And then you came along and broke them all. You challenged me. You fucking infuriated me. I've never in my life come up against a woman with as much fire as you." He looks out at all of us and gestures before taking both of her hands in his once more. "And you've met the women in this family."

Arianna's laugh rings out above everyone else. "You love it!"

He grins at her, then looks back at Dani. "You scared me more times than I can tell you, but you're a fighter. You're an incredibly strong and brave woman who chose me for some reason. You chose me and this family even though you could have run far away as fast as you could. If I had the chance to choose any woman in the world to be mine, it would be you. Only you. I love you, baby. I can't wait to spend the rest of our lives together, and show you all of the love you deserve to be shown."

I lean my head against Luke's shoulder. He gives me a sweet kiss on the forehead as he squeezes me. Nick reaches up to wipe a stray tear from Dani's eye. Dani smiles and takes a few deep breaths as she composes herself.

After a few moments she takes Nick's hand and kisses his fingers. "When you busted through my door the night we met, I didn't realize you were symbolically busting through the wall I'd built up around me. I'd resigned myself to live my life alone and on the run. But that just wasn't you. You wouldn't let me run. You always tell me I'm strong and brave. The truth is, I'm none of that without you. You gave me the strength and bravery I have. You gave me the will to fight and live. And you gave me the strength to love. The courage. You gave me so much more than that. You gave me this family. You gave me your heart. You gave me everything I needed and wanted, but never admitted to myself I needed or wanted. You swept me away. I love you so much."

I can't resist. Their vows are so beautiful. My heart is filled with so much emotion and love for Luke that I lean up and kiss him. Seeing Dani and Nick share this moment makes me want my own moment like this with Luke. I love him so very much that thinking of not being his in all ways possible physically hurts my heart.

As Ryan reads their promise, Luke kisses me just as softly and lovingly as I had him. He smiles when he pulls away, but keeps me close to him. We turn back just as Dani and Nick kiss. I smile and applaud and whistle with everyone else. We all laugh when Nick lifts Dani and runs down the aisle to the house, disappearing inside.

After moving the chairs to the side and everyone dishing up their food while Nick and Dani deal with their needs, I lean against the wall of the house. I watch everyone with a sense of happiness and lightness I haven't felt in a while.

I laugh when Arianna takes Luke's hand, dragging him to the makeshift dance floor. I laugh even harder when he attempts to dance without stepping on her toes and fails spectacularly. I smile at Ryan when he leans against the side of the house with me.

"Josh said you guys had quite a day," he says.

202

"Yeah." I look up at him. "You know Jessa is going to be pissed off about missing this."

He shakes his head with a chuckle. "I don't think so. She once told Nick that he needs to take Dani to the courthouse and get it over with. Jessa has never been fond of big weddings."

"But she is fond of family and special events like this."

Ryan laughs. "Jessa hates weddings with a blinding rage. She does like the family time, though. Which is why when we get her back, we'll be celebrating getting her back as well as this and the life of my parents. We missed Josh's and Lyric's day for Jaxon, so we'll be doing that. That's the kind of stuff Jessa likes."

I smile and nod. "Okay."

He nudges me. "So. Tell me about today."

I sigh and look up at him. "I don't know how to react to it. There was so much shit that happened, I'm not sure I've really caught up. I mean a fucking sex trafficking ring with girls that have a striking similarity to Jessa. But what really got me was learning that Jessa had been taken somewhere and has a girl with her." I look over at Alec. He's alone by the firepit absently stoking the flames. "It just pisses me off. The shit he's doing, and not being able to stop it."

"You feel helpless."

"Yeah. Helpless is one emotion. Anger is another. But there are so many more that I can't put my finger on."

"Well, the truth is, you aren't the only one. I think we all feel exactly as you do. You know how we deal with it, though."

"We gather information, and we act."

"Exactly. You have to look at the information you gathered today. We know that we have a sex trafficking ring that involves officers with numerous different police departments around the world. We've cleaned up departments before. We'll do it again. We know each of these girls were taken from my territories to make it look like me. But Matthew underestimates the sheer number of allies I have. He has no idea that I'm everywhere. Even in places he'd never fucking guess. Like Interpol. The ATF. FBI. CIA. ICE. The fucking Royal Air Force. I have very secret allies everywhere."

I nod. "I know."

"It's time we use them. Matthew doesn't understand the storm he's bringing to his doorstep, Robby. He doesn't understand the war. He thinks he's amassed so much power. But you know as well as I do that he'll never beat me. Especially now that we've teamed with the Lucinio Mafia. Our resources are doubled."

I nod again and look up at him. "You seem more determined."

His eyes darken dangerously. I'd be terrified if it was directed to me. A chill still finds its way down my spine. "He killed my parents. He took my sister. He's tried to kill my brother. You. He tried to kill Jas. He's dead. He doesn't know it yet, but he's fucking dead. He was already. Long before this. But now? It's going to be far more violent than it has to be. Far slower. Because I want him to suffer. I want him to feel all of the pain he's caused this family. He wants to fuck with us? He can find out just how dangerous and ruthless I can be. And trust me. I'm on a whole other fucking level than he could ever dream."

I smile a little dangerously myself. "You know, you can be scary sometimes."

He smiles with a low chuckle as he nods to Luke. "Go save my wife. Your boyfriend is going to break all of her toes."

I laugh as I head for the dance floor. I smile at Arianna when the song slows to a ballad. "Mind if I cut in?"

Arianna smiles up at me. "Go for it. But I warn you. He's a terrible dancer."

Luke cracks up. "I am not."

Arianna laughs as she walks away. "You totally are!"

I smile as I step into his arms. He locks his arms around my waist. I lock mine around his shoulders and kiss him. "You really are."

He grins as he sways with me. "This is more my style."

I smile into his neck after I lean my head on his shoulder. I lose myself in the music and his earthy scent. The feel of his muscular arms holding me and his strong body next to mine is my idea of perfection.

I don't notice the song ends, but when Luke gently pulls away I'm brought back to reality. He kisses me so lovingly that my heart melts. It's like it's just me and him. No one else in the world.

When he drops to one knee, though, time stops. Everything pauses. Sound. Movement. It all stills when his eyes meet mine, and he takes my hand in his.

"Oh, shit," I whisper with wide, shocked eyes.

Chapter Twenty Four

✗ Luke ✗

Looking up at Robby from bended knee is the most nervous I've ever been in my entire fucking life. And that includes finding out if I passed the academy to be part of the NYPD. It includes being recruited to the ATF. And it absolutely includes any of the calls or missions I've ever been on.

What I'm about to do is something I've never done. It's something I've never thought to do. I've never had the desire to do it with anyone. If I'm being honest, I'm probably more nervous now than I was when I kissed him for the first time.

My heart feels like it's going to pound out of my chest. It's like a jet plane is running through my ears. I can feel the blood pumping through my veins. I'm hyper aware of everything right now. Including the shock and wonder in my boyfriend's eyes. The way his lips are parted slightly. How the light from the tea lights bathe him in some kind of ethereal glow.

I can even feel the slight tremble in the hand that I'm holding in mine. I see his body shivering ever so slightly. I don't need to turn to feel everyone's eyes on us. The gun metal ring with the red strip in the middle that I hold in my hand is warm. I squeeze it tighter in my fist to keep my own hand from shaking.

I take a deep breath, not taking my eyes off Robby's. "I've loved you since the second I saw you." My voice is hoarse, and it shakes with my nerves. "I've held this ring in my possession for a long time because I knew I'd marry you one day. The problem is I didn't know when to give it to you. It never really seemed like the right time. So much going on. But I realized tonight that I don't want to wait anymore. I want to start our lives together. I've never wanted anyone like I do you. I've never loved anyone the way I love you. I don't want to. Everything in my life has led me to this moment. To you. Marry me. Please. Make me the happiest man alive. Be mine forever."

I watch Robby lick his lips. My heart feels like it stops beating. I hold my breath waiting for Robby to answer the question I've been wanting to ask him for longer than I dare tell him. The longer it takes him to say anything, the drier my mouth becomes, and the more shaky I get.

After a few moments, Robby smiles and kneels down slowly. I'm sure I could hear a pin drop as I watch him. He takes my face in his hands and kisses me. It starts out soft and warm, but he deepens it. It quickly turns hot and needy. I have to pull away before either of us embarrass ourselves, but I do it slowly, not wanting to break the contact.

He nods with a sexy as hell smile. "Yes," he whispers, his voice just as hoarse as mine. "Holy God, yes, Luke."

My smile is probably bright enough to see from the International Space Station. I lean forward and drag his lips to mine for another toe tingling kiss. I pull him up with me and hold him close, still kissing him with everything I am as we sway gently together.

The applause and whistles around us fade into the far distance. As our tongues tangle together, the pats on the back and congratulatory words spoken to us are hardly noticed. Robby's hands on my back and warm lips against mine is all I care about right now. Nothing else matters to me in this moment. Everything that's happened to us all over the past couple of days falls to the back of my mind.

Him.

Robby.

He's all I need right now. All I want.

So with the family celebrating Dani and Nick around us, I take Robby's hand and lead him away. He follows me into the house to our bedroom. He says nothing as I close the door behind us. I can see the emotion swimming in his eyes. It's the same as my own. Deeply seeded raw emotion. So much love for each other.

I haven't let go of Robby's hand. I pull him close and wrap him in my arms. The kiss I started with him outside continues. I run my fingers through his hair as slowly and thoroughly as I'm kissing him. He slowly drags my shirt up my back until I have to pull away to remove it. I impatiently toss it as he pulls his off.

I reach up and cup his cheek in my hand. He grabs my wrist as he watches me. A soft smile plays on my lips as I lean forward. I catch his lips in a slow kiss once more as I back him towards the bed. I love the feel of him in any way I can get him, but when he drags his fingernails up my back so softly, like he is right now, it gives me goosebumps and makes me shiver.

"Fuck, Robby," I whisper as I start kissing his neck. I let my hands find the waistband of his jeans. I nibble on his neck as I make quick work of both his jeans and mine.

We both step out of them and tumble onto the bed. Our lips and limbs are locked tightly to each other. I roll onto my back with him on top of me. Keeping him tight to my chest with one arm, I tug his hair with my hand so he's looking at me.

"Don't make me wait, Luke. Please. I want you." He presses his hard length against mine and grinds.

I groan. "Patience. If you keep doing that, I'll come before either of us get what we want."

He only smiles. He doesn't stop. He does it harder and faster until I'm moaning. I run my hands down his back and grip his ass as he starts kissing my neck. He nips and bites. It takes everything in me to stop him. But I do because I have plans tonight. Plans that don't involve either of us coming against each other's dicks.

I slap his ass. He jumps and looks at me. I nip his lip and guide him so he's sitting up and straddling me. I drop my hands to his thighs and let them gradually move up to his ass once more as I allow myself to drink in every part of his body.

I spread his cheeks as I slowly drive my length deep into his ass. When his head falls back and he closes his eyes, I smile. His neck is perfectly elongated for me, and his Adam's apple bobs as he swallows, making me want to lick every inch of it. Sort of like I want to lick every ridge of his hardened stomach.

I start thrusting slow and deep, holding his hips so he can't take the pace where I don't want it to go. I move him with me and watch as every gasp and moan escapes his beautiful lips. I give into my temptation and trail one hand over his muscles. I trace each and every line of them while driving him to the brink with each deliberate and sure thrust.

It's not until he opens his eyes several moments later that I give him what I can feel he wants with every clench around my dick. I thrust harder and faster. When he grabs his for his own dick, though, I give him a warning growl and grab his wrist.

"You coming on my stomach isn't where I want that come," I say with a half-smile that I know portrays both my cockiness and my dominance.

His eyes widen, but he obeys. Instead, he grabs my wrists and allows me to take him the way I want. I roll my hips against him and rock him in the opposite direction when I once more grip his hips.

"Oh... Fuck, Luke," he moans as his eyes roll back.

I'm rewarded with another clench that makes him so tight around me, my head falls unwillingly back to the pillow. I close my eyes and relish the feeling. He moves his hands up my arms and grips tighter.

The slight shift in his position brings out a moan that I have no hope of holding in. "Holy God, baby."

I'm so close to coming that I force my eyes open. One of my favorite things in the world is watching his face when I fill him. It's one of the sexiest and most peaceful looks I've ever seen. Missing it because of how fucking good he feels is never an option.

I give him a few more hard, deep thrusts before I bury my dick as deeply as he can take me. I push his hips down so he can't move. He spreads his legs further, taking me deeper, and looks down at me.

"Oh fuck." My dick thickens so much it actually hurts with how tight he's clenching around me. When I come, it's so hard, I almost black out. I dig my nails into his ass as my hips jerk against him. I try to clench my teeth to stop the animalistic scream, but it doesn't work. "Robby!"

I refuse to close my eyes like they want to because Robby's head falling back and the soft moans that escape his lips when I come is the most alluring and exquisite sight I've ever had the honor of beholding.

After I'm emptied inside his perfect ass, I fall limp against the bed and finally allow my eyes to close. Robby slowly leans down and kisses me. I allow my dick to fall out of him gently as I wrap him in my arms.

"You don't have any idea how good you feel," I whisper in his ear right before I kiss just below it.

He grins against my neck. "I would assume probably close to as good as you feel."

His deep voice reverberates against my skin, sending chills throughout my body. Robby is the entire package and so much more. He's everything to me. He's the part of me that I needed to make me whole. I know how cliche that sounds, but all I want to be with him is cliche. I want every cliche thing that love entails. Or at least our version of it.

When I open my eyes, I catch him staring at the ring I put on his finger. I smile and take his hand. I kiss the ring before entwining our fingers together and looking up at him. The love emanating from him is breathtaking.

I smile. "What are you thinking, baby?"

His smile is thoughtful as he looks back at the ring. "How did you find the perfect ring? I love it."

"Well," I begin as I look at the ring. I run my thumb across it while keeping his hand in mine. "Gun metal. That should be obvious." I give him a teasing wink. He laughs. "The red line, though, is for my heart. You own it." I focus back on the ring, but his eyes are on me now.

He gets a little misty eyed and leans down to kiss me. His lips brush mine so lightly it tickles. "I love you, Luke."

"I love you, too."

He smiles and looks back at the ring. "We need one for you. It's perfect. Symbolic of our love."

I grin. "Funny you should mention that."

I gently guide him off me. He settles at my side with his head propped up on his hand as he watches me. I reach in the nightstand and pull out a black box. I lay back down on my back and open the box as he looks down at me.

"Oh, damn," Robby gasps when he sees what's inside. He smiles as he takes the ring. I close the box and toss it onto the nightstand. Robby takes my hand. "I said yes to you." He tries to keep a serious face, but the corner of his mouth twitches. His eyes are laughing. "It's only fair. Be mine."

I smile and laugh. "You call that a fucking proposal? I want to be wooed!"

Robby laughs and gives me a bright smile. "Then wooed you shall be." He sits at my side on his knees. He looks at the ring and gets a very serious expression before looking down at me. He takes my left hand in his.

I smile. "I was kidding, baby." But my heart feels like it has butterflies. I don't want him to stop. I want to hear what he's about to say.

"Shh... Let me." He bites his lip as he thinks. I watch him. The butterflies have moved to my stomach. I've never had fucking butterflies. He takes a breath. "You said downstairs that you loved me from the second you saw me. Honestly, I think I did, too. I just didn't know what I was feeling. What I do know is that when I think of losing you, I know I'd never survive it." He looks at me. "I can't live life if you aren't in it because you are my life. You've owned my heart since I met you. You'll own it for eternity. You've given me a reason to believe in a love I wasn't truly sure existed. My heart is so full I'll never be able to put it into words, but you're my life. I love you, Luke. Marry me. Let me shower you with all the love I have for you for the rest of our lives and beyond."

I can feel the tear slide down my cheek, but I make no move to stop it as I sit up. I kiss him languidly and pour all of my feelings into it. I only pull away when we both need to breathe, but I don't let him go.

"I will marry you. I'd marry you right now if you asked me to," I say with my lips still against his.

He slides the ring on my finger without looking away from me. "Good. Because I'm already wearing your ring. You can't say no."

I laugh and tug him down with me into another kiss that lasts longer than any of the others. I'm so wrapped up in putting everything into it, that I don't realize he's managed to somehow get out of my arms until he sits up on his knees again. The pained look that crosses his face is alarming, but right before I'm about to ask him what's wrong, I realize I left something unfinished.

I give him a wicked grin. "You know I'd never leave you wanting, baby." I sit up and shift so I'm on my knees for him. I brace myself with my hands against the wall.

He lets out a small groan when his fingertips make contact with my ass. I spread my legs more so I drop further into the position he likes. His hands make their way up my back to my shoulders. I bite my lip when I feel the tip of his large, thick cock nudging against my ass where I'm craving him most. It's not often either of us need to feel him inside me, but something about tonight...

He doesn't make me wait. He pushes in with a low groan as my head drops. His hands splay across my abs as he thrusts and takes what belongs to him. What's never belonged to anyone else.

Me.

I can tell by how hard and thick his dick is that he is trying desperately not to come and enjoy the feeling of being inside me. But he also knows I hate when he holds back. He's taking it slow. He hasn't slid in all the way like I know he wants to. So, I arch and push back against him. He can't resist the feeling and shoves himself in as deep as he can as he bites down on my shoulder.

"Jesus, Luke. Oh fuck." He thrusts harder and faster, just like I know he wants to.

I purposely clench around his dick again and again to the rhythm of his thrusts. When he's close, his hands find mine against the wall. He puts his on top of mine and twines our fingers together. He turns his head so his lips are against my neck.

His hot breath against my skin as he pounds my ass is exactly what I wanted because it brings him to his peak. He spills into me with his cock jerking and hips slamming into mine with every thrust as he comes.

I turn and kiss him as he trembles against my back. I take my time, making sure that when I brush my tongue against his, I suck lightly. When I deepen it, I suck just a little harder until he finally lets loose and moans into my mouth with a last jerk of his dick.

We stay just like that for a long moment until he stops shivering. Lovingly, I take each of his hands and bring them to my lips. I kiss them as he slowly pulls out of me. I get out of bed and help him to his feet.

After we're both cleaned up, I lead him back to bed. I pull him down with me and wrap myself around him. I pull the blankets up and run my fingers through his hair. He holds me tightly, burying his face in my shoulder, using my arm as a pillow. I kiss the top of his head.

"I love you," he whispers.

I smile against his forehead as I slowly close my eyes. "I love you, too, Robby."

My Robby.

Chapter Twenty Five

⚔ Robby ⚔

Sometimes it's necessary for a man to do sit ups in order to think properly. This is one of those times. I don't know what it is about working out and putting things together in my head, but it works like a charm every single time.

I sit up after my last one. I take a drink of water and jump back to my feet. It's only then that I notice Luke standing in the door leaning against the frame with his arms folded over his chest.

I laugh. "Like what you see?" I pull my shirt back on.

"Very much. I especially like that ring on your finger telling the world who the fuck you belong to because the idea of anyone else touching all of that sends me to a dark place I don't think very many people would survive."

The purely dominant tone does things to my body that makes me groan out loud. I wouldn't be able to stop myself from walking to him if I tried. It's like my body is simply doing it on its own. I wrap my arms around him and kiss him hard. I only pull away when I hear someone coming down the hall towards the den.

"To be continued," I say, kissing him again before heading for my laptop to see what my search has brought up. I sigh when it's nothing and sit down feeling a little defeated.

"What is that look about?" Luke asks as he sits down next to me, looking at my screen.

"I thought I might have a lead on Jessa, but it's an empty lot. I broke into the Department of State and used some of their imaging from their satellite based Earth observation systems. There's nothing."

Luke blinks a moment before shaking his head and chuckling. "You're fucking scary when you want to be."

I smile. "If you want to blow up Iraq, just let me know. I'm pretty sure I can angle the nuclear warhead in Ohio and blow Iraq off the map."

He laughs. "I'm going to say this again. It's a good fucking thing you're on the side of good and not evil. God fucking help us all if you decide to switch teams. I mean, the fucking State Department? Don't they have firewalls and shit? Safeguards for people like you?"

I shrug. "Nothing I can't bypass. It's a challenge, yes. I have to disguise myself and be fast in case they detect me." I log out of the system and look up as Lance and Ryan come in deep in conversation.

Ryan looks at me as he sits. "How'd the search go?"

I shake my head. "Nothing. Vacant lot. There's nothing underground where anyone could be hidden, but I want a few guys to check anyway. Just to make sure."

He nods. "I'll take care of it. In the meantime, Lance. Tell him what you found so he can help track it."

I look at Lance as Luke settles back. "What did you find?"

"I don't know. I can't get further than what I did. All I know is the company is fake as fuck. Doesn't exist anywhere. At least not legal. IRS has no record. There's no business ID number. Fucking nothing. But it's connected to Viper's Venom."

I raise an eyebrow. "I didn't see anything off with any of their shit."

Lance shakes his head. "No. You wouldn't have. This comes from Matthew's side. I think this is the Berlusconi Mafia. But I can't get further than what I did. I can't connect them."

I study his screen for a second before I open my program and start my own track starting with the account numbers he has. I hit the same brick wall he did, but I have what I've already done for both Viper's Venom and the Berlusconi Mafia.

After a few moments of cross-referencing, I link my fingers behind my head with a smirk. "You're right. That company doesn't exist. This restaurant is a cover for it." I lean forward and turn my laptop for everyone to see as Luke laughs, already seeing what I have.

Ryan just looks confused. "What the fuck? What the fuck are they even trying to do? What am I even looking at? Isn't that some famous restaurant in New York?"

Lance laughs. "Ry, look closer."

Ryan leans forward as I point to the address on the screen. "Arianna's favorite restaurant. Eleven is in New York. Not Chicago. I don't get it."

Luke looks at him. "Ryan, the address. Look at the address. It's one of the most well fucking known address's in Chicago."

"Uh… 3510 South Michigan." Ryan shrugs. "I don't get the joke."

"It's the address of the Chicago Police Department's Administration building," Taylor says as he walks in.

Ryan shakes his head. "That isn't a restaurant. What the hell am I missing?"

"He's calling you out, Ry," Luke answers. "He's made up a fake as fuck business using Chicago PD's address. And he covered the fake business with another fake business that he's used to cover other businesses in the past. Look." He points to Lance's screen. "This business was used as a cover a few years ago. And it's used here just last year, then again a few months ago. Now he's using it for this fake restaurant that it looks like Viper's Venom has invested in."

"Which means it's something we need to ask them about," I finish. "I didn't see it when I was looking at Viper's Venom. So, this is something that's under the table. It's being used as an investment firm to invest in fake companies. My guess is money laundering."

"So, they're involved in money laundering?" Ryan asks.

I shake my head. "Nope. They wouldn't know this company is fake and being used for money laundering. There are several investments by regular people. It's being used as a pyramid scheme, if you will. And one of the best ways to launder money is through a pyramid scheme."

216

Taylor nods. "We've taken a few of these guys down over the past couple of years. This one wasn't on our radar yet. My guess is the scheme is new. No one knows they lost money yet. Pretty funny they're using "

"Okay, I can't take anymore fucking surprises. Just figure this shit out, please. All of this seems insignificant at this point. We need to get Jessa back here." Ryan leans back. "Luke, go get Alec. He's outside doing something to the shed. Something about soundproofing. Probably a wise idea."

"On it." Luke squeezes my thigh as he gets up and heads out of the room.

"Robby, hand that over to Taylor. His team specializes in shit like that. I don't want you dealing with it unless it gets us closer to Jess."

I nod and quickly give Taylor the information he needs to deal with the pyramid portion of it. When Josh and Alex come in with Jason, Nick, and Chase as well as Gavin and Dane, I quickly explain to them where we are with everything. Moments later, Luke comes with Alec.

Alec sits, looking more exhausted than I think I've seen anyone. I clear my throat. "Do you happen to know what Skyfalls Investment is?"

He watches us all for a few moments before speaking. "I feel like this is an inquisition. But to answer your question, after I took over, I wanted to expand. I've opened a couple businesses. I've invested in a couple of businesses. I invested in a restaurant called Eleven about a week ago. They haven't broken ground yet, but that's the firm they're going through seeking investments."

Lance hesitates slightly before taking a breath. "Uh... They're a fake company linked to Matthew Lucinio and the Berlusconi Mafia. They both use the company for covers. We think money laundering and pyramid schemes."

"Probably funding the sex-trafficking ring," Josh says quietly and definitely on edge.

Alec sighs. "I should have fucking known. It was a few days after I made the investment that Dallas went missing. Go figure, huh? Cassidy fucks up again."

I crease my eyebrows. "Who's Cassidy?"

Alec leans forward and rests his elbows on his knees. He drops his head in his hands. "My real last name. Viper is what my dad changed it to.

217

Thought it was cool. I'm still in the process of changing it all back. I don't want to be known as Alec Viper. And Dallas hates the last name Viper."

"Wait. Your last name is Cassidy?" Josh asks. I watch his eyes flick to Ryan. Jason's eyes widen. Alex's mouth drops.

I glance at Luke. He shrugs, just as confused as me. "What am I missing?" I ask, not sure I'm going to like the answer.

"Does Jess still keep that keepsake box in her top drawer?" Alex asks. Alec looks up just as confused as the rest of us.

"Right underneath her favorite red bra. We don't go anywhere without it. She made sure it came with us here," Jason says as both he and Josh get up. The two hurriedly leave the room.

"Son of a bitch," Ryan says. "It would make so much fucking sense."

"Far too much. The question is how the hell he found out before we did," Alex says.

"Okay, what the fuck are we missing?" Alec asks.

"If we're right? The missing fucking piece of a very fucked up puzzle," Ryan answers. "A twisted piece."

I shake my head. "What does any of this have to do with Jessa?"

"Everything," Alex says. "This has all had to do with Jessa ever since he laid eyes on her."

Nick chuckles. "I honestly don't fucking believe this. The answer being here this whole time. It's too fucking easy."

"So fucking easy it's hard," Ryan says.

We all look up when Jason and Josh come back in the room with a box. They both sit down. Jason opens the box and starts taking things out. He lays them in a neat line on the coffee table in front of us. We all lean forward to look.

"Jessa was adopted," Jason begins. "She loved the fuck out of her adopted parents. They were the only family she knew since she was old enough to remember anything. She was barely four when she was adopted. Here's her birth certificate." His finger taps on a piece of worn paper.

"Mother. Amelia Cassidy. Father. Richard Cassidy," I read.

"That's... My mother's and father's name," Alec says quietly and maybe a little in shock. "But that's not possible."

"Holy shit," Luke and I say together.

Ryan points to a picture. "This is her with her twin brother." We all look at it. Alec looks like he's about to hyperventilate as he leans back. Ryan leans back watching Alec. "You."

He looks up and shakes his head. "No." He stands up and paces. "No. No fucking way. They told me she died." He looks back at all of us. "They said she fell into a well on our property and died!" He sits back in his chair and swipes everything off the table they laid down. "No fucking way they'd keep my own sister from me!"

Alec breaks down in gut-wrenching sobs that I never thought I'd ever see from a man as big as him and covered in as many tattoos as he is. But fuck if it's not happening in front of my eyes. It feels like a knife is being twisted through my heart watching it.

Just when I'm about to get up to comfort him because I can't watch it anymore, Josh kneels in front of him. I kneel down and help Alex pick up everything on the floor instead.

Josh puts a hand on his shoulder. "Alec. I know this doesn't make a lick of sense to you. There's a letter in there from your mother. It explains why she did what she did. It doesn't go into a lot of detail. All it says is that she wanted to protect her. She wanted her to have a better life. Given what we know about your father and what he tried to do to your sister, Dallas, I would say he had the same plans for Jessa. Your mother was protecting her in the only way she knew how."

"If he wasn't dead I'd kill him for putting us through that," Alec growls out over his sobs.

"She had a good life," Ryan puts in. "Her family loved her like their own. Jessa grew up in a good home. A very safe and nurturing environment. She never blamed your mother for what she did. She knew it was for the best."

It takes Alec a few more minutes to calm down. I stand and slowly walk back to Luke. I sit next to him. Luke always knows exactly what I need. He puts his arm around me and pulls me slowly to his side. He kisses my forehead sweetly and keeps me close to him.

"You okay?" he whispers. His voice rumbles against my cheek.

I shake my head. "How much more pain are we going to uncover until this fucking ends?" I bury my face in his chest because I need that strong earthy and fresh scent to center me again. Keep my heart from shattering.

219

"We're not done yet, baby," he whispers.

Luke takes over for all of us. He explains everything to Alec. Everything about Nick and his family. He takes turns with Josh, who explains everything about Matthew. How Jessa is involved. And at the end, Ryan tells him something I don't think he needs to hear. I think he already knows.

"Putting it all together, it all starts to make sense," Ryan begins. "Dallas was taken because she's related to Jessa. This is something we've kept close to us. Jessa never really brought it up to anyone else because, well, it just never came up in the conversation. It's not that she was hiding it. It's just that she found it to be something not important."

"She did want to look into her family," Jason says. "But her life hasn't been that stable for quite a while. Just when things seem to calm down, something else happens. So, she's put this on the back burner for a long time."

"How he found out is something I don't understand," Josh says. "I don't know how he could possibly figure it out unless he did some deep fucking digging. Cole doesn't even know. He's her best friend."

I can't help but chuckle at that. "Maybe after you. Where is he anyway?"

"He's helping Zekeih, Jesse and Reed. He's staying at Reed's house," Josh says. "With Taylor and Dane with us, they need someone to help them with everything we throw at them."

Taylor smiles. "I'll be honest. For not wanting Dane's position, Jesse is pulling his weight."

The room falls silent as we all process everything we just learned. My eyes fall on Alec. I don't think the guy has stopped crying since we found out Jessa is the sister he thought died. While he's not sobbing, the tears still fall. It makes me want this to end even faster and more than I already did.

But I also know that Ryan is right. We need to do this systematically. Take out each rung of his ladder until he has nothing to step back on. I can't wait to see the fall. It's going to be something so epic. The memory just may be one of my favorites.

I lean up to kiss Luke's cheek, but stop. "Fucking hell." I jerk out of his arms and immediately grab my laptop. Everyone in the room watches me, slightly startled at my sudden outburst. "I might know where Jessa is."

My fingers fly across the keyboard with a speed that surprises even me. Everyone gathers around me as I bust through wall after wall of security measures on my way back into the State Department's satellite system. I smile a little evilly when I get to the point where I should be blocked. But I've already been through and told their system that I'm okay. I get through far quicker than I had before. With my continued speed, I quickly gain access to what I need.

"Fuck me," Lance says. "The State Department again? You're going to get us all killed."

I give him a half smile as I find the satellite I want. "Nah. They'll never find me." I angle the satellite to see the area near Chicago PD's Administrative building. I grin when I see an abandoned building. Large. It looks to be some kind of apartment building. Or perhaps a warehouse. All I know is there are rooms.

"Why not just use Google Maps?" Taylor asks. "Or ask me what's there. That's an old bar with some apartments at the top. Used to be an old cop's hangout."

My smile grows wider. "Because I wouldn't be able to do this." I zoom into the building until I can see inside it with near picture perfect quality. I search each room quickly, looking for anything that looks like a human.

"Holy… shit… What the hell are you? Some kind of hacker on the FBI's Most Wanted List?" Alec asks in pure shock. Maybe a little terror.

I have to laugh. "No. At least I don't think so. I'll check that later."

"Fuck. Holy fuck. He's using fucking international satellites to spy," Alec says as he rubs a hand down his face.

I shake my head. "Not international. This one is controlled by the United States."

"Stop!" Ryan commands. "There." He points to a blob on my screen. "What is that?"

I move the angle slightly and tilt my head. And then the blob moves. Clearly we can see two bodies, one much smaller than the other, but they look as if they're spooning. Suddenly, the satellite gives us all the proof we need. Clear as day, we can see Jessa with another young human who looks quite a bit like her. Alec gasps. Luke's hand on my thigh grips me tighter.

"Everyone move out!" Josh commands. I grab my laptop, not caring that I could very well get caught. I'll rely on my brother the fucking supervillain who has contacts everywhere if it means getting Jessa back.

Alec tries to follow but Ryan, Chase, and Jason hold him back. I can hear him protesting as we all run out to our SUV's. I put my laptop on the seat and quickly start throwing on my gear. Josh is barking orders into his phone. So is Luke.

In record time, we all jump in the vehicles ready for a battle and peel out of the driveway. We speed towards the city. My eyes are completely focused on the satellite imaging I have on my screen. I can see the two move to the corner of the room. They're sitting next to each other and curl into each other.

At that moment, though, the image starts to get fuzzy. "No. No! No! No!" I start hitting command after command to get my images back.

"What's happening?" Luke asks me.

"I'm losing the signal!" I force myself to breathe and think. Despite the WiFi connection these vehicles have, my signal is getting weaker. It can only mean one thing. "I have to block them. They're blocking me. Which means they found my signal in there. Or rather something that doesn't belong."

"How the fuck are you going to do that?" Luke asks me wide-eyed and panicked.

"Drop a virus to buy us time."

"Jesus Christ."

Seconds later, I'm doing exactly that and praying to God it works. Whoever they have on the other end is good, though. And fast. It takes me a little longer to get past him then it would anyone else, but I manage to do it.

"Just give me a few more minutes. I promise I'll fix the damage I just caused."

"Damage? Robby, what the fuck did you just do?"

"I gave them a cold, in the words of Jeff Goldblum from Independence Day."

"A cold? You're going to end up in Guantanamo and tried for treason!"

"The thought crossed my mind. But at least we'll have Jessa back."

"Robby, Jesus! Do you think I want to fucking lose you? Fix it!"

I look at him. He shoots me a withering glare, but it's not the domination that gets me to submit to him this time. It's the utter terror in his eyes. Without another word, I turn back to my laptop and quickly fix everything I just did to block the State Department from blocking me.

As we hit the edge of town, I'm closing out of my laptop and swallowing hard. I would never want to do anything to upset Luke, but the idea that I just scared him as badly as I did puts me in a place I don't like. Somewhere between feeling like the worst boyfriend in the world and the precarious ledge of disappointing the man I love.

Luke takes my trembling hand and squeezes it as he kisses it. "I love you, Robby."

"I love you, too."

Just like that, his words make the world right again. As we fly towards the building, I exhale a relieved breath.

For the first time in days, I'm filled with something other than fear, exhaustion, and dread. Something I haven't felt since Matthew waltzed into our lives.

Hope.

Chapter Twenty Six

☒ Luke ☒

I slam on the brakes in front of the building. Everyone else skids to a stop behind or next to me. We gain a lot of attention very quickly from passersby and Chicago police officers across the street. All eyes are on us as we start jumping out of the vehicles armed with more weapons than the police themselves.

A lot of people look at us curiously, but I ignore them. There isn't time to try and be secretive right now as we usually are. Trying to stay away from prying eyes while we do what we do is one of the most important things in our line of work. It's how we're able to exist.

"Get them out of here!" I command one of my guards as I point to the people on the street. He immediately does as I say as I finish grabbing my gear.

"What's the play, Massena?" Josh asks over our earpieces.

"We go in with all we have. Fast," I respond. "Overpower them. They don't have many guards. Robby saw four total. All upstairs."

"I sent in Zekeih, Jesse, Reed, and Cole with a team," Taylor says. "Haven't heard back."

"Let's move. No teams. We go in together," I say. Robby is behind me as we plaster ourselves to the side of the building. Josh and Alex are across from us. There's a door between us. I nod.

As we move to kick open the door, my heart starts hammering in my throat. The door crashes open, hitting the walls on the inside. The noise echoes through the empty building as Josh and I enter with our guns raised and ready. We lead with our gun as we start searching the building. Everyone spreads out behind us.

"My team is upstairs," Taylor says in our ears as he chuckles. "They asked very nicely to not be shot."

I can hear the smile in Josh's voice. "Then tell them to be good boys and keep their hands up."

Taylor laughs quietly. "Clear down here. I don't see any fucking thing."

"Be on your toes," I say. "You know better than anyone how fucked up things can get and how quickly."

"Better than anyone," Taylor responds. I choke down the anger when I think about how not too long ago, the precinct he was working at was started on fire with him and Nick still in it.. The doors were wired to explode if they were exited.

"I'm clear," Josh says.

"Clear," Robby says.

"Clear," Nick says. "Heading upstairs."

"Not without backup, you asshole," Alex says.

"Then catch up," Nick chuckles.

I smile as we start heading upstairs, leaving some downstairs just in case. Robby taps my shoulder when we get to the top. Using hand signals, he tells me Jessa and Dallas are in the third to last room at the end of the hall to our right. I nod and lead the team down the hall. We check each and every room on the way.

I hear a chorus of whispered voices saying they're clear coming from the team we sent down the other side of the hall. I'm suddenly very uneasy. There have been no guards. No sign of life at all since we've been here. No gunshots ringing out at us from anywhere in the building.

When we get to the open door of the third room, I get my answer. Jesse, Cole, Reed, and a couple of other cops are standing in the room looking around. Cole is holding something in his hand. Jesse is taking a picture of something. Reed is talking to the two cops. A few of our team finishes clearing while the others spread out to guard us.

Jesse looks up at me from where he's kneeling. "All we know right now is that she was here."

I let out a shaky breath as the anger starts to build. I close my eyes and shake my head. "How the fuck did they get out? I don't understand. You guys were right across the street. Robby was watching them until about three minutes before we got here."

"It took us a bit of time to get a team. The department is still reeling from the trafficking shit you found," Jesse says. "Not a lot of people want anything to do with our team right now. Probably scared they're going to go down next since we have a habit of sniffing out bad shit."

I chuckle. "Can't argue with that."

"What did you find?" Taylor asks.

"I don't have any idea. I can tell you it looks like two people were lying here where I am," Jesse answers as he stands. "And I can say it looks like they were sitting where Cole is. Other than that, what we have is shit we can't make sense of." He shows Taylor the phone. Josh and I look over Taylor's shoulder.

Taylor tilts his head. "It looks like a couple people were standing there."

Josh traces something on the phone. "It looks like a word, but with the footsteps, some of it looks like it got rubbed out. Look. There's a 'C' for sure. Looks like C-Z-U. Underneath…" He squints and zooms in before kneeling down where Jesse just was. He tilts his head. "M and X maybe?"

"C-Z-U-M-X," I say. "What the hell does that mean?"

"Could be where they're taking them," Robby says. "Send me the image. I'll see what I can do with it."

"What did you find, Cole?" Josh asks.

"I don't know. It looks like Jessa's handwriting, but it makes no sense." Cole hands him a piece of cardboard.

"VV. Allies. Dallas Cassidy." Josh hands the cardboard to me. "Looks like she knows who Dallas is and probably that he's her brother."

I nod. "So, she's telling us Viper's Venom are allies. And that she has Dallas with her."

226

"We knew Viper's Venom were allies, though," Cole says. "But what are you talking about? Brother? Dallas's brother?"

I shake my head as I look at him. "We just found out, but a few already knew. Ryan and Jas. Alex and Josh. Nick. Jessa is adopted. We all just found out that the brother she's been looking for is Alec. Her mom adopted her out when she was like four. Faked her death."

"Oh, fuck." Cole runs his hands through his hair in shock. "So, she figured out who Dallas is? That's Alec's sister, so hers, too. Maybe that's why she's so protective and demanded Berlusconi take Dallas or face Matthew."

"Looks like it," Josh says. "Looks like she's telling us to contact Viper's Venom. That design she drew looks a lot like the custom patch on Alec's jacket."

I reach for my phone in the pocket of my vest when it starts to vibrate. I look at the caller ID and quickly answer. "Hey, Lance. What's up?"

"Where are you guys?" he asks frantically.

My heart starts racing as I put him on speaker. "At the old cop hangout. Jessa and Dallas aren't here."

"I know! She's at the airport!"

We all take off running. "Where?" I yell as we run down the stairs.

"Chicago Executive Airport!" Lance yells. "The hangar is at the end. I looked up the location on their website, and all I can tell you is it's Hangar N. She turned her phone on just a couple minutes ago!"

Robby slides in beside me as I jump in the SUV. I slam it into gear and punch the gas so hard it makes the tires squeal and rear end fishtail when the vehicle starts moving. I drop my phone as I grip the wheel. I take off for the airfield at a rate of speed no one has any business driving in the city limits.

Robby grips the door handle. "Shit..."

I'm laser focused, though. I speed through the traffic like it's nothing. Looking behind me, I see the others have no issue keeping up. Either they're used to a million cars on the road and know how to get through them, or they're just as anxious as I am. Probably a mixture of both.

"I sent squads," Taylor says over the earpiece.

"Good. Fucking good," Robby breathes as he holds on. I take a turn hard and send him crashing into the door. "Fuck, Luke. Try not to kill us."

"Sorry," I grumble. "I don't want them getting away with her."

"Neither do I, but we can't fucking help her if you kill us."

He reaches over and grips my thigh just below my dick. It may seem strange to some, but he's learned that gripping me there calms me down. Steadies me. He rubs his thumb over my thigh as I breathe and focus. I know he's right. Getting there in one piece is top priority.

"Squads coming up on your left," Taylor says. "I'm with them. Lights and sirens. Follow us."

"That will make this navigation shit easier," I say as I move over for him.

When he flies by, I step on the gas and follow him like he told us to. It's nice seeing the traffic, for the most part, move when they see six squads and a line of unmarked, black SUV's coming up on them. It helps even more with the four squads behind us. It keeps them from thinking it's a good idea to try and cut us off, something Chicago drivers are known for. Probably all drivers in large cities.

It doesn't take us long to get to the airfield, but I'm beyond surprised when we aren't stopped at the gate. "You call ahead for us?" I ask Taylor.

"Only the best for you, boss," Taylor teases. "Even stopped the air traffic for you just because I like you so much."

I grin. "Well, damn. I do like the VIP treatment."

I hear a few laughs as we accelerate onto the tarmac heading directly for the end hangars. But just as we make our final turn, a jet plane is heading right for us at a rapid rate of speed. The engines roar as the plane gets closer.

"Fuck!" Taylor yells as he swerves out of the way and spins out in a spray of rock and dirt.

"Luke!" Robby yells, gripping my thigh tighter as I swerve to avoid the plane.

"Son of a bitch!" I grind out through gritted teeth as I swerve myself. I slam on the brakes and start to spin out as the wheels of the jet hit the roof of the SUV.

We come to a stop on the other side of the runway. I watch in unadulterated horror as some of our team jump out of their vehicles and start shooting at the jet as it takes off.

"Stop! Stop fucking shooting!" Josh screams into the ear pieces as he gets out and motions for everyone to cease what they're doing. "Stop shooting!"

"Are you all fucking crazy?" I yell. "We don't know if that's our plane or not!" But that doesn't stop the thoughts of the plane crashing to the ground, killing Jessa and everyone else on board.

"Air Traffic Control just said that was an unauthorized takeoff. It was Sean Berlusconi," Taylor growls.

"Argh!" I pound on the steering wheel. "One fucking break!"

Robby leans over and wraps his arm around my waist. He kisses my shoulder. My muscles are tense as I grip the steering wheel. My knuckles turn white as I watch the plane in the sky become smaller and smaller.

"I thought we had her," Robby whispers. "How does he keep getting away?" he asks softly.

I instantly soften and turn. I wrap him in my arms. "We'll get her. I promise." I run my fingers through his hair.

"I don't understand how he's always a step ahead of us," he whispers. "We weren't that far out when I closed out of the satellite. How did they get out that fast? How did they get here so fast?"

I shake my head as I kiss his. "I don't know. I wish I had the answers for you, but I don't. What I do know is that we have some clues to work with. We can see about getting a flight plan. There has to be some record of where that jet is going."

"I'll take care of it," Josh says as I hold Robby while he cries.

I take my earpiece and Robby's out. I shut them off and put them in the cup holder, still keeping Robby in my arms. "Baby." I kiss his neck, then tilt his chin up as I pull gently away. "We'll get her back. She's smart. She's helping us."

"I know. But I don't understand how it happened so fucking fast."

"I don't either. I don't know if they got tipped off. I don't know if they were already on their way out. What I do know is they got here before us. They were prepared. Now we follow the clues and find them."

"They're on their way to him. I know it. I can feel it. We aren't going to get to her before he does."

I hug him tighter. "We have to follow her. She left us clues to follow. All we need to do is figure it out. You're the smartest fucking man I know, Robby."

He nods and tightens his grip. "I feel overwhelmed."

"I know we throw a lot at you, but I know you'd tell me if it's too much. Is that what you're telling me? Because I won't hesitate to take it all off your plate and give it to Lance if that's what you want."

It takes him so long to answer that I know for the first time he's seriously questioning his life decisions. As his boyfriend, my heart feels like it's being squeezed at the thought that we've given him too much to handle. Sometimes, I forget that he's barely twenty-one.

Being such a valued member of a huge mafia has to be hard in itself. But everything happening right now with our family above and beyond him being nearly killed three times has to be throwing him. I hug him as hard as I can, feeling like a terrible boyfriend.

"I want to finish this. I want Jessa home. It's a lot. But it's necessary. It's my part to play. Without me, it would take longer."

I smile into his neck. "It's not always going to be like this."

He nods. "I know."

We both look at the driver's side window when someone knocks on it. I turn and push the button for the window to go down when I see Taylor. Knowing Robby still needs the contact, I take his hand in mine and hold it in my lap.

"What's up?" I ask.

"I figured you took out your earpiece when you didn't answer me," he says quietly with a soft smile. "I didn't want to interrupt, but Reed found something. He didn't get the chance to tell us before we took off."

I raise an eyebrow. "What did he find?"

"A note." He hands it to me.

I read it. "Meet me at the Tomb of Anton Cermak in the Bohemian National Cemetery. Tonight. Midnight. I could get killed for this. This is a serious betrayal of my boss. I'll only talk to Josh. Anyone else shows, I walk." I glance at Taylor. He's leaning against the roof of the SUV looking down at us.

"Well, that's not fucking suspicious," Robby mumbles.

"Did you tell Josh?" I ask.

"Not yet. He's busy threatening the lives of those who shot at the plane." Taylor winks and smirks.

I chuckle. "Let's get the fuck out of here. I'm not sending him alone. You need to wire him."

"How do you want to play this?" Taylor asks.

"Tell him on the way home. Right now, we're wasting time. We have clues to unravel. I need Robby and Lance working together on this. We'll get Pierce to help with the wire if you want him to."

"You got it." Taylor pushes off the SUV and walks towards his truck yelling at everyone to move out.

I kiss Robby's hand. "What do you say to getting our sister back?"

He gives me a pained smile. "Sisters. Looks like we gained another one."

I smile. "The girls are going to outnumber us pretty soon."

It was meant to make him laugh. Instead, he gives me a soft chuckle and leans his head against the window. He closes his eyes, but he's still squeezing my hand. As I drive towards our safehouse, I let Robby take the time to regroup.

I know my boyfriend well. When he goes quiet, he's getting his head back on right. Working through things. Sometimes, it takes minutes. Sometimes, hours. For him, silence is his Ativan. It's the way he gets his racing mind to slow down.

He keeps ahold of my hand, gripping it tighter as he allows himself to zone out. Right now, I know he's afraid we've lost our chance at saving Jessa and Dallas. He fears we failed them. But there's one thing he hasn't lost. Something he's using as an anchor. Something he'll never have to worry about not being there when he needs it.

Me.

Chapter Twenty Seven

⚒ Robby ⚒

"Doing okay?"

I look up at Josh as he sits next to me on the couch. "No. But I refuse to sleep until I figure this shit out."

He looks curiously at my laptop. "What is that?"

I smile and focus back on my work. "I imputed the letters from that picture into a program that gives me options on what the fuck it means."

"Oh. That's kind of cool. What do you have so far?"

I shake my head and squeeze my eyes shut as I rub them. "Nothing. I have nothing. Nothing that makes any sense anyway."

Josh chuckles. "I think 'the cat's zebra's uranus is my excalibur' is my favorite."

"Not as good as 'China's zany udders is macaroons xenox'."

He laughs. "It doesn't look like this is helping at all."

I smile. "It's giving me a good laugh. And it did actually give me a little bit. The m and x could be Mexico. I'm looking for cities that start with a c or z or u in Mexico. Or cities that have all those letters."

Josh nods and watches me as I scroll over my map, writing down my options. I have to give myself a pat on the back when it comes to Alex and Josh. I've managed to figure out their differences so I can tell them apart.

While they're both tall and well-built with the same eyes and hair, Josh seems to stand taller than Alex. His confidence exudes from every part of his being. He's darker. More dominating. He could be scary if he wants. His voice is deeper. He carries himself with power.

Alex isn't nearly as dark. While he's intimidating and doesn't usually have to raise his voice to be heard, he's far less dominating. His voice isn't as deep. And he carries himself with more grace and confidence then he does confidence and power like Josh.

But the biggest difference between the two is the edge they portray. Josh's experiences have affected him far deeper than Alex. Alex's edge comes out when he's on missions and protecting the ones he loves. Josh's is there all the time. It's like it's plastered to his features. All of them. Even Josh's hair has a dark edge to it.

"Are you ready for tonight?" I ask him.

"Yeah. I'm ready to go. I was just checking on you. Ryan said he'd like you out there as my sniper, but I figured you'd need to get me wired up."

I give him a slow nod. "Who is he having go with you?" I don't look at him because it would let him see all the worry and angst I've been feeling about this meeting. I don't let anyone see that much of my emotions. Luke is the only person I've let in that far. Not even Arianna has seen me truly vulnerable.

"I'll have Alex with me. And you. Ryan says you don't miss when you take a shot."

I smile. "He's right."

"I'll also have more of my crew. They'll be hidden. I have a lot of guys in Chicago, too." He bumps me teasingly. "Maybe not as many as Ryan."

"I don't think anyone has as many as Ryan," I say softly.

"So, tell me what's bothering you."

I chuckle. "What isn't bothering me? I feel like a part of me is missing."

"Believe it or not, so do I. But we'll find her."

233

"I know we will. I think what's bothering me the most is Jason. He's quiet. I mean, I would be, too. But if he's anything like me, he's plotting ways to destroy Matthew. It's a hard thing to come back from."

"I get it. It worries you."

"He's a good guy. I would hate seeing him take a life. No matter how fucking horrible the person is. And I know Ryan's rule. Ryan wouldn't allow him to take the shot. But I don't think even Ryan would be able to stop him if he came face to face with Matthew."

"I agree with you. But there's something you're missing about Jason."

I lean back with a yawn and look at him. "What?"

He leans his elbows on his knees and looks back at me. "Jason used to run missions. He grew up in this. Just because he walked away doesn't mean it's not still in him."

I had forgotten about that. I sigh. "I guess you're right."

He pats me on the knee. "You're a lot like Jessa. A kind soul." He smiles as he stands. "How about you get me ready and wired? We need to leave soon. Lyric's getting more anxious than you. I just want to get this bullshit over with."

I chuckle. "On it, boss."

He laughs. "I fucking hate being called boss. Makes me cringe."

I grin. "I know. It's why I do it."

He shakes his head as I stand. "Asshole."

"Learned from the best." I wink at him.

He laughs. "I am kind of an asshole."

I raise an eyebrow. "Just kind of?"

He grins. "Okay. I definitely am. I'm glad you're learning from the best."

I smile as I stretch. "I'll be there in a minute."

He nods. "He's out back."

It's kind of amazing he knows what I was talking about. Josh might be just as intuitive as Ryan. I didn't think that was anywhere near possible, but I suppose getting mentored by him, things like that would rub off.

I step outside and see Luke talking to Ryan. He's poking at the fire in the fire pit. The sparks shoot in the air when he drops a log on it, then stokes it more. Ryan is leaning forward with his elbows on his knees speaking low. I hate to interrupt them, but Luke isn't coming with me on this one. He's needed here to help Ryan formulate our next course of action. I take a couple of steps towards them, trying to stay quiet.

Luke looks up with a smile. "Hey, baby. Heading out?"

I glance towards the door. "Yeah. I'm just going to wire Josh."

"Okay. We're coming up with a battle plan. You find anything out about Jessa's message?" he asks as he stands.

I sigh. "Not really. I have a few ideas, but nothing really to go too far on."

"How about you tell me what you have, and I'll help you." His voice is low and husky when he reaches me. He puts his arms around me and pulls me in for the hug I would never admit to needing.

The tension melts when I put my arm around his back. "How the fuck do you do that?" I murmur into his solid chest.

He hugs me tighter. "I just know you. Tell me what you need."

I groan into his neck. "I've narrowed down a list of cities in Mexico. I don't know why, but instincts just keep screaming at me that she's somewhere in Mexico. I think she was trying to tell us the city she's going to. I looked at the image closer. I think there was a letter between the m and x. It's why I'm thinking Mexico."

"Okay." He pulls away a little, but keeps his arms around me. "What cities did you come up with?"

I hand him the paper I was using. "There's a lot. I used the letters c, z, and u."

He takes it and looks as he lets me go. He stays close. Close enough for me to lean on him. "Shit... That's... There's a lot."

"Over a hundred. I was going to look at the spacing between the letters in that image. I think maybe the city name has a c,z, and u in it. It doesn't look like a long name."

"Do you think it starts with a c?"

I hesitate a little. "I don't know. I was hoping that maybe someone with a more trained eye could look. I don't see anything else that could look like a letter before that c. But I really don't know. Maybe I'm barking up the wrong tree."

"It's more than we had. I'll take it." He looks up at the house. I turn and see Josh standing by the door. "Looks like that's your cue. You going to be okay?"

"Yeah. I wish you were going, but I know Ry needs you."

"You have Alex and Josh. You'll have a lot of Josh's guys to back you up. I'd say routine, but nothing is ever routine. I will say easy, though." He grins the loving and cocky grin he reserves only for me.

I smile and lean into him. I kiss him. "Thank you."

"Be careful," he whispers. He gives me another kiss and a quick hug. But it's still warm and strong. The kind of hug I need.

It's not that I'm unable to do things without Luke. I've run missions without him. I'm capable. The issue is that since Matthew got to me, I haven't been away from him. My confidence is slightly wavering because I'm letting fear get in the way.

I know I can't let myself do that, so I take a deep breath and walk into the house. I force myself to do my job because it's what I have to do. But there's still a niggling part in the corner of my mind stuffed way in the back in the dark that's freaking out.

Luke makes me feel safe. I feel invincible next to him. While there isn't a single person that I'm with right now that I don't trust, Luke is the one who makes me feel secure. Protected. It's unnerving to me that, for the first time in days, he won't be by my side.

After getting Josh set up, I climb in the back of the SUV next to Lance. Alex sits in the front next to Josh. I open my laptop and start to set up things on my end. Lance follows my lead. He'll be doing audio while I do video.

"Josh, can you move the camera on you up a little?" I ask as soon as I get my feed up.

"I got it." Alex leans over and moves the camera I have wired into a button on the pocket of Josh's black leather jacket.

"To the left a little," I say. Alex moves it just a little. "Perfect. Is it clamped back in?"

"Yep. He's good to go," Alex says.

"Give me an audio test, Josh," Lance says.

"Check. Check," Josh says. "Testing the audio."

Lance chuckles. "Smart ass."

Josh grins in the rearview mirror. "You reading me okay?"

"Loud and clear, b-"

"If you call me boss, I will kick your ass," Josh growls. But the smile gives him away.

Lance and I both look at each other. We smile and turn back to Josh. "Yes, boss!" we say in unison. Alex laughs.

"Fuck you both. Get out," Josh says with a chuckle.

We all laugh as Josh drives. At his rate of speed, it doesn't take us long to reach the Bohemian Cemetery. Josh parks a little ways away from the monument. We all get out and arm ourselves. I grab the long range rifle and set the sights as quickly as I can. Josh gets into another SUV as Alex gets in the driver's seat of ours. Lance and I follow. Alex follows Josh into the cemetery, but stays a distance away from him.

"Ready for this?" Alex asks. "Pulling double duty?"

I chuckle. "If it means watching his back out there, I'll do whatever I need to. Make sure we're well hidden, but can see him. I'll need to be on the roof, but I'll need to line up my shot if I need to take one."

"Let's hope you don't." Alex pulls over.

We're far enough away and hidden in the dark so we can't be seen, but I have a perfect view of the monument. I get out quickly and put my laptop on the roof. I put my rifle up, then climb up. I lay prone on the roof and set up my shot, keeping my eye in the scope as well as on my laptop. I can see Josh is still in the SUV.

Moments later, I can see a figure dressed all in black with his head down walking quickly towards the monument. He quickly looks around then puts his head back down. He does it several times before he reaches the monument.

"Looks like game time," Josh says.

"You're good to go," I say. "I've got you covered."

"Okay. Here we go." Josh gets out of the SUV and heads for the monument.

I watch the guy watching him closely. Josh stops a few feet away from him. The guy watches him before looking around nervously again. He stays quiet as he keeps his eyes on the shadows. I can tell he's scared just by looking at him.

Finally, he takes a deep breath. "You come here alone?"

"As alone as you're going to get me. Who are you?" Josh asks.

"Heath Anderson. I work for your father." He waits for Josh to react. When he doesn't get one, he backs away a step and puts his hands in his pocket. "He'll kill me if he knew what I'm doing."

"I don't doubt that. Why am I here, Mr. Anderson?"

He regards Josh with confusion before sighing and rubbing his eyes. "He's involved in a lot of shit that I just can't deal with. Shady shit. Not the usual stuff. I can deal with drugs. I'll shake people down if I have to. Fuck. I'll even sell automatic weapons to the cartel. But this? This is my line."

"What? What's he doing that's so bad you're coming to me at the risk of getting shot by him or the sniper I have here with me?"

Heath inhales sharply as his eyes dart around. "Fuck! You said you came alone!"

"I said as alone as you're going to get me. I'm not fucking stupid. Now, tell me what's going on. Now. Or I'll give him the signal to take off part of your ear."

I chuckle. "Just give me the signal."

Heath backs away a little more. "Okay. Just... don't let him shoot me."

"Then tell me why I'm here. And stop backing up. You're freaking me out. You have someone waiting around here to off me or something?"

He shakes his head and steps back a few more steps. "No."

"Take one more step, he shoots," Josh says. "Just tell me why I'm here."

I watch as he takes another step. I chuckle again. "Want me to warn him?" I watch Josh. He keeps his hand at his side but closes a fist. "You got it." I aim just above Heath's head and slightly to the right. I pull the trigger with a smile and watch as it hits my mark. The bullet slams into the monument behind him. Right next to his ear.

Heath lets out a shrill scream and covers his ears. "Holy fuck!"

"Next time, he'll aim for your head. Now, what the fuck am I doing here? If I have to ask you again, I'm not going to be happy."

"Okay! Okay!" Heath shakily puts his hands down slowly. I can see his entire body is trembling. "He's running a sex trafficking ring."

"I know that. Tell me something I don't."

"Okay. He has two girls on the way to him now. I know you know Jessa is one of them, but he has another girl."

"Who?" Josh asks, though he knows the answer.

"Her name is Dallas Cassidy. She's Jessa's sister. Like full-blood real fucking sister. Matthew has a deal with Viper's Venom. It's a motorcycle crew here in Chicago. He's using them for money laundering.

238

Only they don't have a fucking clue. They think they're investing in some bullshit restaurant. And they think the deal is with a bogus investment company. If they were to look into it, it would just look like a legit firm. Unless they dig deeper. Then it would come back as a cover business for the Berlusconi Mafia. But they're an ally."

"What does that have to do with the girl?"

"When Matthew was checking them out, he found out that the crew president took over after a war with his father. It was because his father wanted to marry off his young daughter. His son wasn't having it. That was a few years ago now. The girl is now fourteen, but while he was researching, he found out that this president of the crew had a twin. They said she was killed when she was a kid, but Matthew saw a picture."

Josh is quiet for a few moments as a few of us suck in a breath. It's quite possible we seriously underestimated this fucker. To be able to dig that deeply, or think to, for that matter, is something I never expected from him.

"The picture. How does he know who it was?" Josh asks.

"He was curious. He dug into it. The girl he knew about didn't fit how old the girl in the picture would be. He figured out it was Jessa through that and images I guess he had from before when he was spying on her. Images of her showing you things from a box. I didn't see them, so I don't know, but he said that he matched the pictures."

"Son of a bitch," Josh growls.

"Easy, tiger," Alex says. "We need to know where the fuck he took them."

Josh lets out a low growl. "So, this Dallas. She's Jessa's sister. He has Jessa and her sister. What's the plan?"

"Well, the plan was to sell Dallas into his sex trafficking ring. But Jessa threw a fucking fit."

"Jessa talked to him?"

"She demanded to after Berlusconi tried to put Dallas with the other girls to sell. She wasn't having any of it. So, Matthew agreed that if she cooperated and came to him willingly, he'd spare the girl."

"Where? Where is he?"

The guy clears his throat. "You have to keep me safe, man. He'll fucking kill me."

"If you don't tell me where the hell he is, I'll kill you."

"Josh. Please." Heath sounds terrified. "He will kill me. He probably knows somehow I'm talking to you. He's already pissed the fuck off that you all are taking out his smaller factions one by one."

Josh chuckles. "Good."

"I'm not asking for your trust. Fuck, I don't expect it. I'm just asking for your help. Keep me safe until you take him out. I know you're going after him. So does he, but he doesn't think you know where he is."

Josh is once more quiet for a few moments. Finally, he sighs. "Tell me where he is, and I'll keep you safe. But if I find out that you're fucking with me, I'll execute you medieval style. Chopping block and all."

"Fine. You have my word."

"Turn around."

The guy looks at him, confused, but does what he says. Josh quickly cuffs him and pats him down. He removes a gun, putting it in his own waistband. After he's finished, he turns him back around to face him.

"Cozumel, Mexico," the guy says quietly.

"That's where he is?"

"I'll even give you the exact location."

I don't move until Josh is back in his SUV with the guy in the backseat. I trust that Lance is already contacting Ryan. I keep my scope trained on the guy until one of Josh's guys gets in the passenger seat of his vehicle.

When Josh tells me he's good, I jump down from the roof. I quickly put my gear away and jump in the passenger seat with my laptop. Alex peels out after Josh. Lance is talking to Ryan. I breathe the first relieved breath I have in days.

Finally. Finally we're on the right track. My instinct about Mexico was right. We're going to get her. We're going to get them back.

Fucking finally.

Chapter Twenty Eight

✗ Luke ✗

I check my watch again. The meeting should be close to done or already finished. I want a check in. It's not that I don't trust my team or think they can handle themselves. It's that Robby is with them. He hasn't been without me at his side since Matthew got to him. I don't like him being away from me.

So, I continue pacing around the room while Pierce continues narrowing down Robby's list of cities in Mexico. I fold my arms over my chest and look at my watch again. I glance at the ceiling when I hear a thump. It's followed by a shrill cry.

Taylor lets out a low growl. "Fuck me." He rubs his head as he gets up. "Tait is testing my patience lately."

I give him a reassuring smile. "It's nice of you to take care of it, though. Nicole is exhausted."

"You're telling me. He's not adjusting well to not being at home. I don't think he likes that he has to share everything with two other kids. Including his bedroom." Taylor heads for the stairs.

Ryan rubs his eyes. "I'm getting too old for this shit." He's laying on the couch with his feet up on the arm of it. He drops his forearm over his eyes. "Where did the days go where I could stay up for two days and not bat an eye?"

Nick laughs. "They ended the day you took over."

Ryan smiles and chuckles. "Such an asshole. What happened to the sweet little brother who was always so supportive of us? Even though he hated our playboy ways?"

Jason snorts as I smile. He looks at Nick. "Is he for real? When have you ever been sweet?"

Nick grins. "Not a fucking clue. Maybe before Penelope ran off with my inheritance."

Jason groans. "Don't remind me of Peneloslut."

I laugh. "Is that what you guys called her?"

Ryan smiles. "She deserved it. That and many, many other names. Penelowhore. Whorepe. Slutbag. Gold digger. The list is endless."

"I'm just glad she's gone. She was the worst decision Nick ever made." Jason leans back against the couch.

I'm about to ask more questions to keep my mind occupied, but I'm cut off by a chime on Pierre's laptop. I raise an eyebrow as he looks at it. His eyes widen and his fingers suddenly fly across the keys. I'm hoping that's good news.

Ryan sits up. "What's going on?"

"Jessa," Pierre says. "She just came back online. Or just turned her phone on, I mean."

We all gather around Pierre just as Nick's phone rings. He looks at it. "Jessa." He answers it quickly and puts it on speaker. "Jess?" he says quietly.

"Nick," she whispers, sniffling. "I tried calling Josh again. He didn't answer... I don't know where we are. They were so secretive."

"Josh had a meeting with someone saying he knows where you are. We're hoping he's not fucking lying. We're tracking you, honey. Just try to keep your phone on," Nick tells her.

"I don't have a lot of time. They told us that they're going to get Matthew. I know I'm in the basement of a large house. It's cold and dark. No light. I don't have a lot of battery left, so I haven't tried using the light from it to look around."

"It's okay. Tell me what you saw on the way to where they took you. Anything?" Nick asks.

242

"No. Nothing. We were blindfolded. I left you a message at the last place they held us. I don't know if you were able to get it or not. I overheard them saying Matthew was in Cozumel, Mexico, but I don't know if that's where we are or not. On the plane they were saying they knew you were after them. I don't know if Matthew moved."

"Just keep your phone on, honey," Jason says.

"I'll try."

"I almost have you, Jessa," Pierre says. "I have you in Mexico. Just narrowing you down now."

"Okay," she whispers. "Jason, I'm terrified. I'm trying so hard to be strong."

"I know, baby. You're doing so well. Just keep doing exactly what you're doing. Play to Matthew. Do whatever you need to do to keep him from hurting you or Dallas. Lie. Whatever you have to."

"She's my sister. I figured it out when she was telling me about her parents. Everything clicked."

"We know, sweetheart. Your brother came to us asking for help finding her. We put everything together," Ryan says.

My eyes flick to Pierre. "We get her?"

"Cozumel. Just zeroing in on her location. Give me a couple seconds, Jessa."

"I can hear them coming," she whispers. "Tell me what to..." She lets out a sob.

"Do not shut your phone off, Jess," Ryan tells her. "Hide it. But under no circumstances do you shut it off."

"Okay. I love you all. I love you, Jason. I have to go."

She hangs up before we have a chance to say anything more. "Fuck," I whisper, rubbing my chest. "I feel like I'm going to have a heart attack."

"Don't have a heart attack yet," Pierre says. "She didn't shut the phone off. I'm logged in with my CIA credentials. I didn't get her exact location, but I can still get her using the GPS and other intelligence that we have. Just give me a few minutes."

"Between Robby being out there without me and Jessa in Matthew's fucking grasp, I'm going crazy here," I say.

"How about you go grab Alec?" Pierre says to me. "Tell him we're heading out."

"What?" My heart flutters. I don't dare hope that means what I think it does. "Did you get her?"

"Cozumel, Mexico. I got the coordinates for the house." Pierre grins.

My phone rings just as Ryan's does. I quickly look at the caller ID and answer. "Robby. Thank fuck. How did it go?"

"Cozumel, Mexico," he says. "Lance is talking to Ryan."

"Jessa just called. Pierre got her. We have coordinates," I tell him.

"Josh is getting them from the guy now. We're bringing him to a Lucinio safehouse. Josh's guards will deal with him. Do you want me to call for the jet?"

"I'll take care of it. Just meet us there. We need to coordinate who will be staying with the girls."

There's a flurry of motion around me as everyone starts moving at the same time at Ryan's command as I hang up with Robby. They all head for the girls as I walk to the den for Alec. He's sleeping on the couch on his stomach. His crew are all scattered throughout the room.

I make my way carefully to the couch calling his name as I walk. It's never a good idea to walk up on anyone in the line of work we're in. "Alec."

"What?" he grumbles.

"We got them."

He shoots up. "What?" He rubs his eyes and looks at me hopefully. "You found them?" His crew starts to move around as they sit up.

"Cozumel, Mexico. We're heading out. I was talking to Ryan earlier about the other girls that you had taken from your crew, and we think we found them, too. We sent a crew out to check into it. Looks like one of them is in Nashville. The other might be in Canada."

"Jesus," Tyler grumbles.

"I'm coming," Alec says. "I'm not fucking staying here when my sister is there." He looks up fiercely.

I nod. "We need a couple of guys to stay here and help Chase, Dani, and Lyric. There will be guards here, but no way in hell are we leaving the girls without as much protection as possible. If something were to happen, they need backup right here."

Alec nods. "How many do you want here?"

"As many as you got. We thought you'd want to take Tyler."

"I'll take care of it while we're getting ready to go," Alec says.

I nod and pat his shoulder as I head out of the den and outside. I start gathering gear, making sure we have everything we need. We're going to go in with so much force it will make Matthew's head spin. He's not going to know what hit him.

"Luke?" Arianna calls softly from behind me.

I turn. "Hey, honey. What's up?"

She hugs herself and looks over her shoulder. She sniffles. "With the loss of Ethan and Jenny…" She trails off and looks back at me. "Ryan isn't showing it, but I know he's deeply affected. I'm scared that…" She covers her face with her hands.

I quickly cross the garage to her and wrap her in my arms. "Arianna, I know how scared you are. I do. But you have to do what Ryan tells us all to do all the time when our confidence is wavering. Trust the team. I'm scared to death letting Robby out of my sight, but I know he'll be okay. He has a fuck of a team watching his back. So does Ryan." I kiss the top of her head and tighten my grip. "I will not let anything happen to Ryan, Air. I promise."

She nods but keeps her arms wrapped around me. She takes several deep breaths as she starts to calm down. I sway gently with her, running my fingers through her hair. After a few minutes, I see Ryan walking down the hall strapping on his vest. He immediately looks concerned when he sees me hugging Arianna.

"You okay, baby?" Ryan asks, voice laced with concern as he reaches us.

Arianna nods as she shakily lets go. She turns and buries herself in Ryan. "Scared," she whispers.

Ryan hugs her as tightly as he can. He gently kisses her neck. "I know. I do. But this is coming to an end. One way or another. He's not walking out of there this time."

"I'm scared for you, Ryan. Please, please come home. Safe. Alive." She starts crying again.

"Oh, honey." He leans down and starts whispering in her ear as he sways gently with her like I had been.

I smile and rub her back before turning back to the garage to finish packing our gear. When I have everything done, I start pulling out vehicles.

I call the pilot to be ready and make sure Josh's is ready. Because we're bringing so many people, I call in Chase's and Jason's as well.

By the time I'm done with the busy work, everyone is coming out. Ryan jumps in the driver's seat of our SUV. I follow trying to think of anything but Robby. I know he's okay. I just talked to him. I try to shake it off, but I can't help feeling something is wrong.

"What do you say we get you to Robby, huh?" Ryan starts driving.

I look out the window. "Am I that obvious?"

"It isn't that hard to see."

I sigh and glance at him before focusing on the road speeding by underneath our tires. "I don't know what the fuck is wrong with me. I know he's capable of handling himself."

"You've almost lost him three times. After almost losing Arianna in that fire in Hawaii, I didn't let her out of my sight for months. You know that."

"So, the fact that I feel like I'm a crazy, possessive asshole is normal?" I chuckle a little, but it doesn't make me feel a damn bit better. "This isn't who I am. I trust him. I trust he's okay."

"Luke, he's the love of your life. He's the one you've given your heart to. You're engaged to marry the guy." He glances at me. "The primal instinct to protect the one you love isn't you being an asshole. It comes from a place of love. And if you want me to be honest, I bet you that he's thinking of you and feeling a little vulnerable without you around. Arianna felt the same way for a long time after."

I shake my head. "Doubtful. Robby is one of the strongest people I've ever met. He doesn't need anyone to make him feel safe and secure."

Something about what I said makes Ryan laugh. "I should crack you in the back of the head! Stop being an idiot. If it were you who'd gotten shot at, no way in hell you wouldn't feel a little off without Robby with you. He makes you feel just as safe and protected as you make him feel. Arianna is one of the strongest women I know. She doesn't fall apart in front of very many people. She'll pretend she's a fucking warrior if it means people don't view her as weak. But in front of me, hell, even in front of you, she'll show her vulnerable side. She feels safe enough with us to do it. It's no different with you or him."

I'm quiet a few moments before I finally sigh. "Okay. You're right. I fucking hate the idea of him being out there without me. I need him near me. I need to know he's safe. I keep telling myself he is. I know he can take care of himself. But you're right. I don't feel right without him near me right now. It scares the hell out of me."

"It's normal. You'll feel like an asshole, but it's normal to not want him out of your sight. He almost died."

"Three times."

He reaches over and squeezes my shoulder. "It's normal to want to be with him. You feel like you're the only one who can keep him safe. Trust me. I understand completely. The idea of leaving those girls home is killing me. It's killing all of us. Nick didn't want to leave Dani. Taylor didn't want to leave Nik. I sure as fuck don't want to leave Ari. And guess what? Even though they're not together anymore, Josh hates leaving Lyric."

"I know…" I scrub my hands over my face. "I'm sorry. At least I'll have him with me. You guys won't."

"Don't apologize. There isn't a need for it."

I nod and take a deep breath. "Talk to me about something else. Anything else."

"Okay. What do we have for the jets?"

"I called in Chase's pilot. I have Jason's, yours, and Josh's as well."

"Four jets. We'll have the guards on the other three jets. We'll take us and Robby. Taylor, Jas, and Nick. We'll have Alex and Josh. We'll take Alec and Tyler. And we'll take Lance, Gavin, Damon, Cole, and Dane."

"That's a lot on our jet."

"It'll be fine. It's big enough."

I nod as I focus on the road. I reach up and rub my chest. "Fucking hell. My heart hurts."

"Almost there," he says in a calming voice.

"I've never felt this way before. I don't know what I'd do if something happened to him."

"I can't answer that. I feel the same way. We'd probably go on a fucking rampage. Sort of like what Jason's about to do."

I laugh because he's right. "There's no way in hell you'll be able to stop him from taking the shot if he gets the chance."

"I know. And I won't. It's not that he can't handle it. The only reason I've ever stopped him before is after he left and struck out on his own, I didn't want his reputation tarnished. I may be legit, but it's still hard for a man of his stature to be associated with the mafia. There's a stigma that comes along with that. It could ruin him."

I look over at him. "So, why let him take the shot in this case? It could still ruin him."

He nods as he takes the turn to the airport. "It could. But that's where the overprotective brother, badass mafia boss, comes into play." He smiles and gives me a wink. "Anyone who tries deals with me."

I laugh. "I'd never want to come up against you."

"It's definitely in people's best interest to do what I say. Jason will be fine. I have the connections to keep him far away from this."

I laugh again as he grins wider. "Thank you. For getting me out of my head."

"That's what brothers are for."

He drives to our hangar. I'm pleased beyond reason to see that Josh is already here. It means Robby is here. My chest instantly loosens. I feel like I can breathe again. I'd almost given up hope that it was going to stop hurting tonight.

I don't wait for Ryan to stop completely before I'm opening the door and jumping out. I wrap Robby in my arms as soon as I reach him.

Fucking hell. I've turned into a sap, and I don't even care. As long as he's near me, everything is right.

Chapter Twenty Nine

⚔ Robby ⚔

(The Next Day)

I grip the pillow in front of me and bite down as Luke grips my hip and slams his dick into me over and over again. I clench around him as I moan. He pulls me back into each thrust. I swear he gets harder and thicker with every plunge into my ass.

"Fuck! Luke!" I scream into the pillow. I reach back and tangle my fingers in his hair as I arch.

He moans into my neck and slides his hand down to my hard as a rock cock. He takes it in his hand and starts stroking. "I'll never get tired of this."

"Holy God, please don't ever get tired of it." I push back into him harder, relishing in the feel of him sliding deeper. "I never fucking will."

He squeezes my dick as he strokes slowly. He slows his thrusts to the same pace and rolls his hips. I tighten around him and slide my hand down to his neck\. I meet his thrusts. His thumb hits the spot just below my tip that he knows drives me closer to my release. My dick throbs and twitches in his hand.

He starts thrusting faster and faster again until he's slamming his hard and deliciously long, thick cock harder and deeper into my ass. His strokes continue to keep pace with his thrusts. My stomach tightens as my ass clenches tight around him. I jerk my hips as I keep meeting him thrust for thrust. His large hand strokes me at the perfect pace. He gives me the right amount of pressure.

"Jesus, Luke." I let my head fall back against his, my back flush against his chest. He kisses my neck. I turn and kiss him. Our tongues meet and explode into fireworks, igniting us all over again.

He deepens the kiss with a moan. "Fuck, I'm gonna come, baby."

"Me too," I whisper.

"Come with me," he whispers against my lips. "Now."

My body obeys him on its own accord. A jolt shoots down my back. My lower back tightens as hard as my stomach. I come hard into his hand as he slows his strokes. My release explodes in what feels like a waterfall. Powerful and strong. My dick jerks and throbs as come gushes out of me.

"Oh… fuck…, Luke…"

I close my eyes when he slams his dick into me hard and comes at the same time as I do. His dick jerks into me in a delicious rhythm as he kisses me long and deeply, filling me with all of him. Greatest feeling in the world.

"Holy shit, baby," he says against my lips as he slowly pulls away. He keeps my dick in his hands as he slowly stops stroking and thrusting.

We lay snuggled into each other for a while before either of us make any kind of an attempt to move. But when we see the time, we force ourselves to. Luke pulls out of me slowly with a low moan. He gently lets go of my dick as we sit up and head for the bathroom.

"I didn't realize how much I needed that," I say after we start cleaning up.

"Honestly, I didn't either. But it helped. A lot. I'm not as fucking on edge."

I smile at the thought that I can do that for him. All I want is to make sure he has all he needs and is happy. Content. I want to give him all that he's given me and more. I feel like it's the least I can do for the man who made me the happiest I've ever been.

I've been able to express my true self with Luke. And not only has he accepted me, but he's loved me in every single way a person should be loved. And then he surpassed it and loved me more. Luke has shown me what love really is. He's breathed a life into me that I never knew existed. A life filled with happiness and contentment. A world filled with a sweet and passionate love with all of the romance and hot sex that I could ever dream of. He's given me everything.

I look at him as we're getting dressed. "You know, when I was out there without you, I was a little scared." I say the words quietly.

He gives me a soft smile and nod. "I was scared you were out there without me. I know you can handle yourself, but I've been by your side since…" He trails off, biting his lip.

"I know." I take a breath and hug him because I need that contact. I sink into his arms when they wrap around me. "It's not that I feared I couldn't do my job, or that I didn't trust those I was with."

"You felt a little less safe."

I nod. "How much of a dick am I? Not feeling safe with people I should feel safe with? I mean, Josh and Alex are family to us."

He kisses my temple and tightens his grip, rubbing his hands up and down my back. "It was something I struggled with, too. But Ryan actually put it all into perspective for me. He said that me feeling possessive and you feeling unsafe without me is normal. It happened with him and Air. And same with Taylor and Nikki. Nick and Dani. Bree and Chase. Jas and Jessa."

I smile into his neck. "That actually makes me feel a little better. Less weak."

He pulls back and kisses me. "You're not weak, Robby. Anything but." He kisses me again before taking my hand. He leads me from our hotel room to Ryan's suite.

"Did he say when we're going in?" I ask.

"He's had a crew out all day surveying. We have an in with his guards."

I look up at him in shock as Ryan lets us in. "What?"

"Yeah. There's a guard with him. He used to work for him before Josh took over Lucinio Mafia. He recognized Jessa. Called Josh right away."

"How do we know we can trust this guy?"

"Good question. I don't know the answer to it, but I can tell you Josh trusts him."

I sigh as I sit down. Ryan hangs up his phone. I'm surprised to see a spread of food and drinks on the kitchen island. My stomach immediately growls. I realize I haven't eaten in a day. I gravitate to the food just like everyone else in the room.

When we're all settled, Ryan begins to speak. "Alright, listen up. We're going in with over two hundred men, so we have teams with very specific goals like usual, but we're going in with more than four teams."

Josh clears his throat and puts down his plate as he leans forward. "We're doing a perimeter this time. Yes, I know that we usually do it, but this one is bigger. We're doing a total and complete takedown. The first perimeter will be set about a mile from the house. No one gets in or out. Second will be set a half mile in from that one. The third will be directly around the house like our usual surveillance teams are set."

"Each team has been assigned to a leader. We're all meeting at different locations. Leaders will have the team's assignment and will meet their team in the designated team meeting location. From there, leaders will lead their teams to their assigned locations."

Josh stands and starts handing out papers. I lean into Luke looking at the one he was handed and kiss his shoulder softly. It lists the names of the team leaders and location they're to meet their teams. It also lists their assignments.

Josh leans against the arm of the couch. "You'll see everything is going to be different from how we usually run missions."

"You aren't fucking kidding." Taylor looks up at Ryan. "You want me leading a team? I mean like an actual team? Not like one who just searches? You've never wanted me to do that before."

"I've never needed you to, Taylor. We've never gone in like this before." Ryan sighs and stands. "Look. I know things are not at all like anything we've ever done. But if we expect to succeed against him, this is how we run it."

Josh nods. "Now. We know he has a lot of guys. He wasn't fucking around with that. The reason our perimeter is so large is because he has guys patrolling a larger area. About a fourth mile from the house. We're going in with a lot of men. We're obliterating him and all of his forces this time."

"Because we have so many people, we have these armbands."
Ryan holds up a red armband. "We're going in with black tactical gear and
these armbands on our right arm. If you or your team come across anyone
not wearing an armband or wearing one on the left arm, shoot them. He's
not one of ours."

"We know Jessa is being held in the basement. She was able to
send a text," Josh says. "We don't believe it was intercepted or anything.
We don't think Matthew knows about her phone. But even if he did, Pierce
is doing some CIA shit to make sure she's okay."

"You have me leading a team," Alec says. "I've never done any of
this shit before. I go in and do what needs to be done. I'm not this
organized. I overpower and fuck people up. I don't think this is a good
idea."

Ryan chuckles. "You aren't going in. You can shoot a gun. Your
team's job is to watch our asses. Take out his men that are in the closest
vicinity to the house. You'll be guarding anyone we take out of the house.
Jessa said it's just her and Dallas, but she's only seen the basement."

Alec visibly lets out an obviously relieved breath. "I don't want it
to seem like I can't do this. I just don't run my shit the same as you. And
my sisters are in there. The last thing I want to do is fuck something up."

"You won't," I say reassuringly, sensing he needs it. "Shoot the
guys who aren't wearing red armbands on their right arm. Tell us if anyone
is coming at us."

Alec smiles. "I can handle that."

Ryan smiles. "I know you can. It's why we're trusting you to do it.
Everyone on those perimeters has United States military with them.
They'll do what needs to be done just like anyone else will." He looks at
his paper. "Luke. You're leading Team Five. Your entrance point is door
four. Flip the page, you'll see a map of the house."

"Courtesy of Homeland Security," Josh chuckles.

I can't help but laugh. "You really are every fucking where. US
military. Homeland Security. CIA."

"Damn right I am." Ryan grins as arrogantly as possible.

"Alright. Next. Alex," Josh begins. "You're leading Team Four.
Entrance door is two. Lance. Team Six. Surveillance. Gavin. Team Seven.
You'll be on the half-mile perimeter. Damon. Team Eight. We want you on

the outer perimeter. Your team is the biggest because you have the most area. You have Marines and Army Rangers with you."

Ryan clears his throat. "Taylor. Team Three. Your entrance door is five. Alec. Team Nine. You'll be our eyes on the outside. Surveillance says someone is coming in or out, your job is to protect us. No armband, shoot unless you hear from one of us otherwise. Unlikely, but you never know. Jason. Team Ten. Your door is six. That door is in the back of the house off the kitchen. There's a door that leads directly to the basement from there, but let me make it clear. We clear the house before we go down there. I do not want anyone trapped down there."

Jason nods. "I don't want to waste time. We need that house cleared fast."

Ryan nods. "I agree. But you *do not* go down there until me, Josh, Alex, Nick, Taylor, and Luke get to you. I'm not even close to fucking around. Chances are Matthew is down there. At least that's what surveillance believes. Most of the guards are in the basement. There's a room with four people in it down there. We think that's Matthew. We know two of the others are Jessa and Dallas. We don't know who the other person is. I'm Team One. I'm taking door three. Josh is Team Two. He's taking door one. When we get into the house, we'll break off again. Kill team is me, Josh, Alex, Taylor, Jason and his full team, Luke, and Robby."

I swallow and sit forward. "What about Renza? We know she's there."

"Kill her," Josh says simply.

I look up at him. "It's not that I have any issue doing that after what she tried to do to Arianna, well, the whole fucking family, but don't you think we should talk to her?"

"No. I don't." He shrugs. "She knew what she was doing. She's not a toy under Matthew's control. She fucked up. And now it's time for her to face the consequences."

I nod and lean back. If I'm being honest with myself, I know he's right. But there's a part of me that can't figure out what happened with her. A part of me that has to understand. Maybe it's the part of me that loved the girl once. At least in some way.

"Any questions?" Josh asks.

"Nope. Just want to get this over with," Jason says.

254

"Okay. Then let's go. We head out right now. Meet with your teams. Brief them." Ryan looks down at me as we all start standing. He's rubbing the brown, worn leather bracelet on his wrist. It comforts me more and more. "You're with Luke."

The tightness in my chest is immediately gone. I give him a grateful smile. "Thank you," I whisper.

He gives me a brief hug. "I get it. And I'll always have your back." He pats my shoulder as he pulls away.

"Everyone's gear is in the vehicles already," Josh says. "Earpieces are set to the channel we'll be communicating on. Make sure you're wearing vests. I know I don't need to say that, but I'm going to because it's important. Armbands for your team are with your gear. Wait for our command to get set up in your locations. We're doing this on a schedule. We're going in hard and fast."

Everyone starts piling out and heading for the vehicles. I jump in the passenger seat of ours. I wait for Luke to get in the driver's seat and start to drive before I turn to him. I take his hand in mine and kiss it.

He chuckles. "What was that for?"

"I'm starting to feel like a weight or something lift. I'm getting excited at ending this chapter in our lives and starting a new one. One where Matthew Lucinio doesn't exist."

He runs his thumb over the top of my hand. "I'm just hoping he doesn't know we're coming. The fact that he's appearing to be in the basement scares me."

"Do you think that's why Ryan is surrounding them like he is?"

"I think it has a lot to do with it. We have close to three hundred people. Ryan said over two hundred, but if I counted right, Team Eight is around a hundred people. Team Seven is pretty damn near the same number."

I chuckle. "We're going in with a fucking army, US military aside."

"Did you really expect anything less? I think he learned from the first time they went after him. And the second. The first time, from what he told me, they were outnumbered and outgunned. Ryan vowed never to make that mistake again. The second time, they had the element of surprise, but he still slipped through their fingers."

"Hence the DNA tests on the targets. To make sure."

"Exactly."

We arrive at our meeting location. I'm relieved to see our team has already gotten there. Luke parks. We get out and quickly start handing out armbands and gear. We make sure everyone is wearing their armbands on the correct arm, and that they're all armed and geared up.

After putting our earpieces in, Luke leans against the back of the SUV. "Listen up." His dominant voice carries without raising it. It never ceases to send shivers throughout my whole body. "Our assignment. We're going through door four. That's in the back of the house. It's off the pool. We'll be entering the library of the house. You're wearing the armbands because it's how we're going to tell you apart from the bad guys. Don't lose it. Keep it on your right arm. Shoot anyone who isn't wearing one or wearing it on the wrong arm. Questions so far?"

"Mr. Massena, we're all a little on edge here. We have no information beyond what you're giving us now. All we know is there's a fuck of a lot of men and teams," one of the guards says.

Luke nods. "There's a reason for that. Our target is Matthew Lucinio."

I look around as guards gasp and murmur. I lean over and speak low in Luke's ear. "How the fuck do they not know that?"

"We pulled them in from all over. Ryan and Josh didn't tell them why. Just that they're needed. They'll explain when they get here. The only people who know why they're here is us and the military."

"That explains a fuck of a lot," I mumble.

He kisses my head before turning back to the grumbling guards. "Quiet down!" He waits until all attention is back on him. "Now. I know there are men here from the Lucinio Mafia as well as the Crane Mafia. Other teams have military. I know some of you have an idea of what's happening. Others are in the dark. The gist is Matthew got to Jessa. That's Ryan's brother's wife."

"Mr. Massena, we heard Ryan is dead," another guy says.

Luke nods. "It's part of the plan. It's the only way we could pull this off. Matthew put a hit on him. He thought Ryan and Jason had been killed the night he took Jessa. I assure you, he's alive and well. As is his brother, Jason. His parents... uh... They didn't make it." He pauses as another murmur rushes through the guards.

"So, our mission. It's Matthew Lucinio?" another asks.

"Yes. When we get into the house, our goal is to take out any guards not wearing an armband or wearing it on their left arm. The band is large enough that you can't miss it. When we get into the house, Robby and I will break off. Your mission is upstairs. You'll be joined by Team Five. They will continue to floor three. You will clear floor two. We have intel that Matthew is in the basement. Our mission is twofold. Take out Matthew and his guards. Rescue Jessa and Jessa's sister, Dallas. It's possible there are more girls that Matthew took for a sex trafficking ring he's operating. So, we may be rescuing more than just our two girls."

I clear my throat. "One more thing." I pass around papers. "If you see this girl, she's to be detained. Not killed. We don't know who she is. Her identity has been kept hidden. All teams are getting this same image. This girl was seen with Renza and Matthew recently at a resort. We don't know if she's a prisoner or someone we need to worry about."

"Renza is Matthew's wife," Luke finishes for me. "She's also a target. She's the one responsible for nearly killing Ryan's wife in the fire in Hawaii. I know you all know about that. Does anyone have questions about their responsibility?"

A chorus of 'no sir' echoes throughout the team. Luke tells them our set up point. We all get back into our vehicles and head to our next point. It's a little bit of a hike after we park our vehicles, but it's necessary. We don't want to get too close and risk raising suspicion.

"All teams," Ryan's voice rumbles over the earpieces. "Exterior guards have been eliminated. Team Nine. If anyone approaches the house, it's not us."

"Got it. Team Nine is in position," Alec says.

"That's our cue," Luke whispers. "Team Five. Prep position. Stay low."

I follow Luke to the edge of the property. We stay low in the hedges and lay prone. It's then I see the layout of the property. The image we had to go on was just the house.

"Fuck...," I breathe.

Luke looks at me. "What?"

"The driveway. It goes all the way to the back of the house. The garage is right there."

"Garage is clear," Alex says. "We cleared it on the way in. Our door is on this side of the house."

"That's not it," I say. My chest tightens it. "It's an easy way to surprise us."

"Team Nine has our back, Robby. Anyone comes up the drive, we'll know," Luke whispers.

I nod because I know he's right. But it's an unknown I wasn't prepared for. I don't like unknowns any more or less than anyone else in this family.

Especially ones like this that could cost us our lives.

Chapter Thirty

✕ Luke ✕

I glance at my watch a little nervously. It's getting late. Ryan and Josh never gave us an attack time. I understand the reasoning, but I hate just sitting here twiddling my thumbs. It doesn't help that Robby's nerves are permeating the air and mixing with mine.

He doesn't like that the driveway goes around the house to the back, leading to the garage. The more I stare at it, the more I feel like he's right. It does give anyone an opening. I know we have a lot of people on our side, but I don't like the driveway.

"Son of a bitch," Damon says over our earpieces. "It's her. The girl in the image from the resort. She's heading your way."

I look at Robby. "Luck or not?"

"Guess we'll find out," Robby says.

"Don't stop her," Josh commands. "Let her through."

We wait, holding our breath, until a red Maserati comes flying into the driveway. It pulls around the back of the house and directly into the garage. We wait until we see her come out. Her dark hair flows down her back. She walks with purpose and confidence. Her slender body moves with grace and poise.

"What are we doing with her?" I ask. "We can't let her get in the house. Not if we want to find out who the fuck she is."

"I got her," Alex grunts. He pops up from his hiding place and sprints the few steps to the garage. He hauls her back into the bushes kicking and screaming, but his hand is over her mouth, so the screams can't be heard. At least not to anyone who doesn't have an earpiece.

"I'm on my way to you," Alec says. "I'll keep her in the SUV."

"Ssh… Don't fight it, honey. Just go to sleep," Alex grunts. "Sleep. Good girl." It's silent a few moments later. "She's out. Alec has her."

"Good. There's no movement in the house, so I think you went unnoticed," Josh says. "My contact says it's time to go. He's walking out right now. No one shoot. As soon as he's clear, we go in. He's coming out door four. Let him walk to the garage. Let him drive away. Team Seven. Stop him. He'll be looking for you. He'll tell you where Matthew is. Relay back."

"Yes sir," Gavin responds.

I watch as a guy walks out of the library. He looks around nervously. I will him to keep walking, and not do anything stupid, but I don't get my wish. When he gets to the truck parked outside the garage, he hesitates. He looks around again and turns back towards the house.

Robby sucks in a breath. "What the fuck is he doing?"

"Josh, you're guy is heading back for the house. He's walking slowly. Still by his truck." I watch as he turns back for the truck. "Looks like he's having an inner battle."

"Robby, you got a laser on that rifle?" Ryan asks.

"Always, sir," Robby growls.

"Point it at his chest. Let him see it. He'll know not to attempt to walk back into that house," Ryan commands. Robby does as he's told. The guy looks down at his chest when he sees the red dot aimed at his heart.

"I just sent him a message," Josh says. The guy looks at his phone, then back at the house. I can see the war he's waging in his head. In the end, his fear wins.

But not his fear of us.

"He's walking back to the house," Robby says.

"Drop him," Josh commands.

Robby takes the shot. The guy drops right by his truck, out of sight of the house. It's silent thanks to the silencer on his rifle. "Done. What about the information on Matthew?"

"Last information I got was that he's downstairs with Jessa," Josh says. "I have nothing to indicate he was lying, so that's the information we're going on."

"We were waiting on the informant," Ryan says. "Time to go. Go straight to your door and bust in. On my count. Three… Two… One… Go!"

On Ryan's command, we all rush the house and kick open our doors without hesitation. Usually, the entry team meets at the door. When we're all in position, we get counted down again before we all bust through the door. This time, the hope is that doors busting in at different times, even if it's only seconds, confuses anyone in the house. The element of surprise is a powerful thing.

"Teams, break off!" Josh commands.

I see no one in the library, but I search anyway on the way to our meeting point. My team finishes clearing the room and exit, leaving Robby and I alone. I hear a few pops when someone shoots, but everything is relatively quiet.

Keeping our weapons at the ready, I lead Robby out of the library. Making our way down the hall towards the kitchen doesn't ease my mind at all. I can feel Robby is feeling exactly what I am. Something isn't right.

"It's quiet," Alex says.

"Too fucking quiet," I agree.

"Coming up behind you," he rumbles.

"Why does this seem too easy?" Robby asks.

"Because most of your guards are in the basement," Lance responds.

"What's our count?" Ryan asks.

"We counted fifty-two outside guards," Lance responds. "Thirty seven were taken out by Team Seven. The other twenty-five were taken out by Team Nine. We had thirteen guards in the house. Not counting the basement. You've taken out twelve."

I smell the distinct scent of tobacco sting my nose before I turn the corner. I stop Robby and Alex with a closed fist in the air so they don't keep walking when I stop. I don't have a chance to tell them why before I'm being slammed against the wall.

"Fuck!" I grunt when I hit the hard plaster. The barrel of a rifle pushes against my neck. I use my rifle to push against it and shove him off.

Out of the corner of my eye, I see Robby helping to throw him off, but the fight is on. They guy punches Robby in the face, infuriating me. I slam him against the wall when he comes after me again. Robby recovers quickly and punches the guy in the stomach with so much force, the guy loses his breath.

But he doesn't stop swinging. He connects with my hip and reaches for his gun once more. It's then I notice that he'd also hit Alex. I growl and knee the guy in the groin. Alex uses the butt of his gun to hit him in the back of the neck.

"Oh fuck...," the guy groans as he slumps. He grabs onto me as he sinks to the floor. I shove him as I gasp for air. Robby shoots him between the eyes.

I watch the blood pour from the bullet hole as I rub my neck. "Fuck."

Robby is instantly at my side looking over the injury. "Are you okay?" He moves my hand and runs his thumb lightly across what I'm sure is a bruise already forming.

I smile at the tenderness and kiss his head softly. "I'm okay. Are you? I saw him hit you."

"Got me in the shoulder. His elbow hit my face. I'm okay. Just knocked me back." He leans in and kisses my neck before pulling back. "Scared the fuck out of me. His rifle against your neck."

I can feel his hand trembling against my arm. I take his hand in mine and look at Alex. "You okay? Looked like he got you, too."

"Elbowed me in the mouth." He runs his thumb across his lip, wiping off the blood. "I'm okay."

"Coming up on you now," Josh says as he, Ryan and Taylor run to us.

"You okay?" Ryan asks. He tilts my head to look at my neck. "Fuck."

"I'm fine," I say. "Nothing broken. It's sore, but I've had worse. Robby's bitten me harder." I wink at him with a smile.

He blushes a furious shade of red. "Luke..."

262

Ryan laughs as he looks down at the guard on the floor. "Thirteen guards down. Tell me what we got, Lance."

"No more in the house that we've been able to see. Everyone is in the basement. If I had to guess, I'd say fifteen, but I can't be sure, man," Lance says. "I can only see heat signatures. There's a few larger ones that look like possibly two guys. I don't know, man. I'm saying fifteen for sure, but there could be more."

"You guys need to hurry up," Jason whispers. "We've been completely silent, but they're making fucking plans to storm us. I have ten guys. Get us more."

"On the way," Taylor says. "Team Three. On me. Kitchen. We're going to overpower these fuckers with sheer force."

Ryan takes the lead. We follow him to the kitchen. Taylor's team shows up moments later. Jason points to the door. Ryan leans closer as he listens. Suddenly, he backs away.

"Back up. Get down. Take cover where you can," he whispers in the earpieces.

"Looks like they're storming up the stairs," Lance says.

I pull Robby behind the kitchen island. We kneel next to each other. The other's quickly get down and hide where they can. We aim towards the door and wait.

"Let them come out," Josh whispers. "Start taking them before they leave the kitchen."

"Yes, sir," one of the guards say.

A few moments later, the door to the basement creeps open. Very slowly, Matthew's men start quietly making their way out. They all have their guns raised and are looking around for us. But we're all hidden well. The one thing I can say for Matthew is the guy has an immaculate kitchen. Not only does he have the island, but he's also got a bar, and a nice little lower bar that I'm thinking serves as a breakfast table.

Silently, I move to the other side of the bar closest to the kitchen's exit into the house. Just as two of them reach the door, Taylor and I both shoot. They both fall into a heap on top of each other. I duck back behind the solid wood of the kitchen island, just as one of them take a shot. It splinters the wood near me.

I hear a few other shots before I sneak around the island again. More shots ring out around me, but I'm zoned. I pop up enough to drop another guy and the one next to him. Looking around, I see no one else.

"How many didn't come up?" Josh asks quietly, not wanting to alert anyone who may still be on the stairs that we can't see.

"Three," Lance says. "Four people are still in the room at the bottom of the stairs."

"Location of the three," Ryan commands.

"Two on the stairs. One of them is a little over halfway up. The other one is near the bottom. Last guard is near the door of the room."

"All teams," Josh says. "Be on guard. Kill team is going down."

I take a deep breath and reach for Robby's hand. I look back at him a moment. The gesture is meant to calm my nerves, but I think it serves to calm his just as much. He squeezes my hand before we both let go.

I watch Ryan closely as he crouches. Staying low and using the wall and door frame for cover, he peeks around the corner. He quickly moves back when one of them shoots. The bullet pings off the wall at the top of the stairs.

I can't help but chuckle. "Missed!" I call out.

"Come down here then!" the guy calls back.

I laugh. "You don't want that. How about you just put down your gun like a good boy and make it easy for us?"

"Not a fucking chance."

Ryan laughs. "Don't say you weren't warned." He moves quickly. Using his Glock, he lays down cover fire. Josh crouches as he moves. He aims down the stairs. After he shoots, I hear a thunk followed by a few more. Almost like someone is falling down the stairs.

"Fuck!" someone else. "Would you fucking shoot them?"

"Second warning!" Ryan growls. "Just give up. You're going to die anyway."

"No chance of that happening, Crane! But if you want to try and come down those stairs, I'll gladly put you out of your misery!"

"Fair enough. But don't say I didn't ask nice!" Ryan drops to the ground and peeks around the corner, quickly moving back as more shots ring out. "Stair three. Crouched. Using the stairs for his cover," he whispers.

I chuckle. "You're up, Robby."

"My favorite kind of shot. The hard ones," he drawls.

I watch as Robby jumps up on the counter of the kitchen island. I swear to fuck. He could be the next Chris Kyle if he wanted to be. He's a hell of a shot. Give him a high powered sniper rifle, he'd end any war we're ever in within a matter of seconds. I don't know how the hell he got so good, but I don't question it. He's saved my ass more times than I care to admit. Fuck. He's saved everyone's ass on more than one occasion.

I grin when he lays down prone on the counter. It's an added bonus that he's hotter than the devil himself. And it doesn't matter his nerves. When he's getting ready to pull the trigger, he never misses. I don't know why the fuck I find that so sexy. It should be scary as hell.

As Robby settles and sets his sights, I can't take my eyes off him. He's calm. His muscles are coiled, but not tense. He's relaxed but not lax. He's fucking perfect. I have to tear my eyes away before I embarrass myself.

"Sights are set," he whispers.

"Take them both," Josh rumbles.

"You got it, bro." Robby inches and angles himself so that he can see whatever he needs to but not be seen. I grin because the fuckers downstairs have no idea what's about to hit them. Quite literally. "Taking out target two by the door. Just because I want to scare this fucker."

"You have way too much fun with this," Taylor jokes.

I can feel Robby's smirk. I don't need to see it. I swear I hear him laugh when he pulls the trigger. There's a thunk followed by a scream that has all of us snorting back laughter. I'd love to see the expression on the guy's face when he sees his buddy hit the ground.

"Uh oh," Robby says. "Nice try, but I don't think you're going to get that shot off." He takes his second shot with a chuckle. "Targets down. I don't see anyone else down there."

"Only people down there are the four in the room. I don't see any other heat signatures other than the two Robby took out and the one that fell down the stairs," Lance confirms.

"Okay. Time to go to work," Alex says.

We all stand and ready our weapons. Ryan goes first, followed by Josh. Alex is right behind him. Jason follows Alex. I nudge Robby ahead of me so he follows Taylor down. I'm unwilling to let him out of my sight for a second. This way, I know he'll have both his front and back watched. Our guards start following me down the stairs.

When we all get down there, leaving a few guards at the top of the stairs, I breathe my first relieved sigh. No other guards are here. The basement is wide open, save for one room. We all plaster ourselves against the wall.

"How do you want to go in?" Josh whispers.

"We kick the door. I want Robby and Taylor to go in first. They're both the best shots with the most control," Ryan whispers back.

I suck in a breath as I look at Robby next to me. He smiles and kisses me softly before moving next to Ryan. Taylor stands next to Josh.

I tell myself over and over again that we have a good team. We'll get through this. We'll take out Matthew this time.

But what's behind that door scares me. There are so many unknowns. I don't know what we're going to see. I don't know what's going to happen.

What scares me the most, though, is that I don't know if Jessa and Dallas are okay.

I do know that if they aren't, Matthew will have to face Jason.

Chapter Thirty One

⚔ Robby ⚔

I've never been one to get nervous on missions. I'm usually very calm. Cool. Collected. Being without Luke on the last one caused me to be slightly anxious. And I understand why now, even though I really didn't get it before. With Luke here now, I'm far more calm.

But I'm beyond anxious. I don't know what we're going to walk into, and it terrifies me beyond belief. I'm scared of the condition we're going to find the girls.

I take a breath, and put it all aside. When we go through that door, it's game on. There can be no hesitation. No fear. I have to choke it all down and do the job we came here for. Take out Matthew. Anything that comes after that can be dealt with as it comes.

"You need to move," Lance says over our earpieces. "It looks like two people have taken the other two hostage. I'm sorry I can't give you who or what's going on. It's just heat signatures."

"It's okay," Ryan whispers.

He uses his fingers to count Josh down. Taylor and I get into position. When Ryan closes his fist, the two kick in the door. Taylor enters first. I follow. Both of us stay low just in case they start to shoot, but neither of us are prepared for what we see.

"Drop it!" I yell, pointing my rifle right between Renza's eyes. Ryan and Josh come in right after us, followed by Jason.

"Fuck…," Jason murmurs, his gun leveled at a smiling Matthew. "Just fucking let her go."

"Aww… Mr. Jason Crane." Matthew gives us all a sickening smile, though he seems a little confused to see him and Ryan alive. "So nice to see you again. Alive." He keeps his gun against Jessa's temple and levels a glare at Ryan. "I see you've taken out my guards."

"Did you think I'd come in here with puppies and fucking glitter? Let my sister go," Ryan growls.

"Where's my son?" Matthew asks.

"He's got the perfect shot," Nick says from the other side of the room. "Drop the gun."

Matthew laughs. "No thank you. If you shoot me, I shoot her. So, what's going to happen is you're all going to walk away. We're going to walk out of here. And we'll call you with the location of Jessa and her sexy little sister. Can't promise they'll be alive."

"Not going to happen," I say, keeping my gun trained on Renza. Dallas is in tears. She looks like she's been drug through the mud. Her clothes are torn. I can see scratches and bruises. But there's something else. I can't figure it out.

"I thought you'd say that," Matthew says. "So, I took out an insurance policy."

The calm tone of his voice makes me immediately nervous, but it's Renza's maniacal laugh that actually has my heart racing. I look carefully between the two of them. Jessa's clothes are just as ripped up as Dallas's. She's also scratched and bruised, but there's also something off about her.

"What the fuck is wrong with you?" I ask Renza. I need to keep them talking until I figure out what's going on. What it is I'm not seeing.

"Me? Nothing is wrong with me, baby," she drawls. Her calling me baby makes bile rise from my stomach.

"Why are you with him? Why betray your best friend and marry the man you know is causing her torment?" I ask. But my eyes aren't on her. They're looking Dallas up and down. Every inch of her is being carefully dissected.

"Because Matthew offered me the life I've always wanted. The life I deserve to have. Luxury. Power. He's given me everything you couldn't. I mean, just look at him." Renza glances at him with an adoring smile before focusing back on me. The gun in her hand stays nestled against Dallas's head. "Look how hot he is. How in control he is. So many guns pointed at him, but he's facing you all down. The bravery he exudes. And the love for me. Using these two bitches to get us out of here so he can be with me."

Ryan laughs. "You think he wants you? Why the fuck do you think he stayed instead of running? Why do you think he took Jessa in the first place?"

Renza's eyes flick to him. The gun shakes slightly before she glares. "He has plans. I trust my husband knows what he's doing."

"You were always destined to be just a side piece, Renz," I say with a chuckle. "So blinded by the flash of the money and power, but Matthew never fucking loved you. Did you, Matthew?"

"Shut-up!" Renza screams at me. She tugs Dallas's hair.

"Ah!" Dallas screams. But she doesn't move to stop her. She just cries and clenches her fists at her sides.

I glance at Ryan. I know instinctively that he can see it, too. Looking at the faces of all of our guys, I know they all do. The question is what exactly it is. Something is wrong. Very, very wrong. I don't like it.

"Drop the guns, or they both die," Matthew says deathly calmly.

"Not going to happen," Josh says. "What's your play here, Matthew?"

Matthew laughs. "Not dad? I'm fucking hurt."

"You were never a father to us," Alex growls dangerously.

"You were a disappointment. Just like your brother," Matthew says. He looks at Nick. "Both of your brothers."

"So, let's get this straight… Dad…" Nick growls viciously and venomously when he says the word 'dad.' It makes me chuckle. "You want Jessa because she reminds you of my mother, the love of your fucking life. Even though you killed her."

"Fuck you, boy. I didn't kill her. I never gave those fucking orders. I loved Aubrey. I always will." Something like regret passes over Matthew's face. "My father gave the orders to kill her."

"So, you decided Jessa is a good replacement." Josh's voice drips just as much darkness as I feel. Probably as much as everyone in this room feels.

"The resemblance is uncanny, isn't it?" Matthew brushes his lips against Jessa's neck. She whimpers and tries to turn away. He tugs her hair, then licks her neck. Jessa cries.

"You son of a bitch," Jason growls as he makes a move for her. Ryan stops him as Matthew's gun digs into Jessa's temple. His eyes bore coldly into all of ours.

But I'm watching Renza. I see the way she looks at him. The way she bites her lip. The anger that flashes in her eyes. The hurt. And being the asshole that I am when it comes to her, I plan to exploit every single bit of it. I see the weak link in this entire thing.

It's her.

"You know, Renz. He doesn't love you," I say softly. I lace my voice with the kindness and love I used to show her. Even though it twists my stomach in knots and makes me want to throw up. She looks at me. I smile softly. "Not like I did."

She watches me. I watch her hand tremble just a little. She sniffles. "No. You're wrong." She tries to say that with hatred. But her voice gives her away.

I feel Luke's eyes on me, but I don't look at him. I know he trusts me. I keep my eyes trained on Renza. I let them soften. "I'm not. You know it."

"Oh please. What can you offer her, little boy?" Matthew spits. "She knows you're fucking Ryan's second."

I ignore him, staying focused on Renza. "Maybe. But you also know how good it was with me, Renz. You know I can offer you so much more than what he does. I wouldn't treat you like a toy. You'd have everything with me and more."

Matthew laughs. "Come on. She knows better than that."

Renza chews on her lip. I can see the fear she's trying to hide. Deep within the cool depths. "He does love me," she whispers.

I shake my head slowly, keeping my soft smile in place. "He doesn't. You know he doesn't. You know he's using you. He wants Jessa. He's fucking obsessed with her. But what does she have that you don't? Huh?"

"Renz, come on, baby. Don't listen to him. He's just fucking with your head," Matthew growls.

"Renza," I whisper, holding her eyes. "Put the gun down, baby. Let her go."

Her hand trembles. I know I'm getting to her. Deep down, she knows I'm right. Her eyes fill with tears. "Robby…"

"Come on, honey," I say softly. "Let her go. She has nothing to do with this. You know Matthew has plans for her. Plans that involve his sick fantasies. Not you. He doesn't want you. Not like I do. I'm the one who loves you. I always have. Luke is nothing to me. Just a fun distraction, baby. Come on."

"Enough!" Matthew bellows. Renza jumps and flinches. "Drop that gun, and I'll kill you like the fucking worthless bitch you are."

The tears that threatened to fall moments ago start spilling from Renza's eyes. I feel bad for her for a split second. Until she pushes Dallas to the ground with a scream and spins to Jessa. "I hate you! You've ruined everything!" She points her gun at Jessa, but she just did exactly what I wanted her to. She gave me a shot.

I pull the trigger, dropping Renza just as Matthew shoves her away from them. Renza pulls the trigger on her way down, hitting Matthew in the shoulder. Jessa screams and falls from Matthew's grip to the floor.

Matthew roars. "Fucking whore!" He aims at Renza and starts shooting.

Shots ring out around me. Matthew's body is riddled with bullets. I watch it all unfold in slow motion. Like a bad fucking movie. His body jerks with each hit. Blood sprays from his body and splatters all over the floor and walls behind and around him. He finally falls down to the floor choking on his own blood.

Dallas and Jessa are both screaming on the floor. They're covering their ears, but instead of curling into a ball like I would expect, they're trembling on their sides where they fell. It looks like they're terrified to move even a millimeter.

I watch as Jason runs for Jessa. He drops to his knees next to her. "Jessa!"

"Stop!" she screeches, holding up her hand as she covers her head with the other.

Jason freezes. "What? Baby, what's happening?"

"Stop!" she cries. "Don't. Don't come closer! You all have to get out of here!"

"Jessa, what the fuck?" Jason trembles, fighting himself to pull her into his arms. Josh kneels next to Dallas.

"Don't!" Dallas shrieks, holding her hand up against his chest and physically pushing him back. Her shirt moves up her stomach.

And I see it.

"Holy shit...," I say, dropping to my knees and feeling instantly sick to my stomach. "She's wired."

Jessa and Dallas both cry harder. Ryan kneels down next to Jason. He very lightly lifts her shirt. I watch him. My chest constricts so tightly, I can't breathe. Sure as shit, Jessa is also wired. Everything suddenly makes sense.

"Fucking shit," Nick chokes out. "That's why he was so fucking cocky. He knew we wouldn't allow him to hurt them. He just didn't get the chance to show the fucking ace up his sleeve."

"I'm fucking sorry, Jess," I say over the sob caught in my throat. "If... I hadn't played Renza against him." The damn breaks. I drop my head in my hands. "Fuck, it's my fault."

"Robby, no. Fucking no. You're a genius. Playing Renza like that." Luke wraps his arms around me. He pulls me into his chest.

I shake my head. "This is my fucking fault." My heart feels like it's being ripped out of my chest. I shake uncontrollably as I cry into Luke's chest. "I knew something wasn't right."

"Robby, fuck. We all felt it," Luke whispers in my ear. "This isn't your fault. It's Matthew fucking Lucinio's. No one else's."

"I'll video call Reed," Taylor says over a hard swallow. He takes out his phone. I shakily look up at him. "I have bomb experience, but not anything like him."

"Hey, Lieutenant," Reed says. "What's up? You get the fucker?"

"Yeah. Reed, listen. We have a problem," Taylor turns the phone to Dallas and Jessa.

"What the fuck am I looking at, boss?" I can hear the fear in Reed's voice. It's the same that's coursing through my veins.

"They're wired, Reed. I fucking don't know how to disarm it," he whispers. "I've never dealt with anything like this in training. It wasn't as extensive as yours."

272

"Is it a vest? I need to see it, Taylor."

My eyes grow wide. "Taylor…"

He nods. "They're afraid to let us touch them," he says as calmly as he can. "They're afraid it will detonate."

"It won't, Lieutenant. I need to see it. You need to cut their shirts off. Don't pull it up. When we get to the point of taking it off, the shirt needs to be gone anyway. Be fucking careful you don't cut the wires."

Taylor only nods as he slowly kneels down to Jessa. He and Josh both take a knife out. Luke and I hesitantly make our way to Dallas.

"Did I just hear what I think I did?" Alec asks. His voice cracks.

"Hold your position, Cassidy," Ryan demands. "We'll take care of her."

"Fuck you, Crane. That's my fucking sister! I'm coming in!"

"No. You aren't. All teams," he says calmly, never taking his eyes off Jessa. "Evacuate the house. Keep Cassidy out."

I hear Alec screaming obscenities as he's obviously forcefully kept away from the house. The only people who remain are the family. Nick kneels between Jessa and Dallas with Alex. There's no way any of us would walk away right now.

"God fucking damn you, Crane! I'm going to fucking kill you when I get my hands on you!" Alec threatens.

"I don't need more distractions, Cassidy," Ryan growls. "Trust us to do our fucking job!"

Alec continues ranting. Ryan pulls out his earpiece. We all follow. We need to concentrate on what's going on in front of us. That's the most important thing.

Taylor starts cutting Jessa's shirt carefully as she whimpers and cries. Josh slowly moves closer to Dallas. She looks at him wide-eyed and terrified. She squeaks as she sobs, but she's too afraid to move.

"Dallas," he says low and dominantly, but still somehow managing to come off calm and soothing. She tearfully looks up at him as she trembles. "You need to trust me. I'm not going to hurt you. I promise. I need to cut your shirt off. Okay? Can you trust me?"

She watches him but slowly nods. "Y-yes."

"Good girl. I will *not* let anything bad happen to you. I promise." He leans forward to start the cut, but stops when she holds up her pinkie.

Her hand violently shakes, but she bravely holds it up anyway. Josh links his pinkie with hers and gives her a genuine smile. "Pinkie promise."

She smiles a watery smile. "You can't break a pinkie promise," she whispers.

"Never." He gives her a reassuring smile. He speaks soothingly to keep her calm. "My best friend, Lyric, once told me the same thing. She said pinkie promises are sacred. And she'll tell you I've never broken a single one." He holds her pinkie a moment longer before letting it go. He slowly starts to cut the shirt.

I hold my breath and watch, though I want to turn away. I take Luke's hand in mine and squeeze tightly. So many visions are running through my mind that I find myself trembling just like them. I pray to a God I don't know if I believe in to save them. To save us all.

"Shirt is cut," Taylor says. "What next?"

"Show me," Reed says.

"Taylor, here. Give me the phone," Nick says. Taylor does. Nick focuses on the bomb strapped to Jessa's chest.

"Show me the back," Reed commands.

Jessa shrieks. "No! What if it goes off?" She cries, but tries to keep her breathing steady.

"Jessa. Honey, it won't. It would have already," Reed says. "Trust me. I disarm bombs all the time."

Jessa cries but lets Taylor help her sit up slowly. "Please, please don't let it go off."

"I promise, Jessa," Reed says confidently. I can feel the shift in the entire room. We all take a relieved breath and trust him. Nick shows him the back of the vest. "Okay. Good. There's a detonator somewhere. It's probably a phone."

"H-he... in... h-his pocket...," Dallas says softly.

I spring up and start checking Matthew's pockets. I find two phones. "I have two, Reed." I hold them both up as Nick turns the phone.

"It's the Nokia. Don't touch any buttons on it. Go back to, Jessa, Sarge," Reed commands. Nick obeys. "Do you see any kind of a timer? Anything like that?"

Taylor looks her over. "Just wires attached to TNT sticks."

I stay right where I am, watching everything unfold. I hold both phones like they could explode at any time. Truth be told, they probably could. It makes me breathe so fucking shallow, I'm not sure I'm breathing at all.

"They have to start somewhere," Reed says. "Get me closer. Full view. Front. Back. Sides. I need to see where the wires are coming from."

"You got it." Nick slowly moves the phone around a trembling Jessa. Josh watches him, but makes no move to touch Dallas.

"There!" Reed says. "Stop. See that? On her left side."

"Got it," Taylor says.

"Do you want me to follow your commands with her?" Josh asks. "We have two girls with the vests."

"Don't you dare, Lucinio. Hers could be different, or they could be connected to each other," Reed says.

Josh takes Dallas' hand when she whimpers. "It's okay, honey," he whispers, soothingly. He keeps speaking low with her to keep her calm and distracted. He tells her about Alec outside, waiting like a prince to come in and rescue her. He tells her an adorable story about how Lyric called him Goliath for weeks after they first met.

"Taylor. Carefully, open that flap. It's velcro," Reed says. Taylor obeys. I hold my breath. "Okay. Good. The red wire. Cut it."

Taylor looks at us all. I can tell he's not breathing. None of us fucking are. "Fuck," Taylor whispers as he slowly takes the wire between his fingers. I can see his hands are shaking. The most confident of men are in this room. Not a single one isn't shaking.

"Trust me, Lieutenant," Reed says. "See how that's the only one not covered? Don't cut any of the wires that are covered. Just that one."

"Fuck," Taylor breathes. He takes a breath and cuts it.

I look down at the beep in my hand. The Nokia phone in my hand suddenly has a timer. "Uh… Reed? This phone is counting down."

"Move the phone to Dallas. Hurry up!" Reed commands. I don't know how the fuck he sounds so confident. All of us are starting to panic.

"There," Nick says as he moves quickly next to Josh.

Dallas very visibly squeezes Josh's hand as she trembles. Luke looks at me wide-eyed before hurrying to my side. He wraps me in his arms. I know the move is symbolic. If we all die, at least we'll go together.

"Josh, sit her up. Slowly. What's my time, Robby?"

"Two minutes," I say far more calmly than I feel. My heart is fucking racing.

Alex helps Josh slowly sit her up. "Trust me, honey." Josh doesn't break eye contact with her.

"You pinkie promised," she whispers.

He gives her a smile that drips with all the sweetness he can muster. "They can't be broken."

"One minute-thirty seconds," I crack.

"Show me all around, Sarge," Reed says. Nick does as commanded. "You need to stop shaking, man. Trust me. I won't let it go off. The two are connected. I was counting on that. One gets cut, the other will start going. Stop! Her right side. Open the flap. Slow."

Josh quickly straddles Dallas and leans to her right side. He slowly opens the flap. "Red. Green. Blue. Yellow. Black."

"One minute," I say nervously. My eyes want to move from the timer, but they won't.

"Listen to me carefully. Red. Cut it. You need to be fast. You hesitate, we'll be in trouble," Reed says.

Josh nods. He cuts the red wire. "Cut."

"Fuck!" My eyes widen as the timer starts counting down faster. "It's going fast!"

"Blue! Now!" Reed commands.

Josh cuts it. "Cut."

"Going faster!" I croak. "Ten seconds!"

"Black!" Reed says.

Josh cuts the black wire. "Cut!"

I fall against Luke as the timer stops. "Fucking hell. Fuck…" I gulp in air. Deep breath after deep breath. "Holy fucking hell." I drop the phone and bury my face in Luke's neck. "Fucking less than a second."

"Is… Is it over…?" Dallas whispers. I look over at her, praying like hell Reed says it is. "A-am I dead?" Her eyes are squeezed tightly shut.

"It's over," Reed says. "It's disarmed. You can take the vests off."

"Shit…," Ryan says. "Holy shit." He rubs his chest like everyone in the fucking room is.

Jason carefully removes the vest from Jessa. Josh does the same. Both of them hand the vest off to the closest person and pull the girls in their arms. I continue taking deep breaths as Luke rubs my back.

"What do we do with the vests?" Taylor asks.

"Leave them, Lieutenant. They'll make a really pretty show when you burn that fucking house to the ground," Reed answers.

"Not a bad fucking idea." I stand slowly. Luke follows. Jason stands with Jessa. He picks her up in his arms. She presses against his chest. It's only then I realize that she's not wearing anything up top. She's completely exposed. "Jesus. How the fuck does that fucker put that vest over them without a shirt? That had to fucking hurt. Rubbing against them."

"I don't think he cared," Josh growls as he does the same with Dallas. He carefully tucks her against his chest, effectively hiding her exposed tits so they aren't seen. She cries into his neck as she holds him tightly. "I got you, honey. You're okay. We'll have you back with your brother in no time. You're safe now."

After he takes DNA samples, Luke takes my hand and kisses it sweetly as we follow everyone else out of the house. I don't think anyone truly breathes until we reach the dark night air.. Suddenly, the freshness of the blackness surrounding us seems like the most important thing in the fucking world. We all breathe deeply.

"Dallas!" Alec yells, breaking free of the guards holding him. He runs full speed at us, crashing into Josh. He hugs both of them as he buries his face in her hair. "Fuck. I'm so fucking sorry. I'm so, so fucking sorry." He breaks down in gut-wrenching sobs.

"It's not your fault," she whispers as she melts into his arms. He tucks her into his chest. Her hand keeps hold of Josh, unwilling to release him. Josh whispers something in her ear. She shakily turns to Alec and wraps her arms around him. Josh lets her go so Alec can pull her more fully into his arms. He hugs her so tightly, I question if he might break her.

I smile a little when I see Josh hand his gun to a guard. He takes his vest off and hands it to another. Tyler starts to wrap his arms around Alec and Dallas, but stops when he hears the warning growl Josh gives him.

"Well, that was…" Luke looks down at me then back at Josh. "Not fucking Josh. That's what that was."

I smile a little bigger, gripping Luke. Josh takes his shirt off and hides Dallas from everyone while he helps her get it on with Alec holding her. When she's covered, he lets Tyler join Alec and hug her. I join in with the family and hug Jessa, who is now wearing Jason's shirt. We all tremble a little, grateful we're all alive.

"Douse the whole thing in gasoline," I hear Josh say to some guards. I look up at him when he joins in our family hug. The guards nod and do as they're told.

I take a deep breath and turn to Luke. "I don't want to wait. When we get home, Ryan is performing the ceremony. I want to marry you now."

Luke's grin spreads like wildfire across his face. He crushes his lips to mine, kissing me so deeply my head spins. The ground beneath me fades to nothing. Luke's arms around me and tongue tangoing with mine is all I feel.

I don't know how long the kiss lasts, but I slowly come back to Earth when I feel intense heat against my back. Luke slowly pulls away. His beautiful eyes reflect the light from the fire behind us. I turn in his arms and lean against his chest. His arms lock around me.

As promised, the TNT makes a pretty show. As the fire ignites it, what could be mistaken as a firework shoots up from the flames. It causes a nice explosion and sparks that crackle in the air. Alex and Josh watch the house collapse in a heap of flame and sparks. They both have the same expression on their face.

Peaceful. Content. Like the past is finally put behind them. I glance at everyone else and notice that everyone looks the same way.

For the first time in many months, my family will be able to move forward. Live the future we all fucking deserve.

While I don't doubt there will always be threats, it comes with the territory after all, at least we'll never have to deal with the likes of Matthew Lucinio ever again. With him out of our lives, the time for healing from the devastation he's caused is now. We can finally grieve for all he's taken from us.

But what's more... I smile as I look at my family. What's more is that we can finally appreciate all we've gained.

Epilogue

✗ Luke ✗

Looking into the deep depths of Robby's beautiful eyes as I sway with him to the soft music in Ryan's backyard might just be everything I've ever wanted in life. He's my husband now. By law and heart. He's mine. All mine.

As I bury my face in his neck, I can't help but think of what it took for us to get here. The events that took place throughout the Crane's family history is a sacrifice I'll never be able to fully grasp or repay. But I appreciate it. All of it.

The loss of Ethan and Jenny is felt so deeply in my soul every time I look at the Crane brothers. My brothers. Their pain is worn on their sleeves as they all try to move on and live. It's hard not to feel it. Even if I wasn't as close to this family as I am, I'd still feel it. It's all around us in all we do.

Though our DNA test proved Matthew is gone for real, the true devastation he caused will forever be imprinted on our souls. It's touched us all in different ways. He's left his mark. And it's fucking deep.

It hasn't stopped us from clinging to what we have, though. We've taken comfort in our family. We've spent the past couple of weeks doing nothing but spending time together. It's what we've all needed. Just to be close to each other.

Kent and Rebekkah are inseparable. I smile at them as I hold my husband close. They're looking as adoringly at each other as I am to Robby. I kiss his neck and run my fingers through his hair as I smile and look once more into his eyes.

"I'm glad we did this now," I say, my voice clogged with more emotion than I know what to do with.

He smiles softly as he looks around at our family. "We needed time to regroup. Grieve our losses and appreciate what we have." He looks back at me and leans in. He kisses me just as softly as he's smiling. I deepen it with a low moan before pulling away slowly and holding him close.

Jessa and Jason have slowly started to recover from the terrifying experience of Jessa's harrowing ordeal. Today was the first day the two of them did any kind of work related to Crane Industries, but they didn't leave each other's side for a single second. Jason has become far more protective of her than I ever knew he had in him. Then again, I never knew the guy could shoot someone in cold blood and not fucking flinch.

Chase, Breetana, and Lyric have turned out to be the rocks we've all needed. For days after our battle and rescue mission, the three of them ran the household. They made sure we were all fed. They made us all go to bed when they thought we were supposed to. If not for them, I think we all would have completely fallen apart. Chase even arranged our move back to our complex. By the time we all got back from Cozumel, they all had made sure the complex was safe and ready for our return.

Taylor and Nicole spent the entire first few days locked in each other's arms. Where one went, the other followed. Nicole's unmatched maternal instinct kicked in, and she made absolutely certain that the kids were cared for while everyone else was too exhausted. Though, it wasn't often any of the kids were out of their parent's sight.

Arianna forced Ryan to take a break from everything that has to do with the Crane Mafia. I've never seen anyone be able to bring Ryan to his knees, but Arianna doesn't seem to have any issues at all with it. While everything with his empire moved on flawlessly while he recouped and spent time with his wife and child as well as all of us, Ryan is back where he belongs. At the helm of his vastly large kingdom. The King of the Crane Mafia doesn't seem to have missed a step.

Dani was and still is Nick's calming force. She's what grounds him and keeps him from becoming so angry at what happened to his parents and his adopted parents that he becomes engulfed by the darkness that is always just on the edge of his mind. The evil that he feels inside himself and is terrified will drag him back down the dark hole he worked so hard to claw his way out of. He's just as much her support system. He's the one who keeps her from breaking. Learning who her father was and what he did, has been something she's had a difficult time recovering from. Losing her sister after learning who she was and all of the treachery she caused has also had an effect she doesn't know how to deal with.

Lyric struggled a lot when we first returned. Her submissive nature had her hovering and trying to take care of not just Josh, but of us all. She helped Chase and Bree when they were looking after us, but she went a level higher in making sure that they were looking after themselves, too. So much so that her own health suffered. She rarely ate or slept. It didn't take long for Josh to pick up on it once he had gotten a good night's sleep. He took control and got her back into a routine. One I know she will follow once she is home.

Josh and Alex are flying back to Gainesville with her in a couple days for a business meeting. They will return a few days after that. I know they plan to check out her apartment. Josh hasn't seen it, but her brother, Luca, let slip to Josh that he didn't think it was up to code. I have no doubt that they will make sure she has everything she needs. And if they don't like her apartment, they'll find her somewhere better and safer. I'll admit it. I'll miss her when she leaves, but we've already made plans to visit later in the year, and she'll be back to visit Jaxon's garden on the anniversary.

Until tonight, I haven't seen Dallas since Alec took her home, but Josh said she's doing well. He's struck one hell of a strong friendship with the leader of Chicago's most notorious Motorcycle Crew. Tyler's sister was returned to him safely. As was every other girl taken by Matthew from the Viper's Venom.

Alex and I sat down with the girl who showed up at Matthew's house in Cozumel. The girl we couldn't identify from our surveillance at the resort. She gave us absolutely no information other than her name and her relationship to Matthew. Apparently, Raleigh Jennings is Matthew's daughter. At least according to her. Lance and I have been spending a lot of time researching it. They don't share blood.

It shouldn't surprise us, really. Matthew didn't like to do things legally. Raleigh was homeschooled, grew up in a very nice home with a loving nanny and father who she claims doted on her whenever he was home. She always had everything she needed and wanted. She told us she was raised right.

It's pretty obvious that while the rest of us may believe her, Alex absolutely does not. And because they can't find any family, he refuses to allow her out of his sight. He's suspicious of her, though, so I doubt he'd let her out of his sight even if we had been able to figure out who she was and where she came from. Even with DNA we have yet to find her real parents.

Robby and I chose today to marry because it's given us all time to come down and adjust to things after all that happened. We were able to truly mourn our losses and it gave us the opportunity to spend time with Lyric and Josh as they remembered the child they lost.

Truthfully, I think this was what we all needed. A happy moment in our lives to truly end the shit we've all been through over the past few years. Something to put it all behind us and start fresh. Something new and bright to bury the darkness we've emerged from.

I smile at the thought and lean into Robby. I kiss him as I pull him close. I wrap my arms tightly around him. I pull back slowly from the kiss. I know just how I want our brighter days to begin.

I push his hair back out of his eyes. "What do you say we leave these guys out here to celebrate, and we take this somewhere more out of the way of prying eyes."

He grins. "I thought you'd never ask." He reaches down and uses me to hide himself as he adjusts himself.

I grab his wrist and step closer. "You aren't going to need to hide that." My husky tone makes his eyes darken and a visible shiver travel down his spine.

He licks his lips with a low moan. "Hurry."

It's all the words I need to pull him into the house in search of the closest room with a door. I reach down and adjust my own cock. But only because it's painful as fuck pushing against the unforgiving fabric of my jeans.

I ignore all the cheers and teasing as I tug Robby into the bathroom. "I can't make it any further."

We tear at each other's clothing. We toss shirts and don't bother stepping out of our jeans or underwear. I lift him on the bathroom counter, tug him to the edge, and sink deep into his ass with a groan as he grips the counter clenching around my dick with moans of his own.

I trail a hand up to his neck as I thrust. I don't squeeze, but I know Robby. He loves when I take control of him like this. I drop my other hand to his throbbing cock as he leans back and stroke firmly to the pace of my punishing thrusts. Hard, deep, and fast. It's what we both need right now.

"Oh... fuck..., Luke." He slams his ass against my dick and clenches around me with each and every thrust.

We both moan and pant as a thin sheen of sweat starts to slick our skin. The fast pace I've set is doing exactly what I wanted. Relieving the pressure we've built up the entire night dancing with each other in such close proximity that not rubbing against each other was impossible. The friction built up made me want to explode.

Which is exactly what I'm going to do in mere seconds. I keep stroking his dick as I pound hard into his ass. My dick swells with my insatiable need for him, but the possessive asshole in me loves the fact that he's just as thick for me.

"Luke. Fuck! I'm gonna come!"

I move my hand from his neck to his mouth and push into him again and again. "Come for me," I growl against his neck while I bury myself deep inside him and continue stroking his dick.

With a roar that could wake the dead if my hand wasn't over his mouth, Robby drops his head back against the mirror. "Luke!"

"Robby!" I groan as I jerk my hips against him, filling his ass with hot jets of come.

He lets out an almost animalistic growl as he spurts out his own come into my hand and all over his stomach and mine. He jerks hard as his ass milks my dick of everything I give him. I smile at the pure pleasure emanating from his dark eyes.

"Shit...," he moans as we both start to come down.

"You're going to ruin me," I tease.

He laughs. "Fuck. I think that's what you just did to me. I was innocent and naive before I met you."

I grin and pull slowly out of him. "Happy to be of service, Mr. Massena."

He smiles at me. Happiest smile I've ever fucking seen. "I love you."

"I should hope so. I did just give you my last name."

He laughs as he sits up. He leans in and kisses me long and deeply. I forget completely about his come on my hand as I grip his ass and pull him against me, making a mess of us both. I deepen the kiss, swiping my tongue along his and sucking lightly. After the kiss ends, I'm damn near seeing stars.

It's always been like that with Robby. Dizzying. Like I'm trying to grasp reality from the dream world I'm constantly dragged into with him. Not that I'm complaining. I love our little world. A corner of the universe reserved for just us.

I pull away slowly and kiss him softly. "I love you, too, Mr. Massena." He loves when I call him that.

His smile could light the darkest corners of the world. And it's all for me. I can't stop the grin that spreads across my face as we quickly clean up. While I don't want to go back outside right now, I know that Robby does. He loves being around everyone. Which is just fine with me. I have my entire life to get my moments with him.

As we walk back outside, the pure, innocent happiness seeping from my husband gives me all the warm fuzzies I don't believe existed before him. Unwilling to let him stray too far away from me, I pull him over to the benches by the firepit and wrap him in my arms.

"I don't think Alex likes Raleigh," Robby chuckles.

Raleigh sits curled into herself next to Dallas. She sneaks glances at Alex, but quickly ducks her head away from his searing stare. The glare he's shooting her as he stands against the wall of the house with his arms folded across his chest tells us all we need to know.

Lyric has moved from where she was sitting next to Josh to lean against the wall next to him. She says something and slaps his arm, causing him to look down at her, giving Raleigh a break. He wraps an arm around her, hugging her to his side as she talks. Whatever she's saying seems to be working, though. I can see the tension seeping out of him.

I shake my head as Robby rests his back against my chest. "Nope. Too bad because I really don't think she's lying. But Alex is insistent."

Dallas yawns and rests her head on Josh's shoulder. He glances down at her before going back to his phone conversation. I smile a little. I'm hoping Alex figures out whatever he thinks is going on because I think Raleigh is going to need some support. She just lost the only family she's ever really known through no fault of her own. She's become close to Dallas, but Dallas is still young herself and recovering from what she went through.

Robby snuggles closer. He contently watches our family with a soft smile on his face. My eyes fall on Lance and Damon. I've wondered about them. They're quiet. They keep to themselves. But the way their heads are close together as they talk makes me wonder a little more about them.

Ryan and Arianna are playing scrabble against Jessa and Jason. I grin when Tyler, who is looking on, fist pumps. Arianna wiggles happily. Jason's face falls while Alec laughs. I'd guess my little sister just got hella points on a good word.

Breetana yips and squeals before she cracks up laughing while she runs. I can't help but chuckle as Taylor chases her with a paintball gun. Nicole pops out from behind the house and shoots a shocked looking Chase in the ass. Robby and I both laugh.

Dani and Nick have a game of beer pong going with Dane and Cole. I don't know who's winning but they all look sloshed. Nick shoots a ball into a cup and cheers, but almost falls flat on his fucking face. I've never heard him giggle until this second.

Kent and Rebekkah skipped out long ago. I have no doubt they're getting a little more acquainted. They have years to make up for, after all. I chuckle when I catch Shane and my mom ducking into the house. My mom is giggling and blushing like a schoolgirl. Out of the corner of my eye, it looks like one of the guys from Alec's crew is wooing Eve.

But what catches my eye the most is Gavin. He's dancing with all three kids like he doesn't have a care in the world. Sort of like he's starting over right now and couldn't give a fuck about his past. He's grinning from ear to ear while all of the kids squeal and laugh.

I jump and look up when I see a paintball gun pointing at me. "Don't you fucking dare, you asshole." I grin in both warning and challenge as I hold a hand up to ward off Taylor's attack.

He grins back, but it's fucking evil and full of mischief. "Don't what?" He lowers the paintball gun and shoots Robby in the thigh before taking off running.

"Ow! You fucker! I'm an innocent bystander!" Robby says, mock hurt.

"Come join the fight, then, Massena!" Taylor says, holding his arms wide like he's just waiting.

"Oh, it's fucking on!" Robby says. He darts to grab another paintball gun. He tosses me one. "Ready to show him who rules this course?"

I grin as I stand. "Fuck yes." We both join the fight. Breetana and Nicole cheer when we jump in on their side.

"No fucking way!" Chase says, realizing they're outnumbered. "Alex! Lyric! Get in here! Help us even the score!"

Alex smiles for the first time since Robby and I said our vows. He picks up a gun as he jogs into the yard. "You're all in trouble now!" Lyric giggles as she takes the gun he hands her. "We've got the scrappy Briterican." He laughs.

And the war is on. We all dive for cover as a team and strategize. My heart feels lighter than it has in a long time. For the first time in years, my entire family is breathing easy. And I know when our heads hit the pillow tonight, we'll fall into the first peaceful sleep we've had in longer than we care to admit.

Like Gavin is portraying in his carefree dance with the kids, we're all looking forward to a bright future filled with the love and a strong family bond that we've all desired our entire lives.

It's over.

The weight of Matthew Lucinio is gone. But for the Crane family, it feels like it's all just beginning.

And I can't wait to see what's to come.

The End

Introducing...

The Lucinio Family Series

The devilishly dark and alluring Lucinio Family Series begins!

With a strong and brotherly bond with the Crane Mafia, the Lucinio Mafia has risen up from the ashes they were left in to become one of the most powerful and largest mafias in the world.

While the family grows, they become untouchable as they form unbreakable relationships under the leadership of sexy, dominant, and fearless Josh Lucinio.

Throughout the series, the Lucinio family face challenges that are meant to burn them to the ground. But instead of weakening them, it only serves to make them stronger while Josh earns his crown as the King of the Lucinio Mafia.

Order *Rising From The Ashes* Today!

The Crane Family Series

Available Now

The Reluctant Mafia King
Sweet Lies
Billion Dollar Love Story
Be Mine
Protecting Her
Dangerously Forbidden Love
His Heart
Love In The Dark

Box Sets Available

The Crane Family Series

Other Books By Melony Ann
The Beautiful Dream Series

Available Now

Loving You
My Love, My Heart
Softening Lyric
Undercover Temptations
Captain Charming
Breaking Boundaries
Crashing Into You
Tactical Inferno
Ravishing Our Queen
Cherished By The Texan
Unveiling Our Passions

Box Sets Available

The Beautiful Dream Series: Box Set: Part 1
The Beautiful Dream Series: Box Set: Part 2

The Deimos Trilogy

Available Now

Connor's Legacy
Aryan's Alpha
Kade's Redemption

Box Sets Available

The Deimos Trilogy

The Forbidden Temptation Series

Available Now

The Detective's Forbidden Temptation
The Running Back's Forbidden Temptation

The Lucinio Family Series

Available Now

Rising From The Ashes
The Player's Rebel
Encrypting My Heart

Multi Author Series
Piper Falls: Firehouse 49

Available Now

Ignite My Fire by Melony Ann
Regain My Fire by Kindra White
Playing With My Fire by D.L. Howe
Fight My Fire by Darley Collins
Against My Fire by Anneke Boshoff
Relight My Fire by Louise Murchie
Harness My Fire by Ayana Lisbet
Quench My Fire by Havana Wilder

Let's Be Friends

Follow me on

Bookbub

Facebook

Goodreads

Instagram

Tik Tok

Visit my website
www.melonyannauthor.com

Subscribe to my newsletter and get a FREE never-seen-before NOVELLA
just for subscribers!
https://www.melonyannauthor.com/exclusive-content

Join my Facebook Reader Group!
Jason's and Melony's Sizzling Book Nook

The official Crane Family Series Playlist on YouTube
https://youtube.com/playlist?list=PLGEiD5wbQmDc78K7gNeODh-
janqmIFiie

Dedication

To our universe and world. Your sun and moon will forever shine brightly as you guide us and keep us within your strong arms.

Acknowledgements

Brad - Your love shines so brightly that I never have to fear finding my way home. I love you so very much.

Laura - I love you more and more every day. You're always my little ray of sunshine. Thank you for stepping in and keeping me from drowning.

Jay - It's not easy being a constant support system to all of us. Yet, somehow, you manage to keep doing it. I love you.

Ayana - Thank you for being my cheerleader. I love you.

Anneke - Thank you for always being the voice of reason when I find it hard to continue. I love you.

Jason - In stormy seas, you're my life raft, and I'm proud I get to be the same for you.

To the Bookstagram Community.

To my family.

To all of those who believe in me and support me.

To all of those who don't.

Cover by: Carter Cover Designs

Edited by: Alyssa Skaggs

About Melony Ann

Melony Ann began writing short stories and poetry as a child. She continued honing her craft over the years until she took the plunge and began publishing her work, despite having severe anxiety.

Melony writes contemporary romance stories that are full of suspense and a lot of steam.

When she isn't writing, she is loving her family and working to make her life something she deserves.

Melony believes that if her writing can inspire just one person, then all of her hard work is worth it.

Her hope is that her writing allows each and every one of her readers to escape for a little while. To dive into a different world one book at a time.